ADVANCE PRAISE FOR

STATIONS WEST

"What a lovely book. Allison Amend has just the right touch, and her people are alive on the page."

—RICHARD BAUSCH,
author of *These Extremes*

"*Stations West* is truly an American epic. It is the story of immigrants and natives, of the evolution of the land, of culture and of people, of attitudes and lifestyles, of belief, of family, of America itself. I know of no other piece of literature like it. Written in a style as starkly beautiful as the landscape of the Oklahoma territory it describes, Amend's prose is unflinching and unsentimental; it takes on difficult truths with wide-open eyes. I'm quite awed by the novel's tremendous reach and its generosity."

—THISBE NISSEN,
author of *Out of the Girls' Room and into the Night*

"There are no other books like *Stations West*. It speaks to something new, a kind of Jewish *Angle of Repose* . . . Stegner mixed with Singer. It struck me throughout as beautifully written and this alone makes a serious contribution to literature. But novels should also plow new ground and this story certainly does this. Boggy and Moshe and Alice and Garfield are real to me—living and enduring a landscape that is as familiar to them as it is to anybody else out there."

—PETER ORNER,
author of *Esther Stories*

"Allison Amend possesses the rare gift of being able to fully transport her readers to an uncharted land. Her version of nascent Oklahoma reshapes the mythology of the Old West, telling an enthralling family story that reveals the role of Jews in shaping the American frontier."

—HANNAH TINTI,
author of *Animal Crackers* and *The Good Thief*

STATIONS WEST

Yellow Shoe Fiction
Michael Griffith, Series Editor

ALLISON AMEND

STATIONS WEST

A NOVEL

LOUISIANA STATE UNIVERSITY PRESS
BATON ROUGE

Published by Louisiana State University Press
Copyright © 2010 by Allison Amend
All rights reserved
Manufactured in the United States of America
LSU Press Paperback Original
First printing

Designer: Michelle A. Neustrom
Typefaces: Whitman, text; Egyptienne D, display
Printer and binder: Thomson-Shore, Inc.

LIBRARY OF CONGRESS CATALOGING-IN-PUBLICATION DATA

Amend, Allison.
    Stations west : a novel / Allison Amend.
        p. cm. — (Yellow shoe fiction)
    ISBN 978-0-8071-3617-1 (pbk. : alk. paper)
    I. Title.
    PS3601.M464S73 2010
    813'.6—dc22
                                                2009035580

A cartographer of sorts—I measure
earth with words. I have drawn roads
and made them impassable. I have laid
railroad tracks to serve as escape
routes. I have surveyed rivers and
seas by touch and taste. And yet,
I ignore my point of departure or
destination: only know the lands
that lie in between.

—BEATRIZ BADIKIAN-GARTLER,
"Mapmaker," from *Mapmaker Revisited*

She stood in tears amid the alien corn. . . .

—JOHN KEATS, "Ode to a Nightingale"

CONTENTS

PROLOGUE

Boggy Haurowitz arrives in Indian Territory during the hottest part of the summer of 1859. The horse slows; Boggy jumps off its hulk, gets tangled in his satchel, and rolls in the dust. He stands up, rubs his shoulder. He is on the outskirts of a town whose name he doesn't know. It is printed in childish handwriting on the sign outside the makeshift Baptist church, but Boggy can read neither English nor Cherokee.

Boggy wears the one pair of trousers he owns. In the pocket a pack of chewing tobacco presses his thigh comfortably, and his cotton shirt is open in the dry heat. His head is covered by a slouch hat taken off a dead man somewhere in eastern Missouri. The man was freshly murdered when Boggy found him, his skull beaten in so that the brim of the hat shows specks of brown flaky blood that will scrape off in a few weeks. The horse Boggy leads by the reins belonged to the dead man as well. Boggy's leather satchel contains a bedroll, a tin cup, a canteen of water, some beef jerky, a trusted pocketknife, two bits, and a small, worn copy of the Torah, no bigger than a fist, printed in Hebrew script on parchment and bound tightly with horsehide.

The town—south of Kansas, west of Arkansas—is home to Indians, prairie dogs, and skinny cattle. Its nearest neighbor is barely a settlement. It exists as a place for locals to buy candles, fabric, soap, burlap, and grains. A place to gather for rotgut or lemonade and to spit on the floor and swap stories if the languages match. This town has no civilized pretensions. It stretches in all directions, a flat palm offering itself to him, miles of bluestem grasses and tangled oaks, goldenrod, and sandbur. He shifts his weight, spits, and walks west until the smoke of a fire turns his footsteps slightly south.

The Cherokees in the small settlement, who number about a hundred, tolerate rather than welcome him. Not many words are exchanged as the dogs surround Boggy, sniffing his crotch and barking excitedly. By the next spring, Boggy marries a full-blood named Taya and is grunted at familiarly in the larger town when he goes in monthly to buy supplies.

Boggy and Taya live in taciturnity, grazing cattle and collecting what others do not want. This they have in common, a need to surround themselves with possessions, just in case. Boggy has fashioned a wagon by the time the first boy is born, and when the second utters his first cries, Boggy has modified it so that the two oxen he received in exchange for the dead man's horse can pull it. It's heavy now with pots, pans, blankets, and tools, a contraption that melts down old wax for new candle stubs, grain barrels, old milk jugs, skins for beading and skins for clothing and skins of ugly animals, products of the plains' godforsaken cruelty.

The cattle travel with them. They stay patiently inside the temporary fence Boggy constructs for them near the settlements he and his wife visit in the Cherokee and Creek territories. When the boys are old enough, Boggy takes them with him through the podunk locales, and they sit on the porch of the inn keeping cool in the shade as Boggy goes from house to house, visiting the lawyer's wife and the medicine man's house first with his best wares.

He trades for food or for banged, dented, or otherwise damaged possessions, which he can fix up while his wife cooks dinner over the fire, easier to light now that he traded for a set of flints near Okmulgee. He has learned enough English to answer to "Jew," which means peddler now and not a worn-out religion. He still keeps his small Torah in the family's trunk.

They travel the wagon roads and follow the rivers, venturing into the Cherokee Outlet, where the cattlemen are happy to see them, see anyone. They travel to where the tall grasses give way to gypsum dunes; crusted, dry steppes populated sparsely by stubborn shrubbery and scrub. They wander down through the Chickasaw and Choctaw Nations, into Texas, and back north again.

The Territory protects them, buffers them from the outside world. Plans for a coast-to-coast railroad skirt by it for now. The train avoids the Indians and frontier outposts for fear of their reputed savagery. This isolation shields Boggy and his wife from English words too far away to learn:

Tammany Hall, blockade, secession—concepts to which neither pays any attention.

But then the United States government seems to remember that it deposited and afterwards abandoned thousands of Indians to be courted by the Confederate army. By the time it realizes that Indian Territory is worth defending, Boggy and his wife are east of Park Hill, supplying Confederate troops with tobacco, paper, candle stumps, and socks.

Boggy and his family travel back and forth, through the Outlet and the Civilized Nations and the white settlements, posing alternately as white or Indian. Like hungry dogs they follow the bloody battles, then head northwest, just ahead of the neutrals and the pursuing Confederate army, crossing the path of large supply trains escaping into Kansas. They wait west of the Arkansas River, huddled in a cold "soddy" built into the side of a hill, making the butchered cow last all winter.

When spring comes, they emerge from their hibernation into a changed Cherokee Nation. Traveling down the Arkansas they visit Taya's village to find the men gone, recruited into the Confederate army and slaughtered by Unionist sympathizers. Though her clan is too poor to own slaves, they are southerners in dress, speech, and customs, and are therefore stripped of property and livelihood. The houses are charred shells, the fields scarred with trenches and shallow graves. So Boggy and his wife head west, where there is no one to care if they are neutrals, northerners, southerners, or apparitions.

In the fall of 1865 he completes the cabin near the willow grove just under the rise. The enormous cottonwood that grows at the edge of the grove is out of place but provides shade, and can be seen from far off. The site is far enough from the nearest town, Denton Station, that the Plains Indians won't bother them, but close enough to get supplies when they need them. The cabin is charming—two rooms, separated by a curtain, with a blackjack-log front door. Boggy fashions a bed from straw. On his next trip to Tahlequah he trades a literate man a mixing bowl in exchange for the man's skills. He sends a letter to the old country, hoping everyone is well.

Taya gives birth again, and the little girl—conceived in a bed and therefore born soft, unlike her brothers, who are the result of hard unions on the flat, flat plains—dies of pneumonia her first winter. They bury her soundlessly behind the house, the first little tombstone in the family plot. From the makeshift graveyard, the plains stretch on for miles, interrupted only by the mirage of future train tracks, the promise of postwar prosperity.

Boggy is gone for months on end, and his wife makes kaffir cornbread daily from the meal he buys, hunts the plains rabbits, and tries to make the vegetables grow. When Boggy returns, he lays out his new acquisitions next to the fireplace and she nods approvingly, picking up a ladle or a mirror for a closer look. By 1875, Boggy and Taya have five children in their small home.

Boggy's letter must have been received, for one day the cousin arrives. Boggy has never met this cousin, who, uninvited, took the boat and the miles of trains and coaches to the rural Cherokee Outlet to live with him, the American, as Boggy is proud to be known. There is simply a knock on the door. Luckily, Boggy is home from his travels. The cousin is a long-legged scholar from Boggy's mother's side of the family. He has been to university and has a tranquil and pensive air. He smells as though he is indoors, as if indoors had a particular smell, like potatoes, Boggy thinks as he kisses him in the Old World way. The cousin brings with him a satchel, as Boggy had years ago, only this one is filled with books, a Sabbath suit, and a shadowy, wrinkled drawing of Boggy's parents.

The cousin encroaches on Boggy's life in a way Boggy wasn't aware was possible. He hadn't realized his routine was so structured as to be closed to another person. But Taya likes the cousin. She serves him the best piece of meat, the biggest yam, the choicest apple. Her smile is shy, but her black eyes light up like windows in an otherwise dark house.

Boggy confronts her one night. They are in bed, the blanket and mattress stuffed with feathers of everything winged, from goose to turkey to chicken. His wife denies that she favors the cousin. She serves her husband, she says, who provides for her, and as proof she opens her nightgown, though it is cold in the bed. But Boggy can think only about the five children and the cousin who eats as though his voyage left him with a tremendous void, and he turns over to sleep.

The cousin reads during the day, and after the children have finished their chores he teaches them to write the old language by candlelight. They are eager to study, to turn the symbols into sounds and words, and they write poetry on the dust floor of the cabin with long iron rods that Boggy has collected. Suddenly, it is like Boggy's home in the old country. Suddenly, it is a Jewish house.

One night at dinner, after the cousin says the motzei, Boggy passes the cornmeal bread, steaming from the brick oven and browned on top with soot. He notices that the hand the cousin takes the basket with is white and soft, and when it touches Boggy's duffer hand it stiffens with repugnance at the stubby brown fingers, dirty under the stunted nails. Boggy leaves the next day.

Boggy goes west, is bumped west, follows the sun and any river, game trails, wagon tracks, or military roads he can find. He trades pails and dented pots to grateful cow farmers, for food, cloth, and books. He receives pennies for delivering packages on the condition that their destination is West. He stands, three springs later, in new denim overalls, in Monterey, California, having futilely panned for gold that no longer flows like mother's milk, having traded harvest labor for English lessons, having managed a team of silent railroad-building Orientals. He envies their faces, flat pictures of serenity. He sees them bluffing card games behind tightened dark brown eyes, sunburned nostrils flush with their round cheeks, and knows their seeming incomprehension belies a sagacity. He has sold his wagon to a painter in Yosemite for what he considers a favorable sum, his red buck horse to a rancher farther north.

He turns now, away from the sun setting into the white ocean. In his right pocket he feels the hard wad of dollar bills, the fruit of his travels, the reward for his wits; in his left, a cardboard train ticket sticks into his thigh. The front flap pocket has a pipe, which he takes out now, along with a pouch of tobacco. It will take all night to walk to the station, and he should start now, but he stops to light his pipe, waiting for the last chords of the sun to fade away before he heads back home.

Home is always farther when you're headed toward it instead of away, Boggy muses. The train stops in Chouteau, sighing steam. Boggy jumps down without waiting for the metal stairs to unfold. A boy with a dirty face and hat in hand asks him if he can help with the luggage. "What luggage?" asks Boggy, amused. He fingers the money, its edges crisp inside his trousers. He takes the stagecoach west to Denton Station. The town is not much bigger than when he left; its dusty paths and faded signs comfort him.

He walks to the log cabin. It is as he remembers. The fence surrounding the meager garden sags as though it has missed him, and Boggy silently curses his worthless cousin. The house looks tired; the brown wood has faded to gray under the weight of the winters Boggy has passed traveling, and the door hangs to the left. A shadow hides the blinding sun for a moment, and Boggy shivers involuntarily. He counts the number of tombstones in the family plot: still only the little girls, one stillborn, another less than a year old, the dog's small wooden stick and the mass grave for the other pets. Boggy sighs with relief.

As he approaches the house, Boggy notices a carved metal mezuzah on the jamb. He touches it and kisses his fingers, as they did in the old country, and wonders what other changes the house has undergone. The door swings open to his touch, and the sun entering behind him glints off the dust in the air. There is a fine layer covering the table, the seven chairs, the wash basin. The room smells deserted, musty. Boggy can hear the rustling of mice behind the small nest atop the cabinet. Then he sees the three envelopes gathering dust on the uneven table.

The first contains a letter written by his oldest son, Moshe. It is folded into careful thirds, and Boggy reads the script slowly; he is unused both to reading and to English letters.

"Dear Papa," it says. "I'm very sorry. I was in Fort Gibson. I met a girl there. They said they buried them in the churchyard near the accident. And I sold the animals." His son has signed the letter without a close. The money from the sale is not included.

Boggy is not so much puzzled by the letter as disappointed. He had known there was something wrong, something that made him leave and made him stay away so long. The second letter is from the police in Jefferson, Texas. It regrets to inform him that his wife, cousin, and children were killed when their wagon attempted to cross the railroad tracks just outside of town. Boggy puts the letter down and arranges it next to the letter from his son, smoothing out the creases with his fist and placing the envelope on top.

The third envelope bears the curved writing of his cousin. It is in the old language: "She cannot write so I will, Cousin. We are going away from your dusty house, and your dirty fist. You do not love me, nor do you love her, and the town does not like to see me take her arm without your consent. You must bless us, and do not worry about the children, who will grow up with heads swollen from knowledge instead of feet sore from walking, hands calloused from the pen and not from work."

Boggy is thankful to have opened the letters in the order he did. He feels simultaneously weighed down by the lump of loss in his stomach and lifted by the marvelous pull of the heavens, which makes his shoulders light. He pictures the graves and is disturbed to think of them next to some clapboard church, but it's too late now. He takes the tobacco from his pocket and packs and lights his pipe. Then he flicks the match onto the neatly placed letters and watches as they burn from the outside in, edges curling as they turn brown. The table starts to smolder, and a breeze enters the open door, spreading the flames across the wood.

As Boggy exits, an impulse makes him grab the mezuzah from the door. It is only barely attached. He grips it tightly; the smooth metal fits well in his palm. Once he's outside, though, the object feels heavy and foreign. Boggy draws his arm back and tosses the mezuzah into the woods. He cannot hear it land.

Boggy walks back to the town and enters the saloon. He orders rotgut, standing at the bar, then downs a beer and lemonade mixture. He leaves a bill for the bartender, who nods, aware of the tragedy, and in recognition of the too-large tip. He knows it is a farewell dollar.

Boggy catches the next train, jumping on even before the wheels have stopped. He goes from car to car, looking for a window seat that faces forward. He sticks his head out of the window and imagines the tracks spread out in front of him, the two rails pointing like arrows to the future.

STATIONS WEST

PART 1

Arrows to the Future
1880–1893

1

Moshe Haurowitz rescues Alice O'Malley from her family. Her eleven siblings sound a chorus of demands, and Alice dreams at night that she is multiplied, so that one of her will do the washing up while another can feed the baby and another sweep and another sew, and a last, luckier one will primp in front of the mirror, strap on shoes, and lace up a dress, curling her hair for a dance.

Alice's father fights with the land every day, but the land is more obdurate than he. The blows he deals it reverberate up his arms, causing them to shake even after he has left the stubborn fields. Whether they vibrate with rage or pain Alice cannot tell. Alice's mother has not been out of bed since the baby was born almost two years ago. She sweats and soils the sheets and whispers directives in her daughter's ear when Alice wipes her brow.

How can Alice leave them? And where to go? She is walking home from Fort Gibson's sole apothecary, when Moshe steps on the back of her dress. He apologizes too profusely, dropping his parcels in the dust. His hands flail as though he cannot control them, and he is comically disheveled. Can he walk her home?

A mere two weeks elapse before Alice is ready to leave her clamoring family, their roughhousing, and their angry stomachs. It takes only a fortnight for a maladroit peddler's son to win the heart of a girl who remembers with nostalgia the days when a potato was worth its weight in gold. Alice does not expect much; she is half afraid she'll get caught as she leaves the house to pass water in the moonless night and sneaks away, but no one sees her or tries to stop her. Alice's family, immigrants themselves, understand the need to leave, are sympathetic to the impulse.

The journey is slow; Moshe and Alice must first travel south to Denton Station, then walk to the cabin. This boy is clumsy, laughably so. She

3

giggles for what seems like the first time in her life. He looks at her while they walk, so that each rock or rut becomes a potential hazard. He trips, recovers, only to stumble again. Alice feels a flutter of panic—what has she done? With whom has she joined her lot? But then a wagon rumbles past, a baby wailing under the canvas, and Alice reassures herself that no matter what her new future holds, at least it will be separate from her family's.

While he stares, he talks to her—not in the angry, heightened tones of her father and brothers, but conversationally. He tells her everything he is thinking, when he thinks it, so that it is as though he thinks on the outside. He explains about his mother, the cousin, his siblings, the accident. His words are a stream, a flood of babble. He is worried as well; he doesn't know what to do to please her. He's afraid he will fail, and so he distracts his mind and fills the space between them with purposeless nervous chatter. He knows he is lucky to have her, and he must do everything in his power to keep her. He speaks with the accent of one raised in near isolation. Stilted communication, to which she gradually grows accustomed. She, too, speaks with the accent of her old country, mixed with the nasal vowels of the sequestered farm. She listens until sleep overcomes her, fully clothed, on the tarp Moshe has set down for them as night falls on the road. Moshe watches her eyes close, then says a quick prayer in the cousin's language, asking for a blessing on their union.

When they arrive, she sees his home as a mirror image of her own rundown wooden barracks, though his is inverted, empty. And though she's disappointed, the familiarity is comforting, like the smell of boiling potatoes. They sleep in the dusty featherbed, and she shows him what he must do, though he does it reluctantly and not without difficulty. She takes his hand and puts it here, then here. He taps her tentatively, as though checking to see if a pie is cool enough to eat. Finally, she takes his shoulder and pulls him on top of her, guides him inside her with her hand.

"H-how do you know?" he wonders aloud, alarmed but thrilled, amazed.

She does not answer him. She is incapable of speech just then; she feels as though a heavy cloth has descended over her mind, and when she searches for words there is nothing but viscous mud.

But he does not really expect an answer. They have already settled into this pattern: his prattle, her silence.

She watches him while he sleeps, beads of sweat on the downy hairs of his upper lip. She scrutinizes him and begs him, can they stay? Can they stay here in the deserted house of his youth? He explains to her that it is his father's house. Though his family is dead, it does not belong to him. She feels small tears start, then blinks them back. She wants to stay. Why does he not want to?

It cannot be the pain of memories, for they are almost completely submerged, by the narrative he generates constantly. It cannot be the hope of something better, for who has instilled in him the idea of hope? It must be the restlessness of his father; can such a thing be inherited? Was it baked into the bread? Alice wonders. Did it travel airborne like influenza? Moshe feels a desire to wander, and he can do no more to master it than he can his extremities. It propels his legs as though downhill.

At sunrise Alice watches Moshe write, his gestures slow, methodical like drawing. He leaves the letter on the table. They too go west. When they cross the Territory boundary, both feel regret, but they are too embarrassed to share their emotions with the other. Their future is a cascading boulder; it cannot be stopped, nor can its course be altered.

They are married in Orerich, Colorado, one Sunday afternoon, after Alice is too big to sleep on the tarp, and the inn will not let them take a room without a marriage license. The minister smells of spirits, and the church is small, built of a cheap pine that has lost its scent but retained its splinters. The service is short, and Alice signs her name with an X. Moshe tells her he will teach her to write when the baby is born.

Moshe works in the bar as a pearl diver, scrubbing dishes heavy with the grease of meals. He tosses the bones, gnawed white, into the yard, where the dogs and wolves chomp ungratefully. When they are finished, there is nothing left except the occasional morsel of cartilage. When the bones are heaped, Moshe starts on the stack of white plates, biblical in their exaggerated, precarious pile. He dips them into the soapy basin, scrubs, rinses them in the tub, and sets them on a rack to dry. Soap, scrub, dry; soap, scrub, dry.

Moshe sings to himself, music with rhythms in thirds, to the tune of his chore. Songs he learned from his mother: soft chants; from his brothers and sisters: mocking, singsongy melodies; from his cousin: solemn dirges. He praises God, the doe, the wicked child, mindlessly, mechanically. He does not sing for joy. Instead he sings to tamp down the worry that sits in his stomach like too-yeasty bread. It crawls up like a belch unless he actively suppresses it by vocalizing.

As a dishwasher he is a remarkable failure. His hands, their long, awkward fingers curled from immersion in water, refuse to grasp the dishes properly. He must pay for each one, each piece recovered by the broom on the floor. The discarded dishware—bowls and plates and ashtrays and coffee cups—composts next to the bones, competing piles of white castoffs.

Alice sits upstairs in their small room, the silence a welcome relief. She watches a spider spin a web in the lower corner of the glass pane. Outside the dirty window she can see the rail yard, empty cars resting like horses in a barn. The only live trains appear at 10:00 a.m. and 10:00 p.m. exactly, daily, save Sunday. Alice hears them first, announcing their approach with a loud, low whistle, then the chugging wheels, the sigh of steam. The brakes sound then, a screech of effort, and Alice closes her eyes.

She is uncomfortable; the only bearable position is on her side. Her back aches. Her bladder clenches. She has charley horses in her calves. She knows she's carrying a boy, knows because of her size, her exhaustion. He's stealing her beauty; she can glimpse the distortion of her features in the mirror as she washes her face in the basin. All the brothers at home stole her youth, her ability to laugh, her time. And now she has time and no beauty, only the unnatural imbalance of noise and silence, noise and silence.

She can hear the clank of the dishes as Moshe stacks them, the extended crash when he mishandles them. The days are hot here, like in Indian Territory, but the nights are cool, cold even, and Alice burrows under the thin quilt, which smells of pine. She looks at her hand, a thin tin band for a ring that Moshe promises he'll change soon to a silver example of Orerich's—their new home's—abundance. And when she learns to read, he'll have it engraved. After the baby comes.

The cold reminds Alice of the Ireland of her childhood—the long, freezing winter nights, when the women sat around the table, a bin of lit coals underneath, using the tablecloth pulled up as a lap blanket so the warmth strayed up their skirts. She remembers sitting between her mother's legs, close to the embers. In that circle of warmth, the heart of the forest, the trees were women's stockings, crude cotton socks above the knees, skirts rucked up to reveal lumpy, white, hairy thighs and dark patches of pubic hair.

The baby kicks, and Alice rubs her distended belly. This imminent child is everything her husband is not: forceful and silent. Strong hands and stiff tongue. But for how much longer can she keep him inside her, before he emerges, screaming and demanding, like all the others—like the strident voice within her, grating, pleading, insisting, on what? What does the voice want?

* * *

Alice has never felt so much pain, as though her limbs are being torn from her body. To make it stop she would gladly give all she owns, the sum total of which is herself: an organ, an eye, a hand. But in the end she gives her spirit. It escapes down the long cord that wraps around the baby's neck.

The midwife cuts it off with a sharp knife, and the boy's features turn red. She holds him expertly by the legs and thumps him soundly on the back. When she hears his cries, she smiles triumphantly, dunks him in the hot water next to the bed, and wraps him in the rags provided by the innkeeper's wife, who stands by in attendance.

"Almost there," the midwife says to Alice, who is still writhing. "A healthy baby boy." Alice turns on her side and vomits again on the drenched pillow, grateful that the words are devoid of compassion. The midwife has witnessed enough births to understand that the emergence of life is far from a miracle. Rather, the hand of God is in the fact that anyone continues to live afterward.

They name him Garfield after the dead president, give him middle names to honor his ancestors, and brand him with his father's transparent, transplanted surname: Haurowitz. Alice is even more tired after his birth, which was the longest the midwife has ever seen, over thirty-six hours. After Alice pushes out the afterbirth, Moshe takes it in back to bury it in the yard, where he knows it will be dug up by the voracious wolves. It is still warm from the heat of his wife's body, and he cradles it to him, as though it were the child. He imagines it pulsating softly, and he sings to it, a cradle-song his mother sang to the younger children. He loves it as though it were the child, this silent mess of blood and passion, and it breaks his heart to put it in the ground. But he can already hear the throaty sobs of what he has created, the baby crying from inside the inn, and with streaming tears he sings louder, patting the last bit of grave dirt with the back of the shovel.

Orerich grows like a precocious child, by leaps of miners and bounds of tradesmen. It's the hard way through the Rockies, the summit of the mountains—simultaneously the relief of the pinnacle as well as the apex of exhaustion. The town is a throwback to a time when nature ruled oblivious to the constitutions of man. It is where grown men eat each other, caught in a ten-day whiteout thirty miles from an outpost, where avalanches roll over prospectors, where bears eat the thawed remains come spring.

But the celebrations are legendary, the spirits freely flowing down throats and out of joyous voices; they are happy to have made it so far, happy to be here, anywhere that has a name, finally. Moshe barely hears the orgiastic melees. He is ensconced in the steamy kitchen, the dishes in epic abundance, the call for drinks so constant that Moshe mostly scrubs the small bullets of shot glasses, leaving the multitude of plates until morning. The moans of waking revelers soothe him to sleep as the sun rises. Sometimes he is so exhausted he falls asleep on his feet, hands in the soapy, gray water.

Moshe knows that his wife entertains the men, but knows it in a place so deep inside that the pain of the knowledge feels like a crick in the spine, a bruised tailbone. It is easy to invent other purposes for the men who go upstairs. He can pretend he does not see his wife in her low-cut dress serving liquor, adding a flourish of the buttocks for free. The baby sleeps, oblivious, in the corner. He is a good baby, everyone comments, mostly silent in contrast to the tumult around him.

Alice glances his way occasionally, detachedly. She was born with a finite number of smiles, she figures, and she saves them for the men who grunt and spit and grab her bottom. She has to force herself to turn up the muscles in her cheeks. Her days are filled with boredom, a bottomless despair and listlessness. She has shirked the duties assigned to her, those she promised to complete when still hopeful with the flush of her arrival in Colorado. She doesn't milk the cow, distribute slop to the pigs, or thrust her hand under the warm skirts of the hens to steal their eggs. The wedding ring is still awkward and foreign on her fourth finger. She turns it with the other hand, an unconscious habit.

One afternoon after dozing in the lumpy bed, she rises at twilight to comb and braid her hair. Moshe watches her, just awakened from his four nightly hours of sleep. He relates stories of the chickens and dishes, what the cook said, the news the men have brought at the rail yard where Moshe goes to collect supplies. He reads the newspaper aloud to her, rattles on about the shooting of Jesse James, old news to most. "Thirty-five years old, how about that? Sixteen years on the lam and then pow, they get him. Wonder what he felt when that bullet was coming at him? I'd be relieved just as much as scared, wouldn't you? After all those years running from the law, jumping trains to save your skin. Ever jumped a train? I tried once, and let me tell you, it takes know-how as much as strength, timing it so you don't let it outrun you, wind up with your legs under the wheels, then pfff." He makes a knife sign across his neck.

Alice can see him in the mirror. She does not respond. If she never responds, will he stop?

Moshe tries harder. He clears his throat, turns the page. "Now here's a thing I can't believe 'cept it's right here—artificial light. Like a sun inside a glass globe, they say. It doesn't burn oil or kerosene or wax, just uses what's in the atmosphere. You'd have to show me that afore I'd believe it. You can put anything into print, just set the type and go."

Alice studies herself, undoes her braid, starts again. She can feel Moshe's eyes on her, and she takes cruel pleasure in denying him even a nod of acknowledgment.

"I have something for you," he says. He gets out of bed and tickles the baby under his chin. Out of his jacket's threadbare lining he removes several magazines. He places them in front of Alice, opens a page at random. Alice can see they're old and dog-eared, advertising clothes and wares they cannot afford. Moshe turns the pages, pointing out cartoons of comic Africans and cannibals, the sanguine battles in the Indian Wars. All the while Alice braids her hair into plaits, pins it back. She gets up from the chair and Moshe sits, reading from *Collier's*. Alice goes over to the stand and washes her face. Then she shoos Moshe out of her chair and sits applying rouge to her cheeks and mouth. She tucks and untucks lace from her cleavage. Her fingers move quickly, faster even than Moshe can read. She concentrates on her hair because she knows if she sees her eyes in the mirror she will start to cry.

He shows her the illustrations, shoves the magazines under her nose, and she turns away toward the wall. With her elbows up so her fingers can manipulate her hair, Moshe can smell the faded, sour smell of her armpits, the rotting of her nipples, which only gave milk for one week. Since then, Moshe has nourished Garfield by his own hand, with milk from the inn's goat.

President Garfield lingered for two months and seventeen days. A nurse turned him over, drained the pus and redressed his wounds twice a day until his groaning grew dim, his breath merely a whisper, and finally he expired. According to a months-old *New York Times*, the assassin's letter read: "Life is a flimsy dream, and it matters little when one goes."

Alice cannot stand these stories, and each night she thinks she might scream, might tear the taut braids out of her head and beat her husband with them. She imagines herself a vessel that is brimming with Moshe's words, his songs, his incessant need to be audibly present. Already baby Garfield is copying his father; he coos and gurgles and smiles stupidly. She has given birth to an idiot, she thinks, to a child that is only her husband's.

She studies her décolletage in the oxidized mirror and shuts out Moshe's tales of presidential infection and hero Deadwood Dick. Why had she thought she might learn to read if this is what it brings you? Useless knowledge, more detritus in her already bursting mind.

She prefers the company of the rough drinkers in the downstairs bar. Their sure, knowing hands, not Moshe's spidery tickles. Men who know what they want and insist on it, not like Moshe's begging, his quick capitulation. There was no guilt the first time, just as there was no pain. She had been faithful, given Moshe a son, and received nothing in return.

Tonight, something snaps; the last thread of a flimsy rope breaks, and Alice decides she doesn't care. She doesn't care if her husband catches her in bed with another man. She doesn't care if her child turns away from her. Suddenly, it makes no difference, and just as suddenly, the pain is gone, replaced with a blessed feeling of calmness she hasn't felt in a long time.

Moshe takes the baby and goes downstairs into the kitchen, and soon Alice comes down, too, into the inn's great room. She approaches the man with the newest hat and sits on his lap, breathing, "Will you buy a girl a drink?" in his ear. She has not misjudged. He is unshaven and dirty, but she can feel his muscles beneath his trousers. His fingers are callused. She stands and takes his hand, and he follows her upstairs.

The baby cries; she can hear him all the way up in the bedroom, and Moshe starts to sing. The stranger's moans and thrusts are the bass to the light melody of Moshe's singing, his climax the crash of yet another dropped dish.

But tonight Garfield will not stop screaming, his face pink with unattended rage, his fists clenched and pounding. Moshe puts down the rag. He sings and strokes the baby's face, gives him his finger to suck, then one of the less picked-over bones, and finally a thimbleful of whiskey he steals from the bar, to no avail. When the baby cries Moshe feels it physically, like the edge of a broken plate piercing the pad of his finger. He cannot bear to see his son unhappy; he would do anything to soothe him. Garfield continues to shriek throaty stabs of sobs. Tears run down his cheeks, and even after Moshe picks him up, cradles him, and sings his favorite lullaby, still Garfield will not stop. Moshe's failure to quiet the boy seems a judgment against him.

Frustrated to the point of tears himself, Moshe carries him upstairs. The baby's cries should act as a warning; Moshe's approaching footsteps should sound the alarm, but Alice is oblivious in the grubstaker's arms. The baby's cries could be her lover's; she is unaccustomed and unattuned to the sounds of her son. She has decided not to hear. So when the door bursts open and Alice hears her name, she can pretend she is not in a dirty little attic room in bed with a man not her husband, a man whose name she does not even know. Alice looks up at Moshe. She feels nothing: no shame, remorse, or guilt. No pride or satisfaction. She knows he will do nothing, say nothing, and his pathetic acceptance makes her want to weep.

Moshe does not break down, does not scream and cry to match his son. He falls silent. The display of body parts, of secret places exposed, is enough to finally quiet him. Garfield, too, sensing the change, closes his mouth to gum his lips, whimpering softly.

Dazed, Moshe returns to the kitchen, puts the now-quiet infant back into his basket, and returns to his rhythm: Soap, scrub, dry. Soap, scrub, dry. When the cock crows morning and the first strains of light are visible out the window at his back, Moshe dries the last of the dishes. If he leaves now, it will be as though it never happened. If he pretends this night never occurred, if he goes far away and doesn't ever think about it, it will seem as though it was all a dream.

The saloon is silent, all the customers gone home or passed out under the gaming tables, and Moshe folds the dishtowel over the chair. Garfield sleeps beside him, so soundlessly, so intensely that he does not stir to his father's kiss on his cheek, does not register the sounds of his father's good-bye, does not open his eyes to see his father's retreating figure making its way toward the rail yard.

It is a short train ride to Denver, a simple process to sign up to be a flag-man or a call boy or a coal shoveler on the budding Denver and Rio Grande Railroad. They are glad to have Moshe aboard, they tell him; someone po-lite, they slap him on the back; someone who knows his place, they shake his hand; someone who won't go bothering the guests with chatter. And Moshe simply smiles. He has been struck dumb. He can hear the words of response in his head, but his tongue lies like something dead inside his mouth.

He takes his first pay and buys himself paperbacks. Adventure books like *Tumbleweed Tom Treks West* and *California Colin and the Indian Wars*.

Heroes like Fred Fearnot and Tricky Sue steal his imagination and his free time. He goes through them like wildfire across a brush plain.

The Negro shoeshine boy smiles to watch him read like that, wonders what is in those pages that commands the attention of a taciturn man like Moshe. He does not realize that if Moshe stops reading, if he exits the world of the book and returns to his current life, then the flood of tears he has never shed will be unstoppable. They will cover all the earth.

He is happy to be known as silent. It was not an appellation he ever thought he'd earn, but he has mastered it quickly, learning that a slight nod of the head or a sly point of the finger will do for most situations. He clears his throat occasionally, and sometimes he climbs on top of the passenger car to sing out into the desert night, but mostly he is known as "Mopey Moshe." It's not a term he's familiar with.

One fall day in 1890 he steps down from a train terminating in Salt Lake City and sees his father. Boggy has grown leathered and chapped like the arid earth. He does not recognize Moshe immediately, doesn't return the bear hug given him, pretends not to notice the tears that Moshe wipes away before he can control them.

Moshe starts to talk before he can stop himself, his tongue animated by the unexpected, unimaginable coincidence. They walk from the station to the outskirts of town, where Boggy has set up temporary camp until he is rehired as a brakeman. Over a supper of some desert animal warmed on the fire—squirrel or groundhog or rattlesnake, it is impossible to tell—Moshe relates his tale in exacting detail. He speaks in his father's language, the words unfamiliar but comfortable in his mouth. "I have a son, Pa. He must be eight years old now. Every Jewish New Year I send him money, to Goodmoore, the owner of the saloon in Orerich. You should see Orerich sometime, Pa. It's—well, it *was*, when I was there, which was a long time ago now. Truth be told, I'm not even sure they live there anymore. I'm sorry you haven't met Alice. She's prettier than I can say." He talks up a storm of description, a barrage and tempest of facts: His wife's face, her high cheekbones, her rounded chin and blue eyes, dark hair and long neck. The body of his infant child, plump with goat's milk and crushed apples with sugar, his soft coos and toothless smiles.

Boggy hasn't been talked to in a long while, and the words barely make sense to him. It is not unpleasant, this idea of attention being paid to him, of being addressed with questions instead of orders, but it is foreign, and

Boggy is unprepared to answer. The ground feels lumpy beneath his sleeping roll.

When Moshe runs out of talk he begins to sing, all the songs of his youth, the ballads of the old country. Boggy stares at the fire and watches it melt into the memory of his arsoned cabin; the sparks become the memories of the first meal in the makeshift kitchen, his cousin's grateful blinking, his wife's thin smile. He remembers her long black braids, her taut stomach, her exaggerated forehead, the way her hands could knead away the knots in his muscles. He never thought he would miss her, hadn't missed her much, but Moshe's trilling brings up an emotion he never thought he'd feel: regret.

Memory is stealthy; it sneaks from behind like a silent thief. And it is selective, so that when Boggy struggles to remember something else—the old country, or the first time he learned to hitch a gooseneck link, or the vast roiling of the ocean—all that comes to him is a picture of his wife, so perfectly detailed he might have seen her yesterday. Some memories are as clear as a freshly shined window, while others are as opaque as coal dust. Whole decades are elusive, yet certain brief stretches, unbidden and unwanted, flash so vividly through his brain that they seem current, present. And it frustrates him that he has no choice which memories are which.

The anger grows; by morning it is the familiar rage at being cheated. By God, by his wife, by America. Boggy's eyes are barely opened when he sees the lump of his son sleeping across the fire under Boggy's harsh wool throw. It is easy to feel anger at his son. To be angry at Moshe's words, which have brought the memories back, linked them to the fire he builds nightly. To be angry at his return, the resurgence of the life he tried to reduce to ashes.

And it is easy for Boggy to leave. To simply walk back into town and return to his life as a detached brakeman. To sign up for the first eastbound train, a train on which he assumes Moshe will never think to look for him.

Moshe is unsurprised to find him gone, resigned more than hurt. He wonders briefly if his words have scared his father away, but he recognizes the same instinct for flight in himself. He feels disappointed, his throat scratchy with smoke. He wishes he were whatever his father wants him to be. He folds the scratchy blanket his father has left and finds, under the canvas bag he's used for a pillow, his father's tattered copy of the Torah.

Moshe puts it in his pocket and fingers his stubbly beard. He puts his pack on his back and wraps the blanket over his shoulders like a shroud.

He sprinkles water on the fire. It hisses, then settles. Moshe feels himself empty out, his words retreating back inside, fading with the embers. He watches, concentrating on the coals as they turn from red to black to gray, finally dead, finally harmless. Behind him, the Great Salt Flats stretch out, rounding as they reach the horizon. Bereft of trees, they shift with the vagaries of the wind, the salt like dried tears, the sand rolling on toward an unknown destination.

2

O rerich, Colorado, might be the most vile, filthy, iniquitous, and un-
christian town in the soulless country that is America. Or maybe it
is no worse than any other frontier outpost created in the wake of
technology or the search for its fuel: Cheyenne, North Platte, Reno. If cor-
ruption can be measured, depravity quantified in a simple equation such
as brothels per capita, or saloons per block, then Orerich must rank close
to first. Though perhaps this is just the criticism of those who do not share
in Orerich's debauched good time, those whose religious or social beliefs
prevent full immersion in Orerich's deviant culture.

Certainly, Orerich is no place for a boy to grow up, left basically on his
own since his father abandoned him as a baby. Garfield and his distant
mother, low-class in a town of the lowest social ilk in a country that supposedly has no class system, are swallowed up by the town's dirt streets,
wallow in its mud in spring and drink its dust in August. Without her
husband's support (after innkeeper Goodmoore takes his cut as banker,
Moshe's yearly remittances are a pittance), Alice simply turns her pastime
into full-time work, renting a room in a house on Gilges Street, in the Irish
part of town.

It is a house of "sporting women," a perversion of some feminist uto-
pian ideal, since the women's subsistence depends entirely on the men
who come to call, some as regularly as the milkman, most passing through
on their way west: poor or stupid or wanted by the law. The options for
women are limited. Like Alice, the girls of Gilges Street have chosen the
only available career for women with children, or fallen women, or ugly
women, or women from a family of twelve hungry Irish mouths, or those
whose club feet and cleft palates render them unable to secure a life in
the service of just one man. And, really, would one man be better than the

stream of faces that swim in front of them when they open their eyes? The echo of the same insecurities, the same uncomfortable demands, the endless cycle of desire: there is no joy in repetition in the harsh mountains, and at least the spice of variety makes a change from potato and cabbage soup.

During the day, there is laughter pouring out of the windows as the washing, the dishes, and the animals are cared for communally. Afternoons are their own. Alice sits on the porch if the weather is fine. Colorado is blessed by sunshine most days, and even in the mountains it is warm enough to close your eyes and bask in the sun's long arms. Some of the other women knit or sew, raised on warnings of the evils of idle hands, but Alice prefers the porch rocker. It is practically her chair now, wear marks on the cushion from the two hard bones of her buttocks and on the wooden floorboards from her relentless rocking back and forth, back and forth.

Her son Garfield is a strange-looking boy, the features of his mismatched parents having failed to synthesize properly. He has his father's dark curly hair and thick lips, his mother's light, freckled skin and eyes that are dully brown, the same color as the dusty Orerich roads. He is short, with lanky limbs that never tan but rather turn a magenta color, as though he has rolled in wild raspberries.

In 1890, winter lasts so long that Orerich's residents begin to fear that spring will never come, then grow resigned to that fact. Finally, the snow gives way to a grudging change of season, and Garfield is given his first official grown-up task: mail pickup. Orerich has not yet developed a delivery system; the town is too migrant, too chaotic, too rural. So eight-year-old Garfield is dispatched to the post office every day at three o'clock with a handful of letters from the women of the house to their mothers, sisters, or sometimes husbands far away. There is never anything from or for Alice; there is no correspondent anxious for news, no one with a desire to share anything with her. She still has not learned to read or write.

Garfield kicks the dirt up with his feet as he walks. There are deep ruts about three feet apart where wagon wheels have eaten the ground away at the surface, leaving the middle rippled like a washboard. To his left, Garfield can see the majesty of the higher peaks to the north, but he keeps his eyes to the ground, looking for dropped treasures.

The post office is in the center of town, near the station. The railroad reached the town in 1886 when for once fortune smiled on Orerich, and a line from Denver to Salt Lake City was routed south around the Rockies right through town. But then the Union Pacific bought the company and the claim got mined out soon after. Now rail traffic is scarce. The platform, built with such hope and promise just a few years before, looks sad with neglect, the weight of winter showing in its sagging beams and faded paint.

It is this desolate scene that Garfield passes on his way to the post office. The mail still comes daily, mostly by stagecoach. It is sorted by the postmistress, who doubles as the town curiosity. Rail thin, with beady eyes, she is what the church ladies (as the denizens of Gilges Street name the respectable women in town) would call "addled." She has one black dress, threadbare from years of use, in the old style, with a high waist and a wide collar.

She likes Garfield, smiles when he reaches up to pull the door handle above his head, always calls him by the full name on his birth certificate (she also keeps the town records): Garfield Shimon Patrick Haurowitz, a real mouthful. She has the mail already bundled, and frequently yesterday's newspaper. Sometimes there is candy or fudge in a package for a person who has since moved on, and she shares it with Garfield, watching him eat it greedily at the postal window.

She is also in charge of the town's weather, which comes from Denver via telegraph. Orerich shares little with Denver—neither its size, nor its civilization, nor its climate. The spring mountain weather is reliable: a morning of sunshine followed by afternoon clouds and thundershowers, each day a duplicate of the day before. When the postmistress flies the rain flag in April though there is no hope of the temperature climbing above freezing, or when she forecasts clouds on a day so clear you can see to California, the townspeople laugh (when they can remember what the weather flags stand for). She has to fly these flags; it is part of her job as postmistress for which she is paid two hundred dollars a year.

No one actually reads the newspaper Garfield brings home—they use it for toilet paper or kindling or to wrap purchases or for cleaning—but if they did, they would be well versed in American history: the Dawes Act, which would further close in on the already claustrophobic Indians; the first camera for individual use invented by Mr. George Eastman. They would even have read the final stanza of "Casey at the Bat," reprinted in the *Denver Observer*, and perhaps recognize themselves as the joyless, bandless, silent fans of a town for which a more accurate name would be Mudville.

Luckily, Garfield is one of those children born old, with innate common sense. He knows, intuitively, to look out for the wagons that travel the

streets, to dodge the rotten apples that fly his way as he scrounges in trash
bins. His fingers tingle as a bar fight turns into target practice, the pricks
an internal warning, more imperative than any parental directive.

His nights are spent in the kitchen, where he has his own set of bedding
on the floor like a dog, next to the house's servant—a large Negro woman
named Tallulah who performs the most grotesque of the household chores.
Even society's lowest rungs have servants who are less well-off than they.
Tallulah was a slave, not so much freed as abandoned in the aftermath of
the War Between the States—that distant, inconsequential skirmish back
East. She followed her master out West just before the end of the war, enduring the harshest mountain passes in the dead of winter. When word of
the war's end finally reached Colorado, he stole away in the night and left
her in Orerich, five months pregnant. The child, at age four, fell down a
mining shaft. Garfield's lullabies are the sound of Tallulah's tremendous
sobs, the heaving rhythm of her sorrow.

The two sleep near each other but not touching, close to the fire if it's
winter, near the door if it's summer. The parlor rattles with the noise of
entertaining women and their escorts for the night. Light floats around the
door, ice clinks in glasses, and the smell of tobacco is strong, even in the
kitchen. Sometimes they can hear the grunts and groans of the men upstairs "going about their business," as Tallulah calls it. She sings when this
occurs, loud spirituals about heaven and salvation, but they are an empty
consolation, since the singer doesn't really believe their message.

Alice notices Garfield only tangentially. She is in a fog, as if stunned
each morning to wake up in her life. Garfield is like a doll, and she is
happy to cuddle with him occasionally, when she remembers or when it
suits her. The men she receives with stoic acceptance of her concubine's
fate. She neither seeks their affection, nor particularly pays them any, yet
the rough-and-tumble men—con men, bounders, and criminals—take her
reticence as coyness, and she is a favorite in the house. As a result, her low-
cut dresses are of a particularly fine grade of cotton, and the ribbons that
encircle her neck are of the smoothest satin.

Alice's moments of pleasure come at the hands of the other girls in the
house, plaiting her hair or sponging her back. They preen each other like
cats during the long twilight hours, and Garfield fits well in her lap, playing with the tassels on her chenille dressing gown while Laura or Mary-
Caroline winds her long black hair into cords. These are Garfield's favorite
moments, too. It is like finding gold, these little nuggets of warm atten-

tion: calm, unthreatening snippets of time. He gazes at his mother's face, her hair, the lace on her dress, all up, up, up. And up, Tallulah informs him, is the Kingdom of Heaven.

The house is an enclave, an island. The church ladies walk blocks out of their way to avoid it. Dr. Hymore will not visit with his black bag unless coerced (though he has been known to drop by late at night dressed in weekend trousers, his nightshirt tucked clumsily into his suspenders). Gilges Street is noisy; Goodmoore's Saloon hosts the brutal sounds of Spanish monte or faro or poker, and the ensuing scuffles or the occasional cock fight (illegal, though the sheriff can avert his eyes if the incentive is right— ten dollars should do it) keep the townspeople awake. The street is bright, even in the wee hours, with barroom lanterns and the Gilges Street house's kerosene lamps, scarves draped artfully over the shades.

School opens in 1890, but Garfield refuses to go and so is harassed by the church ladies, especially the doctor's childless wife, Mrs. Hattie Hymore, who tries to give Garfield a proper upbringing—years of ethics lessons, family values, religion, and manners—in a public mini-course conducted over the five minutes she succeeds in holding him by the collar on Main Street. Not surprisingly, it doesn't take.

Neither does learning. Garfield shows a remarkable aptitude for incomprehension. He can barely read and write and is unable to add until he starts loitering around Lead Street outside the taverns and watches the men play poker or euchre, or that strange, loud game with only the black cards.

Each morning, Tallulah wakes Garfield with her singing, the clank of her fork against the bowl as she whips eggs for omelets. Garfield stretches, drags the bedding over to the chest, and goes out to the privy. Tallulah makes him a plate of bacon, eggs, and a biscuit with gravy. His ankles stick out below his trousers. Tallulah cannot let them out anymore.

Today there is a knock at the door. No one ever knocks at 14 Gilges Street. The men sidle in quickly like prairie dogs into a hole, and the butcher leaves his packages on the porch. Tallulah gives Garfield a look and waddles heavily to the front door, the staccato intake of her breath like a third step in her gait. There, outside the heavy door, is Mrs. Hattie Hymore.

"G'morning, Mrs. Hymore," Tallulah says politely, the years of training as a housemaid overcoming her surprise at seeing such an elegant lady here. Mrs. Hymore is dressed in a long black princess skirt, the petticoats of which are covered in the dung that lingers in the unkempt street outside, the refuse of patient horses in their long waits for their card-playing, hard-drinking, whoring masters. She holds a white parasol with paisley designs cut into it and a small pocketbook from which she removes a handkerchief and pats her face. It is a warm spring day.

"I've come for Garfield," Mrs. Hymore says. "All boys are to go to school. By law." She reaches again into the pocketbook and pulls out a piece of paper, which she shoves in Tallulah's face. The paper means nothing to Tallulah. There have been many official papers in Tallulah's life, yet she still makes breakfast every morning. She still cleans out latrines and sweeps living rooms, scrubs clothes and pretends not to have seen the stains or smelled the odors, still answers the door for white ladies. She doesn't even bother to look at Mrs. Hymore's document.

"Garfield," she calls. "Git."

Garfield approaches warily, his eyes on the ground.

"Mrs. Hymore say you going to school."

Garfield shuffles his feet. He steps onto the porch, blinking in the sun.

"He needs a quarter for books," Mrs. Hymore says. "If you don't have it, I'm sure I can sponsor him . . ."

Tallulah grabs her pouch from where it hangs on her belt. She shakes some coins into her hand and gives one to Garfield. He pockets it, still looking down.

"Good-bye then," Mrs. Hymore says.

"Ma'am," replies Tallulah, closing the door.

What Garfield cannot appreciate, as he struggles to keep up with Mrs. Hymore's hurried steps—she is anxious to leave the ghetto, the street of sin—is the courage it must have taken Mrs. Hymore to travel to 14 Gilges Street. How she courted misadventure (perhaps even rape!), dirtying her clothes and her reputation, for won't the church ladies' tongues wag when they find out she's been there, been seen inside the house, actually talked to the colored woman who works there? All for this little dirty half-breed with no father and a whore of a mother. This ungrateful brute, who will never succeed.

The unfortunate schoolmaster is one Mr. Napoleon Pickney, educated in the Jesuit manner at some since-defunct college. He is a religious man, one of the church ladies. Or he pretends to be, which is why they have hired him, an inexperienced teacher of undetermined origin. He is a particularly ugly example of America's melting pot, an amalgam of each race's worst characteristics: a long, sloping forehead covered by cowlicked red Scottish hair; a flat, truncated nose, which is red in the Irish way and lies flat and lazy against his pale, Scandinavian skin. He has burly Italian forearms and a skinny English torso. In short, he is unsightly and imposing enough that no one thinks to ask where he comes from. Everyone comes West hoping it will deliver on the casual promises made in the East. Maybe he is looking for a wife; maybe he thinks he will strike gold (though the surrounding mountains are so riddled with failed miners' assays that the hills appear pocked as plucked chickens). Maybe he succumbed to the siren song of the transcontinental railroad and simply detrained here, in the ironically named Orerich.

Mr. Pickney is a harsh teacher, unschooled in even rudimentary pedagogical techniques and quick to reach for the switch or the paddle. Garfield comes home with eraser prints chalked on his behind and coal marks from the poker's sharp jab on his arms and legs.

Class is held in the Gilmore Opera House, which is both church and community center, and now schoolhouse. It is a grand building with a mansard roof and a large three-hundred-seat auditorium. The students sit on the stage, which adds to Garfield's discomfort; it is as though his scholastic failures are being scrutinized by an invisible audience. The respectable children sit up front, near the teacher. They have appropriate clothes, the kind Garfield sees in newspaper illustrations, with lacy ribbons and sashes, matching muffs in the winter, tight suspenders, dainty boots the girls can hardly walk in.

Garfield fights with the other charity cases for the seats near the coal stove, though he is scorned even by the outcasts. He cannot sit still in his chair. He is distracted by the bugs on the wall, sparks and shifts in the stove. Each raindrop calls to him with a sad and surprised sigh as it hits the unyielding ground. Garfield imagines he can hear these things—the roar of the tumbleweed, the creak of distant wagons, even the hum of the rails across town, hours before the train is due to arrive.

Mr. Pickney he cannot hear. Or, rather, he hears but cannot listen, cannot interpret the sounds the old windbag makes. The class is eventually divided into those who can read and those who can't, and Pickney spends hours with the alphabet written on the blackboard, coaching the squirming degenerates to memorize, using blows as the method to cement the acquisition of the building blocks of literacy. "I can't teach idiots," he has been known to murmur. Truth be told, he can't teach anyone; the literate children copy their lessons out of a few worn textbooks ordered from

Denver. They write essays on topics like urbanization, labor unions and unrest, the electoral college, and other subjects remote and foreign to their rural existence.

Truancy is Orerich's newest and most prevalent crime; it is the latest way to offend the sheriff, who has taken to fining families one penny for every unexcused absence. Garfield is often dragged to school by the ear-lobes. Alice has started to pay for his truancy by "entertaining" the sheriff a few evenings a month.

"I don't see the point of school," she complains to Tallulah. The women stand in the kitchen. "If I could read, I might know what I'm missing."

Tallulah nods and continues to grind the meal for cornbread.

"I didn't get learning, and it didn't hurt me none." Alice picks at the edge of the kitchen table. She has come to look for Garfield, who is out playing ball with some German boys. "Now his father . . . ," she continues to a half-listening Tallulah. "A booky type he was, liked to read. Reading out loud to me all the time like his top teeth never met the bottom half. Guess Garfield favors me after all. In temper, not in looks."

Tallulah adds milk and starts to beat the mixture with a spoon.

"Well," Alice sighs, "you see that boy, tell him it's the law to go to school, even if those church ladies are making laws for all of us, never mind our opinions. Unless he's wanting to pay those fines himself, he better get to that school each morning."

"Yes'm," Tallulah answers. Garfield will do what he wants, she thinks. Garfield's got his own sense of purpose.

By November, Garfield has finally managed to learn the alphabet, A to Z. The song, like Tallulah's spirituals, is a series of empty notes and a pattern of moving lips, signifying nothing. Single-unit addition, too, he can recite: "one plus one equals two, one plus two equals three," and so on, though he has no idea what those numbers correspond to. He can count, of course; he buys at the general store for Tallulah sometimes, but the notation system is lost on him. He stops going to school on all but the coldest days, when even the most brutal beating from Mr. Pickney is not a deterrent from sitting in the warm opera house.

Most days Garfield can be found by the nearly silent railroad tracks. The train arrives when it wants, and the poor stationmaster, an Irish immigrant unimaginatively named Smith, passes lonely days in the old depot. He tells Garfield stories—when the boy will sit still long enough to listen—of the old days as an engineer on the Burlington Northern, about the bridges and the steep grades, the politicians and actors he carried, the time the Johnson brake failed and the freighter derailed and caught fire, and he had to walk twelve long miles to Schenectady with a broken ankle in a snowstorm. Smith repeats the tales again and again, in a still-thick accent. Each time, they are exaggerated or changed just enough to make Garfield suspect he is inventing everything. Smith is a drinker, which is how he, a fully trained engineer, has ended up here, a stationmaster in a town that is no one's destination. Once, into his cups, he neglected to switch the southbound over to the auxiliary track. He watched the northbound engine slam into it, locking grilles in a screech of brakes.

When the train rolls through, Garfield can hear the whistle and rumble announcing its approach. Then the tracks begin to hum and the ground to shake, and Garfield hears the rhythm of its wheels—*Heine Marouche, Heine Marouche*—like the name of a villain in an action comic. The engineer will doff his cap. Usually there is no passenger car, but if there is a "varnish," Garfield and Smith wave furiously.

Though he is not aware of it, Garfield looks into every passing passenger coach, at every swimming face, on the off chance that one day his father will come home. He has no idea what Moshe looks like, and only the slightest notion of what kind of a man he is. His mother says little about his father, and what she does say is not flattering. Mostly, Garfield hears about his father when he misbehaves and his mother claims that he takes after Moshe. Is Moshe tall? Handsome? Is he a dandy with a pocket watch and a white hat? Or is he tired, worn-out, and plump? None of the passengers is ever his father.

Sometimes the train stops to unload items ordered by catalogue or mail, or supplies for the general store, fabrics and dry goods and magazines. Garfield will help the train hands, earning a nickel for his efforts if the hands are in a generous mood. They laugh and swear and threaten to kidnap and enslave him, though they're not serious. The hands migrate, looking for seasonal work. In the fall the high plains area is busy; the winter takes them out West for produce; in the summer they work the passenger lines back East. These men have seen San Francisco, New York, Chicago, St. Louis, the long grassy plains, and the hot, distant desert. They've climbed passes and lolled in valleys. And now they are in Orerich.

If the train stops to turn around, the men have a couple hours off and Garfield directs them to Gilges Street; they return happy and sated, smelling of spilled beer and the warm sweat of the women in the house at

Number 14. Meanwhile, Smith and the fireman uncouple the engine and wait for the engineer to ease it onto the side track. Then the engineer pulls it around to what was the caboose and rehitches the now-empty rattlers. What was forward has become backward, what was right is now left. And, reattached, its men safely aboard, it will chug off back to where it came from.

Sometimes when the rail hands go into town, Garfield spots a hobo climbing out of a freight car. Dressed mostly in rags, hatless, carrying his meager possessions in the proverbial bindle, the hobo is a national legend. Smith tells Garfield all the popular tales of Frypan Jack, Supertramp, Boxcar Bertha, Steam Train Mallory, Three-Day Whitey, A Number One, T-Bone Slim—the heroes of stealth rail. He even sings him a song or two about the life of a hobo: the travel, the excitement, the cold of a boxcar night as the train thunders across the plains. Smith teaches him to differentiate between the types of vagrants: the hobo who works and wanders, the tramp who dreams and wanders, the bum who drinks and wanders. Then there are the subcultures: the homeguard, who doesn't leave his own rail yard, just watches the trains roll by from under a tipped bottle, and the yeggs, railroad criminals.

The travelers Garfield watches look less like nomadic heroes and more like bums, sneaking off in search of a jungle, which they won't find because Orerich is too small, too poor, too nowhere. They slink back, sober, and wait for the train to leave again, look at Garfield with pity in their eyes. They can leave, their legs are wheels, but Garfield is stuck in this town.

They are not the only ones who pity Garfield. There must be something about the boy, something neglected in his demeanor, something needy in his wide brown eyes and disheveled hair that asks for the attention of the childless old women in town. What Alice callously disregards, Mrs. Hattie Hymore cries for nightly. Even her husband, the doctor, can't fix the problem—nor can repeated prayers and donations to the church, nor an endless litany of good deeds. The postmistress, too, has taken to Garfield with an attachment beyond fondness, adding clothes and shoes to the myriad goods she bestows on him as presents.

Garfield tolerates this as he tolerates Tallulah's kneading his scalp through his hair as she cries at night. He was born, it seems, as a vessel, ready to be filled up with others' woe and misery, to embody their failed hopes and dreams and to offer a small comfort to the inconsolable.

And perhaps he needs this attention, too, the only kind he receives. Garfield is lonely. Maybe he needs surrogate mothers, and maybe without them Garfield would be another boy, become another man, have a different tale to tell. But Garfield carries this melancholy through his life. It enters and infects him, subtle as a cancer and infectious as a fever, until he is a snake that bites its tail, poisoning and repoisoning its own body.

3

It is a particularly rowdy night in Orerich, Colorado, 1892, cold and clear. It's well past midnight, and Goodmoore has sent Garfield home from the saloon for the night. Three dollar bills lie in Garfield's pocket. When Garfield breathes, it is as though his mouth produces small crystallized stars. As he turns down Gilges Street, the lights from Number 14 burst out of the house, creating a mist as though it were giving off steam. He can hear artificial laughs, even from this distance, so crisp and windless is the air. The upstairs windows are curtained, with shadowed silhouettes like reverse cameo brooches.

Garfield slows his steps, though his wool sweater and jacket are painfully inadequate for this extreme weather, and his hands, jammed into the pockets, are starting to lose feeling. He watches the house, its sagging porch, faded paint, and sorry junk pile of a garden buried under snow. It seems to pulse with activity, and he knows they are all bustling inside: pouring drinks, dancing, flirting. He can imagine Tallulah in the kitchen, stirring rum on the stove for toddies.

But even slow steps advance him, and soon Garfield is on the porch. He walks around back, peering in the parlor windows. He sees a couple of rail hands he directed this way earlier. There has been a successful strike somewhere south, and a resulting increase in rail traffic moving the unrefined silver north for processing. There, on the couch, Netta waves a scarf over the face of Billy Knowles, who works in the general store. Millard Tinker, the milkman, is pouring himself a drink from the bar in the corner. Garfield can see Tab Strunks, the blacksmith, whose wife has pleurisy, and Woody Harbison, the sign maker, laughing with Tabitha, a Mexican resident of the house. Her dress is low-cut, and Garfield can almost make out the darker pink of her nipples when she bends over.

The strategic display of flesh is the girls' special skill. The soft line of a thigh, the curve of a hip through a slit in the fabric, ample arms through lace sleeves can drive a man crazy. Garfield knows this already; though he has never been with a woman, he is already an initiate into the game, the challenge, that is sex. He knows the dance, and the act itself will disappoint him. It is as though he has been backstage at the circus and seen the wigs, makeup, and mirrors; the show has lost its thrill.

"Don't be standin' there peekin' in windows, boy," Garfield hears Tallulah say. She has come out onto the porch without a coat. She tips a large bucket over the rail. It steams in the cold air. "It's cold out here, boy. You comin' in?"

"Yes," Garfield says. "I'm hungry."

"I got some leftover gravy you can put on the potatoes."

"That'd be all right." Garfield is about to turn from the window when he sees a familiar hairy forearm on the sill directly in front of him. It belongs to Garfield's worst enemy in a town of antagonists: the schoolmaster, Mr. Pickney. Garfield draws a sharp breath. So much for the churchgoer's piety. It has been overcome—like Dr. Hymore's, like the butcher's and the blacksmith's—by desire, by lust, by the charms of the girls of Gilges Street and the carefree moments they provide. Garfield is hardly surprised, yet can't help but be disturbed, for the substantial ankle that now careens into view (a sign of a body covering another on the couch), swathed in fishnet stockings and a well-worn boot, belongs to his mother, Alice O'Malley Haurowitz.

Garfield takes a sudden step back, and Tallulah says again, "What you see in windows, Mr. Peeping Tom, ain't none of your business."

"He's here often?" he demands. "He's been here before?"

"I don't know who you're talking about," Tallulah says, resting the bucket on her hip. "You ain't got no right to talk about things you see lookin' into rooms where you ain't been invited."

Garfield swallows and follows Tallulah into the overheated kitchen, where she gives him warm beer to thaw him out and places a shallow bowl of gravy and lumpy mashed potatoes in front of him. Garfield eats it hungrily. He has a feeling in the pit of his stomach that this liaison between Alice and Pickney will end badly—for Pickney, for Alice, and for himself.

There is no reliable thermometer in Orerich, but the news from Denver is that the temperature is below normal even in that sun-blessed location. Up in the mountains it is even colder. Garfield is throwing stones from a small pile at a dead bird on the tracks below. Though he is shivering, he has not had the courage to face Pickney at school. He does not know what he'd say. He can hardly defend his mother's honor, not at this point, in this town, but he still feels somehow violated. He's not even sure Pickney knows that Alice is his mother. He concentrates on his task, listening to the rocks hit the rails with a ping, or making a duller thud when they strike the bird's frozen flesh.

Smith sighs behind him. He is reading the *Union Pacific Rails* for old times' sake. "Says here," he calls to Garfield, "they've invented some sort of new gauge system for the wheels. Won't be rocking quite so much inside."

Garfield nods. He has never ridden a train, not really, not farther than just around the yard, the time it takes for the engine to turn around, and he has only been inside a passenger car once, when a man in a suit gave him twenty-five cents to deliver a note to a lady. The man smiled and patted him on the head, and Garfield walked him to the only respectable hotel in town, the Six White Horses Inn, where the bar had a Bible and a sign above it saying "no swearing." No one knew whether the owner, old man Granger, had intended the joke or not.

There is a silence. Garfield throws another rock, hits the bird square on, rolling it onto its back so that its spindly legs stand up like tent poles.

"Did you hear?" Smith looks at Garfield.

"Hear what?"

"'Bout Mrs. Guiteau. Laid up with pneumonia, it seems, and no family to care or pay the doctor's bill."

"Who?" Garfield asks. He has never heard this name before and is surprised, for he assumes he knows everyone in town.

"Mrs. Guiteau. The postmistress. Ain't she the one so nice to you, got you them new pants?"

Garfield pitches all the rocks onto the tracks. They splatter like hail. He begins to swing his legs to warm himself. The postmistress's sickness is not of interest to him.

"I would've thought you'd been down there already," Smith says. "Give her back some of what she give you."

"I don't like sick people. And I don't hardly know her." He has a sense of where this conversation will go, and he wants to avoid it.

"Still, she don't got many visitors." Smith gives him a look over the top of the magazine that implies Garfield's visit is more of an order than a suggestion.

Garfield stands up; his head hurts from the cold. "All right, I'll go," he says. "Where's she live?"

"Down the hill. Garden out front. Here you are; you take her this." He hands Garfield the magazine he's reading. "And this." His sack lunch.

Garfield walks as slowly as he can. The solitary house seems to sag. The gate hangs only by its top hinge, but the garden seems well-kept, with burlap bags over what must be the rosebushes. It is difficult to get anything but wildflowers to grow at this altitude, but Mrs. Guiteau has made a valiant effort. There is a flagstone path, and Garfield walks up it now, knocks on the door.

There is no response. Garfield hikes around back. There is an abandoned ice chest next to a window, and Garfield climbs on it to look inside. The kitchen is a mess. A pie lies in pieces on the floor, and field mice are having a convention in its ruins. Dishes are piled unwashed in the sink, and laundry is strewn across an interior line.

The back door is ajar, and Garfield lets himself inside. The house is small, just a few rooms. He surveys the sparsely decorated salon. The furniture is fading but was once grand, he can tell: a loveseat of smooth horsehair, tarnished kerosene lamps with leaded glass shades, and a candelabrum on the mantelpiece. Garfield moves closer to inspect it. Gold, unmistakably, a four-candled piece with a smooth long neck and ornate vines winding around its wide base and up the fingers of the lamp. Next to this treasure is another piece of gold, a frame, with a daguerreotype fading to black under its glass. A beautiful woman poses in front of a train station with a dapper man. Both are dressed in the dated fashions of the postbellum East, the woman in a long, heavy skirt and a tight-buttoned bodice with puffed sleeves, the man in a suit with high trousers, a pocket watch chain peeking out from underneath his long waistcoat. He has spectacles dangling from a chain around his neck, and his arm around the woman. She leans into him, a distant smile of joy on her face—a smile Garfield has never seen in person, a real smile, absent of guile and artifice. This woman is happy; it is obvious. This woman is in love. Behind them, the train smokes as though alive. Puffs of steam curl into the rafters of the grand station, and the background is full of supernumeraries busy with various station tasks, waiting for trains, loading and carrying luggage, oblivious to the posing couple.

Garfield is aware of a pulse in the house, the staccato rhythm of breathing somewhere. He passes a small room that must be a water closet (he has never seen one) and a linen shelf lined neatly with white sheets and towels. The door ahead is open; the room is shrouded in darkness.

"Who's there?" a voice whispers.

"Garfield," he answers, whispering as well. Suddenly he is struck with the most palpable fear, Tallulah's tales of the devil fresh in his mind.

"Garfield Shimon Patrick Haurowitz," the voice whispers.

"That's right," Garfield says.

"Garfield Shimon Patrick Haurowitz," it repeats. It sounds like one of the hymns they are made to recite in school. "Come closer," the voice says.

Garfield's eyes gradually adjust to the light. He can see the postmistress in bed, the covers pulled up to her chin, the black dress on the chair in the corner of the room. She looks small, so much smaller than she ever seemed from her elevated perch in the post office. Her legs make insignificant ripples in the otherwise flat covers.

"You're sick?" Garfield asks, though he already knows. He can smell it in the musty silence of the house, the scent of the beginning of decay.

"Yes." Mrs. Guiteau's voice is small.

"Would you like a hot rock to put in your bed?" It is what some of the Gilges Street women want when they take to their beds, complaining of womanly troubles.

"No. I want to see you. Come here. You came through the living room, yes?" Mrs. Guiteau asks. Garfield nods. "On the mantel, near the candles, is a picture. Can you bring it to me? And the candles?"

Garfield jumps up, glad to be dismissed. In the living room the sun is shining, the air is breathable again, and he takes his time removing the items from the mantelpiece. It is low, and though he is short he can see the rings of dustless wood they leave when he removes them.

He reluctantly returns to the bedroom. "Turn on the lamp," Mrs. Guiteau directs.

Garfield reaches over and, at her pointing, rotates the knob of a lamp on the night table, though he is confused about how this is supposed to shed light. "I forgot," Mrs. Guiteau says, smiling. "No electricity. Draw the curtains."

Garfield peels the heavy velveteen curtains apart. He ties the sashes, and the light tumbles in, filtered through the cotton undershades. Mrs. Guiteau blinks. Her skin is loose on her face, her eyes red and sagging. She picks up the frame from her lap.

"I was pretty, wasn't I?"

"Yes, ma'am," Garfield answers.

"That's something, then. To be pretty. That's lucky."

"I s'pose." Garfield feels as though he must say something. Already he is planning his escape. His headache is worse; it is pounding now against his skull. After her next sentence he will say good-bye.

"You should know. Your father told me before he left that I should look out for you, because he couldn't anymore. He didn't want to leave. I'm telling you this because I could see it in him. He wanted to stay, but he couldn't." She is gripping Garfield's arm fiercely now, with a strength he hasn't suspected she could muster. Her words are quick, feverish.

"Come back tomorrow to check on me. There's no one else," she says. She slumps back onto the pillow, spent.

Garfield nods. Her eyes have closed, and her breathing is measured. He backs out of the room, clutching the candelabrum to his chest. He doesn't stop running until he has reached the familiar chaos of Gilges Street.

There, clammy from the cold air, with sweat running down his temples, Garfield debates where to hide his treasure. He knows he must keep it hidden, well hidden, if he wants it to be his. And he does, he desperately wants it—*something*—to be his and his alone. For what has he owned in his life, this near orphan? A pair of pants, a secondhand sweater . . .

He scurries under the porch and continues under the house until there is no more light and his way is blocked by a load-bearing beam. Then he uses his hands to dig a hole, pawing furiously until his back and knees start to hurt. He digs through the pain for a while, sweat soaking his long johns, until the hole is big enough. He lays the candelabrum down carefully, gently, as if burying a child, and scoops the dirt back over it ceremoniously.

He has to back out of the crawl space. He scoots slowly until he can feel the air on his legs and then his back. He looks to the right and sees the stout, swollen ankles of Tallulah.

"What you doing under there, boy?"

"Nothing, ma'am," Garfield says. He is instinctively protective of this, his first real treasure.

"Sheriff come by. You ain't been to school again." Garfield studies his scuffed brown boots. They are too big, but already Tallulah has had to re-sew the sole to the toe in front.

"Where you been?" Garfield still says nothing. "And what you hiding under that house? You a mess." Tallulah brushes the dirt off his shirt, then puts her arm around Garfield and steers him toward the back door. "You look cold, boy. You downright shivering." Tallulah warms some milk in the kitchen while Garfield takes off his boots and puts on a clean shirt. He does feel cold; he is trembling. He takes a sip of the milk and feels it travel down the tunnel of his throat. He has the small ball of a pleasurable secret in his belly.

By the time the kerosene lamps have been lighted and the sounds of men's low voices mingle with those of women in the parlor, Garfield's fever has spiked. Tallulah wipes his brow with a cool cloth and arranges his bedding by the fire, though he shakes with chills. His head is warmer than any she has felt, and she is scared. Alice has been in to see him, but she is busy entertaining Pickney again.

Tallulah rocks him when she finds a spare five minutes away from the demands of the women. She sings him spirituals, and they merge with Garfield's delirious dreams so that he believes he is in the fires of hell, burning. Finally, the fever breaks slightly and he sleeps, so still that Tallulah comes over with a glass from time to time to check for the condensation that means he is still breathing. She has come to regard Garfield as something of her own. She'll be damned if she will lose another child.

It is four days before Garfield regains full consciousness. He has been given one of the upstairs rooms, but he doesn't like its printed wallpaper and heavy curtains. He wants to be back in the kitchen, which smells like fire and coffee and dinner instead of musty old mattress.

When he opens his eyes, Alice is there. She smooths back his hair and hums to him, soft quiet ballads unlike Tallulah's effusive melodies. They seem to come from Alice's head, from her plaited brown hair. They have no words, and they soothe Garfield back to sleep, although he feels as though he had something important to do. Something that demands his attention immediately. "It can't wait," he wants to tell his mother, but he is hypnotized by her crooning, and his eyelids flutter once, twice, then close.

The next time he wakes, Tallulah is standing near with coffee and porridge and two eggs, just the way he likes them, fried crispy on both sides. He sits up on his pillow and takes a sip of the coffee wordlessly. It is too hot, and he opens his mouth to let out the steam, which makes Tallulah laugh.

"You feel better?"

"Better," Garfield says. He takes a slow bite of porridge. The texture is strange, and he has difficulty swallowing. But when the first mouthful hits his stomach, he realizes how hungry he is. He finishes the porridge ravenously and moves on to the eggs. "No toast?" he asks.

Tallulah shakes her head. He takes a large drink of coffee and wipes his mouth on the bedsheets. Tallulah says, "You had it bad. I only seen one other soul get better from a sickness like that and that's my papa. Yessir, he tossed and turned one week, devil of a fever in his brain, all shouting and speaking in tongues, and we had the preacher ready, but then he just sat up and asked for porridge and ate it all down."

This is the first Garfield has ever heard about Tallulah's family. He has assumed she has no kin. "Your father?" he asks.

"I don't remember him much. He got better and then took his hat and left to fight on the North side in the war. We ain't never seen him again."

Garfield starts. "I was supposed to look in on the post lady. She was laid up, too. I was supposed to go over there tomorrow. Is it tomorrow yet?"

"Boy, you've been lying here five tomorrows." Tallulah laughs. Then her face returns to its concerned pout. "Lord, are you serious? Sweet Jesus, that poor old woman." Tallulah hurries out of the room, leaving the tray on the bed. Garfield moves it to the floor. It is all he can do to stay awake for this action before sleep overcomes him again.

Tallulah has never been inside the station house. She hears the distant sound of the railroad's passing like harmless thunder's meaningless noise. As she reaches the end of Gilges Street, Goodmoore's Saloon unnaturally and uncannily quiet during the day, she turns right, east, instead of her customary market-bound left. Ingor Street boasts no residences, just largely abandoned structures built grandly in the optimism of a vein strike. A well-weathered sign for a blacksmith's shop swings, bored, in the breeze. Tallulah identifies it by the picture of the workhorse and his shoe.

The tracks loom ahead, the station hidden by the buildings on the left. She looks in both directions and crosses the tracks gingerly, her sharp heels sinking in the gravel between the rails. She can see Smith napping on the station's bench. The open magazine on his chest rises and falls with his rhythmic breaths.

"Sir?" Tallulah asks. Smith doesn't move. "I said, sir?" Tallulah repeats. She is standing beneath him, one foot on the rails, next to the platform. Smith gives no response, no sign of having heard. She looks for stairs, but there is no polite way up onto the platform. It is the height of her low bosom, and she has no choice but to climb. She leans her body forward, using the rail for extra height, and manages to get her torso onto the wood. It groans with her weight. She swings her right leg up onto the platform. Her skirts lift, exposing the welt of her wool stockings above the knee and the knobby lumps of flesh resting there. She gives a large grunt as she rolls over.

"Jesus Christ!" Tallulah cannot see the speaker; she is on her stomach. She rolls over another half turn. Smith is standing over her. They stare at each other in an embarrassed impasse.

"I'm looking for the post-office lady," Tallulah says, finally. She has straightened her skirts but remains sitting on the cold platform, winded.

"Down Carbonate Hill," Smith says, pointing with the magazine. "Only house there. Sent that boy down there a fair number of days ago, I did. Ain't seen hide nor hair of neither since."

"Garfield's had the fever," Tallulah explains. She is going to try to get up.

"He recover?" Smith asks. He would like to offer her a hand, but he can't. Can't because she is colored and can't because she lives on Gilges Street. Even with no one around to see, the postmistress laid up, the train hours or days away, he cannot offer her a hand.

"He will." Tallulah is breathing hard now. She has managed to grab the arm of the bench, but she can't pull herself up sideways. She struggles, stops. Struggles, then stops again. She looks up at Smith.

Smith looks around twice, a gesture Tallulah does not fail to notice, and moves behind her to grab under the warmth of her armpits and hoist her quickly onto her feet. Then it is over, and they have a tacit agreement to pretend it has never happened.

Tallulah pulls her skirts straight and walks through the station, passing the waiting room's vestigial ticket window. The benches stand in attentive rows like church pews, and the floor slopes gently so that there are no stairs to negotiate when Tallulah steps through the open door onto the angle of Carbonate Hill. Down the path she stumbles, her ankles swelling with the unexpected exercise. She can see the house in the distance. The lack of chimney smoke in the cloudless sky is a sure sign of trouble.

Tallulah walks as Garfield did around to the back; children and Negroes are accustomed to back doors. She knocks once for the sake of decorum, but she does not wait for an answer. She knows what she will find. In the kitchen the mice are gone, as is the pie. The tin sits on the floor.

Tallulah walks through the living room and into the bedroom, where Mrs. Guiteau lies, eyes open, hands clutching the picture. Death Tallulah has seen, more times than she ever dreamed she would. And even the first time, a stable boy kicked in the head by a horse, was unsurprising. Birth is just the first step toward death, and death, at least, requires minimal effort.

Tallulah lifts the woman out of the bed. Mrs. Guiteau is light, Tallulah thinks; life is much heavier. She sets the body down on the floor and makes the bed. Then she takes the black dress off the chair and opens the back all the way so that it spreads out as a blanket on the bed. She bends over and removes the dead woman's nightgown, which smells of sweat and urine. Tallulah balls it up and leaves it on the chair. Then she takes the woman in her arms and places her facedown on the bed. It is like dressing a doll, only the arms are stiff. They will not relinquish the picture frame, so she tries to pull the dress up around it.

When she is finished, the last button done, the dress hangs loosely. Tallulah gathers her hair in a long braid down her back and rolls her over. Her arms cradle the picture beneath the dress; the sleeves hang oddly empty.

Then Tallulah goes into the kitchen and starts a fire. This woman clearly had money once, Tallulah thinks; the stove is a fancy double-compartment wood or coal burner. What Tallulah would give for a stove like this. She throws the nightdress in with the existing wood for fuel. She collects water from the pump in back and sets it to boil. Tallulah does the dishes. Steam rises from her hands and dissipates. She does not forget the pie tin. With the same water, Tallulah scrubs the kitchen floor, the work table, the shelves. Then she looks for a rag. She finds one, along with nesting newborn mice, under the sink. Tallulah takes the nest and carries it to the garden. One small mouse falls out over her index finger and dies soundlessly on the floor. Tallulah picks it up by its tail and sends it sailing out the back door.

She takes the rag and moves into the living room. She dusts the low tables, the window sills near the front door, straightens the antimacassars on the couch, aligns the big chairs and goes over to the mantel. She can see her reflection in the mirror above it. She is what she expected she would be, and she looks away before the image can sink in. On the mantel, though, she notices two spots of dustless wood: the long "T" of the picture frame and a circle. She knows, suddenly, that this is what Garfield was hiding under the house: a treasure he has stolen from a dead woman. She wipes the traces clean.

She stares at the indoor privy and marvels at its lack of smell. Though there is no plumbing, the downward slope of the hill and the water rushing beneath keep it relatively odor free. She has never seen a privy indoors, and it strikes her as indecent, filthy. Still, she scrubs it clean; she has completed worse tasks.

When the house is in order, Tallulah begins the hike uphill. She stops to rest several times, and it is dark when she arrives back in town. It is extremely cold now, and she pulls her shawl close. Her steps are instinctive; she has never been where she is going now, but she knows where the house must be. The biggest one in Orerich. She finds it easily near the center of town—a large, square box of a building, the remnants of a garden in front, a neat, waist-high fence surrounding it.

Tallulah walks to the back door and knocks. She waits. Mrs. Hattie Hymore opens the door. Tallulah has expected a maid. Her mouth is open, but she makes no sound.

"Yes, what is it?" Mrs. Hymore wipes her hands on a flour-covered apron. So the woman cooks as well, Tallulah thinks. She has assumed that all rich white women have help, even if the houses are not as big as those she remembers from the South.

"Speak, woman," Mrs. Hymore says. She shivers a little. The light and warmth from the kitchen escape.

"I found the post lady. She dead," Tallulah says.

Mrs. Hymore nods. "Well, then it'll wait until morning, won't it?"

"I didn't know nobody else to tell," Tallulah explains.

"No, you did the right thing. I'll notify the pastor in the morning. Good night." Mrs. Hymore steps back inside and closes the door. It latches with a deep noise, and Tallulah feels dismissed in a way she thought was no longer possible, not after years of exclusion have made the feeling so banal as to be unremarkable.

She starts to walk home. The streets are dark, but the light of the quarter moon and the gas lamps in the windows make her way sufficiently visible. Suddenly a thought comes to mind: This is the way the doctor walks when he comes to Gilges Street at night. This is what the doctor sees, what he smells, the cold he feels. His feet fall where mine do, she thinks; he touches the same fence post; he hurries along toward the same warm destination. Tallulah is comforted, and her step quickens.

4

ickney's hiding places have one major flaw: they are aboveground. He has dollar bills stuffed among the husks in his mattress, in the bottom of his trunk, in the leaves of his books, in the vase of dried flowers on the mantel in his small boarder's room in Mrs. Oliver Tinker's house. They peek out sometimes, as though sending out roots from a bulb into the daylight. He must be careful to stuff them back in place. This money is his "collector's fee," his unofficial salary for the insufferable job he holds as schoolmaster in Orerich, Colorado. It is the payback for all his bad luck, all the hard knocks and unfair twists of fate. And it is at the expense of the generous Episcopal churchgoers.

Because of his supposed superiority at mathematics, Pickney is treasurer of the church's funds. They are saving for their own worship hall, not just a slot in the Sunday morning time schedule in the all-purpose building they have to share not only with the school and the Baptists, but also with the Catholics, the Lutherans, and the Evangelicals. They are saving slowly, over time. Their little congregation is growing, as is the town.

Orerich may yet see prosperity, though Pickney doubts it. Regardless, he'll be long gone by then. He will have enough money to buy up tracks from Philadelphia to Richmond, bridges especially. He is a man of action, a strong man, born of America, educated in her bosom and set free to play in her skirts. Anything is his for the taking; America owes him, her son. Here is his plan: He will take Alice, that pearl of beauty among the swine, and run. They will leave at night, as soon as first thaw, on Tinker's horses, the team he uses to pull the dairy cart. They will ride all night to Leadville, where they will hide, like Pickney's money, in plain sight in the lawless town. They will lie low, like Jesse and the gang. They will rent a room— he will be able to afford it—and make love. And then (and this he longs

37

for more than he longs to see Alice's body completely naked in the light of day) he will sleep with her, next to her. He will listen to the soft noises she makes in her sleep, the grinding of her teeth, the suck of her tongue against the roof of her mouth, her sighs as she readjusts her position. He will rest his hand on her breast, feeling her chest rise and fall. And she will wake up in the morning and want it, too. This is his fantasy: that she will turn to him, breath sweet with morning's scent, and she will kiss his mouth with hers, let her tongue travel lightly over his teeth, wrestle with his own, dart in and out like a firefly. She will reach for him with her long fingers, rub his back crossways, her nails a soothing rake, the striations like the lines of a sunset across the sky. She will want him as much as he wants her.

Not long now. Just one more cold, snowy Colorado winter until he can make a home for his rescued bride. Once the trail is cold, they will emerge from their den of safety and take the northern transcontinental route to California. And then it will begin—the rest of his life.

In the meantime Pickney squirrels away cash, buries what he can, and waits. The winter's hibernation will be brutal. But there is the hope of sunshine at the end of it, and his photographic rodent's memory of buried treasure.

Garfield is regaining his strength, though his back aches where he was bled and cupped with a cow horn to draw out the fever. Tallulah rubs a poultice of tobacco and lard on the wounds, sealing them. Her fingers are soft grass. He sleeps in Alice's big bed, next to her. Once it's dark he sits in the kitchen with Tallulah throwing woodworms into the flames and listening to them hiss. Tallulah is teaching him basic bartending, and he can now bring the men their drinks. He knows how much water to splash in the liquor, how to pour the beer without losing its foam. Finally, he is useful. When the men leave, Alice calls him, and they change the linens together. The fabric smells of cologne and dirty socks, and Alice balls them up quickly. She throws them down the laundry chute, and they remake the bed with white sheets of harsh cotton and fall into slumber together, resting in each other's arms.

If Smith suffers in Garfield's absence he does not complain. He still sends rail hands to Gilges Street, but does not himself come by to inquire after Garfield. Perhaps he is afraid that the house has some pull, like the magnetic force of the Pole, or the gluelike stick of flypaper, and will trap him. Perhaps he no longer thinks about Garfield. The nature of working in transportation is that things are always coming and going, he comments to his wife. She is mostly deaf and says, "Yes, dear," when she sees his lips move. Sometimes he calls her names, just because he can. Garfield came and went, and that's as simple as that.

Winter descends on Orerich like a heavy tarp. Everyone is frozen in place, settled down for the season like bears. As stagecoach and even rail travel over the pass become practically impossible, the bustle of the market slows, and the town diet dwindles to stored items: potatoes and pickled vegetables, old apples and preserved eggs. The snow piles on top of houses; warm windows and dripping mansard roofs melt round holes around jambs and sills. The sky looks like the air, blizzard white, insulating the town and cutting off its tenuous connection with the rest of America. It is just Orerich now, a stage with limited players.

Moshe looks out the window as the train hurries through the prairie states. He should be in the kitchen stirring stew for dinner. The mess bubbles and gurgles without him. Moshe's face is red with soup steam; there is a thin line of moisture under his nose. He opens the window and sticks his head out to let the air blow on his face. This is strictly against the rules, and if the brakeman sees him he is sure to notify the conductor. Then Moshe will have to run back to the kitchen and innocently spoon the soup around in its pot.

They passed Dodge City, Kansas, just before lunch, and now, at supper-time, they are so close to the Outlet that he can smell it. It is an acrid aroma, of rancor and salty tears, but it is familiar like nothing else is. He can almost see the deserted plains and government outposts, the failed fields and small conglomeration of houses and gin mills and stores. He hears the footsteps of the brakeman above him and ducks his head in, hitting it on the sill, disorienting him just for a minute.

In the fog of his injury, rubbing his head, Moshe thinks he sees Alice. She appears out of nowhere in front of him in her nightshift. Her long, dark hair is brushed flat against her back, but every time the train rocks he can see it shift into view, like the tail of a comet. She is tall and straight and lovely pale, and Moshe is ready to run into her arms, to forgive her everything, to beg her to forgive him, too. And then Alice is simply the dining room coat rack, an apron, and the round Pullman dish mounted on the wall. Moshe's heart sinks.

His fellow cooks stare as he enters the room, wondering where he has been. He must look shaken. Bloated squirrel pieces float in the stew, along with potatoes and lentils and carrots. Moshe adds a little pepper. Squirrel tastes like any game, and tonight they are passing it off as venison. No one will be the wiser. The head chef, French-born Jacques, comes over. He takes the spoon from Moshe's hand, dips it, blows on it softly with pursed lips, and tastes. "*Bon*," he pronounces and lets the spoon fall; Moshe can only stare at its handle disappearing in the goopy mess.

They are all watching this exchange—Paul, the assistant cook; Dickie, the dwarf in charge of the cold kitchen; and Justice, the kitchen boy. They return to their tasks as Jacques walks away. Moshe is relieved. He is not a cook; he had wanted to be a porter, but those choice jobs were reserved for Negroes. It seems that whites are more comfortable ordering around colored men. Plus, the porter jobs are handed down, father to son or nephew; you have to know one to be one.

So Moshe took the job as kitchen helper and learned to cook the repetitive menu of the Pullman car. Mondays, "veal" cutlet with Béarnaise sauce. Tuesdays, prime rib with horseradish and potatoes au gratin. Wednesdays, chicken supreme with buttered carrots. Thursdays, lamb chop. Friday, "veal" again, with rice pilaf. Saturday delivers game pie, and Sunday is leftovers thrown into a "venison" stew. Dinner is seventy-five cents, prix fixe, including dessert and coffee and a glass of Pullman wine. Not a bad deal, all things considered.

When the stew is simmering satisfactorily, Moshe starts to spoon it into small bowls on top of bread. Outside, the dining room bustles. Moshe can hear the waiters pulling chairs out for the first seating and the clank of silverware. The kitchen begins to get crowded with waiters entering to pick up the large silver trays that Dickie has laid out with crudités in a vinaigrette dressing. They fill the matching silver water pitchers from a large cooler in the corner of the car and pass through the door again.

Moshe works methodically, trying not to spill the stew down the side of the bowl, but the ladle doesn't seem to work properly. Justice has set out five trays of bowls, and Moshe has only filled three individual bowls when the first waiter appears, gloved hand outstretched.

"Hurry it up," the waiter says. His gloved hands clap together. "I got people waitin.'"

Jacques materializes. "You, again, no can do it more fast?" He sighs, exasperated. "Here, I do." He pushes Moshe backward until Moshe catches the cutting table with his hands. The chef begins to ladle the stew sloppily into bowls. "Like zat, *idiote!*" he says once the tray is full, and storms back to the oven, where he is baking tartlets for dessert.

Moshe starts again on the bowls, but now his hand is shaking from the reprimand. Jacques' insult becomes a chorus of voices inside his head that harmonize and harp on his stupidity. The entire world is at a different pace; Moshe is a player piano winding down, unable to keep up. His head hangs low, his tongue swelling in his mouth. It rests against his teeth, paralyzed. And the decay is spreading. Already he can barely smell, hardly taste. His brain reacts slowly; he doesn't dodge when he should, doesn't pull his hands away from the hot plates or open flames. Is he dead, or merely sleeping?

Then a white glove takes his hand and eases the ladle from it. "I'll help you," a soft voice says, and magically, the stew leaps from the pot into its bowls. "Just you calm down and do your job," the voice continues. "It ain't no big thing, you just drop it in, like that, and then into the bowl. Don't be worrying about the number of pieces of meat. It just prairie dog anyhow, ain't it?"

Moshe nods and looks up. The waiter is a deep shade of black. His eyes are bright in the light of the car, and Moshe can see small flecks of green in the irises. His collar is too tight so that his head looks swollen and bloated, like a jack-in-the-box.

"There we are." Astonishingly, the task is done. The bowls on all the trays are expertly filled to the top with the red stew. Very little is left in the pot on the stove, just the sugar from the tomatoes burned into the bottom. Moshe or Justice will have to scrub it.

"Moshe," he says, before he can help himself. No one has asked his name; everyone calls him "you." But this waiter has been kind to him, helped him.

"'Scuse me?" the waiter asks.

"Moshe. I'm called Moshe," he repeats.

"Well, I'm Jackie," the waiter answers. He speaks in a high tone, as though to a child. He thinks I'm addled, thinks Moshe.

"I got to go now." Jackie takes the tray and walks off.

Three weeks later, Moshe is again where he shouldn't be. He is wandering through the sleeping cars back to the caboose, where the mechanics will be playing cards and smoking cigarettes, throwing the butts outside, watching the points of light trip lightly down the tracks before receding into the darkness.

Moshe lets his right hand trail along the red velvet trim that runs under the hallway windows. The cars are wide and open, and the rows of bunks separated from the aisle only by flimsy curtains reveal the usual debauchery that Pullman brochures try to hide. Moshe hears several sighs and groans and the self-solaced sob of a child. A woman hangs her legs over her bunk so that only her calves and shoes extend below the curtain.

A pair of hands grab Moshe's elbow and pull him back into the porter's room at the end of the car. It smells of chicory coffee and sweat. He looks up the gray Pullman uniform, too tight in the collar, until he sees the face, recognizes it. "Jackie," he says, as though glad to see an old friend.

"What you doing in the sleeping car?" Jackie asks. He still has him roughly by his upper arms. He gives no sign of recognizing Moshe.

"Aren't you Jackie?"

"Yeah . . . ," Jackie says.

"We met in the kitchen," Moshe says. "With the stew."

"Oh, right." Jackie loosens his grip. "I ain't waitering no more. I'm a porter now."

"Oh," Moshe says, impressed.

"That don't explain what you're doing on my car in the middle of the night." Jackie whispers; his voice is soft, unreproaching.

"Going to the crummy to watch the tracks," Moshe says.

"Now you know you ain't allowed in my car," Jackie says, and for a minute Moshe is shocked. He has never seen a Negro scold a white man, no matter the infraction. Jackie sees him bristle. "It's not me," he says. "They's the rules. You get fired they find you in here."

"I just gotta get some air," he explains to Jackie. He feels as though he might suffocate. He has adjusted to the train's constant movement. He can sleep through whistles and conductor's calls and sudden stops and small grades. But he has never become accustomed to the lack of air. He feels constantly as though he is in a glass box, the sun beating down on him as he moves like a snake through the country.

"I sure do know how that is. OK. You go on back to that caboose. Anyone ask you what you doing, you tell them I sent for you 'cause I'm out of coffee, and that you going back there see if those boys need anything. OK?"

Moshe has the urge to say "yessir," but catches himself in time. He nods and Jackie lets him go. Moshe rubs his arms where Jackie grabbed him. There will be two bruises: a thumb and finger print.

Moshe hurries through the last two cars, desperate to stand on the caboose's platform and watch the cigarettes bounce away in the dim light of the safety lamp. Finally, he opens the door to the last car and jumps over the hitch to the opposite platform. The caboose men swing their legs back into their bunks to let him pass. Moshe smells the coals in the small stove as he pushes past the tables to the platform. He throws the door open, surprising the watchman, and inhales deeply, letting the air fill his lungs. He can see his breath as he exhales.

"Needing a blow, were ye?" The Irish lilt reveals the watchman to be a recent immigrant.

Moshe nods.

"Cigarette?" the man asks.

"No. I don't smoke," Moshe answers.

"Was asking if you had got one, but I guess I've got my answer," the watchman says. He takes a rumpled paper sack from his back pocket and shakes it. Out fall two rolled cigarettes. He takes one and lights it with a match he strikes on the iron railing.

"Was a bear a bit back there," he says. "Don't see that every day."

"Oh," Moshe says. The man's verbosity is ruining his air. "Good night," he says.

Moshe enters the hot room. The men are sitting in their bunks playing some sort of bluffing card game.

"Wanna join us, kitchen boy?" one man asks.

"No money," Moshe says. He doesn't waste money on nonessentials. He saves some and sends the rest to Orerich. He hopes it arrives and that Alice and Garfield haven't moved on.

"Well, then." The men laugh. Moshe opens the door and crosses back over to the sleeping cars. He sneaks through them again, this time on tiptoe, and the oblivious porters doze, shine shoes, or write letters home. They can't see Moshe. He is stealthy, invisible, invigorated by the cold air.

He reaches Jackie's car and knocks politely on the glass, startling the man. "Get the coffee?" Jackie laughs.

"Yup," Moshe smiles. "Thanks. For not turning me in."

"What's the profit in that?" Jackie asks. "Now you owe me something."

Moshe moves his body inside the small door. "What're you reading?"

"Holy Bible," Jackie answers. "Word of God. You ever read the Word of God?"

"Not since I was a kid, and never in English," Moshe says, thinking of his father's worn Torah, which he has never opened, though he sleeps with it under his pillow every night. He is saving it for a time when they are together again, as a family, and this wandering has ceased.

Jackie laughs again. "This ain't the kind of thing they sell at the Harvey stores."

Moshe chuckles at the idea of the Bible next to *Railroad Bill Hits the Brakes* or *Bessie's Six Lovers: A Summer Idyll,* or *Of the World Worldly,* all popular in 1892. He can just see the description of the book, listed beneath it on the shelf: "A stirring tale of intrigue and romance by the world's most popular author, God Himself. A book of cultivation and taste for discerning readers." He tells this to Jackie, and the two of them laugh, although he doubts Jackie has ever been in a Harvey store. It isn't illegal, exactly, but Moshe has never seen a Negro inside.

"If it ain't too rude, can I ask, are you a Jew?"

"Half," he admits, reluctantly. His religion has always made him the butt of jokes, if not worse. Once a group of boys asked what church he called his own, and he was forced to admit that he worshiped in no church, and that he didn't accept Jesus Christ as his savior. The boys beat him up, punching and kicking until Moshe's passivity made them lose interest. Moshe learned that it is easier to manufacture an imaginary church and swear devotion to it. But something about this man invites confidence.

Jackie nods his head in admiration. "What's the other half?"

"My mother was a Cherokee."

"That's a combination! Don't you get confused about which religion is which?"

Moshe is incredulous. Amazingly, being Jewish seems to raise him in Jackie's eyes. But he doesn't know how to answer this question. He's not sure what he believes. He has always assumed that somewhere between his uncle's atavistic stories of slavery and redemption and his mother's missionary songs lies the real truth, the true Divine Spirit. But he practices no religion, prays to no God, because he assumes that both his mother's God and his uncle's abandoned them, taking his brothers and sisters. He has escaped by some oversight, he reasons.

This he finds himself telling Jackie, the man eager to listen to Moshe's disjointed tales and half-cooked philosophy. Moshe tells him about his mother, about Boggy and his disappearance, about the arrival of the uncle with the unblemished hands. The little cabin in Oklahoma, the stubborn garden, his brothers and sisters. Then he describes Alice, her beauty, her unhappiness, and finally her betrayal. Then he talks about little Garfield, just months old when he left. About ten now.

Jackie listens until Moshe has finished. It feels good to Moshe to get it all out. He hasn't spoken to anyone in a long time, and the story feels as if it has been lodged in his throat the whole while.

Jackie does not tell his story in return. He simply says he is from St. Louis. His father was a rail man, too, who ran off when Jackie was twelve. Since then he has been the man of the house. He has a wife and two daughters, another one on the way. He sees them one weekend a month on a layover.

Moshe hasn't realized how lonely he is. This intimate chat has awakened a deep thirst in him, like a sip of water on a hot day. "Can I come and we can maybe talk again?" he asks.

Jackie smiles sadly. "I never been friends with a white man before. Not since I was old enough to know better. But all right," he says. "We'll try it."

Their conversations are hurried, like lovers' trysts. They are frequently interrupted by bells that summon Jackie to the bedsides of traveling passengers. Some want water, hot or cold, some food, others to make sure they haven't missed their stop. Can Jackie tuck in the blanket? Can he shine the shoes? And buff them good, now.

The trip west ends and so do their conversations. By the capriciousness of the rail system, Moshe is sent north, Jackie south. Then Jackie lays over in St. Louis. His wife has the baby. Moshe catches the influenza and rests in a hotel outside Santa Fe. They meet up infrequently, but are always pleased to see each other, subdued happiness in front of rail hands and other Pullman porters and, of course, in front of railroad brass.

Jackie may be Moshe's first friend. He is laughing regularly for the first time in a long while, and the old talkativeness is back with a vengeance. Whenever he sees Jackie, especially if they have been separated a while, he talks incessantly, narrating each day, almost minute by minute, that they have been apart. Jackie tolerates his streams of words the way Alice used to, with an amused smile. For Moshe, this friendship is a strange sensation—a risky choice. Moshe stands taller, it seems. Jackie's respect and admiration bolster him. He regains his tongue and his senses. His eyes open in the mornings, his lungs take in air, the tips of his fingers feel surfaces when he touches them. And the men continue to give him wide berth, but now not because of his strange abnormality or his status as an outsider; rather they now see a powerful man who has *chosen* not to associate with them.

All through the hot summer they ride the rails in tandem, Moshe and Jackie. Moshe almost jumps a train in St. Louis to visit Jackie's family, but at the last minute is offered a place on the Denver and Rio Grande West to the coast at a slightly higher salary than usual. Secretly, both men are grateful. They can avoid the potential awkwardness of having Moshe meet Jackie's wife, his secret life, and the stares and clucking tongues of neighbors who would not approve of a half-breed (which half is worse, he wonders?) staying in a colored man's living room.

Fall descends like a shadow over the plains. The land is too tired to be grateful. Tilled out, parched, and sun-baked, the fields seem to sleep in the fast-falling nights and cooler days. Moshe's head is always out the dining car windows, taking in whatever air he can gasp. Jackie will join the train in Jefferson City, and Moshe has plenty to tell him. The train flies through the small towns along the way, the names too blurry to read, but then all small towns are named the same thing in every state. Names of hope: Pretty Prairie, Mount Zion, Water Falls; names of founders: Meade, Kearney, Jackson; names the Indians gave the area, the Indians themselves long gone but the names enduring: Wachatuchkee, Meeniteko, Korawanoo. Moshe waves to the people standing on the platforms or sprawled on their summer porches, though he knows they can't see him.

And as the towns rush by, Moshe is infused with a sense of hope that has no other name but Faith, a fluttering of his heart that he thinks is evidence of the presence of a Creator, a joy derived from the notion that he among all others is chosen by God, that his life has a purpose, a meaning. He sees proof of the hand of God in every working mill, every flowing stream, even in the rushes and eddies of air created by the train's agitation. Jackie has done this to him.

This time they are to meet up on the eastbound. When the train stops in Jefferson City, Moshe is busy plating beef medallions. The train begins to move again, to pick up speed as Moshe lays the round fillets on mashed potatoes. The first seating is almost over when Moshe hears the engineer's screaming whistle. The train stops abruptly, with the screech of emergency brakes. There are frantic footsteps on the train roof. Moshe sticks his head into the dining room where a few customers, surprised by the sudden arrest of movement, wear soup like bright ties on their lapels. Moshe finishes his last fillets hurriedly, leaving the dishes for the kitchen boy to start, and walks to the rear of the train. A bold move; he must sneak there even in the dead of night. But he walks with purposeful step until stopped by the oversized bartender in the second-class car.

"You from the kitchen, ain't allowed back there."

"You know what happened?" Moshe is afraid to ask. A sudden unexpected stop can only mean bad news. Even a busted water pipe or a fire makes the train slow gradually. The churning of the crank pins grinds to a warped chug, and the whistle lets out steam languidly as the valves close. A train stops like this for only two reasons: a head-on collision or a dead body.

"Lost somebody."

"Shit," Moshe says. He rarely swears, but he knows this is the appropriate reaction in front of the bartender. His first instinct, to pray, would be received by a strange look followed by no further information.

The bartender leans in. "You know Jackie Potsman, the porter?"

Moshe's mouth is dry. His head nods on his neck, a little too emphatically, but he can't stop it as it lolls up and down.

"Drunk white man done pushed him between the cars."

Moshe wants to cry. He turns and runs through the bar car back toward the sleeping cars. When he sees the passageway blocked by craning heads he turns around, throwing open the connecting doors between the cars, and leaps onto the gravel next to the dormant tracks. As he runs it seems to him that it is the train that is moving, that he is standing still and the world is turning around him.

A fireman stops him. "Whoa, Nelly." The man is large from shoveling coal.

"I have to look," Moshe says.

"There's nothing to see," the fireman says. "There's nothing left. The engineer already did the long walk home, and there weren't much of him." Moshe has seen bodies mangled by the train, and he knows there won't be much to bury. Jackie's body is reduced to specks of food for vultures and crows.

That night, Moshe does something he has never done before. He seeks the company of the men in the caboose and tips back a bottle of whiskey. It feels right, the windows open, sucking the air behind the train back into line as the tracks fade. They are all shaken up, even those that don't care about "some nigger porter" who makes more money than they do. Railroad work is dangerous, and this has simultaneously made their conversation sober and their minds drunk. Moshe wants to be with the other porters, to feel in their uniforms the proximity of his friend, but his friendship with Jackie transcended barriers that have closed behind them, like weighted doors, and Moshe must seek his own kind.

His head spins, unaccustomed to the alcohol. The train has been made hours late by the delay of paperwork. Moshe wonders if he should write to Jackie's wife and children. But what would he say? All the letters he composes in his head seem empty and condescending. When a Negro comes into the room, offering his hat for donations to Jackie's family, Moshe drops his entire month's wages into the black standard-issue cap.

The train turns its back on the accident, racing toward the civilized part of the nation, the cities with their tall buildings and technological advantages. The death of Pullman porter Jackie Potsman seems to be forgotten as soon as the hangover fades. If Moshe thinks of him often, every day when the sun noses its way over the plains, or at night when the dogs howl as the train slows for the station, he never lets on. And the letter he is intending to write Jackie's wife gets shorter by a word for every mile the train covers, until even the imaginary paper flies away in the train's wind. A year goes by before he decides.

Moshe waits until the train is stopped, just outside the tracks in Denver, and climbs out the window of his berth. His sleeping companions don't turn over or even break a snore. The next day he takes a train heading south. Destination: Orerich.

Though she tries hard not to, Alice O'Malley dreams at night. After the hours spent staring at the ceiling, relieving the urges of the doctor, a visiting drayman, the blacksmith, the schoolteacher, she closes her eyes and sees yards of taffeta, delicate champagne glasses, carriages, and corsets. Others remain sleepless. Tallulah hums and mixes dough. She can hear Garfield rummaging underneath the house, digging up his treasure to look at in the moonlight. He rubs his fingers over it, as though he expects a genie to appear. Pickney tosses and turns on his bed. Dollar bills make poor mattress-stuffers; desire promotes insomnia, and anxiety produces nightmares.

Though uninformed of Pickney's plan, Alice can tell something is afoot. Pickney has grown unreasonably attached to her. He refuses to visit any of the other girls when she has her monthly. He grips her tightly, holds her arms so they wear permanent bruises she must cover with makeup. He kisses her endlessly, strokes her, caresses her, and puts his fingers, his tongue everywhere he can in a futile attempt to pleasure her. He gazes into her eyes as he climbs on top of her. Still, he is her favorite, if only for his gentleness. His interest in her is flattering, and he never tries to take anything for free or on credit. He pays beforehand, puts the coins discreetly on the dresser behind the vase of fake flowers.

Alice does not have the luxury of liking or disliking her work. She is living completely in the present. When Garfield crosses that present, she is glad to see him, admire him, the one thing she's ever produced in the world. Except for that horribly ugly Jewish surname he bears, she sees nothing of Moshe in her son; she has separated Garfield's birth from his conception.

The men come in, and she is used to them. In a small town the faces are rarely new; they simply rotate like a roulette wheel. Even the migrant rail men seem familiar, poorly shaved and dirty, eyes bright. She lies down and waits for them to get undressed. They cover her with their bodies, hairy or bare, in varying degrees of bulk or thinness and different pitches of grunts to let her know they've finished, and all the while Alice looks at the ceiling. There is a knot in the beam directly over her bed, a squarish darkening of the grain. Alice imagines it is a boat, then a wagon, then realizes it is a train. Every evening it is there, and she imagines it huffing down the length of the joist. It is Alice's personal carless steam engine, above her bed on the second floor at 14 Gilges Street, Orerich, Colorado.

PART 2

The Tracks Single Out
1893–1894

5

M oshe arrives during the cold snap of October 1893. Orerich is quiet as the train pulls up to its destination and achingly halts. A deep layer of snow has settled over the town like silent meditation. The sun is shining strongly, as though mocking the to-do of the previous night's storm.

Moshe steps onto the platform. The train seems only to pause as hands throw bags of supplies to the tracks, and it leaves almost immediately. Smith picks up the drawstrings of one bag and tries to drag it to the station house, but it sticks on the rails. Moshe walks over, plucks up the bag, and carries it effortlessly, then returns for the other.

Smith looks at him. "You're here for the boy, I s'pose," Smith says, finally recognizing Moshe. Years of working in rail yards have inured him to surprise—trains take people away and bring them back with a rhythm known only to the rail gods.

Moshe nods, though his son is not what he came here for, not exactly. He picks up the second bag.

"He's a good boy." Smith spits onto the rails. The chew slinks down the sides of the metal tie. He studies Moshe now. In the years away he's grown stockier, though his face has thinned. He has lines around his eyes now, wisdom lines, and an unkempt beard. "Boy's done his best."

"Where can I find them?" Moshe asks.

"Gilges Street." Smith points his twisted finger. He wonders if he should warn Moshe. The man looks older, sure, but different in another way, too. He has the world-weary furrowed brow that Smith has seen in alcoholics and crippled veterans, the eyes filmy with a layer of protection between viewer and world, as though they can filter out what they do not want to see. Smith hopes it works, this intricate system of denial. He hopes Moshe's tolerance for unhappiness is still intact, that a blow like the one he is about to receive will not permanently injure him. He has sympathy for a man like Moshe and his son Garfield, Americans for whom America has been a lesson in the worst of humanity's myriad cruelties. Smith should know; his small violin screeches out the same tune.

But Smith holds his tongue. His moment of sympathy passes like a cloud. He reverts to his defense of privacy. It is none of his business. "Fourteen Gilges Street."

"I thank you," Moshe says. His heart cannot help but speed, though he wills it silent in his expanding chest. He hopes he will find Alice, beautiful Alice, and that she will want him, too, and they will fall into an embrace. That is as far as Moshe lets himself speculate, as far as he lets his optimism wander before he checks himself. It is equally possible, he knows, that Alice has not waited, or that she doesn't want him after all these years; that his son will be angry, that they will be unreceptive to his coming home unannounced.

His steps are the only tracks in the snow. The town has nested in for the day. There is nothing so pressing in Orerich that it can't wait out the storm. Moshe can see his breath form clouds of condensation in the air, and he begins to sing, softly, an old rail tune. He holds his duffel in front of him like a train's plow attachment.

It takes him thirty minutes to trudge the half mile through the snow down Gilges Street. He is lucky to have picked today to return, when the street's sordid chaos is hidden under this white sheet.

The porch of number 14 sags beneath a colossal drift. The windows on the left side of the house are covered to above Moshe's head. Smoke rises urgently from the chimney.

Moshe makes his way toward the back door. He takes his hand from his pocket. It is swollen and red from the cold, stuck in a pugilist's fist of attempted warmth and engorged anticipation. He thumps loudly on the door.

Moshe hears footsteps inside. As much as he wants the door to open immediately and his life to start again after its long hibernation, he equally wants to suspend this moment of potentiality right here, where his most ardent fantasies are still possible. He knows that once this door is opened, the course of his life will be certain, final. Alice could be a thousand things in that house, but once he sees inside she will only be herself. When Moshe left she was little more than a child, and his memories have become confused with daydreams of how a life with Alice could be, countless visions of their reunion, played over and over in his mind. These idealized versions of Alice and his relations with her have replaced the true recollections in the vault of Moshe's memory so that he half expects an apparition.

The door opens slowly, creaking heavily. A large Negro woman stands, blocking the entrance with her extreme girth and panting as though she has run a great distance. "A little early, ain't it?" she asks.

"I beg your pardon?" Moshe says. This was not the reaction he'd wished for. He peers past the woman inside the house. Down the long hallway he can spot the red of the curtains. He thinks he sees lace hanging from a lampshade as though tossed there. Realization hits him like sunlight after a long tunnel.

"I said, it's a little early, ain't it?"

Moshe is at a loss for words. "Umm," he stammers. "A little early?"

"Yeah. Why don't you go get yourself some breakfast and come back 'round dusk?" The woman is impatient, drying her hands on her apron, though they look dry already.

"You don't even know why I'm here," Moshe says.

The woman looks up at him. Moshe can see the scars of acne and old scratches healed into the wrinkles of her round face. "Don't I?" she asks.

Moshe's hands are still frozen into fists. "Alice Haurowitz lives here, right?"

"Alice . . . Alice O'Malley . . . ?"

"Yeah, that'd be her."

"Lord, yes, we got Alice. We sure do got Alice," the woman chuckles. She retreats into the house, begins to close the door. "I'll tell her you're waiting on her at dusk."

"Umm," Moshe tries to hurry against the closing door. "I'm Moshe. Tell her I've come back, I'm home."

The door stops. He can see just the hint of the woman's brown face as she presses it to the wooden frame. "You Moshe?" The woman looks at him again, eyes wide. She surveys him from boots to yarn hat.

"Yes."

"You still best go get breakfast, and I'll tell her you're around."

"Thank you," Moshe says, and the door slams shut. He hears it latch behind him.

Goodmoore serves Moshe two eggs fried crispy. He bangs the plate down, which Moshe takes as a sign of acknowledgment. He did not expect a red-carpet welcome, but certainly Goodmoore, a man in whose house he lived for almost a year, should be glad to see him again. But perhaps Goodmoore feels abandoned, betrayed. Moshe is surprised at this realization, that someone could be attached to him or depend on him enough to feel hurt at his absence. The coffee burns acid in his stomach. He does not ask about the money he has sent all these years; he doesn't understand that Goodmoore's irritation is at his own guilt for having pocketed the lion's share, not at Moshe's reappearance.

Goodmoore takes up a broom and sweeps the bar floor, moving the dirt around in circles. Moshe is alone at the bar except for a large man snoring under a gaming table. His chest lifts and falls with each grunt. Moshe wipes his plate with the toast and finishes the coffee in one slurp. The grounds are lumpy at the bottom of the tin cup. He is anxious; his legs are restless. His mind replays his glance into the living room and attempts to explain away what he saw.

Goodmoore glares at him from the corner. Finally he breaks the silence. "Your boy used to do this for me. But not no more."

"Oh?" Moshe says. He is curious, but afraid that any eagerness will inspire Goodmoore to withhold the information in punishment.

"Yeah. Good worker. Like you were. Didn't give me much more notice either."

Moshe turns around on his barstool.

"Took sick."

Moshe's breath catches. The panic must register on his face, for Goodmoore adds, "They tell me he's all right now."

Moshe sighs. "Why don't I do that for you?" he asks. "Work off some of breakfast?"

Goodmoore pauses, considers. Moshe can see the calculations flicker through his mind like ticker tape. He holds out the broom, and Moshe takes it. The old rhythms come back to him like half-remembered song lyrics, back and forth, back and forth. If he concentrates on sweeping, he can keep himself from thinking about the house at 14 Gilges Street, about what Alice's life must be. He can avoid drawing the only possible conclusion. Goodmoore watches a minute, following the broom with his eyes, hands on hips. The sleeping man snores. Satisfied, Goodmoore humphs, and, taking Moshe's empty plate and cup, retreats into the kitchen, where Moshe can hear the plop of the dishes into the soapy water.

The saloon floor is dirty. It takes several trips to empty the full dustpan out the window onto the snow outside. The dirt sits rodent-gray, lifeless atop the pile of whiteness.

Goodmoore comes out from the back, wiping his hands on an apron. So he has been doing the dishes, Moshe thinks.

"Sticking around?" Goodmoore asks.

"I can't say."

Goodmoore nods. "You ain't been to see them yet."

"Not yet."

Goodmoore nods again. Moshe detects a faint pity in his eyes. He flushes. Goodmoore drops his eyes to the floor. "Well, best of luck."

"Thanks," Moshe says. "Fire going in the drawing room?"

"Make yourself comfortable."

Moshe walks into the next room where the windows are fogged with warmth. He sits in the large chair, puts his feet up on the old ottoman, and watches the logs being consumed by flame. The blaze seems to come from inside the logs, and the change in the bark is negligible—until that moment when the flame goes out, leaving just the charred shell of wood.

When Moshe wakes, the sun is high in the sky. Goodmoore has added a couple of logs to the fire. Moshe stands and reluctantly leaves the saloon. Across the street, he can see the house where Alice lives. Where she is waiting for him right now. Where she is plaiting her hair, putting on her clothes, completing her morning toilet.

In the crisp air, the coldness robbing it of smell, Moshe can remember Alice's scent, the sweetness of her breath in the morning, the damp secret of her armpits, the musk between her legs. His desire is back, awakened finally by his proximity to Alice. He wants to see her hair spread against the pillow, to feel her below him, eyes closed, stroking his back. His feet move quickly, retracing his own footprints in the snow, back toward the house.

This time he knocks on the front door. The house is awake now, and bustling. The windows reveal figures moving behind them; giggles and shouts escape the side panels. The door opens to reveal the same large colored woman.

"Come this way," she says. He follows her through the living room, where women in robes pick up smashed glasses and fold scarves, straighten lampshades. He wants to run ahead, to race up the stairs and throw open

the door. To run into her arms. But then Moshe catches a glimpse of himself in the rusting mirror above the fireplace, rescued from Mrs. Guiteau's
house. He sees a scruffy man, dark and hirsute, his beard full and tangled.
He sees his eyes, small and brown, watching himself as he walks by, hat in
hand, obediently following the large woman.

Moshe flashes with anger now that his suspicion is confirmed. How
had he expected her to make a living? He had to have known that his
money wouldn't be enough. Even after seeing the house, he hoped she was
just rooming there, or worked as a domestic, but it was a feeble fancy. He
swallows, tucking away the realization in the pocket of his mind to conveniently forget. It's as though he has stared too long at the sun and the
comprehension hides behind the spots. Therefore he can know and yet not
know, the shame buried too deep to erupt.

They climb the long staircase to a dim hallway. Tallulah pauses at the
door and knocks. "Yes," he hears from inside; then the door is open, and
the room is bright with sunlight. He is momentarily blinded. He can hear
the door shut behind him, and then he can see her, Alice, pale as snow, the
light causing a halo to form around her white dress. He takes a step forward to envelop her in his arms, to pull her onto the bed that is material-
izing behind her, and then he sees that in front of her is a child.

He is a small boy for ten, with Moshe's curly hair and dark eyes. But
his skin is light, his nose long and pointed like his mother's, and he holds
himself with her grace and bearing. He has created this, Moshe thinks—
something he has actually made in the world. He doesn't quite believe that
this boy is the baby he cared for. He had imagined, illogically, that Garfield
would stay the same. Moshe looks at Alice, then crouches down until he is
the height of the boy. "Hello," he says. "You must be Garfield."

The boy nods. He looks scared, his eyes wet as though he might cry, although Moshe will come to realize that his eyes are always brimming with
tears. From his crouch, Moshe lets himself look up at Alice. She is thin and
older; there are purple semicircles under her eyes, and her hair is done up
on top of her head in a large knot.

She puts one hand on Garfield's head and tunnels her fingers in his
curls. The boy looks past his father to the door. "You," Alice says. It is without recrimination or resignation. She is simply registering Moshe's presence in her life. Moshe says nothing, but straightens. His lungs expand as
he swallows air and fingers his hat. They stare at each other for a while.
They can hear the laughter of the other women. A cold draft comes from

the window; the sun casts a rectangle on the bed. And then Alice leans over and whispers in Garfield's ear. The boy scurries out of the room, closing the door so softly behind him that his father doesn't even notice he's gone, his face buried in Alice's soft robe.

What is Alice supposed to do but let her husband back into her bed? That mattress is no safe haven, but rather a sort of public bench on which she is a fixture. She is so accustomed to satisfying men's desires that it does not occur to her to be coy, or denying or angry. She stares at the ceiling with this one, too, his thrusts making her recall their first awkward coupling on the featherbed near Denton Station. She smiles out of nostalgia at how young she used to be, how young they both were. She supposes she is fond of Moshe, but at the same time she is aware that her heart does not stretch like others' do. She does not feel as deeply, is not capable of emotions other than contentment or sadness, the way some are incapable of touching their toes. But she can tell by his moans that Moshe loves her, or what he imagines her to be, and she envies him that passion.

But with this one she has a problem: how to get him out of the bed afterward. How to convince him that wherever he was, it is better that he return there, and quickly, before Pickney sees him. Alice may be illiterate, but she can read men, and she sees in Pickney the desperate lack of restraint that characterizes the insanely jealous. She has seen it before, in the way Lloyd Hand used to look at Laurel—that burning, exhausting stare of the obsessed. And look what Laurel drove him to, her face still swollen and scarred from the razor blade. Alice wants no part of her life disfigured.

She lets him snore softly using her breast as a pillow, even summons enough tenderness to entwine her fingers in his hair, the same hair her son wears. He is no match for Pickney, she thinks. She feels kindness toward Moshe that she does not feel for Pickney; she wants to protect him. And she formulates a plan. It lacks ingenuity, forethought; it may even be cowardly or unfair, but Alice does not worry about justice. And so she slides out of bed and puts on her town dress. She slips out of the room, just like Garfield, closing the door without a click. Borrowing someone's gloves drying on the mantelpiece, she shades her eyes with her right hand and steps out the front door into the sun.

Pickney is writing a letter to his mother in New Jersey. There is a soft knock, and Mrs. Tinker announces that he has a visitor, the slight crack in her voice betraying her disapproval. "A Miss O'Malley," she says, stressing the *Mal* so that she sounds like a bleating sheep.

The door opens, and there she is. He has never seen her outside the house, in a day dress, and some of her luster is dulled by the lack of sequins and sheen. She removes her gloves and smooths back her hair. Her neck is long, Pickney thinks. It is wrong to see her here; like a fish on dry land, she does not belong in his small rented room. She does not belong out of bed.

She moves closer, places her hand on his neck. He feels the familiar thrill of her attention, the tight buttons of her high neckline exciting him in the obfuscation of their treasure. She leans over and whispers into his ear, tells him, softly, about Moshe. Pickney is still a moment. Then he takes her roughly and pushes her onto the narrow bed, undoing the buttons with haste.

If she smells of another man he does not stop to notice, or care; her smell is a trail of men's pleasure, and he has never known her otherwise. She accepts his caresses, and the bed frame makes porcine squeaks while their bodies rustle the straw and money hidden in the mattress. Pickney can hear the bills rubbing, symbols of their future together.

Afterward, as she dresses, redoing the long row of buttons, reconfining her breasts and belly, he explains what she must do. He takes out the money and counts it in front of her, but does not give her any, not right now. He asks if she is pleased by his planning, and she does not think to question his authority, or to consider her own options. She merely nods to show she understands. She passes his landlady, whose mouth is agape as she furiously stirs a custard. Alice is gone before Mrs. Tinker can formulate the withering Christian invective she wants, and she has to vent her rage on the well-whipped dessert.

Alice, Garfield, and Moshe spend the evening at the kitchen table, listening to Moshe's stories of rail travel and all the sights he's seen. Garfield thinks he is incredible, this mysterious man who holds the title of Father.

Garfield is used to listening to the hobos and rail hands spinning yarns, the facts exaggerated like the rails' miles so that New York skyscrapers tickle God's feet and the Nevada desert continues clear on to China. Moshe's are different; he tells scary stories about rail hands who disappear, trains that move without warning, failing brakes, too-steep grades. He talks about the time the grain car sprung a leak and crows followed the train for miles as though it were the pied piper. He describes Harvey

House girls who serve in uniform, stores that have anything a man could want, pants on the rack and shirts, too, and—he is not immune to exaggeration either—hats so stiff a boulder couldn't crush them. He tells of city streets so wide a thousand men standing arm to arm couldn't span them. He explains how electric lights work, to the best of his understanding, the potential for light lurking in the air all around, the harnessing of God's lightning fury into a small bulb.

Moshe asks if Alice received the money he sent, and she nods her head yes, though Moshe realizes in her reticence that of course his money has scattered all over the country, in the cash boxes of telegraph operators and mail carriers, in Goodmoore's pockets, and only then, much diminished, to Alice.

Moshe doesn't notice that Alice is only half there. She does not appear amused, taking small sips from her beer at regular intervals, studying her hands or gazing past Moshe's face into the fire. He speaks directly at her, as though hoping his words, like a lariat, will draw her closer. Garfield sits at his elbow, hanging on his every word, afraid that if he asks questions he will break the spell. The boy had not even thought to fantasize about a night like this, and the delight he feels in the smoky kitchen is mixed with disbelief, as though it is all a reverie. He would not be surprised to wake in the next minute, to find Tallulah's hands in his hair kneading sweet dreams into his head.

And then all the men are gone, and the house grows quiet. Moshe and Garfield sleep next to the hearth, tentatively. All night long they toss and turn, touching here an arm, there a foot, and then turning away from the connection until morning finds Garfield's hand on Moshe's arm, their faces inches apart, sleeping as close as lovers while the embers glow. Alice sits upstairs for what seems like forever, and then furtively, so as not to wake the house, she tiptoes down the stairs. She glides out the front door without so much as a look behind her and hurries, half running, down the dark, snow-covered street.

Morning dawns cold and dark; the brief respite between fall storms is past, and the clouds have rolled in again. It starts to snow just after dawn, so Pickney's and Alice's tracks are covered by the heavy wet mass, and by the time Moshe and Garfield think to look for Alice, after all the other women are up and dressed, she is long gone. The milk does not get delivered: Alice and Pickney have taken the dairyman's horses to travel the pass through the mountains. Garfield and Moshe stare at Alice's empty bed, the covers pulled back like a shroud fallen away, offering an intimate peek into a secret place. Moshe has proved inadequate yet again, and he is angry and frustrated with himself. Not because he failed to measure up, but because he stupidly thought he might. Because he is still gullible enough, despite all he's seen and lived through, to believe in hope.

"Pack your things," he barks at Garfield, more harshly than he means to.

Garfield shakes his head, his watery eyes brimming over. "I want to stay with Tallulah."

Moshe bends down so he is looking into Garfield's face. "It's impossible," he says. Garfield wants to ask why, but he knows the answer. Because Tallulah is colored. Because he lives in a whorehouse. He has heard the other boys' taunts; he knows this is not the way it's done. He kicks the table leg, understanding that his sadness, his wishes, will influence no one.

Tallulah helps him gather a small satchel. Garfield spends the rest of the day digging a tunnel in the snow underneath the house to unbury the candelabrum. The gold has dulled to a tarnished matte. He wraps it tightly in a pair of long johns and carries it inside. Cradling it, Garfield feels a surge of pride that he owns something. It is heavier than he remembers, and he waits to stuff it into his bag until his father goes out to the privy. That night Garfield sneaks downstairs, leaving Alice's bed, where he was sleeping next to his father. He lies down next to Tallulah and lets her run her fingers through his hair. It stings when she catches his curls, but he says nothing. This time they both cry themselves to sleep.

The next day, once the southbound has plowed the snow from the tracks, they take the train to Denver.

6

There is no greater playground for an understimulated boy than a train. A self-contained world, so much smaller than the immense real one, with its unexplained rules and tacit customs. Garfield races to the front of the passenger cars and then back again, tripping over extended legs and oversized suitcases. He is overjoyed; here is a fresh world, freer and more capacious than the one he left behind. He sneaks into first-class before the porter can stop him and sees ladies in fur coats, men in suits with gold chains leading into their pockets like leashes for hidden pets. The air is thick with pipe smoke. It is as though a different set of climatic conditions exists in this car; it is as though Garfield is in another country.

Then there is a hand on his neck as the conductor grabs him by the scruff and by the waist. Garfield's shirt is too big, his pants too small. The pressure of all of his weight on the tired seams stretches them past their limit. There is a rip, and the pants split down the back. The conductor drops Garfield in surprise. Tears squeeze out of the boy's eyes, deepening his humiliation. He wears no undergarments, and he can hear the snickers of other passengers as he runs through the cars, bracing himself against their arrhythmic swaying.

When he finally reaches his father, Garfield is struck dumb.

Moshe sees the tears and panics. "What's wrong? What is it?"

The burst of attention so startles Garfield, unused as he is to anyone's sensitivity, that he lets out a howl of despair. He turns and shows Moshe the split seam, running all the way down his thigh. His bottom, small and white, peeks through the frayed hole.

Moshe begins to laugh, then stops when he sees how mortified Garfield is. "I can take care of that." He stands up as Garfield begins to cry real tears now, exhausted by the excitement of his first train trip and pitying himself for his predicament. Moshe hands him the bedroll blanket as a cover-up, and Garfield takes off the pants.

"Excuse me," Moshe says to the woman in the next row. "Might you have a needle and thread I can borrow?"

"Surely," the woman says. She is older, and plump. Garfield can smell cheese sandwiches grown pungent with travel in the basket she carries. She begins to rummage through her bag. "Would you like me to fix it? Lord knows I've patched enough seams to be tailor for all of China, what with seven boys."

"Seven?" Garfield says out loud. It seems to him like an adventure book, seven boys to play with, seven brothers of his own.

The woman nods. She finds her sewing kit.

"That's all right, ma'am, thank you, though," Moshe says. "I can do it. I appreciate the offer." He tries to line up the seams.

"Best to do that inside out," the woman offers.

"Right," Moshe mumbles. He turns the pants around, dropping the needle.

"You better let me," the woman says. "It's hurting me more to watch you do it."

Moshe blushes. He hands over the pants. Garfield watches, no longer crying, transfixed. The woman continues to talk as she realigns the trouser legs, holding the thread in her mouth. "Yes, my seven boys, rest their father's soul. He's dead of the croup, what, eight years now, nine?"

"I almost died of that," Garfield pipes in.

"I don't wonder. That's a serious malady. Then all the boys caught it, one after the other like the devil was shuffling cards. Will you find that needle for me, boy?"

Garfield jumps off the bench, gathering the blanket around his waist. "Here it is," he says triumphantly.

"Well, now, aren't you a smart boy?"

Garfield beams. It may be the first compliment anyone has ever paid him. Certainly no one has ever called him "smart."

The woman threads the needle expertly and attacks the fabric. Her stitches are small and even. Later, Garfield will marvel at their uniformity.

"Y'all coming or going?" the woman asks. She has large breasts that rest on her stomach and rise and fall to the rhythm of her breathing. Her hair is a thick blonde braid wound around the top of her head like a wall.

"Going," Moshe and Garfield say together, a little too quickly.

"You got one self-assured boy," the woman says to Moshe. "Not often you see a boy and his pa traveling together. Now a woman and her pups is as common a sight as a drunk Injun, but a man . . . What's your name, son?" she asks.

"Garfield."

"Whoa!" The woman knots the thread and breaks it off between her teeth. "You let his mother name him, huh?" she asks Moshe. He laughs, forgetting that the name was his idea and that he should be insulted.

"There y'are, try them on." Garfield takes the garment and turns his back on both of them as he pulls them on.

"Let's see," the woman says, and gathers his shirt to see her handiwork. That's when she sees how pitifully short the pants are.

"I grew," Garfield explains.

"Go and see if the porter has any lost-and-found things," she says, nudging Garfield. He doesn't move. "Go on now," she says. "A cotton shirt what someone forgot, or a basket liner."

Garfield stands up and seeks out the porter, who is resting with his hat on his belly three cars back. He returns with a denim work shirt and a couple handkerchiefs.

"That'll do." The woman nods. She sews as though she is dancing. She adapts her motions to the swaying of the train car so that the needle jabs as the train rocks forward, pulls taut as it rolls back. Garfield is hypnotized by her fluidity. His eyes flutter, then close. His head falls back, bumps the window slightly, which wakes him up. Then he lolls forward, coming to rest on the woman's great thigh. She smiles and moves her sewing to the other side of her body.

"I'm sorry," Moshe says. "I'll wake him."

"No, don't," the woman says. "That's how I like them best, sleeping."

They sit in silence a while. "Thank you," Moshe says.

"No reason to. Idle hands do the devil's work."

The woman removes scissors from the basket at her feet and cuts to a pattern only she can see. "You boys said you were going, but you didn't say where to."

"I don't know," Moshe says.

"Hmmm, I don't know the place I'm going either. My sister just died, you see, and I'm going to live with my oldest, Lee James. He and his wife already live with her mother, so what's one more old lady?" She laughs.

"If you can cook like you can sew," Moshe says, "I'm sure they'll be glad to have you."

"Your wife pass?"

"Yes," Moshe says, without thinking. Then he realizes she means "die." It is too late to correct the error. "Recently."

The woman frowns at the pants. "She was sick for a while," he says.

"Oh dear," the woman says. "What was wrong, if you don't mind me asking?"

Moshe shrugs his shoulders. "Womanly troubles," he says.

The woman nods in sympathy. "So I suppose you all are going home?"

"I suppose," Moshe says.

"I can't say much, but one thing that I can say with certitude is that you start this life, you wander the earth, and then you end up right back where you started from, like a mill horse. And then the yoke breaks." She pauses to knot the thread and tear it again with her teeth. "And then you wander some more. Sure as sunrise."

Moshe nods, taking in her words. And though he doesn't open his eyes, Garfield has heard their exchange. Both of them, right then, decide that Alice is dead, and hereafter, whenever they are asked, they both concur that she passed away in Colorado, though they never speak of it between themselves. This is the way things should be; so this is how they are.

When she is done sewing, Garfield has a new pair of pants, as well as a pair of underwear.

"I'd make you long johns but for a lack of material." The woman extends her arms, letting the pants hang down like a flag. "Try 'em on."

Garfield looks at Moshe, who nods. He puts them on. He is wearing a different outfit entirely; a denim hem stretches the trousers to his ankles.

"Well, I don't know that they're wearing them in Paris," the woman laughs, "but it'll keep the devil from breathing on you."

His son looks ridiculous. Moshe wants to cry, half because he feels guilty that he hasn't been a better provider, half because he wishes they were a real family—he, Alice, and Garfield.

"How do I look?"

Moshe tries to smile. "They look fine," he says. "Just fine."

Because they don't know anywhere else to go, they go to the only home Moshe has ever known. Now it has a name: Oklahoma Territory. The railroads run across the country, promising prosperity they have yet to deliver.

It is as though the entire nation has taken a deep breath and is waiting, chest puffed, lungs burning, to let it out.

They take the Santa Fe line through Fort Worth, Texas, where they spend a long, cold night on the station platform waiting for the connection to the Rock Island line. Moshe looks out into the flat expanse. He sees brush, the occasional prairie dog, smells sharp sage. The wind is a steady rush, more marked by the absence of sound than by any noise.

They arrive after midnight, and though there are hotels nearby, Moshe doesn't want to spend the money for so few hours since they plan to take the first train out. Moshe tries the station doors but finds them locked. Garfield complains a little, but then is too tired to fuss further and finds himself a niche out of the wind. Moshe can hear Garfield moan in his sleep, watches him curl up tighter between the bench and the wall, hugging the candelabrum he insisted on bringing to his chest like a doll. Moshe walks the platform, wishing that he smoked, that he could allow himself at least this small diversion. Instead he paces, concentrating on placing his feet between the wide boards. He imagines he wears a groove in them.

The sun begins to come up, and Moshe must have been sleeping, because it is the train whistle that alerts him. He takes Garfield's head out of his lap, and they both stand. It is a new train, from the Rock Island line, which means it will have cars with vestibules and a smooth, mostly steel ride. The windows are clean; they close solidly, preventing the whistle of disturbed air that resonates, ringing through the eardrum long after the journey is over. Moshe and Garfield settle into wide upholstered seats and stare out the window.

"There's nothing here," Garfield says. "How will we know when we're there?"

Moshe answers by telling stories about the place he comes from. Alice never told Garfield that his grandmother was Cherokee, that his grandfather was a Jewish immigrant. Moshe talks about the cousin and the way he made Moshe's mother laugh. She had a beautiful smile, he tells his son, with strong white teeth. When she laughed, it was as though she was telling a joke back, inviting everyone to share in the mirth. She had a braid down her back. The cousin had long locks of hair at his temples. He cleared his throat often; he smiled shyly.

At first Garfield feels special, singled out for adventure. They are going to Oklahoma Territory, O.T. And he won't have to go to school. This he makes Moshe promise over and over. No school, Moshe agrees. There probably still isn't a schoolhouse anywhere near the property, and Moshe can teach him just as well at home. But as the miles jostle their way into Garfield's bones, the excitement vanishes. It is replaced by a feeling of being lost in a vast country, of spinning away from his home.

On the long train ride, Moshe begins Garfield's religious education. He has not realized how ignorant Garfield is of his heritage. Moshe's guilt at having been away so long—a coward, unable to face his son, his wife— transforms itself into religious fervor. Moshe explains to Garfield the Sabbath, Creation, the Ten Commandments. Garfield thinks that this is just like school, equally useless. He doesn't want to be lectured to. Garfield momentarily perks up at the Israelites' trek across the desert. It seems to him that he and his father are making a similar journey. But mostly he is silent; his ears take in the words, but his face betrays no reaction.

The more Garfield resists his teaching, the more determined Moshe becomes. This is Moshe's punishment, then, for abandoning his family. He will have to educate his son in order to achieve God's forgiveness, his own forgiveness. Yet the more insistent Moshe's proselytizing, the more Garfield's scowl deepens. He begins to associate Judaism with his father's boring lectures, with this interminable train ride. If there is anyone to blame, Garfield reasons, then his sadness, his disappointment must be God's fault.

What they will do when they get to Oklahoma Territory is not clear. Farm, Moshe supposes, when he thinks about it, though he has no real affinity for or experience with farming. But perhaps he can hire someone to help. Or raise livestock instead. It is not something he puts his mind to. He does think about the night he first spent with Alice there, the magical thrumming of her fingers on his arm matching his staccato breaths. He remembers how she laughed, out of nervousness and kindness, so unlike the derisive snarl he inspired later on. This is what he will remember, then. He will pretend that they lived there, in the house where he grew up, making fires, tending gardens, tilling fields. He will pretend that Garfield was conceived in that very house on one of the multitude of nights in which they joined their love together. He has half convinced himself by the time they change trains in Enid.

After Enid, the tracks single out. Moshe can see a flying branch, snapped by the front car, hurtle past the passenger window now and again. They are close; he can smell it in the desperate foliage, see it in the quality of sun as it reflects off the dusty soil, dull and jaundiced.

Denton Station is almost unrecognizable as the town that Boggy first set foot in. A bustle of men, women, and children brush past each other to unload and load the train. Burlap bags of grain and meal, barrels of substances unknown, packages tied with twine and wrapped in course paper, bags of mail, large cast-off rusted pieces of farm equipment, dull and broken, wait in silence: still lifes in brown against the brown platform. Onlookers throng the station house—sad dirty faces, eyes squinting to keep out the dust, hair covered by hats or kerchiefs. Children run circles around the benches, playing a disorganized game of tag in which everyone and no one seems to be "it." A gaggle of older children sell competing newspapers, their hawking adding to the general hubbub. And a band of missionaries stand in a corner, shouting out psalms and drumming reveille. Garfield takes Moshe's hand.

Moshe stands Garfield under the board for train schedules and wanted posters. He tells Garfield not to move, no matter what, and that he will be right back. As Moshe turns his back, both father and son have the same thought: *I should run away.*

Garfield dismisses the thought first. Where would he run? Back to the house on Gilges Street? His mother is gone, and even if he did find her, there would be Pickney to deal with. A lump rises in his throat, a ball of travel dust. He swallows it back down.

The flight instinct in Moshe is stronger, involuntary, as though he is gagging. Without a son, he could keep traveling, spend his whole life soothed by the bicoastal rhythm of back and forth, back and forth. But no, this is duty; he will rise to the occasion no matter how much his frantic pulse protests. He steels himself to step into the bright sun and find someone to give them a ride out to the old house.

Garfield looks at the posters of wanted men on the board. They are bearded, with pupils too large for their eyes, as though they were surprised to be caught inside a drawing. Garfield cannot read their offenses, so he stares at their faces, memorizes their contours. They are lifelike renditions, so real that Garfield becomes frightened suddenly of Oklahoma Territory. He begins to cry, hiding his head in his hands.

"What'cha crying for?" a freckle-faced boy sneers. "Your pa lost a claim and ran away?"

Garfield has not considered that perhaps Moshe left him here, never to return. Why wouldn't he? Garfield's mother left him. There is something about him, he suspects, though he can't say what it is, something horrible.

It's what makes Pickney beat him and his mother leave. And now his father has left him, too. Again his eyes well up, and the boy laughs.

"You ain't alone. Lots of boys got losers for pas. Where'd you get them shoes, the rag pile?" The boy is a couple of years older than Garfield, and a thin line of dark hair has invaded the space between his upper lip and his nose.

Garfield looks down. His little toe has worn through the leather of his right shoe. He can see the stitching straining to hold the heel to the hide.

The boy scoffs and, turning, takes off in a jog through the crowd.

"Wait!" Garfield whines, but it is too late, the boy is gone. Garfield takes a second to consider. What if Moshe has left him? And wouldn't he be better off anyway with a gang of boys, close to the railroad, which sounds as much like a lullaby as a human voice?

Garfield takes off after the boy, pushing his way around women and their babies, their skirts so dusty it is like running through an anthill. Then he is outside, ducking under the legs of impatient horses and around creaking wagon wheels.

Garfield stops. He realizes he has no idea where the boy has gone. And now he is lost. He spins around, but the train station has disappeared from view, obscured by the thousands of dresses and sheets and tents that balloon around him. There are more people all in one place than he has ever seen before. They stretch out like stalks of grass in a meadow—as far as the eye can see, and as dense and wild, waving to a wind only they feel. Garfield begins to weep in earnest.

Moshe strikes a deal with a Swedish man who owns a wagon. He offers fifty cents, and the man takes it without hesitation. He agrees to meet Moshe on the outskirts of town. Shaking hands with the stranger, Moshe notices that the man's nails are gray, as though the dust of the plains has blown its way clear down to the cuticle. The man has dust in the creases near his eyes, in the small cleft in his ear, and in the part in his hair. He might be made entirely of dust for all Moshe can tell. A dust monster from his uncle's tales, formed by infrequent rain. Moshe hurries to get Garfield.

But Garfield is not where Moshe left him. He blinks. He feels, for the first time, the sharp pain of parental love. And parental love, he understands then, is just the staving off of the devastating fear of loss.

He springs into action. "Have you seen a boy, standing here?" he asks a group huddling over their bundles. They stare back at him, eyes dull as dirt, and betray no reaction. Moshe realizes there are thousands of boys standing all over. Garfield could be any one of them.

"Garfield!" he calls, his voice lost in the din. "Garfield!"

He starts running, the panic mounting. And then, suddenly, there is Garfield, crying, the tears leaving streak marks down his dirty face.

Garfield feels a hand on his shoulder; it is his father, coming to rescue him. They embrace, tightly, and it is a new kind of embrace for both of them. It binds them together in a way they have never belonged to another before. It thrills and comforts, a small solace within the tiny space between two arms that the whole wide world cannot provide.

7

Bounced and jostled. Tossed and bumped. Never in his life has Garfield taken such a jolting ride as in the Swedish family's wagon. The wind assaults the canvas, bends the wooden ribs of the wagon in time to the chattering of Garfield's teeth. He learns that to avoid biting his tongue he must keep his mouth open, but then dirt and bugs fly in, so he opens and closes, alternating like a fish. Inside, four scared and skinny children stare at him. The girls wear bonnets, including the baby, who began wailing with the first "Hup, hie there" her father uttered and has not ceased her caterwauling since. There are two boys no more than six years old—twins, possibly—and a girl slightly older than Garfield. They are all gaunt and gray with dust. Even the mother peers at Garfield with gray eyes, the pupils too big. They bounce along without speaking.

Up front, Moshe sits alongside the man, watching the studied purpose with which he drives the team, thin around the haunches. His name is Fredrik, but he goes by Fritz. His wife is Erika, called Rika. Though they've been in America but a short time, Fritz speaks idiomatic, thickly accented English, as though he's just bitten his tongue. He chews a stalk of grass while he snaps the reins, goes straight down the rutted road west of the town.

Moshe surveys the land. Denton Station has changed. It has grown enormous tentacles, gobbled up the surrounding farmland. The Outlet, too, has changed. Not just its name—to Oklahoma Territory—but also its appearance. The dirt has been beaten into submission. The land belongs to humans now.

Moshe cannot help but smile. That is, until the man speaks. "Someone stake that claim for you?"

"Excuse me?"

"I said, someone stake that claim for you, populize it?"

"We have a house there from a ways back," says Moshe. "A shack, more like, but it held us all—I had a big family."

"How far back, exactly?"

Moshe thinks. "About ten years, I suppose."

The man shakes his head sadly. "You sure it didn't get grubbed in the rush?"

"What do you mean?"

"Land rush, September." The man is incredulous. He takes his eyes from the road to question Moshe.

"I didn't know."

"Last one, they say . . . whole Outlet was up for grabs. My team's so slow it was all taken by the time I got there. We've all been sleeping in the wagon ever since. How is it you didn't hear?" Moshe has never seen eyes so clear. How can he see out of such eyes, their color so pale that the man seems blind?

"Concentrating on other things," Moshe says absently.

"Well, maybe the house'll keep people from it. You got a bill of sale?"

Moshe grimaces. They come over the slight hill that marks the start of the property, and the house is nowhere to be seen. The man pulls the horses up tight, and immediately two of the children jump down and run into the woods.

"You sure this is it?" the man asks.

"That cottonwood," Moshe says, "and that little grove there." He turns to his left. There is the makeshift graveyard, the headstones tilted but still in place. Beyond it, there is a sod cabin leaning precariously into the carved crevice of a hill. Moshe walks to where the house used to be and sees the scars where the scorched land is trying to regrow some grass. He picks up a rusty nail and drops it, rubbing the red between his fingers.

Garfield runs to his side, surveying the charred ruins. "Was this the house?" he asks.

Moshe nods.

Garfield sighs. "What do we do now?"

"I don't know," Moshe says.

The soddy is dug out of the side of the rise, a makeshift house built into the land. Moshe enters the darkness and is momentarily paralyzed by the foulest odor he's ever experienced. When his eyes adjust, he sees that its source is a dead man. There is a hole in his chest, and blood has congealed around it in a small, round crust. The smell turns sweet, decay fooling the recesses of Moshe's brain. He runs outside and vomits next to the door.

He and Fritz drag the body into the nearby grove. Tomorrow they will bury him. The man's clothes are filthy, as though he'd traveled a long way before he died. Standing over him, Fritz says that he is not the first would-be Oklahoman who died defending a claim.

The following day the body is gone. Maybe an animal took it. Moshe is equally ready to believe that the man simply vanished into the plain, became another of those claimed by Oklahoma Territory's insatiable appetite.

They rebuild the house. Without discussion, Fritz and his family stay on. At first, Fritz merely helps Moshe. He drives him into Denton Station to buy supplies with the money Moshe has saved. Rika cooks for both families; they say grace before their meals, a pause Moshe finds oddly irritating, though it is akin to the prayers the cousin said over the bread and wine before they ate. Garfield gathers firewood.

They erect a frame and start to tack on the roof. One house makes more sense—it would be impossible to erect two before winter sets in. Without pausing to examine the implications, they build a house big enough for eight. It is slowgoing, and they haven't even started to clear the fields of rocks and other debris. The sun is warm as it reflects off the ground.

"You know, we can't farm here," Fritz says. And with this sentence both men realize they are staying, entwining their futures. "Too dry, too rocky," Fritz says. "At least without clearing."

"I thought as much," Moshe says.

"Ranching, though, that's a thought."

"Uh huh," Moshe says.

Garfield is playing with the baby in the dirt. She has grown up: She sits up now, puts things in her mouth. Her bonnet is dirty.

When he is with baby Annika, Garfield feels a respite from the anger that has seized him since they entered Oklahoma Territory. He saves up all his caring for her, and when he is not with her, he feels a lump begin to swell, lodging in his throat so that he wants to scream. Gone is the relief Garfield felt when Moshe took him in his arms at the station. He is full of hatred, angry with his father for taking him from the only home he has ever known to this forgotten outpost where bugs live better than humans. Garfield misses the mountains; he misses Goodmoore and Tallulah. He misses his mother, about whom he is not allowed to speak, per father and son's tacit agreement. Alice is dead but not dead, a continuous presence in their lives who goes unacknowledged, unmourned.

"Ani," he calls to the baby. She looks up at him. Her eyes are a watery blue, almost lighter than the sky. She has just the faintest whisper of hair at her eyebrows; a few curly strands that catch the sunlight peek out of her cap. She laughs. "What's so funny?" Garfield asks. "Am I so funny?"

Because Annika is so attached to Garfield, Rika and Fritz often let her sleep in the aired-out sod hut with Garfield and Moshe. It is getting cramped in the wagon, and the baby sleeps less fitfully curled between Garfield and his father. Though he would never admit it, Garfield finds the sound of Annika sucking her thumb at night soothing.

But he is not impressed with the rest of the family. The twins are annoyances. They look so much alike that Garfield can only tell Sten from Oskar by the stains on their clothes. They alternately tease him and beg for his company. The older girl, Dora, does not say much. She mumbles when she speaks, and it takes Garfield a while to realize that the left side of her face hangs lower than the right. She usually hides it against her chest, or looks away, muttering out of the side that is normal. Then it takes him two weeks to screw up the courage to ask her why it does that.

"I was born crooked, my mother says."

Moshe is shocked. When she walks away, he says, "That's a rude question."

"Why?" Garfield asks.

"It's just rude is all," Moshe says. "We're not rude people."

It is an ambitious house. Fritz has rented out his team and his driving services to a ranch down the road belonging to a man with the colorful name of Arnel Plumbly. Fritz spends the day gathering the cattle, driving them into the corral for branding or slaughter, or back out for grazing. In the mornings, Rika joins him. She performs the barn chores, milking and feeding and mucking. Then she walks the three miles home in time to prepare the midday meal.

Dora is in charge of chores at home. She sweeps out the sod hut, washes the clothes and the diapers in the meager stream at the property's edge. It is not much more than a trickle now that the water is diverted from the river over to Brock's ranch farther south. The Brocks are hanging on, but barely, as the price of corn and hay has dropped in the series of wet springs up North and the continuing drought of the Southwest.

Sometimes at night Garfield can hear the moans and labored breathing that he recognizes from the Gilges Street house coming from the wagon where the Swedes sleep. He knows Moshe hears it, too, by the way his father shifts and turns uncomfortably in his makeshift bed. The baby sleeps on, oblivious.

One morning Garfield is walking through the woods searching for "treasure" dropped by cattlemen who wandered from the Chisholm Trail when he sees something gleam. It is metal, cylindrical, with script carvings. Garfield can read enough to know that the letters, if that's what they are, are not English. He picks it up and turns it over. The back is smooth and there are small holes in the top and bottom. It might be gold, Garfield hopes. Then he can sell it in town. But when he spits and rubs it, he sees it's made of nickel or tin. Still, it's a find, and Garfield takes it back to the sod hut and hides it under the straw. This is a small joy, a respite from the constant repression of the tears that almost always threaten.

Sometimes, the lump in Garfield's throat explodes, and his fists curl. If Oskar or Sten is unlucky enough to be near Garfield during these eruptions, they can expect to wear bruises for a week afterward. It makes Garfield feel better to hurt someone smaller than he is. It takes the constant throbbing pressure off him.

Garfield holds Oskar's face in the dust, his arm twisted painfully behind his back. Sten is ineffectually climbing on Garfield, trying to pry Garfield's hands away from his twin as Oskar screams. Sten yells, "Get off him, you filthy Jew."

Garfield freezes. "What did you call me?" he asks.

"Christ-killer! Heathen!"

Without a pause Garfield springs up and grabs Sten. He throws him down and climbs on top of him, punching his stomach wildly.

"Stop it. Stop it, you're hurting him," Oskar yells. His lip is bleeding from where his tooth has broken the skin.

"Take it back." Garfield swings at Sten; some of his punches hit the ground and not the thrashing boy, but Garfield doesn't care. He wants the world to stop. He wants to punch his way back to Colorado, back to his mother, back to before he was born. He wants Sten to die, to bleed until he's nothing but skin like an empty bladder.

"He does. He takes it back. He's sorry," Oskar says.

"I want to hear him say it." Garfield stops his punches. Oskar takes the brief pause as a chance to run for help.

"I'm sorry, I take it back," Sten cries. "I didn't mean it."

"Never say that to me again."

"Never, I won't ever, I'm sorry," Sten says between sobs. His eye is already beginning to swell.

"Open your mouth," Garfield demands. He leans over the boy, coughs up as much dirt and phlegm from the back of his throat as he can, lets it dribble from his tongue into Sten's open mouth. "Why don't you go back to Sweden? No one wants you here."

And then a pair of hands grab him, and Garfield sees his father's shoes as Moshe carries him to the grove. Garfield hangs limply from his father's arms. He is exhausted by his efforts, and for the first time since they arrived here, he feels outside himself, the lump momentarily gone.

And then it is back as Moshe sits him down and begins to lecture. Garfield wishes Moshe would beat him. The pain might keep the lump away; tears might wash away the dirt. Instead Moshe talks to him about religion, about a covenant with God. All Garfield hears is yet another reason why he is different, and that it is the same here as it was in Colorado. He is an outsider, shunned, dissimilar in every important way. The knowledge that there is something wrong with him pounds in his head.

Garfield looks at the creek. He concentrates on the flowing water, and he is no longer a boy being punished by ineffectual words in a grove of trees in the middle of nowhere. He is above himself, outside himself. When Moshe hugs him, he feels nothing but pressure.

The house, built of sturdy wood and strong nails, looks almost inhabitable. It has a living room with a puncheon floor, a kitchen with room for a table and a storage area. The clay chimney continues up so that the room above will be warm in the winter. Over the living room are two more rooms, one for girls and one for boys. Moshe has built himself a small room next to Fritz and Rika's, on top of the storage area. He must pass through the bedroom to get to it.

"Why can't I sleep with you?" Garfield whines. He does not consider himself to be in the same category as the twins and is upset about having to share a room with them. He is still smarting over the fact that his father found his candelabrum and insisted they put it on the mantel. "That way everyone can enjoy it," his father said.

Now Moshe says, "Because I'm an adult."

"Don't talk to me in that language," Garfield says. "You know I don't understand it."

"Sorry," Moshe says. But from then on everything comes to him in Yiddish —names of vegetables, jokes, bedtime stories. He has to make a conscious effort not to burst out with curses, comments on the weather, small words of approval or thanks. The next time Garfield fights with one of the twins, Moshe tries to reprimand his son in the old tongue so he won't lose face with the brothers. But Garfield cannot understand him either.

School is a lost cause. The Swedes are literate, but the children have never attended school regularly. Moshe spends the hours after dinner getting them to write the alphabet over and over, using small blackboards Fritz purchased in Denton Station. These lessons don't last long. The brothers bicker, and Moshe confiscates the boards lest the twins break them in their anger. Dora just blushes when Moshe tries to get her to put chalk to board. She looks at her knees, smooths her gingham dress over them, won't make eye contact. Garfield draws pictures on his slate: circles, wheels, cogs.

Quickly the experiment is abandoned. Moshe has spent the long day clearing the fields or working on the house, and drifts into a waking sleep that he calls "the blanks." Garfield spends his time whittling, his new hobby. He is making a train. So far he has constructed the engine and the coal cars. They hook together by a small ball-and-loop mechanism that Garfield carves patiently out of a discarded end of lumber from the construction of the house. He has cleared away the brush in a remote corner of the sod hut, made a secret space. He makes it large enough; eventually, the entire set will sit end to end and then roll out of the hut and not look back.

Moshe has forgotten how long Oklahoma winter can seem. Finally it rains, relentlessly, as though the sky has been hoarding water for years. Luckily, Moshe and Garfield cleared much of the small field before the rain began. The ground is so hard that the first dozen drops simply bead and roll off the top layer. Moshe stands in the garden, bundled in a wool blanket tied like a cape on top of his leather vest. The wool is wet and smells like the muck pit of a stable, but Moshe supposes that it is keeping him warm. He turns some earth over with the toe of his boot. It has a nice reddish brown color, and Moshe hopes it is soaking up some of the rain; they may be able to plant a garden in the wet soil in a couple of months.

The wind blows from the west, bringing the cold down from Colorado and Utah, all the way from Canada perhaps. The cold feels old, resigned, like a tired, trudging traveler, focused only on his destination.

"Papa?" Moshe hears Garfield behind him. "Are you busy?"

"Not very," Moshe says.

"Dora wants to know can you help us get water. The bank is frozen, and she's afraid to step on it."

"I'll be right there," Moshe says. He picks up the hoe at his feet and starts after Garfield, who has already run across the field. Something in his gait reminds Moshe of Garfield's mother—the lope, or the way he keeps turning back to make sure his father is behind him. Moshe feels a pang for Alice, but pushes it out of his mind. It turns into a vague longing for companionship and then into a quick stab of lust.

At the creek's edge, he takes a tentative step onto the ice. It cracks, then settles, and he is able to reach the bucket into the still-flowing middle of the stream. Moshe goes inside and settles into a chair with Annika to wait for Dora to call him to lunch. Rika has started to stay the whole day at Plumbly's, helping inside in exchange for a small salary, leaving Moshe to deal with the tangled children back home.

He lets Annika play with his beard as he rests. The twins are strangely quiet.

"Boys?" he calls. "Oskar? Sten?"

There is no answer. Annika stares at him, giggles a little as his chest rises when he calls the boys' names. She has wide blue eyes, which have just enough brown rimming the pupils to make her seem adoring. She will be beautiful when she grows up. She does not have the angular cheekbones of her mother, or the lazy melting look of her sister, but rather rounded, heart-shaped features. Already she has learned to smile with her entire face, scrunching her nose and narrowing her eyes so that the smirk is infectious.

Moshe settles into the small weight on his chest, the tiny hands tugging his beard. He pretends to chomp on her fingers. She laughs indulgently and kisses his nose. Moshe is pleasantly warm where she spreads her body heat. He pokes her softly in her solid baby stomach. She convulses into laughter.

After lunch he will go upstairs and fix the living room chimney. The boys have been complaining that smoke is entering their room, that it's hard to breathe at night. There is a leak somewhere, but he doesn't know how to fix the draw on a chimney; he'll have to ask Fritz when he comes home. In the meantime, Moshe will poke around up there, see if he can plug it with a little cotton.

Dora and Garfield clang pots in the kitchen. Garfield has a crush on the girl, it is plain to Moshe, though the boy would never admit it. Moshe and Rika and Fritz have laughed about it after the children are in bed. Moshe relaxes; he is almost asleep when Dora calls, "Supper! Supper!"

In the kitchen, the fire is going strong and the room is hot with the smell of cooking. Moshe hands the baby to Dora and sits down at his place at the head. "Oskar, Sten!" Dora calls.

"Not so loud," Garfield begs, covering his ears. "Some people are right here."

"Like who?" Dora teases quietly.

"Enough," Moshe says. "If they don't want supper, we'll eat without them."

"Whoopee. No Oskarsten." Garfield breaks off a piece of bread. The twins hate being called Oskarsten, hate being merged into one person.

"Stop it," Moshe says. "Pass the butter." There is a pause while Dora ladles five bowls of soup. The two empty places sit steaming. Annika gums a piece of bread thoughtfully, staring all the while at Moshe from Dora's lap.

"Are they in the house?" Moshe asks.

"I asked them to hammer out a dent in the other pot," Dora says. "They ran upstairs with it."

"This is good, Dora," Moshe says. "You're getting to be a good cook."

Dora blushes.

Garfield eats as though it is his last meal. When his bowl is empty, he says, "If Oskarsten isn't going to eat their soup, can I have it then?"

"Why don't you go upstairs and see what they're doing?" Moshe asks.

"I'm eating," Garfield says. He picks up his bowl and licks it. When he puts it down he has soup on his nose.

Moshe sighs. He pushes his chair back and goes to the foot of the stairs. "Boys!" he calls. "Come down to supper."

It is then that he notices the smoke seeping from below the closed door to the boys' room. He takes the stairs two at a time and pushes against the door. It sticks. Moshe puts his shoulder to it, and it opens reluctantly, flooding the hallway with viscous smoke.

Moshe begins to cough, falling to his knees as he struggles to take in air. It is slightly easier to breathe on the ground, and he pulls up his shirt collar to form a mask, tucking in his chin. He scrambles, half hunched, into the room. Inside, it is as dark as a moonless night and twice as menacing. Moshe can't even see his hands.

Almost immediately he is lost. He spins around; the door is nowhere to be found. Moshe picks a direction and scuttles, dropping to all fours. He knows that if he follows the walls around the room he will eventually reach the door, the way out.

He decides to head right. He rounds one corner and is halfway across the second wall when his hands feel a solid mass. He grabs; his fingers circle a small wrist—one of the twins. He shakes the arm. There is no response. Moshe grabs the boy as though hefting a cord of twigs and continues around the room.

He can't breathe. He can't open his eyes. His chest hurts from staccato hacking, his lungs expanding to take in air that is not there. He has to find the other boy, he must, but already this one is heavy under his arm, and Moshe feels his senses blurring from the smoke. He continues his insect path along the walls and finally finds the door with an audible moan of relief. He pulls the boy, not caring now what part of his limp body he holds, then shoves him out in front. The weight is immediately lifted, and Moshe begins to fall, fall, as the dark sky recedes into the distance. There is shouting, and Moshe's head begins to pound as the clouds drift farther and farther away. More shouting, and there is the labored, wheezy whine of Moshe's chest, and then there is nothing.

PART 3

Driving the Ties Together
1894–1895

8

Each morning they move about as if the confusion of having just woken up refuses to wear off. There is the numbing ritual of chores, duties that require the vacant concentration of heavy labor. And that is how they get through the days.

It is winter again, the worst of all the bad seasons in the Territory. There is little rain and less sun, just a numbing grayness that rises off the plains like a bad odor. The ground is hard but not frozen; the stream at the field's edge trickles to a rivulet; three chickens don't return to the coop one night and are never found.

Darkness falls early like a sigh of relief, and all can retire to their beds, where they contemplate the cracks of the ceiling by moonlight. Talking is tacitly forbidden, though Rika permits herself the mumbling of prayers as she weaves her way through the Bible. She rocks forward, like a praying Jew, Moshe thinks.

Sten sits and looks at the fire, as though the smoke will bring his brother back. Occasionally, Fritz admonishes him to move away; the phlegmy rattle of Sten's lingering cough is the only response. Annika caught a fever the day of the fire. She has stopped talking, and they fear she has gone deaf. And Garfield is wilder than ever, disappearing each morning as Moshe yells his chores out after him.

Dora has taken over the household. She makes all the meals now, rising before any of the adults to change the baby, rekindle the fire, put the water on to boil for coffee, bake biscuits for the day. She scrubs the floors and has almost succeeded in removing the smell of smoke from the boys' room. The mattresses had to be thrown away and the wood walls rebuilt. Meanwhile, Sten sleeps with his parents in the big bedroom, and Garfield has taken to curling up in the kitchen, as he did in the Gilges Street house in Orerich. He is never far from Dora, following her like a calf. They talk quickly, heads together, out of earshot in the kitchen.

They have all reverted to simpler, more primitive selves, as the sense of responsibility and guilt, sorrow and grief, drives them into the past. Moshe walks with a slouch, reluctant to make eye contact. Fritz's eyes are heavy with sleeplessness, and Rika has grown gaunt with grief.

Only Dora has continued with a semblance of a normal life. She has filled out, her hips wide and her forearms strong. Once a month, Moshe takes the wagon to drive her into Denton Station for the young people's play parties. The Territory accepts everyone; Dora's malformed face doesn't stop the others from socializing with her. Moshe waits for her, drinking sarsaparilla in the saloon. He has never liked the taste of spirits.

Recently he has made inquiries into the possibility of borrowing books. The saloon owner, fond of him for his generous tips and the fact that Moshe never makes trouble, promises to look around for printed matter. Until then, Moshe contents himself with newspapers from Guthrie and Stillwater and Fort Arbuckle, small journals filled with the news of the struggling Territory.

Statehood occupies the majority of the editorial page, with some liberal suffragists arguing in favor of enfranchising women and Negroes. Always, a couple of farmers on the outskirts of town complain about the Indians. Supposedly the Natives are east of the Outlet, confined to their allotments, defending their land from white settlers jilted out of Oklahoma Territory. But Moshe has seen them at the edges of town, buying bottles of cheap moonshine, illegal in Indian Territory. They sneak across his fields at night—in the mornings he can see their bare footprints in the furrows, like traces of the past. The owners of the larger ranches still complain that Creeks and Seminoles drive cattle onto their territories to claim them as their own. Though he is half Cherokee, Moshe considers himself a white man, a citizen of the United States. The Indians should accept the inevitable, he thinks—sovereign states inside great nations stand as much chance of survival as a low-lying island in a swiftly moving stream.

Moshe reads the endless lists that the newspaper prints: Mrs. Agnes H. Knudson dislocated her jaw laughing last Tuesday. Mrs. Effie Others died of congestion of the brain. Two men made State's Attorney Robert Burtt dance to the tune of two pistols outside Kimble's Saloon on Thursday night. Mr. Burtt was unharmed, and there is a warrant for the miscreants' arrest.

Moshe loses himself in these accounts of people just like him whom he has never met, people trying to survive in the American West.

Dora's play party ends at eleven, but Moshe gives her ten minutes of freedom, to do with as she pleases. At 11:10 p.m. Dora stands in the tavern's doorway with toes splayed out to the side, slanted face flushed. Her eyes are bright in a way that Moshe never sees at home. Her lips move as though she wants to tell him about the party, but when he asks her she simply says, "Fine. It was fine." Her mother's dress is too small for her, Moshe notices; the arms sneak up past her wrists, and the front strains around her chest. She is constantly pulling at it. Moshe wishes he had the money to buy her a new one. "The truly rich are those who enjoy what they have," the cousin used to say. But he didn't have to watch his children do without, Moshe thinks, didn't have to suffer from the unbearable weight of inadequacy.

What Garfield has never told anyone is that it is his fault Annika is deaf. During the "accident," Dora thrust the baby into his arms—"Here, watch her"—and ran to help Moshe with the surviving twin. But Garfield set Annika down and ran into the living room to save his candelabrum. He pulled it to his chest and ran out to the soddy to hide it with his train set and the strange cylindrical object. The candelabrum was his, and he didn't want it to melt away, to leave this world as a clump of mist.

Back in the house, amidst the chaos of tragedy, he forgot about his charge. He found Annika, hours later, curled up in the soddy under the straw next to Garfield's treasures. Her forehead was hot, and her little fists curled. As she sank her face into his shoulder he felt her breath warm on his neck. No one had to tell him it was his fault; his neglect served as further evidence that he was horrible, unworthy. And as he hurried across the field with the baby in his arms, he swore he would never again let anything happen to her.

At the house, Dora pried Annika from him, and he felt a sudden chill like a blanket being lifted. Annika opened her hand; Garfield's cylinder fell to the floor. Garfield bent to retrieve it, but Dora yelled, "Get cold water, quick!" He was startled into obedience, and then forgot about it.

Moshe finds it the following day, kicking it accidentally on his way out the door. He recognizes it immediately as the mezuzah that hung on his parents' doorpost, the one brought from the old country. He wonders how it has found its way to the living room, then decides it is a sign of some kind. He nails it to the doorjamb, thinking of his father. He wishes Boggy were here because, though he knows Boggy would disapprove of what Moshe has become, his father would take charge. At least, then, he would be following orders; at least then he would be useful.

Garfield and Moshe are sitting in the living room when Fritz comes in from outside. "What's that?" He points to the mezuzah.

"Protection," Moshe answers.

From then on, Garfield is reminded each time he enters the house that he has failed Annika. Each time he renews his vow to protect her, no matter what, forever.

The sound of humming wakes Moshe up. No one has hummed within earshot in a long time. Someone is singing downstairs and pots are banging. This in itself is not unusual—Dora is often awake and busy in the kitchen. But the quality of the clanging is palpably new. It is, Moshe would almost swear, the bang of happiness. Coupled with the crooning, it sounds almost joyful.

Moshe can hear footsteps on the stairs. They are loud but careful. The noise crosses through Fritz and Rika's room. Then his door opens, and there is Alice.

This is the way he has always fantasized she would return to him, edges softened by the morning light, draped in a smooth white fabric that stops just above her slender ankles. Moshe's mouth opens in wonder at this vision come to life. His eyes tear with gratitude.

"Moshe?" the figure asks. It is Dora. How could he not have seen it before? She looks nothing like his wife. Dora is blonde, and is wearing a headdress of woven straw into which she has inserted several lighted candles.

"Don't—," Moshe begins, as much to warn her about the danger of the candles as to prevent her from sitting next to him on his small bed. She places the tray on his lap.

"Coffee," she says. "In bed. It's a Swedish tradition. And I've baked you Lussekatter. Try one." Dora delicately breaks off a piece of one of the pretzel-like buns on the tray and feeds it to Moshe. It is sweet and cakey inside, both fluffy and substantial. She leans forward to brush away the crumbs, and Moshe eyes the candles worriedly. Everything about fire has made him nervous since Oskar suffocated. He feels responsible, still, and the wave of guilt makes him shiver.

Dora stands and takes the tray. She smiles at him, and Moshe tries to smile back; then she goes into her parents' room, where Moshe can hear Sten's squeals of delight and her parents' praise. Then there is a peal of laughter and the sound of lilting Swedish music as the four burst into song.

Moshe gets out of bed to relieve himself. He must take care to hit the chamber pot without splashing, and his task is made more difficult because confusing Dora with Alice, allowing her to sit on his bed, touch him, has made him swell with longing.

When he goes into the bigger room next door, the whole family is sitting on the bed. They are all eating buns and drinking coffee. Sten bounces in his excitement; coffee and crumbs jump off the tray, but his parents only laugh. Even Annika makes a giggling noise, responding to everyone's happiness.

"It's Saint Lucia's Day," Rika explains. "The girls dress up and serve adults in bed."

Moshe nods, though he has never heard of this custom.

"Come sit with us," Fritz offers. He points to a corner of the bed. Moshe sits on the trunk at the foot. The family launches into a lively Swedish song that has a frequently repeated chorus. Moshe tries to join in, but each verse builds upon the last, adding a line to the chorus itself, and Moshe can't keep up. When the song finally ends, he stands.

"I'll be downstairs."

"Don't eat too much," Dora calls after him. "There's a smorgasbord later."

Moshe continues down without asking what a "smorgasbord" is. He walks into the kitchen to pour himself some coffee. Garfield sits at the table, rubbing his watery eyes.

"She was up so early," he complains. "Cooking, like she didn't see me sleeping here."

"What is this?" Moshe asks.

"A festival, she said. Something about the darkest day of the year. She tried to teach me the song, but—"

"We're not so good at singing, the Haurowitzes."

"No." This is the first time father and son have agreed on anything in a while.

"Do we have this holiday?" Garfield asks. He stretches his arms above his head. Moshe notices he has grown; Dora must have been letting his sleeves and pants out. He feels as though he is waking from a long nap, as though he has missed months of his life.

"Which holiday?"

"This Saint Lucia's Day," Garfield says.

Has Moshe really been this remiss in educating his son? He tries to remember the last time he practiced their religion. He has not said a prayer in months, has not lighted the Shabbos candles, not observed Yom Kippur or Sukkot. No wonder it seems as though God has forgotten them. "No," Moshe says. "We have different holidays. We don't have saints."

"Oh," Garfield says. There is a pause. "Because we're not Swedish?"

"Because we're not Christian," Moshe says. He opens his mouth as though he is going to add something, but then lets it close again, bringing the coffee cup to his mouth.

Garfield looks around the room. "Swedish holidays look like they have good food," he says wistfully.

"They'll share," Moshe reassures him. He leans over to tousle Garfield's hair. Its tangles trap his fingers for a brief second, and then Garfield frees himself and is out the back door.

Moshe stands in the little graveyard where his sisters are buried, the first stillborn, silent as snow, the second felled by a fever before she could walk. Moshe has righted the markers, placing small stones atop the grave as was his father's custom. A newer stone marks where Oskar lies, edges smoothed by the lathe in town. There are two other graves for the dogs.

He recites the kaddish, thinking more about Oskar than about his long-dead siblings, and permits himself a brief thought of his father, whom he has not seen in years. What is clear now, as Moshe surveys the horizon, gray in every direction until it slopes away from his vision, is that no one else wants this land; for now, it is his. Moshe needs to decide what to plant in the small fields around the house. Cotton would bring some money but will exhaust the land, so Plumbly tells him. He thinks he will probably grow corn, or maybe split the fields between corn and wheat. That would be the more practical course, as the price to ship cotton is still steep. If he can get anything at all to grow in the inhospitable soil.

Moshe hears the kitchen door open and watches Garfield run out. Not seeing Moshe, he disappears into the sod hut. So that's where he goes, Moshe thinks. A prairie dog sticks its head out of a hole. Surprised to find Moshe so close, it twitches and ducks back down. Moshe makes a note to flood the hole and fence the graveyard, to do something to keep the sacred in, or the outside out.

* * *

Under the straw at the back of the hut is Garfield's train set. The engine car has tooth marks from where Annika chewed it, hungry in the hours she spent waiting for them to find her. Garfield has carved four cars in addition to the engine. Two are coal, one is passenger, and he is working on a boxcar. If he can find pigment, he will paint them.

He is not sure why he needs to keep the set a secret. Certainly Sten is no threat now that he is practically bedridden, all his mischievousness gone with his twin. And Dora would not be interested in his toys. But they are his in a way that nothing else is in this shared community. Even his candelabrum has returned to the mantel and is covered in wax. Here he can be alone, dreaming of the time when he will run alongside an actual train, will grab the ladder and swing himself onto a car, join the fraternity of singing and laughing men inside. He imagines himself the leader of a gang of hobos, traveling cross-country to seek adventure. They all listen to him and take his orders. He has a sidekick like the heroes of comic stories. They get into scrapes, but Garfield always finds a way to get them out, winking as they run to catch the next train, the next escapade.

He used to tell Dora these stories, but recently she has no time for him. She shoos him from the kitchen, complains that he's getting underfoot. She has stopped asking him to help with the chores. Their former intimacy is gone as Dora gets taller, broader. She is no longer interested in his boy's games. Sometimes he talks to her anyway, though he can see her lips moving as she follows a recipe from the Swedish cookbook, and if he asks her to repeat what he just said, he knows she can't.

Garfield takes his knife from its carved niche in the wall and begins to whittle the doors of the car. All the while he hums to himself, working carefully, straining to see in the low light. He realizes he is humming Dora's tune and puts it out of his head.

Napoleon Pickney and Alice O'Malley's escape is inauspicious from the start. A snowstorm traps them in Colorado, at an inn just shy of the Wyoming border. There are three long days while the wind blows snow fiercely. When it stops long enough to allow them to venture out, they discover that the barn door has blown open, and the damn team has frozen to death.

Pickney should know he is no gambler. What money his daddy didn't drink up in bourbon he lost at the tables by the waterfront. Pickney should know that those tendencies are passed down through generations like the inverse of wisdom. Yet he sits in at the poker table, betting long after he should, raising when he should fold, out of sheer obstinacy. He is owed something. Luck, life, they both owe him his due, and with his ante already in, each card represents new hope that his hand will win, will produce the right combinations of colors and symbols so that the pot belongs to him. In this way he loses all the money he stole from the people of Orerich.

With no money and no horses, Pickney and Alice are forced to linger there, and Pickney, for the first time in his life, shovels and sweeps for his keep. He does not allow Alice to ply her trade, although he suspects she does so secretly while he is out. The men in town smile at him slyly, as though they know his secret. But she still responds to him when he inches toward her in the night, and though she refuses to perform some acts that he used to pay her for, she is still loving and generous. When her belly begins to swell, she swears that it is his.

Just as the squirrel retraces the same route over and over again, Pickney begins to steal, or to "liberate" as he calls it. In late fall, he slips on the slick ground, and from his pocket falls the town doctor's watch, missing since the previous week. Pickney and Alice are driven out of town, and though Alice is pregnant, they decide to press on to California, where Pickney has aspirations of striking it rich.

They are ill-prepared for such a journey, and Alice begins to complain as they climb into the foothills. Her feet hurt. She is cold. Her back is bothering her. She is carrying too much.

Pickney looks at his so-called wife. She seems tired, old, and when the gas lamps aren't shining their soft light, when she isn't draped and perfumed with satin and oil, she looks worn and rather plain. She has deep lines in her face that makeup cannot hide, and the pink of her lips bleeds into the space below her nose. Pickney begins to reexamine the wisdom of running off with a whore who is married to someone else. And does he really want another mouth to feed, a child who might not even be his?

Still, it is hard to leave her. They have almost reached the top of the pass when Alice sits down, exhausted. It has snowed steadily for days, and they are up to their thighs in drifts of it, the tracks of wagon wheels that precede them all but obliterated. He leaves her the tent and almost all the food, building her a fire before kissing her on the lips and heading down the other side of the pass, toward California, toward his fortune. He promises he will be back with horses in one week. Two at most.

The minute she loses sight of him, his leather vest disappearing into the swirl of gray snow, Alice knows she is sitting in the place where she will die. There is little likelihood of a wagon passing this late in the season, and if any Indians find her, she'll be of more use without her scalp than with. Pickney has no money and even less sense. How will he get horses? How will they make it up the mountain if Alice can't herself?

Strangely, the idea of her imminent death does not depress her. She looks around the tent. It reminds her of her first night with Moshe, his inexpert hands cold on her stomach. She felt resigned then, too, but hopeful in the same way she feels now. Her only regret is for her children—that she will not meet the one she carries and that she will never again see Garfield. But he will be better off wherever he is, she thinks, just as Alice herself will be better off where her journey takes her.

She feels sleepy now. The fire is dying. She gnaws on some jerky, but it is too frozen. She is no longer cold; her feet do not ache; her teeth have stopped chattering. The baby inside her sleeps. And so Alice lies down inside her tent. Through the small opening in the canvas she can see the dark sky. Snow swirls above like a silk camisole flowing over her head. The snow beneath her is a downy nest. And when she closes her eyes she continues to see the snow dance its lace patterns; her ears still roar with the rush of wind as it blows over the pass, even as her heart arrests its rhythm, coming to a slow, slow halt.

In the spring of 1896, Moshe wakes while it is still dark to the sound of arguing. Fritz and Rika speak in loud whispers, and though Moshe cannot understand what they are saying, Fritz is obviously livid. Rika says something soothing, and Fritz raises his voice, stopping only when Rika shushes him. Moshe wonders what is wrong; he has not ever heard them fight. Either they do not exchange harsh words, or they do it far from the house where no one can hear them. But this is most definitely a fight. He hears Fritz clomp downstairs.

Moshe tries to return to his dream. Alice was there, sitting on the edge of their bed in Orerich, combing her hair, and Moshe was looking down at a newspaper. All of a sudden he could no longer read the words, and when he looked up, astonished, Dora was in Alice's place, unclothed. Moshe went to her and tried to cover her with the newspaper, but she fought him off. But now the dream is too far away. He rolls over, and the bed squeaks in response. He sleeps heavily and dreamlessly until morning.

* * *

Fritz and Moshe walk the wet road toward Plumbly's house. Fritz kicks at a stone, and it turns over with a halfhearted sucking noise as the mud reluctantly relinquishes it. He sighs. Fritz has arranged for Moshe to work as a hayward at the ranch, reinforcing corrals and doping steers. It is lonely work, and Moshe had been looking forward to the dawn walks with Fritz, but for the week they have been making the trek the Swede has been silent and inaccessible.

Moshe knows there is something wrong. He looks down the road. The rancher's house is not yet visible. The horizon shows some sort of life, though Moshe would be hard-pressed to say what is different. Perhaps it is the quality of the sun, breaking wanly through the clouds as it rises behind them. Perhaps it is simply Moshe, glad that spring is finally here.

Fritz sighs again, and Moshe wonders if he should ask what is wrong, then decides not to: Fritz will tell him. Sure enough, not five minutes have gone by before he says in his accented English, "Was it you?"

"What?" Moshe says.

"Tell me. I won't try to hurt you for it. I just need to know. Was it you?"

Moshe racks his brain for some offense he may have given but comes up with nothing. "I'm sorry," he says, "I don't have any idea what you are talking about."

Fritz stops and looks at Moshe. Then he drops his lunch pail and springs on him, tackling him to the muddy ground. Moshe is so stunned he offers no resistance as Fritz sits on his chest, grabbing his shirt roughly and shaking him.

"You know damn well what I'm talking about."

"I don't," Moshe says. He can see Fritz blanch visibly as Moshe's voice takes on a whine.

Fritz drops the shirt. He swears in Swedish, then puts his head in his hands and rolls off Moshe to lie silently in the road. Moshe gets up and offers him a hand.

Fritz stares up at him and shades his eyes with his hands. "She's with child," he says.

Moshe nods.

"Do you hear me?" Fritz says. "I said, she's with child."

"I hear," Moshe says. "You're having a child."

"Not me," Fritz says. "Not us. Dora."

This takes a minute to sink in. Moshe is surprised to feel hurt, betrayed. It grabs him like a stomach cramp, then lets go. "A baby?" he says stupidly.

"Do you know whose it is?" Fritz asks slowly, seriously.

Moshe looks him in the eye. "No," he says, letting a measure of sadness creep into his voice. "But she's a child herself." Moshe knows as he says this that it's not true.

"Yes," Fritz says. "She's still a child. And she's having a child."

Moshe is still extending his hand. Fritz takes it, and Moshe hoists him to his feet. They are both covered in the dull gray muck. It feels heavy, as though it were dragging him down.

"How could I have thought it was you?" Fritz snorts.

Moshe says, "I never touched her."

"Someone in town," Fritz says.

"Hmmm." Moshe wonders if the father could be his wild son, then decides that at twelve, Garfield is too young.

"You see her with anyone at the party?" Fritz asks.

"No," Moshe says. "We come right home." A small white lie. He feels a blush of shame creep up his face as he recalls the ten minutes he gives Dora. It is Moshe's fault, then, that she finds herself in this predicament.

"I'll find him," Fritz mutters. "I'll find him, and she'll marry."

They walk the rest of the way in silence.

Later, as Moshe cauterizes the bulls after they've been castrated, leaping out of the way so the dope boy can plug the wound with creosote and tar to discourage flies, he finds himself thinking about Dora. He imagines that he is the father, her misaligned smile as he strokes her hair, releases her breasts from her too-snug dress, kisses her in the cleft between them. She smells soothing, and Moshe holds her. And then there is a baby in his reverie. He sees the three of them, a family, close and loving. Moshe comes back to reality long enough to wonder if he can marry Dora, and then he hears the dope boy shout that there's a calf on the prod, and he snaps back to the task at hand.

Sten continues to improve. In a fit of generosity, Garfield makes him a present of a figurine and makes him promise not to tell anyone. He shows the boy his knife, lets him run his fingers down the blade. Sten is appropriately impressed. Garfield considers showing him the train, then changes his mind.

He begins to play with Sten again, batting him around and wrestling him into submission. The boy obviously loves the attention, but that is not why Garfield humors him. He likes to play rougher and rougher, grabbing Sten's frail arm, pulling on his ear, bending the boy's leg back, letting himself fall deeper into the territory where he can no longer control his actions. He hovers on the edge of trying to do harm, grimaces with the release of it until Sten's breath becomes wheezy and he cries uncle.

Sometimes Garfield pretends not to hear him. He makes Sten swear not to tell his mother, admonishing him as a crybaby. Garfield's secret satisfaction, though, is being caught by Rika. Sometimes she'll call from the next room to tell him to stop. Sometimes she will come and investigate, pull the boys off each other. She takes Garfield into the kitchen where she explains again, every time with less patience, that Sten cannot play so rough, that he is recovering. Sometimes she has a tear in her eye, and that brings Garfield a particular pleasure, that he can make her cry.

Moshe and Fritz's employer, Arnel Plumbly, stands on his sun porch, watching the Hebrew and the Swede he's hired take their water break. "I don't know what you're talking about," Plumbly says, bending over a table to look at the surveyors' drawings. "This here's the driest territory in the Union."

"Well, compared to Louisiana, maybe," the man answers. He sits back and loosens his tie. "But you've got a floodplain nonetheless."

Plumbly shoos a fly. The Yankee railroad man is infuriating with his patrician accent and his dandy clothes. Plumbly has a few ideas about what the man can do with his tie. He feels overextended financially. The porch they're standing on is a recent addition, the house so large it has become a monstrosity—a sprawling, prostrate labyrinth of unoccupied rooms. The railroad man has come to stay in one of them, and Emily Anne has brought them coffee, remembering to spike Plumbly's. Now he wishes he'd instructed her to spike it more.

"When the creek swells here, as it will do, when the water table rises one of these years, the tracks you've got laid will be two feet underwater."

"I know what a floodplain is," Plumbly says. "What I'm not reckoning is why your surveyors didn't notice it in the primarily."

"I wasn't in charge then," the man says. He lifts his cup and slurps daintily. Plumbly has an urge to smash it into his face.

"It'll just have to be rerouted." The man looks over Plumbly's head out to the pasture, as if Plumbly were boring him. "I'm sorry," he adds.

"Sorry . . . he's sorry," Plumbly mutters. "LaLa gonna pay for this?"

"I'm afraid the Lafayette and Louisiana can't absorb the cost to purchase additional land. Our resources are stretched as it is, but the ties can be re-used, and the men are still under contract."

Plumbly feels his ears going red. He sits on his hands until the joints complain from the weight. "And where will this so-called rerouting take place?"

"Have to see." The man stands up. He smooths the crease in his trousers, tightens his tie. "I'm meeting the surveyors today. Whose land is up on that ridge?"

Plumbly frowns. It belongs to the Hebrew and the Swede. How can he convince them that the railroad should go through their property? With money, Plumbly supposes. Every problem in the Territory can be solved with money.

"We'll let you know." The railroad man extends his hand.

Plumbly continues to sit on his. "You do that," he says. "You let me know."

Plumbly calls the two men in and surprises them by sitting down with them on the wide sun porch.

"Y'all like beer?" he offers. "Eloween! Have Emily Anne bring these men some beer."

There is no answer from inside. "I don't—," Moshe begins.

"You don't what?"

"I don't drink beer."

"Well, 'course you don't," Plumbly says. "You're a religious man?"

"I'm—," Moshe begins.

"He just don't, is all," Fritz says quickly.

"We got some sugarplum syrup put in some cold water."

"That'd be nice," Moshe says. "Thank you."

"Eloween," Plumbly calls again, "and a sugarade." There is a silence while they wait. "Cool spring," Plumbly remarks.

"Yes," Fritz says.

"Yes," Moshe echoes.

"What do the Injuns say about a cold spring, either y'all know?" Plumbly removes his hat and balances it on his knee. "Them Injuns is mostly right. About the weather, leastways."

Moshe wonders why Plumbly has called them here, when daylight hours are precious. He wants to get back to fixing the stock pen. The contact with his employer is odd enough to be disconcerting, and Moshe can't help wonder about the purpose behind the man's sudden friendliness. That he is unable to discern it makes him feel stupid.

Fritz, beside him, waits placidly, a piece of spoonbread caught on his mustache from his supper. The kitchen door opens, and a Negro maid exits the house with a tray of drinks.

Plumbly says, "That's the gentleman who's a teeterer." He points to Moshe. Moshe realizes he means "teetotaler." "That's our upright citizen. And this here's the kind what keeps the Territory a place I'd want to live." He takes a beer from the tray and hands it to Fritz. "Bottoms up," he says, and smiles.

"Good," Plumbly says. "Now, our whistles whetted, I got a question. Y'all like living in the country?"

Fritz and Moshe give Plumbly blank looks. Does he mean the United States, Moshe wonders? He is American, born in the United States.

"The reason I'm asking," he continues, "is 'cause I wish I lived in a town. Yeah, I know, Denton Station's not too far, but I see all these towns making something for themselves. I want to get in on the action. Now, y'all got kids, right?"

A loaded question. Fritz answers, "I've got three; Moshe's got a boy."

"I have a daughter. Apple of the eye and all that." Plumbly wipes his face with the back of his hand. The beer glass is empty. "We gotta leave them something more than a bunch of cows, right?"

Moshe looks at Fritz. Fritz nods.

"Tell me," Plumbly says. "You're a Swede, right?" Fritz nods. "And you're a Hebrew?"

"Well," Moshe says, "I'm half. My mother was a Cherokee."

"No shame in that," Plumbly says, as though trying to convince himself. Poor summa bitch is damned on both sides, he thinks. "I never met a Hebrew Indian before. Guess you're a double wanderer, huh?" Moshe doesn't know what to say to this. "And you got land east of here?" Plumbly asks.

"A few acres," Moshe says. "My father's."

"He filed on that claim?"

Moshe looks at Plumbly. Plumbly repeats, "Is there a claim on that land?"

"We live on it," Moshe says. "We built a house."

"It ain't yours if you didn't file on it."

Fritz and Moshe look at each other. Moshe's heart drops.

"How do we do that?" Fritz addresses Plumbly.

"Well, whose land is it?" Plumbly asks.

"Mine?" says Moshe. It is more of a question than a statement.

"Then he works for you?"

"No, I—we share."

"How civilized of you." Plumbly stands up. His knees creak. "You mind if I throw my eye at it? We'll take my team. You want to yoke 'em up?" He looks at Fritz. "I'll just go on into town after that," he says.

In the wagon, Plumbly begins to hum. Moshe wonders again what Plumbly wants. It's not that he doesn't trust the man; Plumbly has always been fair with his wages. Fritz has nothing but good things to say about the rancher, and Moshe hears no gossip about Plumbly at the saloon in town while he waits for Dora on party nights. But he knows that Plumbly, like everyone in this godforsaken Territory, acts out of his own best interest, always.

"Hmmm," Plumbly says, surveying the house. He does not bother with pleasantries. He spins, holding up his thumb at arm's distance and squinting through one eye. "Well," he says. "I don't rightly know."

There is a pause. He turns back to the two men. "Well, y'all gonna invite me in, or are we gonna stand here like horses at a post?"

Moshe has a flash of panic. What will Plumbly see when he walks inside? They've never had guests. But the house is presentable. Dora meets them in the living room. If she is surprised she does not betray it, wiping her hands on her apron. She has flour in her hair. Moshe thinks she has never looked so beautiful, so alive, her skin glowing with the heat of the kitchen.

"This is Mr. Plumbly," Fritz says. Dora nods hello. "Can you get him something?"

"You got whiskey?" Plumbly asks. Dora shakes her head. Either she or Rika has let the dress out. Moshe would never have guessed she is pregnant. He swallows, the magnitude of the secret a lump in his stomach.

"Beer? Water'll do then," Plumbly says. He is looking around the little room. Sten must be upstairs; Moshe can't hear his rattling cough. Rika is at Plumbly's, and Garfield is gone, disappeared as always.

Dora retreats into the kitchen. The afternoon hours are ticking away. Moshe feels suddenly anxious, as though he has an itch in an unidentifiable location. He goes after Dora. "I'll go see . . ." He trails off. Fritz and Plumbly begin to discuss acreage.

Dora pours three glasses of water. There is a large bucket of buttermilk on the counter, and Moshe studies it to avoid staring at Dora. He sees the clots, the darker yellow of the edges, a leisurely floating spoon.

He opens his mouth to say something. He is poised, ready to tell her— what? That he loves her? That he'll marry her and be the father of her baby? But he is still married, and Dora is a child. More powerful than the voice of reason is his suspicion: She knows, and she doesn't want him. He is an old man, weak and slow. He can't risk the rejection. His stomach lurches, and he says nothing, leaves his hands at his sides as Dora exits with the three glasses. She seems to take all noise with her so that the kitchen seems the quietest place Moshe has ever been.

When Moshe returns to the living room, Fritz and Plumbly are sitting. "I'm talking with your partner here," Plumbly says, shifting his weight, crossing one leg over the other, "about possibilities. You say it's yours east to Fiddler's Creek?"

It takes Moshe a minute to realize that Plumbly is referring to the creek where they get their water. He never knew it had a name. The whole Territory is lawless and wild; the thought of his land as being so orderly as to have borders and official names, seems ridiculous. All his life, Moshe has heard the land referred to as "here" and "yonder."

"Now Denton Station, ha!" Plumbly laughs derisively. "That sorry excuse for a town. Overpriced, underpopular—a man's liable to go broke just thinking about buying breakfast. And this depression's only barely lifting. "But here's the thing, and I think you see what I'm getting at here—"

Moshe is barely following. He feels a burning shame for his inaction in the kitchen. He forces himself to look at Plumbly. The man is growing excited. He's spitting a bit, foaming like a head of beer.

"What's the Rock Island done for us here?" he asks. "In receivership, government's not going to bail them out. And the Santa Fe's nowhere near us. We get the LaLa up here, run it between our lands, we got an opportunity to homestead. We get the land together, incorporate, and we got us our own little town, put Denton to shame."

"LaLa?" asks Moshe.

"Lafayette and Louisiana," Plumbly explains.

"It's a train line," Fritz tells him.

"And it ain't just glory I'm interested in," Plumbly continues. "Rock Island got a good thing going with the Longhorn traffic up from Texas to the Chicago stockyards. We get in on that, graze some, raise our own, ship 'em north, we got ourselves a real business." Plumbly sits back in his chair, proud of himself. Moshe is turning the name "Fiddler's Creek" over in his mind. It's not bad, he thinks.

Fritz says, "Excuse me, sir, what do you want with us?"

"Well," Plumbly chuckles. "The government's a little suspiciate of me, seeing as how I've made inquiries in the past, and maybe they don't much like the . . . methods I used to persuade the LaLa folks in Baton Rouge. But now *you* could file for incorporation; we could set your town up right here."

"My wife and I are Swedes," Fritz reminds him.

"Well, how about him?" Plumbly points to Moshe. "Nobody needs to know he's half Injun. We just need an entry man. And warm bodies for the census. I got myself, my wife, and our little Maura. Plus the cook and the ranchhand. You all got seven people here, with your wife expecting another one, pardon my noticing." He nods at Moshe, obviously thinking that Dora is his wife.

"That's my daughter," Fritz says.

Plumbly barely reacts. "So we got her family, too. Plus the Reeces and the Macleans and the Brocks, and those folks north of the fork. We're on the road to success."

Moshe's mouth hangs open. How could Plumbly have noticed Dora was pregnant? But he thought she was my wife, he thrills.

"What do we have to do?" Fritz asks.

"Not a thing. Well, if we're going to make a townsite we're going to need some streets, surveyors, etcetera. I'll run the tracks between our properties, and we can build the station right here. I'm just letting you all know, as a courtesy, like." He drinks the rest of his water in a gulp.

"Is this legal?" Moshe asks. He is still worried that Plumbly has designs on his land. He's not sure what he can do to protect it. His head swims with anxiety—about Dora, about Fritz, about Garfield, about the land.

"It's Oklahoma Territory," Plumbly says. "Legal's only a pile of money. Tell your woman thank you for her hospitality."

And then Plumbly is gone. Moshe takes a deep breath. Annika walks into the room. Her skirt drags on the floor. She sits on Moshe's feet, waiting for him to give her a ride, but he barely registers her presence.

"What do you think of that?" Fritz asks.

"I don't know," Moshe says.

"He's got one hell of a ranch," Fritz says. "I seen those railroaders on his property. I guess this thing sounds like it's already done." Fritz sighs. "We'll just have to wait and see."

"Wait and see," Moshe repeats.

The following morning, Plumbly comes out on horseback to talk to Fritz. Moshe can see them from where he is plowing the next field over. They are looking at something, hunched over, their backs to him. The horse stamps impatiently.

Moshe wipes his face. The sun shines through the haze of dust coughed up by Moshe's plowing and the hooves of the team. He did not sleep well last night, his brain a butter churn of images. He remembers being awakened by the sound of Fritz crying to his wife. That's a sound a man never forgets, Moshe thinks, the sound of another man sobbing.

He can see Plumbly's theatrical laugh, even from here. His enormous backside shakes with it. He envies Plumbly not only his wealth but his laughter. It seems like years since Moshe smiled, since he has done anything except scrape by, eat, sleep, and work in an endless cycle. Plumbly's wife, attractive precisely because she is homely, used-looking, is what Moshe is most jealous of. He wanted to grow old with Alice, settle into a life, raise their child together, sag and bow together. It seems like too much to hope for.

9

Humans are adaptive creatures; they have short memories. Within a month, the sound of the hammers clanking steel rails to the ground, the nails driving the ties together, is no more startling than a rooster crowing at dawn, or a rabbit's squeal as it is caught in a prairie coyote's jaws. No one comments on the noise. They simply raise the volume of their own speech or wait for a break in the racket.

Garfield is ecstatic about the arrival of the train. His six model cars are almost done. They are coupled together beneath the straw as though Garfield hopes they will procreate little freight cars in the night. They all are without wheels, and so don't travel as smoothly as they should, but still they are fine examples of twelve-year-old craftsmanship, and Garfield takes pride in his handiwork.

Once the men have been at it for a couple of hours, Moshe travels among them. He carries snacks—dried corn, tobacco, nuts—and the men gladly give him a nickel for a bag. The men drink greedily from the lemonade barrel. They joke with Moshe that beer would be better fuel. He keeps his head down when he goes into the kitchen to ask Dora to refill his stock.

Dora's father will not speak to her. In fact, he speaks to almost no one. It is impossible to tell if his silence stems from anger or from concentration. Fritz has an idea; he is thinking of constructing a cotton gin, if he can get the money together. He has written away for plans, which take three long months to arrive. Fritz drives the team to Denton Station, returning at dusk with the oversized papers in a roll looped through his belt like a sword. He spreads them out in the garden shed, which he has turned into his private workspace. He has set up a table and appropriated four clothespins to clamp the pages down on all sides.

The plans are complicated, drawn in a technical hand, then traced so that the lines don't always meet. Fritz annotates, erases, makes a list of materials, crosses out, plots locations, erases more until the original intention is obscured by pencil smudge. He keeps the door closed.

Even Rika is not allowed to see what he's doing, and she wonders what scheme Fritz is concocting. She doesn't like his recent demeanor. Like a mangy dog, he shrinks from her touch. He snarls in his sleep, tossing and turning so that Rika feels like she's sleeping on a ship, crossing the Atlantic again.

Rika tries to teach Annika to speak, coaching the girl to make sounds and then rapping on her fingers when she is not correct. When Annika. does make noises resembling speech, Rika rewards her with a kiss or some buttermilk. Annika is growing fat with praise. Already she can say "yes" and "no" in both English and Swedish. Moshe sits with her and lets her touch his neck as he reads, or rest her head against his chest to hear the vibrations of his vocal cords.

Recovered, Sten follows Garfield everywhere. The older boy has to run around the fields every morning to lose Sten before he heads to the sod hut to carve his trains. Invariably, Sten cries and returns to the house, where Rika puts him to work in the kitchen. If Fritz were paying attention he would complain that cooking is women's work, and that continued exposure to the kitchen will further weaken the boy. Sometimes Moshe takes him to the construction site and lets the boy run errands for the crew.

The louder the railroad men get—Plumbly plies them with liquor every evening to keep their spirits up and to have someone with whom to carouse—the quieter the house becomes. Fritz spends evenings in his shed, scribbling by lamplight. Rika and Dora cook for all the railroad men, then must clean the kitchen, a massive task. They scrub silently. Sten goes to bed early, and most nights Moshe and Annika fall asleep in the living room. The railroad is exhausting, an enervating tornado greedily snatching everything in its path, only to let it all drop to the ground suddenly, bruised and broken.

Plumbly calls Moshe and Fritz to the porch again, and this time Plumbly's wife, Eloween, brings two beers and a sugarade. A little girl peeks shyly from the door. Moshe waves, and she runs back inside. When Mrs. Plumbly leans over to give Moshe his drink, he can see down her dress. Her breasts are wrinkled; her collarbones stick out at angles. She smiles at him, and he smiles back. "That don't got enough sugar, you tell me," she says.

"Boys, we got ourselves an obstacle." Plumbly cants forward, drops his voice so that Fritz and Moshe have to bend in to hear him. "An abstraction. We're needing to reroute the railroad up to higher land. And that higher land falls under the fairview of you gentlemen's land. We're in too far to stop now, I say. Y'all don't mind, do you?"

Moshe tries to catch Fritz's eye, to communicate his worry. But Fritz looks at the evenly laid boards of the porch. "I don't know, sir," he says. "I just feel I have to ask what we get, besides a lot of train noise."

Plumbly smiles. He is half-impressed that the Swede is not so dumb as Plumbly thought, and half-rueful that Oklahoma has taught even its greenest denizens to find out what's in it for them, to hustle a bit of cash. He could force them out, sic the government on them, or burn the house, but frankly, it's not worth the effort. Easier to just throw them some money, watch them leap to grab it.

"Well, boys, how about a little monetarily reward?"

Fritz looks puzzled. Moshe looks up from his feet.

"Money," Plumbly clarifies. "What do you say to a thousand dollars? Split it up however you like, fifty-fifty or you can rassle for it or whatever you want." Plumbly chuckles. It would be highly amusing to see these two tenderfeet in a fistfight.

Fritz nods and opens his mouth, but before he can speak, Moshe says, "I want naming rights."

"What?" Plumbly nearly sputters.

"You can keep your money. I want to give it a name. Leave something for the children, as you say."

Fritz interrupts, reaching his arm out in front of Moshe's chest as if to hold him back. "We want the thousand *and* the name," he says.

Plumbly sighs. He wanted to call it Plumblytown, or Plumblyville, but his wife flat out refused to live in a town with such a silly name; she threatened to pack up their daughter, Maura, and move to Eloweenland, which she swears will be far, far away.

"Fine," he says. "Done." He sticks out his hand for the men to shake.

"Owenasa," Moshe says.

"You're welcome," Plumbly responds.

"No," Moshe says. "That's the name. Owenasa."

Plumbly sighs. What does it matter what the name is, he tries to convince himself. So it's an Indian town. Makes it seem older, more legitimate. And as far as Indian goes, one name is as good as another.

"You're gonna have to write that down for me."

Moshe cannot imagine what the letter says. He doesn't know anyone who would send him mail, and for a moment he imagines it's from Alice. But immediately he realizes this is silly. Alice has probably not learned to read, and even if she has, why would she contact Moshe now, and how would she find him?

DEPARTMENT OF THE INTERIOR
UNITED STATES LAND OFFICE, GUTHRIE, OKLAHOMA TERRITORY

February 1, 1896

Moshe Haurowitz
RR
Denton Station, Oklahoma Territory

Dear Sir:

Herewith is returned your application from the action of this office in rejecting your claim to incorporate a town located at number 4165354, SW 1/4th sec. 16 TP. 29N. Range 1 W 1 M—as there is no evidence accompanying the same—that you served a true copy of the same on The Oklahoma Territory—this is required in appeals of this kind—by personally serving a true copy of this appeal on the Governor of the Land Office.

Having been furnished the requisite proof of the prior establishment of a residential property on the tract delineated above, this office will reexamine the solicitation pursuant to an assumed and sworn affidavit to the effect thereof.

Respectfully,
O. Jackson

Moshe lets the hand holding the letter drop to his side.
"What?" Garfield asks. "Can I see?"

"Bad news?" Rika asks, seeing Moshe's face.

"I'm not sure," Moshe says. "It's from the Land Office."

"Well?" Fritz asks. "Give it here." He reads it silently, moving his lips and furrowing his brow. He looks up. "Plumbly might know," he says. "We'll bring it to him tomorrow."

"The thing is," Plumbly says, holding the letter close to his eyes as if that will make its meaning more readily apparent, "is that I know what all these words mean, each one on its own, but together it makes about as much sense as a snowflake in June."

"What should we do?" Fritz asks.

"It's definitely got a negatorial connotation," Plumbly continues. There are grease marks on the page where his buttery hands have grabbed it. Moshe wants to snatch it back. He has become attached to the letter, its official handwriting, its cordial close. "We'll ask the Yankee," Plumbly decides, putting the letter down next to his breakfast. "He speaks that flowery government language."

When they bring it to the railroad man, he reads it slowly. He is wearing a new suit today, Plumbly notices. This one has a waistcoat to match. He must be dying of heat.

He looks so pale, Moshe thinks. He looks as though he's never been in the sun. Like the cousin, he thinks. An intellectual.

"This will take further study," the man says finally, removing his spectacles. "But off the cuff, I believe the government is looking for proof of occupancy."

"Occupancy of what?" Fritz asks.

"Your land, and its boundaries. This is a denial of your townsite, but only in the absence of proper evidence."

Plumbly again is tempted to pick the man up by his cowlick and swing him around a few times, his supercilious spectacles hitting the chandelier in his gyrations.

Secretly, Moshe suspects that none of the people who've seen the letter—including its author—has an inkling of what it says. He resolves to sit down and write a line-by-line translation.

"How could we prove it's his land?" Fritz asks. "Other than by sending them a handful of the dirt it rests on."

"Do you have any sort of official document?" the railroad man asks. "A deed or a claim or a permit?"

Moshe shakes his head.

"A surveyor's plan, a map?"

Moshe continues to shake his head no.

Fritz asks, "Can we get those surveyors to make a plan?"

"Or better," says Plumbly, drawing out the syllables. "We make a map of the town."

"What town?" Moshe asks.

"Owie . . . what's it called? The town that's gonna be here." Plumbly is grinning. "The town in the future." He speaks rapidly. "And then we'll have ourselves a map of the future. We bring that to the Land Office. A town with a railroad and a map. That's better than most towns in the Territory."

Dora cannot believe there is a person growing inside her. When it moves, kicks, she has trouble remembering that the source of the flutters is a second being and not her irritable stomach. Though Rika has explained it to her, a combination of God's will and sin, the proportions of which are a little hazy, Dora cannot fathom how *that* with *him* has created *this*. Rika, searching for an analogy in nature, talked about adding yeast to dough to make it rise. But dough remains dough. Dough doesn't kick; dough doesn't ruin your life.

Sometimes she can feel what Rika tells her is a foot; she prays that it is only one baby. The woman who came to see her said that twins run in families, but was unable to tell her whether she is carrying one or two. What if she is carrying three? Her mother knew a family like that once in Sweden.

Rika has been unusually taciturn. She hasn't yelled at Dora and is hurriedly teaching her new household tasks, as though Dora needs to be self-sufficient before the baby comes. As though Rika has to finish her parenting before it is born. Dora can see that Rika is disappointed in her. She doesn't understand that Rika also feels guilty; she should have taken the children to church. She could have prevented this. America has distracted her, made her remiss.

Dora thinks about the baby's father; she is oddly detached from the experience, as though it were someone else involved and not she. She guesses she will never see the boy again. Her father has forbidden her to ever leave the house, and even if she did see him, what would there be to say? She has never seen Fritz so angry. His face tight with tension, he turned pink before giving over to a bluish tone. He spanked her like a child, bent Dora over the arm of a chair. Her bottom hurt for three days, and the angry welts remained for weeks.

Being pregnant is not terrible. It wouldn't be bad at all, in fact, if it weren't for the nausea, like being constantly agitated in the butter churn. It wakes her up at night, the back of her throat burning and her tongue too big for her mouth. She is thankful the sickness has gotten better recently, as her time approaches. Though now the baby presses on her bladder, sends her running for the privy several times a day without warning.

And her breasts have grown enormous. She stands in her room after Annika is asleep and holds them in her hands like infants. They are tender and swollen, the areolae large and flat and smooth like hotcakes, the nipples raised and hard. The tenderness feels good, as though they were something that needed holding, soothing. They remind her that she is a woman, no longer a girl.

One day, her feet swollen and her eyes red from crying, Dora gives up. She drops the scraping brush and goes into the living room to rest. Enough. She's had enough. And as soon as this baby is born she'll . . . she'll . . . She is unable to think of a plan, but just the thought of having options is comforting.

Then there is a tap on her arm, and it's Garfield, looking uncharacteristically concerned. "Are you poorly?" he asks.

"Just tired," Dora answers. "And my feet's swole."

"I made something." Garfield shoves an object in her hand.

"Oh." Dora turns it over. She isn't sure what it is, a lump of wood? Still, the gesture is touching.

"It's for the baby," Garfield says. "A model train. I'm still learning."

"It's beautiful," Dora says, sincerely. This is the first time anyone around her has acknowledged her child, let alone expressed an interest in it. Her eyes get teary as she says, "I'm sure he'll love it."

"Or her."

"Or her." Dora looks at the train figurine.

It is one of Garfield's worst; that's why he chose it to give away, but Dora doesn't have to know that. He weighs his next words carefully. He is as nervous to say them as he has ever been, as though Pickney is making him stand on that church stage and recite a lesson that he doesn't know. "If he won't marry you, I will."

"He who?"

"The father."

"There is no father."

"Yes there is. I saw you two together."

"You don't know what you're talking about," Dora says harshly. She sits up straight. She doesn't want anyone to know. It is *her* secret. No one can share it.

Garfield's face falls. He feels shame like heartburn inside his chest. "Yes I do. I saw you near the woodpile. You were wearing the checked dress and he cried and you gave him your embroidered handkerchief."

So he did see them; Dora is shocked. She thought she had been discreet. Her mouth hangs agape.

"Don't worry," Garfield says, filling with the importance of sharing something so intimate, flush with the power of his gift. He feels his confidence return. "I won't say nothing. Ever. Swear on my life." He spits on the floor to seal his promise. "You can think on it, about the wedding."

"Oh, Gar—," Dora begins, and she leans in to hug him as a fresh sob escapes. Garfield hears the tone of her voice, a patronizing pity, and his disappointment closes a wall inside him as he realizes how foolish he must sound. He will never again allow his vulnerability to show. He'll never again expose the tender flesh.

Dora squeezes Garfield as tightly as her belly allows. She loves him so much right now, loves him in a way she doesn't think she'll ever love anyone again. He has been kind to her when everyone else has turned their backs. She will remember this forever.

Then the baby inside her kicks, and they separate and laugh. Each of them decides never to speak of the matter, though neither will ever look at the other the same way again.

There is a scream. Moshe snaps upright in bed, attentive immediately. He hears the sound of Rika's soft voice, shushing, and then he hears it again. This time it is a wail, almost a lament, building.

Dora. Moshe puts on his pants and opens the door to Fritz and Rika's room.

"Sorry if she woke you," Rika says. She wipes Dora's face. Dora turns to him without seeing, her eyes set and her face red. She grips the top sheet with white knuckles.

"Not up here." Fritz stands at the door.

Rika swears at him. Moshe doesn't know this Swedish word, but it is unmistakably an insult, and he can see Fritz recoil. "Don't stand there," Rika says. "Go and get the midwife."

Fritz pivots without a word.

"Take Garfield," Moshe calls after him, "to keep yourself awake."

Fritz is no sooner gone then the wailing starts again. Dora's cries have a low grunt in them now, like a horse with a broken leg. Moshe doesn't know what to do. He realizes he is gawking, standing in the middle of what is a women's room.

"I'll put on some coffee," Moshe says.

"That's a fine idea." Rika is flushed, too, worried about her daughter, and though her tone is level, her voice reveals strain. "Would you mind putting on the pots to boil some water also?"

Moshe nods and walks downstairs. Garfield and Fritz are already gone. Sten stands at the foot of the stairs, eyes wide and rimmed with tears.

"What did she do?" Sten whispers.

"What?" The screams have recommenced, and he can't hear the soft-spoken boy.

"What did she do to make them beat her?"

Moshe laughs. "She's having a baby. Didn't anyone tell you?"

"Now?" Sten asks. "She's having a baby now?"

"She will. She'll have the baby by suppertime today."

"Then why is she crying?"

"Come into the kitchen and I'll explain." Moshe takes his hand. Sten sits at the table while Moshe stands, hands on his hips, and surveys the apparatus. He is sure he can make coffee, but faced now with the stove and the women's organization, he can't remember what to do first.

"What're you doing?" Sten asks.

"I'm putting the coffee on."

"The pot's under there." Sten points to the curtained cabinet below. Moshe squats. "The coffee is in that tin." Sten points to the brightly colored box on a shelf. He gets off his stool to approach the stove. It's the closest he's been to fire in a while. "You put in three spoonfuls."

"Thanks," Moshe says. He goes outside to get a few more logs. When he returns, Sten is measuring even scoops of coffee onto the waiting cloth, stained brown with use.

Moshe pours the water into three pots and sets them all on the stove. "If you cover them, they boil faster," Sten says, so Moshe bends back down and finds lids that more or less fit.

"Can you make biscuits, too?" Moshe asks.

Sten thinks this is a joke. He laughs and hands Moshe the tied bundle of grounds. There is another agonizing scream above them, then silence. They hear Rika's heavy steps descending.

"There you are," she says. "Oh good, the water's on. It'll be a while yet. Annika's still asleep, yes?" She sits down next to Sten and rests her head in her hands. "That coffee almost ready?"

"Almost," Sten answers. She kisses him on the top of his head.

"I'm going to have you help. Can you tear up some sheets for rags? Can you do that?"

"All right," Sten says. "I can do that."

"Are you hungry?"

"A little," Moshe admits.

"We can eat the rest of the pie." Rika retrieves last night's rhubarb pie from the pie safe. She cuts two pieces and sets them in front of Moshe and Sten.

"We might need your help upstairs," Rika says, "if Fritz is a long time coming."

Moshe nods. He can hear the pot lids thumping anxiously behind him. When the screams sound again, Rika rushes back upstairs.

Sten freezes. "Why is she crying?" he asks again.

Moshe considers what he should say. Alice cried so little at Garfield's birth. It hurts, he knows. At first it hurt Alice when he put himself inside her, and he is much smaller than a newborn. He thinks quickly of being inside Alice; he fit her exactly. He remembers feeling her clamp around him, drawing him closer and deeper, the sensation of being pulled from everywhere simultaneously. The terror of being on the edge of control, and the pleasure of that terror. Maybe that's why they cry, Moshe thinks, in fear of the thing pushing out from inside that they cannot control.

To Sten, he says, "Remember Adam and Eve, in the Garden?"

Sten nods.

"Well, the serpent tempted Eve with the apple, and she took it. Then she gave it to Adam. God banished them both from the Garden and punished Eve and all women by making it hurt to bring children into the world."

Sten nods again, taking it all in. Moshe wonders if the boy is simple, and then remembers that people say that about him, because he is slow and thoughtful. Sten reminds Moshe of himself. He wants to shield Sten from the world, make him somehow hurry up, worry less; he wants to help prepare him more for the task of living.

"When does he stop being mad?"

"Who?" Moshe asks. He is thinking of Fritz, his increasing moodiness, his abruptness, his violence—the time he threw Moshe to the ground.

"God. When does God stop being mad at us?"

"I don't know," Moshe says. "That's a thing I do not know."

Rika calls down from the top of the stairs. Moshe does not want to go up again. In his head he can see Dora's eyes, dull and vacant, but still accusing him of something he did not do. Unless she is accusing him of inaction. Then Moshe imagines he is terribly guilty, and feels ashamed.

The door is closed. Moshe is reminded of the closed door to the twins' room before he found Sten unconscious from smoke. He has the same sense of dread now. He knocks softly.

Inside there is blood, and the room is thick with an earthy, womanly smell, a mixture of brine and sweat. "Here." Moshe holds out the sheets and turns his head away.

Rika sighs, takes a sip. "You're all the same. Butcher each other, a cow, but when it comes to women you're greenbugs."

Moshe continues to look at the wall, his eyes averted like a servant's. Rika thanks him and asks him to keep alert in case she needs him. He has said nothing to Dora but can hear her clench in pain, determined not to cry out while he stands there. He sees the wrinkles of the bedsheets tighten, hears her breath quicken, small gasps of inhalation as she suffers.

Moshe feels worse now, having done nothing once again. He feels the familiar trepidation of life about to change and his resistance to it. The cruelest thing that God has wrought, he thinks, is not pain or punishment, but how long a lifetime takes, the sheer span of hours from birth until death, days hammered in like train rails as far as the eye can see.

Fritz and Garfield return with the midwife, Plumbly's colored maid. She has a fascinating starburst of scars on her neck, and Garfield would have liked to sit in the belly of the wagon so he could look at her, but as a white man, or almost-man, he sits on the driver's seat with Fritz. It is a silent ride home; only the huffing horses and the groaning of the axles when the wagon hits bumps punctuate the night. There is enough moon to see by, but the night is overcast, and the stars are faint.

Emily Anne has attended many births. White people like to give birth lying down, she knows, whereas her people prefer to squat, to use the natural force of gravity to help the baby into the world. She has also noticed that white babies make more noise when they are born, squealing and wailing when you hold them upside down to clear their lungs. Colored babies blink widely and know their place in the world.

The woman has heard the circumstances of this birth. It is all the talk among the railroad men, and her husband has shared the gossip. The girl is unmarried, young, and the rumor is that the father is a railroad worker, a Chinaman, or, she's also heard, an Indian. There is a rumor that she was raped by a Negro, or by her father, or else an outlaw who came upon her alone washing clothes in the yard.

The midwife thinks the girl careless. But when she sees how young the girl is, and notices her misshappen face, something in her softens. The girl's mother is calm but harried; her hands shake. She fears something is wrong.

Emily Anne says right away, "You hurtin'. And you gonna keep hurtin', but you look healthy enough, and I'll get this baby born soon." She looks at Dora, pulls her eyelids up and stares under them, examines her breasts. Dora is in too much pain to care that this Negro stranger is seeing her naked. Then the woman spreads Dora's legs. She looks between them at the enlarged opening. The girl looks small. Normal enough, but small. Emily Anne washes her hands with the soap and hot water provided. She scrubs hard, steeling herself for the long night ahead, and the grotesque tasks she will be called upon to perform soon. Then she asks Rika, "How long she been with the pains?"

Rika says, "Since about midnight. They got worse since sunrise."

Emily Anne nods. She's been here five minutes already, and there has been no contraction. The labor is stalling. Dora is still breathing heavily.

Emily Anne reaches over and inserts her hand into Dora's uterus. She can feel the smooth crown of the baby's head, its still-pliable skull spongy at her touch. She moves past, feels a shoulder. The baby is on its side. Should be easy enough to right.

"I want you to push," Emily Anne says. She has forgotten Dora's name.

"I can't," Dora breathes.

"Come on," her mother coaches. "'Course you can. Push, push hard."

"No," Dora says, but Emily Anne can feel the muscles of her uterus contract, softly.

"Gonna have to push harder than that, get this baby out."

Dora grunts as she pushes.

"That ain't gonna do it. Push harder now. Harder, hear?"

"Go to hell!" Dora screams.

"Oh!" Rika is shocked.

"Don't worry," Emily Anne says. "It's just the pain talking. I've birthed enough babies; I heard a lot worse."

"I'm so sorry," Rika says.

Emily Anne tries to turn the baby onto its back, but it's stuck fast to Dora's womb. She can see the top of the head just beginning to peek through the pink lips. The cord must be tangled, but not around the neck. Farther down then, Emily Anne guesses. This will not be so easy.

She prays for the child, surprising herself by including Dora in her prayers, too. She works the rhythm of the prayer into the massage she is performing with her hands. This baby wants out. It is not doing well in the birth canal. Once a baby is crowned, Emily Anne knows, it should get air soon.

Emily inserts both hands up past the wrists and tries not to think about what she is doing. The baby's shoulders are wide, wider than the pelvic bones will permit. The head is out, but the rest of the body remains inside. Emily Anne pauses a minute. Blood runs down her arms onto the lap of her skirt. Rika stands crying behind her.

Short of cutting the baby to pieces to bring it out, somehow the shoulders will have to be narrowed, Emily Anne thinks. A couple weeks ago she saw a mother pick a child up by one arm. He swung once then opened his mouth with a doglike howl. His body hung at a wide angle to the arm. Emily Anne could see where the bone pushed at his skin. His mother calmly put him down and, taking him between her legs, put one hand on his shoulder, another on his arm, and pushed the two back together like hitching up horses. This was the most practical white woman Emily Anne had ever seen.

Emily Anne takes one little arm and pulls it up alongside the head out of the womb. Then, grabbing the child by his head with her left hand and hooking her fingers under his arm with her right, she gives a tug as she commands, "Push."

The baby's head slips out of her fingers, the shoulders still inside the pelvis. "Sheet," she demands, and Rika passes her a long strip. She puts the sheet on the baby's head for a better grip. She can feel the socket beneath her fingers give way, release, and the baby's head pops out suddenly, followed by the one tiny shoulder and arm.

From there it is easy to pull the other shoulder out, and the rest of the infant falls quickly into Emily Anne's arms. It is a girl. Emily Anne clears her eyes, nose, and mouth. She turns her upside down and slaps her once on the back. The baby coughs and then begins to wail. It is a small sound, high-pitched and weak.

"See to the afterbirth," Emily Anne says. She crooks the baby with one arm and with the other cuts the umbilical cord with the knife on the bedside table. She takes the infant over to the chest and lays her on a sheet. Through the baby's blue skin, the veins show like a leaf's. The socket is still out of place. Emily Anne takes the arm and shoves it back into the shoulder. There is a small popping noise, and the baby screams louder, but Emily Anne rotates the shoulder and the baby seems fine. She ties a knot in the cord and washes her off. It is a beautiful baby, Emily Anne thinks. Prettier than most white ones. She has almond-shaped eyes, light blue, and a few wisps of dark hair.

Emily Anne turns to Dora to hand her the newborn, looking again at Dora's distorted face. "A girl," she says, smiling.

"Thank you," Dora whispers. "A girl. Is she pretty?"

"Sure is," Emily Anne says.

Downstairs, the men huddle in the kitchen. Fritz paces the small room while the boys sit morosely at the table. Moshe continues to boil water, watching the stove intently.

Finally there is the feeble wail, and a collective breath is exhaled from the kitchen.

"Can I go upstairs?" Sten asks.

"No," Fritz barks. He continues to pace, then stops near the stove. He pries up a floorboard and reaches under it. There is a small bottle filled with brown liquid. Fritz pulls out the cork and takes a long swig. If Moshe is surprised, it does not register on his face. When Fritz hands him the bottle he takes a sip. Then Garfield reaches for it. The boy leans back, tipping the bottle all the way up. Then he spits across the room.

"Ughhh," he says. "What is that?"

"Lexington Tanglefoot," Fritz says. "Not for the weak."

Sten begins to laugh. It's infectious. Moshe cracks a small smile, and then Fritz begins to snicker as well. Soon they are all in stitches.

"Stop!" Garfield says. "Stop it!"

Emily Anne descends the stairs to find the men guffawing in the kitchen. So many men. Is one the father? "A girl," she says. "Healthy."

"And Dora?" Moshe's breath comes out in a rush.

"Fine. Happy," Emily Anne says. "I'll just be goin' home now. Make sure she gets her rest. Make her drink liquids, tea, beer, get her milk going."

Fritz reaches into his pocket and hands her a few bills, which she slips into her apron, stained with blood. "I'll take you home," he says.

"I'll go with," Garfield says.

"Me, too." Sten is emboldened by the fun poked at Garfield. It has leveled their inequality somewhat.

"All right then," Fritz says.

Once they leave, Moshe pours the hot water into the wash basin and hefts it up the stairs. He knocks softly at the door.

"Come in," Rika calls. When she sees it is Moshe, her face falls. "I thought you'd be Fritz."

"He went to take the girl home," Moshe says, but he is not looking at her. He is staring at Dora. She is nursing the little girl at her breast. The baby is sucking with her entire body, her little leg moving involuntarily. Dora stares down, amazed. She has created this. Her pain forgotten, she strokes the small forehead. Moshe stands transfixed.

Annika toddles in behind him, awakened by the vibrations that the traffic on the stairs has created. He can hear her uneven footsteps. He puts down the basin, turns. She is in her nightdress, hair tousled from sleep. Her eyes grow wide as she takes in the blood, the child. No one had explained to her what was about to happen.

Rika picks her up. "You have a baby sister," she explains slowly, as if Annika will hear her, as if she is merely simple, not deaf.

"Niece," Dora corrects. "Annika is the baby's aunt."

"Right," Rika says. She sets Annika down in the bed next to Dora and the baby. Annika reaches out her hand. Dora grabs it. "Gently," she warns, and Annika tears up, upset at being treated so roughly. When Dora lets go, she reaches for the baby slowly, touches its hand.

"That's a good girl," Rika says. She smooths back Annika's hair. Her babies.

Moshe stands still, watching the scene. No one has acknowledged him. The three generations of women are smiling, happy. This is how it should have been with Alice, he thinks. This is the scene that should have followed Garfield's birth. He approaches, rapt in his reverie, and sits on the edge of the bed. Annika crawls into his lap, giggling when the baby loses her suction and begins to gulp wildly at the air until Dora clamps her down again.

Moshe stares at the nipple, pink and heavy. He would have loved to watch Alice feed the baby like this if she had let him. If she hadn't pushed him out of the room "for modesty's sake." A false modesty, he understands now. She wanted him gone. Moshe catches Dora's eye. Before he notices that she is staring not at him, but blindly, seeing only exhaustion and creation, unfocused and half dreaming, he thinks that it looks almost like a gaze of love.

* * *

Plumbly stands on his porch, chewing on a plug of tobacco. He watches the effete railroad man step gingerly around the piles of ties stacked like money on the ground. The men around him are sweaty; the heavy scent of work surrounds them like fog on the fields in spring, but the railroad man stays dry. Plumbly tries, but cannot remember his name. It is something Yankee; it has a number after it, the Third, or something. Not Glover, something more passive. Something that has less to do with craft, with labor.

The men are finished ripping up the previously laid ties, and are in the process of curving the train along the ridge toward Moshe and Fritz's land, where the elevation is higher. This is a minor setback. It's still his railroad, Plumbly thinks.

He wishes he didn't have to rely on Moshe. He wonders, not for the first time, how simple the man is. Fritz has assured him he is a thoughtful, cautious, complicated man, that his conflicting parentage makes him hesitate before he speaks. Plumbly is not so sure. Occasionally he'll catch Moshe moving his lips as though having a private conversation with himself. Or with a ghost. Strange, Plumbly thinks.

And then there is the relationship between the men. Stranger still, to merge families like that, and Moshe so sweet on the daughter and her bastard child. The cold Swede, obsessed with his cotton gin. Plumbly has smelled the sharp odor of spirits on his breath more than once and recognizes him as a fellow imbiber. How long can that incongruous partnership last?

It's almost, he thinks, like an interracial marriage. Jews and Christians, Swedes and Hebrews banding together. Like his servant, Emily Anne, who is married to a colored Creek. Man grew up a slave; now that he's free, he's more Indian than colored. Talks with that funny accent, and his family's been here long before Plumbly's joined the New World.

Well, that's the Territory for you, Plumbly thinks, rocking back on his heels. All of nature's misfits, looking to make a go of it. Indians and outlaws and immigrants, and all in Plumbly's backyard. Plumbly watches as the sun crests the ridge, raining orange light on the meadow, glinting like gold off the railroad ties.

Dora is obviously not changing back, and it makes Garfield want to hurt something. She has slipped away into the realm of worry and busy-ness. She has turned—irrevocably, it seems—into an adult.

He always thought he'd marry her someday, and that they'd travel the country together. Garfield's one train trip has kindled in him the family wanderlust. It is like a tickle in the throat, his need to leave. Even his sod hut, the one place that feels like his, is oppressive and tight. He needs to be Out There, wherever that is. And Dora's betrayal, her heavy swollen breasts, the baby tying her to the house, the resignation with which she does her chores, makes the need even more urgent.

As he watches Dora cradle the baby, whom Dora has christened Marira, Garfield thinks of his mother. He remembers her only vaguely: cascading hair, warm belly smelling of baking bread when she took him into her arms. He misses the mountains. They seem to him now symbols of safety, a buffer against the world. Without their hulking mass on the horizon, Garfield feels adrift, untethered.

"Dora," he says, trying to get her attention. "Dora, I'm hungry."

Time was when she would stick out her hand to shake, reply, "Hello, Hungry, I'm Dora," then take a warm biscuit from the pile and hand it to him. Now she says, "You've got two hands; fix yourself some food."

Garfield stands up so quickly his chair overturns. He runs all the way to the dugout where no one notices him, no one bothers him. For the more his father pulls on him, the more Garfield wiggles until he has escaped the grasp. He has no respect for Moshe, who is complacent, cowardly. Fritz, though Garfield is afraid of him, is more like the man Garfield wants to be. Fritz once caught Garfield teasing Sten by tying him to a tree and trying to light a fire under his feet. He beat Garfield, hard. Garfield cried and ran to his father for sympathy. His father asked Fritz nicely, so politely, if he would leave Garfield's discipline to Moshe.

But even as he was bent over Fritz's knee, naked to the world, and Fritz waled on him with a switch, even then, Garfield felt a grudging respect for Fritz. This is the way the world works, Garfield thought. He'd seen it before. The smaller are beaten by the stronger, who are in turn beaten by the stronger still. His father tries to use words—ineffectual, superfluous words—when Garfield knows that words matter hardly more than the breath with which they're uttered.

Garfield has a plan. He tells Sten but swears the boy to secrecy, then Indian-burns his arm to make sure he doesn't tell anyone. Garfield is taking steps to put his plan into action. He pores over maps in the office of the stationmaster, a man from St. Louis, bored since the completion of the train has been delayed. Garfield sounds out the place-names. He can get to Denver without consulting a rail schedule. He can brass-pound the telegraph, and the stationmaster explained the complicated system of dots and dashes that represent the letters of the alphabet. Sometimes he lets Garfield telegraph reports on the sounder. Unfortunately, Garfield's spelling is so terrible that the messages he sends are nearly unintelligible.

When it's time for action, Garfield will know; he'll be ready. And until that time he'll wait, patient as potatoes. The train set is finished now. He has seven cars: a passenger, two coal shuttles, two freight cars, and an engine and caboose. He is waiting for the day when the actual train rolls into the station, just outside his front door. When it blows its whistle and stops, brakes crying with effort. And then, he thinks, and then he'll board that train and ride it forever.

10

P lumbly can see it before it happens, and he moves out of the way just in time. The surrey's wheels hit the puddle with a smack, and the mud splatters. Plumbly jumps back; only a few drops land on his suit pants. He wipes them away quickly with his handkerchief, and the stain is barely noticeable. Behind him, Moshe bears the brunt of the attack; his jacket is sopping and his pants drip liquid on the boards of the sidewalk.

Now Guthrie is a city, Plumbly thinks. This is a place he'd be proud to be founder of. It is hardly an example of beautiful architecture or a triumph of urban planning, but it is an honest city—or rather, a frank one. The Territory's government lends it a note of importance. Guthrie sprang up like a geyser in one day, fully formed, and hasn't stopped bustling since. Forget Enid. He's not going to bother with some two-bit regional government, a bunch of elected blowhards. He's going straight to the source—the Territory capital.

The main street is laid with bricks, and the local government has paved the sidewalks with pine boards stretched solidly over stilts. Women hide under broad hats to save their skin from the sun. They bunch their long skirts modestly in gloved hands to protect them from the mud, so that just a coquettish hint of petticoat peeks out from beneath. Corsets are worn obligatorily here, and men in suits outnumber those in overalls. Society people tip their hats in public, drink socially, and debate politics.

Guthrie is a modern-day Athens of the West, Victorian England imposed upon America. Here there are restaurants and toy stores, sweet shops and a picture house. There is one building that has four floors of clothing for men and women. The top floor sells perfumes and cosmetics. Plumbly himself has bought shaving lotion and a musky fragrance on past visits. But this trip is not about pleasure.

Moshe has never been to the capital, and if he is impressed it is only by its shabbiness, the main street dirty and loud. There are chickens in the road; no one has cleaned up after the wild dogs. And the puddles . . . He has never imagined an O.T. city could be so wet, but then he steps to avoid the mucky dishwater a saloon owner flings out over the sidewalk. Moshe watches the familiar filth hit the wood and trickle down to the street. No wonder it is swampy, even in late fall.

A dirty city, even compared with America's most industrial settlements. Ramshackle buildings with bent backs are arranged in haphazard rows. And the women are like horses, laced into those ridiculous cinches. One leans out her front window to smile at the men suggestively. Plumbly tips his hat, as he does to every person they pass. Like a gluttonous bird, Moshe thinks, stooping to pick up every piece of grain.

At the end of the long block, Plumbly straightens his tie and clears his throat, and the two men turn down the side street. It is early morning; the sun has just crested brightly over the ridge. Moshe squints. After a few steps, they stop in front of a large brick building with a makeshift wood sign: United States Land Office. The porch is crowded with men and women waiting to officially prove their claims, carrying envelopes not unlike Moshe's. They sit tiredly on crates or on the ground, not caring that their skirts are gray from dirt and spatter or that everyone can see the thin soles of their shoes. On their faces Moshe reads wan frustration; their bodies are still, their eyes barely blinking. Weighted down by seals and signatures, they languish in a bureaucratic stupor of waiting.

Plumbly seems not to see them; he has the confidence of a man with an appointment, and mumbling "excuse me, pardon me" he makes his way up the steps and across the porch, where he knocks loudly on the door. There is a collective gasp as the group of supplicants sits up straighter at his audacity.

Plumbly turns the knob. The door opens slowly, creaking, so that the mystery of its interior builds. Moshe can feel the hot breath of the people behind him, pressing, anxious to see what lies within.

"Morning, sir," Plumbly says to the man sitting at a desk inside. "I have an appointment to see a Mr. Jackson."

"I'm Owen Jackson," a voice calls from the inner office. A small man in a three-piece suit steps out.

"Arnel Plumbly." Plumbly sticks out his hand, which hangs, axlike, in

Mr. Jackson's face. He lowers it slowly, so that Owen Jackson shakes his hand somewhere near Plumbly's belly. "This here is Haurowitz."

Moshe shakes Mr. Jackson's hand.

"Let's step into my office, gentlemen." Mr. Jackson spreads his arm. "Paddy," he calls back, "don't let none of the rabble in. Call your cousin if you have to."

Mr. Jackson closes the door and points to the two chairs facing his desk. "Dumb Mick tried to form some sort of line last week, practically got us trampled by the claim-provers." The man talks as though he is twice his size, as though he had muscle and girth to back him up. Moshe feels nervous; his stomach roils from drinking too much coffee at breakfast.

"What can I do for you, Mr. Plumbly?" Mr. Jackson settles at his desk, making a show of crossing one leg over the other as though he is stiff or has a full belly. Plumbly and Moshe remain standing.

"You've read the application, sir," Plumbly says.

"I have." Mr. Jackson's voices rises at the end, more an invitation for Plumbly to remind him than a firm statement.

"We're the ones what are applying for the townsite, and the ownership after the improvement on the land."

"What's your flag?"

"Beg pardon?" Plumbly is confused. "I wasn't aware there was a necessary for a flag."

"It's a figure of speech." Jackson drips condescension. Moshe looks at the diploma on the wall behind him; it is from the Ohio School of Mines. He scans the room: bookshelves of law volumes and a daguerreotype of a Civil War regiment. "What's the town's name?"

"Called Owenasa. It means 'home,'" Moshe says.

"In Creek?" Mr. Jackson asks.

"Cherokee."

"How quaint," Mr. Jackson says, a sarcastic note in his voice. "You have a map?"

"Right here, sir." Plumbly takes the map from Moshe and spreads it out on the table. His voice warbles; he, too, sounds nervous, Moshe is surprised to hear.

Mr. Jackson perches a pair of rimless spectacles on his nose and bends closer. "That's the new Lafayette line, is it?"

"Yessir, the LaLa."

"And these are the streets?"

"Yessir. We marked the school and park and—"

"Umm hmm."

Moshe joins the men in looking at the map. He is unfamiliar with plans, and the concentric circles of the elevations seem like targets. He struggles to make out his house, but he can see only Fiddler's Creek winding around as though lost.

"Let's see the proposal again." Plumbly hands Jackson the long document and rocks back and forth on his heels and toes.

"Go ahead and sit, Mr. Plumbly." Jackson paces while he reviews the documents. Moshe follows him with his eyes. The man's shoes look strange. They have heels, like women's shoes, and small tassels. Moshe's own scuffed boots seem lumbering in comparison.

"A couple of questions, gentlemen." Moshe nods. Plumbly has told him to keep as quiet as possible, fulfilling the stereotype of the taciturn Indian. "LaLa is running freight on this track?"

"They're testing the lines this week."

"And it's all right with him?" Jackson signals with his chin at Moshe as though he's not in the room.

"Tracks pass right by his house. The law says that——"

"I'm aware of the law, sir." Jackson straightens up. His tone is haughty. Plumbly hangs his head. "I sent a letter that says his claim is denied." Jackson points to the convoluted letter from his office.

"Only in the absence of proper evidence. Now we have a surveyor's map, and it clearly has this man's residence right on there in ink."

"You've built these tracks, and now you're trying to prove the claim? Or are you applying for incorporation? Either way, there's no record of him making the run in '93."

"Well, sir, now, that's why we came to see you." Plumbly reaches into his jacket and pulls out a large envelope tied with twine. He puts it on top of the map and slides it toward Jackson. "I was told you were a man who likes deficiency. Two birds with one stone and that sort of thing."

Jackson takes the envelope and puts it in the wide pocket of his pants without examining it. "Where do you plan on putting the—" There is an accusatory tone to Jackson's voice.

"Here's another view of Owenasa town," Plumbly interrupts. He spreads the drawing on Jackson's desk, on top of the surveyor's map. "One of those new ones, from up in the air like a bird would see."

Moshe stares at the drawing, the small homes like dollhouses. How was this drawing made, as though the artist stood at a great height, as though he were God?

Jackson is somewhat less impressed. "And how much of this is built?" Jackson asks.

"A percentage." Plumbly reaches into the other breast pocket of his jacket and removes a second envelope, which he hands to Jackson, who puts it in the other pocket of his pants.

"How many souls are there in Owenasa?"

"Fifty-three," Plumbly says. "With one on the way."

"Small town," Jackson shakes his head.

"There've been smaller."

There is a silence while the men regard each other warily. Moshe thinks that Plumbly will win. Plumbly has to win. It's part of Moshe's plan. His plan to get rich and marry Dora. Fritz will have to say yes once they're rich. It all comes down to money, Moshe thinks. To those envelopes that Plumbly keeps pulling out of his jacket like birds from a magician's cloak.

"I don't know." Mr. Jackson stands up. "You're doing it all out of order."

Moshe holds his breath. He watches as Plumbly fingers the edge of his hat. Plumbly inhales deeply. "With all due respect, sir," he says, "it's Oklahoma what's done it out of order. I'm just trying to keep up."

Mr. Jackson frowns, and there is a split second when Moshe fears it is all going up in smoke. But then Jackson's features break into a reluctant smile.

The atmosphere changes, palpably. Plumbly sits back and assumes the generous attitude of a big winner at the poker tables. He sighs theatrically and reaches back for a third envelope, concealed in the belt above his rump.

Jackson takes it with his left hand and extends his right to shake. "You'll have your claim approval and your townsite as soon as the paperwork is finished. Now if there's nothing else, gentlemen . . ." Moshe is surprised when Jackson extends his hand for Moshe to shake. He does so, weakly.

"Nice doing business with you, sir," Plumbly says. He backs out of the office and puts his hat on.

Moshe's heart soars. He smiles widely, still mute, still playing his role. They nod at Paddy and step out onto the porch, where they struggle to push through the crush of people waiting. Plumbly brushes off the sleeves of his jacket. "Well, my friend," he says, clapping Moshe on the back. "That was a highly successful venture, I'd say. And I didn't even have to use the fourth one!" Plumbly leans over and takes another bundle out of his boot. "What do you say we take this stash and get ourselves some drinks and girls to celebrate?"

Plumbly doesn't wait for an answer, but walks briskly down the street. He seems to know where he is going; he turns left, then right, then right again. Moshe struggles to keep up. Plumbly tucks his hat low on his head, looks furtively right then left, then ducks down a small alleyway. He stops at a door and knocks three times.

The door is opened by the largest pair of breasts Moshe has ever seen. They are immense, high up at Moshe's eye level, barely concealed in a lacy bodice. They are attached to a congruently big woman with a bright yellow wig. "Arnel!" she says, and opens the door wider. She takes his head in her hands (her fingernails are lacquered, Moshe notices) and kisses him on both cheeks, leaving round red marks. Plumbly smacks his lips with each peck, exaggerating the kissing noises.

Moshe has never been inside a cathouse before, except Gilges Street, which was a poor example of the genre. Even at the railroad rest stops he stayed away, faithful to Alice. This is a true house of ill repute, luxurious and velveteen. Gilded mirrors reflect an idealized version of Moshe back at him. Marble mantels and glass-plated lampshades cast a soft sheen over the parlor, and Moshe feels as though he's stepped into a dream. He sits next to Plumbly on a red velvet couch with ornate gold trim. When he's handed a glass, he drinks, a blast of fire that numbs his tongue and travels bullet-fast down his gullet. The dreamlike quality of the room increases. There is a film over his eyes as they line up the girls for the choosing.

"Whichever one you want," Plumbly is saying. "But I ain't paying for a virgin. Whichever *used* one you want."

Moshe feels as though he is in a different world, and that he'd best follow Plumbly's lead or get stuck here forever. He looks at the women arrayed before him. He tries to find the one who looks most like Dora. He searches faces for her droop, bodies for her swollen figure. He is about to pick a slightly homely one until he wonders if Plumbly will know by the girl he picks, if he will guess Moshe's secret desire.

Instead he chooses a girl who reminds him of Alice. They are not so similar in looks, perhaps, but her insouciant frown, her blowsy manner, recall Alice's similar uninterest. She tells him her name is Lily, and she takes him by the hand. Moshe turns to see Plumbly pick a tiny blonde who cannot be more than seventeen and pull her onto his lap as she playfully struggles to get away.

On Lily's bedroom walls Moshe is shocked to see pornographic drawings. Some seem Oriental, colorful and crude etchings of sexual positions. Most Moshe has never contemplated, let alone tried. Others are more baroque, sketches of women disrobing or caught in the throes of passion, men with their pants undone, panting at the women.

"Do you see something you want to do?" Lily asks. She has discarded her silk robe and wears a garter belt, panties, and camisole with brocade flowers and intricate lace.

Moshe stares, speechless.

"This isn't your first time, is it?" The woman is from the North; Moshe can hear it in her closed vowels.

He shakes his head.

"You want me to do it for you?"

Moshe nods.

Lily steps closer and begins to unbutton Moshe's shirt. He watches her fingers as though they are touching someone else's body.

"Relax," Lily says. "Don't worry."

Moshe stares at the woman beneath him as he enters her again and again. If he closes his eyes almost completely and blocks out the woman's artificial moans, he can almost believe it is Alice he is making love to, that Alice has returned to be a mother to their wild son, that she has returned to Moshe's bed, his life.

But even before this fiction is completely realized, it is over, and Moshe is hustled out. He sits on the velvet couch and accepts another drink from the large-breasted woman. When Plumbly hasn't returned after an hour, Moshe stands up and wanders the streets of Guthrie until he finds their hotel.

It takes the Sisters of Charity three days until they are finally able to understand the old man through his matted beard and gurgling lungs. "I think he's saying 'Boggy.' Is that your name? Boggy?" Sister Matthew doesn't quite believe it.

But Boggy nods solemnly. He struggles to breathe. It is as though an engine is sitting atop his chest. He tastes sharp metal in his mouth. He remembers feeling feverish, inside his bedroll near Barstow. He remembers a brakeman shaking him awake, the man's hands surprisingly gentle, his eyes light brown. And then he remembers nothing until waking up here, in what he assumes is a charity hospital, being cared for by nuns.

They turn him on his side and beat his chest with the heels of their hands until he coughs up green phlegm flecked with bright blood. The nurses examine it seriously. They show it to the doctor, who purses his lips, writes something on the chart that hangs at the foot of Boggy's bed.

Sister Matthew must have Indian blood; she has the same impossibly high cheekbones as Boggy's wife, the long forehead and the center-parted coal black hair. It is she who rubs the poultice on Boggy's chest, the warmth radiating into his cold toes and ears. She sings just softly enough for Boggy to hear, and though he doesn't recognize the tune or the language, he can tell it is not liturgy, or at least not Christian liturgy.

She is the one who holds his hand as the end comes. They send for the priest, a young man who seems overwhelmed by his duties in the hospital; he juggles a Bible, two rosaries, a cross, and a vial of holy water as he struggles to remove his hands from his billowing robe. Boggy shakes his head and attempts to form words when the man begins, *"Pater noster qui in caelis es sanctificetur . . ."*

"Shh, shh," says the nurse. "He's trying to say something." She places her head down next to his ear, and he can feel on his neck the tendrils of hair that have escaped her habit.

She sits back up. "He's Jewish."

Boggy feels something drain out of him. Suddenly it becomes easier to breathe. The room sharpens into focus. He struggles to keep his eyes open.

There is an awkward silence. There is no rabbi for miles. The nurse and doctor look at the priest. "I—I—," he stammers. "I don't know about—I only have the New Testament."

"Then *recite* from the Old," the doctor commands, impatient. He has rounds to make, reports to write.

The priest clears his throat and clasps his hands together at his waist. *"In principio creavit Deus caelum et terram . . ."*

This is not right, Boggy knows. You do not recite Latin at a Jewish deathbed. Instead . . . he tries to think of a prayer he can offer up. It may be too little, too late, but he feels wonderfully light at the moment, as though he could get up and walk out of the hospital, though his legs are leaden and his arms useless.

But his mind refuses to focus. He pictures himself in the *schul* as a child, sees his mother straightening his shirt, his wife mending a pair of socks. Then the nurse comes back into focus, and he imagines kissing her on the forehead. No, she is kissing him on the forehead. But he was going to pray. And he can't think of even the simplest Shabbat prayer. He feels his eyes flutter.

And then the nurse who reminds him of his wife whispers in his ear. He can hear her clearly over the droning priest. "You can go," she says. She takes his hand and puts it in her lap, crisp white linen, and rubs it rhythmically. "You just go on, now."

The rubbing makes Boggy feel as though he's being cradled, and he wants to close his eyes and relax into the breathing that finally is effortless, and she has given him permission. So he lets his eyes close and thinks about what the sky looks like from a bedroll on the ground outside a train depot. The last thing he hears: "Amen."

"That's all right then, Father." The nurse stands up. She folds Boggy's lifeless hands across his chest. "He's gone now."

"No kin?" the doctor asks.

She shakes her head and pulls the sheet up over Boggy. The doctor walks away.

Sister Matthew makes half the sign of the cross, then remembers, and hurries across the room to where a bedpan needs changing, or an injection needs administering, or someone else needs her to hold his hand as he passes on.

PART 4

Fallen Trees Make a Dam
1896–1902

11

Moshe watches from behind the counter as Rika strokes the bolt of cotton cloth. Her hands move along its stripes, then one holds it taut while the other runs up a yard's length. A farmer's wife stands watching, as transfixed as Moshe; her husband waits behind her with arms crossed. Then the wife turns to look at her husband, and his frown softens. "Not for all the girls," he says.

"Just Joanne," she says. "For her sixteenth."

The husband nods and wanders over to the dry goods.

"Can I help you?" Moshe says.

"I'm thinking about planting some cotton."

Moshe nods, though he thinks this a terrible idea. He would tell the farmer, except that he can hear Fritz's hammers out back, constructing a monstrosity of a cotton mill. He wants this to work for Fritz. Then maybe the Fritz he knew, the one not crippled by grief and frustration, will return.

"How many acres?" Moshe asks.

"Just eight, I think," says the farmer. His hands are surprisingly clean, Moshe notices, and then he realizes that the man has cleaned up to come here. He thrills to think that his store commands that much respect in the town. "Don't want to put all the eggs in one basket."

Moshe lets out a sigh. "We can order those seeds for you. Be here next week."

The farmer nods.

Moshe says, "You need a plow attachment, furrow the rows the right width?"

The farmer thinks. "I suppose," he says.

"You want the one-piece share and moldboard, then." Moshe goes behind the counter and pulls the seed catalogue out with its heavy binder.

"Been selling a lot of Grover brand seed," he says. "Claim it's impervious to the locusts."

"Ain't nothing imperious," the farmer says.

Moshe hides a smile; the man's misuse of the word makes him think of Plumbly. "My personal preference is for O'Shay. They give you nice big bolls, means more cotton each plant. A little more pricey, but you recover it on the back end."

The farmer clearly isn't following him. This is good, Moshe thinks. He has been reading sales manuals ordered from advertisements in *Frank Leslie's*. "Talk fast!" chapter 1 says. "Discombobulate the customer with jargon foreign to the plebian ear." Then there is a list of economic terms to pepper the sale with, *back end* being just the start. *Recovery to investment ratio, sunk cost, recuperation retrieval, investment earn-out interval.* Moshe is putting his knowledge to work.

Moshe draws out an order form and fills in the boxes. He asks the man for his name and the location of his farm. The man gives him a series of numbers, quadrants that the Territory has assigned in the absence of roads to differentiate claims. He looks curiously at Moshe's scribbling, and Moshe realizes the man is illiterate.

Moshe fills the columns and waits for Rika to come by with the sales slip for the woman's purchases. She is ordering an inexpensive gingham for new curtains, ten yards of the cotton Rika showed her, some linsey-woolsey, and various baking supplies: flour, salt, sugar, yeast. Rika goes in the back to measure out the quantities, and Moshe makes an addition column. With the seeds and the plow it comes to $53.36.

The man breathes out a long sigh when he hears the total.

"We don't got a choice, Joe," his wife says.

"I can give you half on credit," Moshe says. "One year no interest. Pay it back how and when you like."

"I don't like owing nobody." The farmer seems reluctant.

"Joe," the wife cajoles. "What, we gonna have the little ones run around naked because we too proud?"

"Fine," Joe says. "Fine."

"Make your mark here." Moshe points to a line. Joe carves an awkward "J. R." on the page.

Rika comes out with a large crate. There is flour on her apron. "Next time you're in town, come by so I can see the girls' dresses from that cotton," Rika says.

Moshe says, "Plow should be here by the end of next week, unless there's train trouble or weather."

"Thank you," the wife says. The husband nods.

When they are out of the store, Moshe whistles breathily. "Good sale."

Moshe and Rika smile at each other. "I was thinking," Rika says. "Maybe we could start selling upper items."

"Like what?"

"Ribbons, face creams, hair tonic."

"If you think so," Moshe says. "I don't know a lot about that."

"Anything *you* think would sell?"

"Child things," Moshe says after a pause. "I think that kids come in here and want things for themselves. Penny candy, factory toys, that sort of thing. When a child wants something . . ."

Rika puts her hand on his shoulder. "I'll get *McCall's,* see what's in there."

Moshe looks around the store. They have built rows of shelves and ordered glass cases. There are stacks of Indian blankets and pipes, hot water bottles and cloth. There are huge vats of pecans, hides of various provenances hanging from the walls, metal goods such as pots, pans, teakettles, and flour grinders. There are small bottles of tonics, large glass jars of spices, salt and pepper, and Mason jars for canning. There is wire for chicken coops and fishing line. There are chisels and lathes and knives and china, tin silverware, salt-back pork, chicory, and tobacco. There are old newspapers, and a part of the store that can be roped off with curtains when the photographer comes to town. A sign outside says HAUROWITZ SUNDRY in large gold-painted letters.

Moshe cannot help but be proud. The money Plumbly gave him and Fritz for the railroad's ingress onto their property—the man is nothing if not generous—led to a battle. Moshe and Rika wanted to open a store, Fritz his mill. Eventually they split the money down the middle. Rika tries to support her husband, but he waves her away whenever she asks what she can do. So instead she helps out in the store. Moshe considers it half hers.

In the house Dora reigns, keeping home for both families. She cooks and cleans while Annika plays and Marira sleeps in a basket on the floor. It is she who makes sure the flour lasts a month and that the vegetables get properly canned to avoid sickness. Dora has become an excellent cook. She cuts recipes from old newspapers and women's magazines and manages to make do with the ingredients she has on hand. Moshe teases her about opening a restaurant, and then they half-seriously discuss the idea. It would be the first in town. Fritz nixes it, saying it is beneath them, like running a boardinghouse.

Dora does not so much enjoy being caretaker and housekeeper; rather, she is resigned to it, as she is to motherhood. It seems the logical conclusion to what she has come to realize was a grievous sin. She catches glimpses of Marira's father only rarely. He lives on a remote farm and so doesn't come to town but once a month. When he sees her, he hides his face. Marira has his long nose and attached earlobes. They had not exchanged more than a hello in a year when he arrived at the house one afternoon and asked to see his daughter. No one else was home. He held Marira stiffly, and after a minute handed her back wordlessly.

When Dora leaves the kitchen to go out to the garden or the well, she asks Annika to watch the baby. Annika will come and get Dora if she sees Marira screaming. She enjoys screaming back, likes the way it feels in her throat, as though her breath were something solid in the world, something she creates.

As burning and imperative as it felt at the time, Moshe's ardor for Dora has cooled. He realizes he wanted to help her as much as have her, and now that it's patently clear she doesn't need his help, his attachment has weakened. Plus, though they live in the same house, he rarely sees her except at mealtimes; they are never alone together. It's as though his night with Lily has snapped him out of his trance. Now when he closes his eyes at night he sees only Alice, ethereally lovely Alice, and he wonders where in this vast country she might be. .

Meanwhile, Garfield has installed himself as a permanent fixture at the Owenasa depot. The stationmaster is of consummate good humor and lets Garfield run much of the operation—making arrival and departure announcements, receiving telegraph messages, and ringing the departure bell while calling, "All aboard!" Garfield orders Sten around as though the boy were his servant. Sten carries baggage, helps unload freight, and chases escaped livestock off the tracks. Garfield garnishes half of Sten's earnings as commission. The boy is too embarrassed to complain.

Plumbly's predictions were accurate. The railroad was slow to take off, but then the LaLa added cattle cars, and suddenly there are trains running up and down the line daily, and the commensurate population growth has started. Already Owenasa counts seventy-five residents, one store, a lumberyard, a bank, and it looks as though someone is fixing to open a metalworks. Denton Station smells deserted, the air dusty with enervation and failure.

Moshe drinks now, like the rest of the men. After the first in Guthrie, gulped wincingly like medicine, he's come to thirst for it, for the feeling of weightlessness that accompanies a night of imbibing. Drink makes Moshe smaller. He sinks into himself until his voice is a tiny whisper, his body a child's. He does not like to enter conversations or play dice with the others. To him, liquor is not about sinning; it is about escape. He slinks back to the store and spends the night in front of the coal stove.

This is the first party Garfield has ever been to and the first that Sten remembers, and both boys are excited. They offer to help Fritz, who gives them a job touching up the paint on the mill so that it shines in the late summer sunlight. But the painting quickly devolves into arguments over who gets to use which brush, and Garfield throws the can in frustration. It hits Sten square in the chest, drenching his clothes. Crying, Sten runs inside to Dora. She sighs. She's got the cookies to finish, the pies to put out, the chickens to dress, and the pork to fry. She needs to cut the bread and find some sort of serving dish for the butter. Instead she takes the water she was boiling for tea and pours a bath. When Sten gets out, she tosses his dirty clothes along with a bit of soap in after him, and scrubs until the red is mostly gone.

Fritz and Moshe stand inside the mill, where Moshe admires Fritz's handiwork. However misguided, it is an impressive bit of engineering. An intricate churning system agitates the cotton bolls before stripping out their seeds. Within, Fritz has designed a system that can differentiate types so that someone who comes in with Carolina cotton can have the mill tailored to the size of his crop. The mill is operated by a crank system, with toothy wheels and pulleys, but Fritz plans to electrify as soon as that's a reliable option in Oklahoma Territory.

Rika comes in from the garden holding three tomatoes in her apron. "It's too early yet," she says. "They weren't ready." She looks up. The sun glints down through the spaces between the roof beams. She squints and says something in Swedish. Moshe can hear Fritz's name.

Dora sticks her head in the door. She has never been inside the mill, and Moshe sees her gasp. "Pa," she says, "it's beautiful."

Fritz doesn't register this compliment.

"It's two o'clock, Pa. You told me to tell you when."

Fritz takes out his pocket watch. He bought a watch and cufflinks and a real suit with a hat when Plumbly gave him his money, said he was a rich gentleman now and should start dressing like one. Moshe put a portion of his money in the bank in Guthrie, as much to be able to go visit Lily as to keep it safe. The rest he stowed away under the tombstones of the grave-yard, wrapping the bills in burlap and a scrap of denim jeaning soaked in oil to keep the wet from getting to it.

People straggle toward the mill. Because it is harvest time and the mid-dle of the day, the crowd is thin. Anyone with horses has them out drag-ging sleds today. So the guests number ten, including two hobos who have stopped by for the promise of a free meal. Dora puts out plates and plates of steaming food on the rickety table: mincemeat pie (made with pork in-stead of beef, but this is almost undetectable under the salt and rosemary), fried chicken, potatoes, canned corn and carrots, jam, bread, thick butter, and a strong tea for drinking.

Plumbly arrives just after Fritz's speech has started. He has begun to wear Levis, as though he were a cowboy, and because they fit tight his belly bulges over like a watermelon. His wife has fashioned suspenders out of a Mexican serape, and he looks like a joke-book character wearing a barrel because a jackrabbit stole his clothes.

Fritz finishes his speech. He sweeps his hand back and presents the mill. Then he snaps his fingers, and Sten, who has been waiting for his cue, climbs to its top and pours a canvas bag of unmilled cotton into the mouth of the machine. Fritz turns the handle; the gears churn, and amid a cloud of thick white dust falls silky cotton. The audience claps.

And then, because there is nothing more to see, and because they have eaten all the food they can fit in their bellies, the audience leaves.

"Good show." Plumbly hits Fritz hard on the back. Cotton lint rises up in a cloud. "Were I a farmin' man, I'd mill here for sure. For sure," he repeats. "Hey, Haurowitz," he calls to Moshe, who's heading toward the store. "Got any liniment in that sag wagon?"

"What kind are you looking for?" Moshe asks.

Plumbly pulls up next to him. "For chafing," he confides, pointing to his crotch. "On account of these Levis."

"I'm sure we have something."

"What do them vaqueros do, you know? For the chafing?"

"I'm not sure," Moshe says. "Maybe they wear undergarments?" Moshe is attempting a joke.

Plumbly furrows his brow as if this seems odd to him, but he's considering the option. "Lemme try that liniment first."

Fritz is left alone with his mill, the lone shade tree in a plowed field. He walks back and forth across its entrance as though on patrol. Nothing to do now but wait for the customers. Far off he can hear the train as it approaches Owenasa. Let it come, he thinks. Let them all come. Then he'll prove to his wife that he has been right all along, that he is a success.

By that evening, the sense of levity has dissipated. Moshe calls Garfield in to help at the store—the afternoon freight brought in some new canned goods. Garfield curses at Moshe and runs off. Moshe debates going after him, but decides to wait until his anger has calmed. Garfield has called him a word that he should never utter, a word that mocks their heritage. Moshe wonders where he learned that slur—who has been insulting them?

Garfield does not return for supper. Rika and Fritz have obviously exchanged words during the afternoon, as they will not make eye contact at the table. Sten, exhausted from the excitement, falls asleep before the food is served. Dora excuses herself to put Annika and Marira to bed.

Now it is just the three adults at the table. "Rika," Moshe says, "A. J. came by and bought that flat iron his wife wanted."

Rika says, "We're getting low on yellow ribbon. That German family from Denton got their hands on some issue of *McCall's* says yellow is the color of the new century."

"That's four years from now," Moshe says.

"And the catalog is about four years old, too. But they all came in and bought yellow ribbon."

"Women and their stupid fashions," Fritz says.

Moshe wants to remind Fritz that he has been completely seduced by the trappings of success—his gold watch fob, his suit and waistcoat. But he fears Fritz's temper.

"That reminds me," Rika says. "Someone mentioned that in Atoka they're carrying the *Times Record*. If they can get it, we can too, probably."

"Boilerplate sheet," Fritz says dismissively.

Moshe ignores him. "I'll look into it," he says. "Next you'll be wanting a telephone."

"I'd love one," Rika retorts. "But who could I call?"

"You'd find someone," Moshe laughs.

Fritz clears his throat. "I heard that Cherokees were so stupid they thought the telephone would speak to them in Cherokee."

Moshe feels the sting of his words. He says nothing. Rika purses her lips.

Dora returns and starts clearing the dishes. "You finished, Pa?"

Fritz pretends he doesn't hear her.

"We're all done," Rika says. "Mind you leave the pie pans to soak, otherwise we'll never get the crust out. Next time you'll grease them better."

Dora starts on the silverware near the washbasin. They all watch her scrub as though it were the most fascinating thing since electric light. She reaches for a plate, and her soapy fingers can't hold it. It falls to the floor and cracks into pieces.

It is as though a gun has gone off. Everyone freezes for a moment. Then Rika bends to help pick up the pieces. Moshe holds his breath. Perhaps the moment will pass. But no, there is Fritz, stretching up to his full height. "You stupid, stupid girl!" he yells. "You think these things grow on vines? You think I can just snap my fingers and more dishes appear like a magic show?"

"I'm sorry." Dora begins to cry.

"I shouldn't have let you stay," Fritz says. "I should have sent you away, you whore."

Dora sobs. Rika holds her tight against her chest. Fritz slams his fists on the table so that the remaining plates leap.

"Enough," Moshe is surprised to hear himself say. Dora and Rika look up.

"Don't you get involved," Fritz warns.

"Fritz, ease up. It was an accident. Have a drink."

"I don't want a drink, and I don't want advice from some stupid Hebe."

"Stop," Moshe says. It sounds as small as a whine. Upstairs, Marira wakes up and wails.

"Go to hell, all of you," Fritz says. He spits on the floor and storms out. They all wait in silence until they hear the slam of the mill door. Rika looks up and motions Moshe out of the room with the back of her hand.

Just like that Moshe is exiled. He should protest, he knows, or go after Fritz, but he is tired. So tired. He's not sure he can manage a confrontation. And faced with his inadequacy, Moshe goes to the one place that feels like home: the store.

In the store things behave the way they should, the way Moshe tells them to behave. Numbers add up; inventory lists match the contents of the glass cases, shined to perfection. Catalogs are stacked, clothing folded, and pencils sharpened. Every day when he enters he finds it exactly as he left it, and as everything else moves beyond his control, the store becomes a place of refuge, a cave, a pillow for the mind.

Moshe's eyes well up when he receives the package. Straight from Chicago, an entire box of books, magazines, and newspapers he hasn't read. He wants to devour them all at once. But there is work to do, and instead he touches their spines gingerly. He sets them on the shelves in the back of the store, where customers can't see, as gently as if he were handling eggs.

That first night he picks one at random, and after the first paragraph breathes a deep sigh. He is no longer Moshe Haurowitz, homestaker in the Territory; he is Edward Rochester on an English moor. Such a relief, such a burden lifted. In the weeks to come he tries to slow down. If he reads this voraciously, there won't be any left. When he is reading, he hears nothing, sees nothing, smells nothing. Rika has to bang her fist on the table to get his attention. Sometimes Annika sits on his lap while he reads, studying the print as though she knows what it means. Sometimes he shows her which words go with which objects: *pencil, desk, fire, chair.* She pays much more attention than Garfield ever did.

When, in a kind of pleasurable torment, he reaches the end of the last novel, he reluctantly puts it back on the shelf, closes his eyes, sighs, and lets his fingers dance over the spines, choosing whatever novel chance wants him to reread first. It begins on the character's eighteenth birthday, and suddenly it occurs to Moshe that Garfield will soon be turning fourteen.

"Rika, what day are we?" he calls into the store.

"April third, all day long, why?" Rika answers. She is knitting a shawl for winter with the new merino yarn.

"It's Garfield's fourteenth birthday tomorrow."

"I'll tell Dora to make a cake."

Moshe muses on how easy it is to be with Rika. They are like an old married couple, serene and unhurried. She makes him laugh. Sometimes one knows what the other is about to say. It reminds him of nothing so much as his camaraderie with Jackie, the easy exhale of friendship. He smiles at her.

Rika doesn't know why Moshe is smiling, but she smiles back.

* * *

At first light, Moshe rises and tiptoes through Fritz and Rika's room. The couple is sleeping soundly, wearing nightcaps to ward off the cold, backs to each other. Moshe closes the door softly behind him.

Moshe carries Garfield's present. Anyone in the house could tell Moshe that a chemistry set is not remotely what Garfield wants, but Moshe occupies a fictive world in which his son will be thrilled to own Dr. Peats's Advanced Chemistry and Electricity Set for Boys. Moshe is so lost in his reverie that he doesn't immediately register Garfield's absence. He enters the kitchen and sees Sten in the corner, cradling his left arm and crying softly.

"I told him I didn't tell," Sten hiccups.

"Didn't tell what?" Moshe is still confused.

"His leaving plan."

"Plan to leave where?"

"Here." Sten wipes his nose on his sleeve, wincing. Moshe can see smeared bruises on the boy's arm.

Moshe sits on a chair in disbelief. Surely Garfield will come home. He always does, angry and dirtied. But Moshe can tell that something is different, and he fears that he has lost something irrevocable all over again. He asks, "But to go where?"

Sten takes a deep breath.

"So where is he?"

Sten looks Moshe right in the eyes so that the older man can see the firm determination of the younger's brow. "Gone."

12

arfield is unprepared for the cold. He knew it would be chilly, riding a freight car, but he neglected to consider that the train's speed adds to the wind. It blows through the thin cracks in the walls, and with each jostle Garfield's teeth gnash, his bones clink, his spirit flags.

And he is hungry. The piece of bread and the flask of coffee that he took with him are both long gone. Hunger preoccupies him; he feels intermittently cold and crampy. When day breaks he is halfway to Denver, and as the train slows in some little town, Garfield sees a hand grab the side of the door. A foot makes its way onto the floor, followed by a grunt and a body.

"Goddamn," the body says. "It's tit cold in here. What is this, the reefer car?" He laughs like he's made a joke, but Garfield doesn't understand it. "I'm Casher." The man extends his hand. He is wearing gloves with the fingers cut off, like Garfield has seen farmhands wear.

"Garfield." He takes Casher's hand lightly. His voice wavers, as though he might cry.

Casher sits down. In the growing light Garfield can see that he is a boy not much older than himself, maybe seventeen or eighteen. Yet he has the assurance and bearing of a man twice his age. He looks at Garfield, purses his lips. "Let me guess . . . You are new at riding the rails."

Garfield opens his mouth.

"No—don't speak." Casher holds up his palm. "You are new, this might even be your first day, and you are hungry. You have a little money, and you are running away from . . . let me guess . . . from your father who beats you. No, who wants you to become a priest."

Garfield decides the best course of action is to nod yes. It would be hard to explain that he is running away precisely because his father does not beat him, harder still to explain that he is Jewish. Already he has seen

143

that being part Indian demotes him in westerners' eyes, and being Jewish invites only derision and curses.

"I knew it." Casher slaps Garfield's knee. "You're in for a ride, boy."

They sit in silence for a while, listening to the metal drumbeat of the rails. "You want some advice?" Casher says.

"Sure."

"You should work on your handshake. I don't know, maybe you like boys; that's what your handshake says."

"I don't understand," Garfield says. He hates feeling stupid.

"There's men that like other men, in the way that men like women. You shake hands like that, all limp like a snake, and that's what they'll think you are, one of the jockers who likes other men."

Garfield is perplexed. Though he knows the facts of life, a means by which men could have sex with other men defies comprehension. Still, the grave tone with which Casher delivers this news makes Garfield fear this misperception. He will work on his handshake.

"Can we shake again?" he asks. He holds out his hand, and Casher takes it. Garfield squeezes with all his strength.

"Good," Casher says. "Can your stomach hold out? I know a good jungle outside Cairo."

Garfield has no idea where this Cairo is, but he nods. And then he feels drowsy, realizing the night of sleep he's missed. The movement of the train lulls him, and he slumps backward against the wall, head bobbing.

At first it seems like the chores are endless, and no sooner does Dora finish than her mother comes into the kitchen and reminds her of something she's neglected. So Dora makes a list. In addition to the three meals and the washing up, there are canning and pickling to think about. Butter needs to be made the day before, and bread has to sit out under a damp towel in order to rise. Stocks need simmering, and rice needs separating.

And then there are the garden duties. She has to plant, weed, and harvest vegetables for the family. In addition to weeds there are aphids and blight, rabbits and rats and early frosts to watch out for. And then she has to fry the vegetables or drown them in butter so the family will eat them. Sneaking them into pies or breads is also an option. Beet and rhubarb pie turns out better than Dora hoped, though it does have a disturbingly sweet taste, which may be the enormous amount of molasses she put in by accident, forgetting that she'd already added sorghum to the mix.

Then there is the baby, who is beginning to ask for mashed food, but who still wants nursing, comforting, holding, and changing. Rika shows Dora how to fasten a sling to her back, but Dora needs to work out for herself how to keep the baby from pulling on her hair or covering her eyes while she works. And she needs to look after Annika. Luckily, the girl makes a lot of noise, banging pots and stomping around the house to feel the vibrations. Dora is suspicious of quiet. It means that Annika is getting into trouble, and Dora doesn't have time for trouble.

Once the morning cooking is done and the kitchen scrubbed, there are the other household duties to attend to. The floor needs sweeping daily as the wind blows in dust, the men track in mud, and the fireplace ashes migrate onto the floor. The rugs need to be taken outside and beaten, and all surfaces dusted. Floors need to be mopped and waxed. Chamber pots must be emptied, washbasins wiped out, and water replaced. Tired of making soap—she hates working with lye—Dora begs Rika, couldn't they use the soap from the store? There is washing to be done nearly every day, clothes and towels and aprons and diapers. Fritz wants his shirts ironed, just so. Though he still is not talking to Dora, he inspects her handiwork with a frown.

Once a week, beds want remaking, candles need replacing, and the stubs must be melted down for new candles. Fireplace ashes must be emptied and the root cellar inspected for mice or water damage. If there is any time when Dora is waiting for water to boil, she must keep busy with the mending or with making clothes for Marira. Dora has become competent at making things stretch. She takes Rika's old dresses and cuts out the least threadbare parts. These become a dress for the baby, or a bonnet, or the little rag doll that Annika drags around everywhere. Once a week Dora wrestles the girls into a bath and then calls Sten, who claims he is too old to bathe with the girls. He makes her wait outside while he washes in the small aluminum tub.

There is the new porch to sweep, the house accounts to keep, the anticipating and ordering in advance of staples: flour, canned goods, kitchen implements. In December, she balls up the list and tosses it into the fireplace. Dora never realized this is what being a woman is about—the endless cycle of staving off hunger and dirt, only to rise the next day and begin the battle again.

She falls into bed each evening exhausted. She doesn't have time to think about Garfield; since the day he left she hasn't had five minutes to daydream. She misses him in a sort of abstract way, the way she misses her previous life as a child. He seems as irretrievable as that time.

The one thing Dora cherishes is her secret. She carries it always in the forefront of her mind; sometimes she takes it out and unwraps it like a present. She thinks about Marira's father, and then she thinks about Garfield, the only one who knows, the only one who was kind to her. And then she puts the memory away. There is work to do.

Garfield's first glimpse of a jungle makes him forget he ever questioned his decision to run away with the trains. A group of men sit around a fire. One stirs a coffee can of thick soup that dangles from a makeshift spit—a branch in the crotch of two others. The smell is so inviting that Garfield feels faint.

"A new recruit, brothers." Casher puts his hand on Garfield's shoulder. The men grunt. "What's for dinner? Let me guess . . . Mulligan stew?"

Casher pulls open a satchel—a horrible quilt of various skins and hides and denim and scraps of cloth—which he obviously made himself, and tosses a can of beans to the man tending the pot. The men grudgingly move over to make room around the fire.

The warmth of the fire feels to Garfield like he's seeing the sun for the first time. He begins to shiver with cold, now that he's thawed enough to move.

"How old are you, boy?" the man next to Garfield asks.

"Fourteen," Garfield says, proud to be so grown up.

The man whistles. "They just keep getting younger."

"Why?" Garfield demands. "How old are you?"

The man laughs heartily, and the others around the circle chuckle. It is hard to see their faces, not only because of the flighty firelight, but also because their long beards obscure their features. He is reminded that his father told him that holy men never shave or trim their beards.

When nobody answers, Garfield offers, "My father's thirty-four." This statement just seems to deepen the silence.

"Herb, where are you coming from?" asks a man. He leans back on his elbows, stretching his legs out in front.

"East," the man named Herb says. "I took a job." There is a general snicker.

"And what say you?" the reclining man asks.

"Go West."

"Shit, they been saying that for forty years," someone says.

"Then it must be true," Herb answers.

"At least it's warm out West," says someone else.

"You obviously ain't been to Seattle."

The man stirring the pot says, "Dinner's ready."

They pass the coffee can around, spooning hot stew into their mess bowls. When it comes to Garfield he pauses.

"Ain't you got a spoon?" someone asks. Garfield shakes his head.

"Here." The man hands him a dented tin spoon. "Mind you give it back."

Someone else hands him an empty can. Garfield scoops out stew to the top.

"Hey, leave some for the other growing boys," someone says.

Food has never tasted so good. Not only is it warm, but it is full of chunks of some kind of meat, soft beans, and corn. Out of his satchel Casher takes a loaf of bread and rips a chunk off. He passes it around, and by the time it gets to Garfield barely a mouthful remains. Garfield sticks it in his can to sop up what's left of the stew. He brings the can to his mouth to lick it, but the man next to him stops him.

"If you want to keep that smart tongue, I'd recommend against that."

Garfield listens attentively while the men tell stories. Some are gruesome, discoveries of murders or dead animals, their stomachs swollen with rot. Some are scary, flights from railroad scags, or near encounters with train wheels. Others are sad, tales of true love lost. But most are funny, practical jokes played on other hobos. Garfield tries to remember them, so that he will not fall victim, but his eyes are fast closing.

Casher nudges him. "You don't got no bedroll, do you?" Garfield shakes his head. "Hey gang," he calls out. "Tenderfoot's got no bedroll."

"Take Sam's," says someone across the fire. "He's pinched."

"Already?" someone else snorts. "It's hardly December."

The men are still laughing and talking when Garfield nods off.

The baby is running a high fever. Dora dabs her face with cold compresses, but she continues to sob. Her cries have a pattern: a small moan escalating to a larger whine to a piercing scream, and convulsing sobs to small hiccups. Dora is shedding tears also. This is the third night she has been up with the baby. Yesterday she begged her mother to take a shift, but Rika refused, saying Dora was her mother, Dora should take care of her.

Dora is not sure which is worse, her father's wordless disdain or her mother's active disapproval. She can mostly avoid her father, but her mother's disappointment is insidious, and Dora is withering under its gaze.

Late at night, sleep-deprived and emotionally depleted, Dora indulges in a rare tickle of anger. What she did (she still cannot bring herself to put a name to the event) with *him* was certainly not worth *this*. And though her situation would not be much different were Marira not around—there would still be all the chores, and the kitchen, and Annika—it is easier to blame Marira for Dora's unhappiness.

Though the reality of the situation is far different, still Dora dreams, in her half-awake reverie as she rocks the baby back and forth, that Marira's father is a different person, a man with means who will ride up one day in a fine surrey and take her to a grand plantation where Dora never has to work. Maybe Garfield will make a fortune, come back for her, and marry her. She can take walks down the long furrows in dresses unmarred by smoke and stain, hand Marira off to servants when she starts to squall. This dream is so powerful that Dora can almost, in the hushed darkness of the house, believe that it could be true, that it is true.

That night, Garfield dreams that he is the engineer on a luxury train of the future. It leaves no gasps of coal dust in its wake and travels at speeds faster than the wind. It is his train, painted green, and he is in charge. When he pulls into Denver's Union Station, he steps out of the engine to deafening applause. The president of the United States comes over to shake his hand and compliment him on the smooth ride. He asks Garfield to be his personal engineer. Or no, that is not enough adventure. He gives Garfield a free pass to travel wherever and whenever he wants.

Garfield will see his mother, somewhere west, probably, Reno or Bakersfield. She will be alone, and he will hesitate but then let her aboard his train, and she will thank him, fall to his feet, and apologize for leaving him. But he will always refuse his father a ride, no matter how much the man supplicates, holding his hat in his hand as the train pulls away, leaving him to wade through buffeting cinders.

Garfield scurries around a corner. He can hear the heavy boots of the railroad bull chasing him. The lawman's breathing is labored; Garfield can probably outrun him. But then he sees the coal bin. He throws his bedroll and hobo stick into the cleft and leaps in after it. He tries to quiet his heart, which is beating so loudly he's sure the bull can hear. Garfield pulls his knees to his chest and sees that he is sharing his hiding place with a family of small rats. Then he sees that the knotted end of his bandanna is sticking out beyond the shelter of the coal bin. He draws his breath in sharply, praying to a higher power he does not believe in to render that grimy red flag invisible. A rat stands on his hind legs and sniffs Garfield's pant leg.

The bull doesn't notice the bandanna. Garfield hears him swear under his breath and turn around. The train pulls out, and Garfield exhales. He pulls the stick and the bedroll closer and shoos the rats with the back of his hand. Then he stretches out as much as he can to settle in for the night.

Dora measures the last wick and ties its ends around the notched stick. Then she checks on the tallow melting in its box. She stirs it; it needs to be warm but not hot. Dora considers: She must add one spoonful of lard for each month after the harvest. It is February, so that makes five spoons. She counts them out. She worries a minute about the wicks. Are they too plaited? Too flat? She once made a set of candles with flat wicks, and they bent to the side as they burned, snuffing the flame. Then there was the time when the tallow was too soft, and the candles guttered over the edges of their holders, creating a gelatinous mess that Dora spent hours scraping off tabletops and window sills.

She dips each wick six times until the candles are fat with wax. She leaves them to dry overnight and pours the rest of the tallow into an empty coffee can. On a lark, the last time she made candles, Dora made a larger one in a can with three wicks. It was a surprising success, ugly to look at but shedding great light so that the early dark had no effect on Dora's ability to see her work in the kitchen. Since then she has always made one or two such unorthodox candles. She keeps them hidden in the pantry, so no one can see the evidence of her inferior housekeeping skills.

She attaches the clothes-drying rack to the bolts in front of the fireplace. The rack has two pulleys, one on each end. She loads one line, turns the wheel, then loads the next. Whenever she passes she can rotate it so that the clothes dry evenly. If she times this precisely, then the clothes are done drying by the time the bread has been baked. Then she can let the fire die down a bit before she has to start supper.

For Christmas, Moshe gave her a vanity. It is beautiful, made of maple with several shallow drawers for scarves and hairpins. But it has a fatal flaw—a large mirror. Dora has never before been confronted so constantly by her deformity. She sees now why people are surprised by her face. It seems the left side has given up, is melting away like tallow and lard. It is almost as though that side shows her future as an aging, resigned, and lonely woman.

Plumbly stands on his new balcony and surveys all that he has wrought. Inside, he can hear his wife humming as she makes the bed. Just a couple years ago he could stand at the tallest rise and see nothing but land, some farmed, some fallow, some unclaimed. Now there is town as far as the eye can see. He is amazed at the speed at which Owenasa has grown from outpost to city. Like a spill, it pushes at its borders, hoping to expand even farther. There are businesses now for everything: tailors and cobblers and a newspaper and a land office and an inn and a druggist and brickmakers and tiehackers and an ornamental sign-painting store, and a few pettifogger pension attorneys. Plumbly is its ruler, master of his pastures, lord of his servants, tenants, horses, cows, pigs, chickens.

The only sore spot, it seems, is Fritz's mill. After the harvest of '97 that seemed like God was showering everyone with wheat until the grain elevators were stuffed to bursting, everyone abandoned cotton to grow Turkey Red wheat. Hardier than its predecessor, red wheat is firmer; it appreciates the cold Oklahoma winters. Plumbly has suggested, more than once, that Fritz change to a flour mill, but the man is stubborn. That's the thing about them immigrants, Plumbly muses. They're all stubborn as rocks.

The flipside to stubbornness, Plumbly knows, is stick-to-it-iveness, which the Hebrew has in abundance. He is reserved, probably a little simple, but day after day he's in that store. He's a big part of what Owenasa is today. The oddest thing about America, Plumbly thinks, is how interdependent everyone is. In this land ostensibly born from freedom and individualism, people still band together, the way fallen trees make a dam. He yawns and stretches and rings a small bell, calling for his morning coffee.

Moshe has sworn off drinking within the confines of Owenasa, seeing what the liquor does to Fritz. Instead he allows himself a small excursion each month, the last Saturday to be exact, to Guthrie, to visit Lily. They have grown quite fond of each other, and their lovemaking is tender and comfortable, like a stuffed chair still warm from its previous occupant. Neither is deluded that this is anything more than a business transaction, yet it has the familiarity and the easy laughter of something more.

Lily arches her back beside him. "I need to *au revoir* you," she says. Lily reads women's magazines, and peppering conversation with French is all the rage. "Miss Tally don't like us to spend more than an hour."

"How much for the whole night?" Moshe asks.

"*Pardonez-moi?*"

"If I were to purchase the entire night," Moshe repeats. "Maybe we could go to dinner."

Lily laughs, a trilling downward scale. "You'd do that? You'd want to be seen with *moi?*"

"How about the Road Inn?" Moshe suggests. It's a rough place on the outskirts of the town, famous for welcoming cowboys, Indians, and Mexicans alike, as long as they can pay. There is a fistfight almost nightly.

Lily lifts the corner of her mouth. "All right," she says. "If you want. I'll ask Miss T."

For ten dollars, Moshe finds himself at the Road Inn with Lily in her "*prêt à foyer.*" She wears white gloves, ludicrously out of place for this cowboy saloon. Still, no one gives them more than a glance as they take a table far from the bar. Nearby, two Mexicans with long mustaches raise small glasses. A cowboy is telling a story to a group of men whose exposure to the sun has made their race indistinguishable. The man mimes throwing a lasso, and a bucking horse, and then the group laughs, some doubled over. One cowboy slaps him on the back, and a cloud of dust rises up.

A waitress approaches Moshe and Lily. She is wearing rouge, Moshe notices. He orders two ales and two steaks, mashed potatoes, and some biscuits. Lily sits excitedly with her hands in her lap.

"I've never been to a restaurant," she says. "Not a real one where they come and take your order."

Moshe smiles. There is not a lot to talk about at dinner, but Lily seems happy, craning her neck to examine the other diners and drinking the ale liberally. It's been a while since he's taken a woman to dinner. Maybe once or twice he asked a nice lady at a station restaurant if she wanted to join him, but it never felt romantic, not the way this does. Although, Moshe realizes, he is paying for Lily's company, and he can predict with certainty the way this evening will end.

Moshe has spent almost twenty dollars for the evening, and Lily rewards him with unusually attentive services in appreciation. Sometime toward morning she gets out of bed and looks at her wall calendar. She crosses off another day. "How could it be April already?" she sighs.

Moshe is too tired to answer anything but "I don't know." He thinks, a week until Garfield's birthday. Two years since he's been gone. Then a panic clenches his gut. It is April already, and he hasn't turned in the order for next month. They do not have a surplus; they will go bankrupt if people begin to shop at Ruede's Outpost or the less expensive Indian trading store.

Once on his horse, who balks at being awakened so early, Moshe curses himself. He has sinned, spent money that belonged to the family on his own personal needs. He spurs the horse faster, though arriving home sooner won't change the fact that it's too late, that he failed. At Cooperdon the bridge is washed out, and Moshe must wade downstream until he finds a place secure enough to cross. He retraces his route back upstream. By the time he reaches the outskirts of Owenasa, it is nearly dark.

And just like that he is Mopey Moshe again, a stupid good-for-nothing who can't be trusted with even the simplest task. He stops rushing and lets the horse lead, dragging her feet along the dirt road. He does not want to arrive home and admit his defeat, his utter uselessness as a man, a husband, a father.

He pulls up to the stable and takes his saddlebags off the mare. "Sten!" He calls for the boy to put up the horse, but there is no answer, so Moshe takes off the saddle and waters her himself. He drops the bags at the back door of the house and walks around to the store.

Rika is sitting on the store's front porch, tatting lace. She asks, "How was Guthrie?"

"I forgot to place the order," he says, sheepishly.

"It's a good thing I did, then."

Moshe lifts his head. Rika has taken care of it? He is both elated and embarrassed. A woman has succeeded where he has failed. "Thank goodness." Moshe rushes up the stairs to hug Rika, but she steps back stiffly.

"Where were you?" she accuses. "We expected you yesterday."

Moshe thinks about Lily. He says nothing.

"I'm going in to start dinner," Rika says. "I don't suppose you've seen my husband."

Moshe looks at his feet.

Rika spins on her heels and walks past him to the house. It is as though all the air leaves with her. Moshe has to sit down.

When Moshe recovers, he goes inside the store, where Rika and her charges have tamed any disorder. He puts his head in his hands. Moshe becomes aware of Sten's presence. He peeks out between his fingers. "She's mad at your papa?" he asks.

Sten nods. "I never seen the like."

Moshe has an urge to slap him, which surprises him. Sten is always the bearer of bad news, and Moshe wonders if their lives would be different had Sten not been so passive. If Sten had divulged Garfield's plans, or detained Garfield, or even if he'd told Moshe right away . . . And what if Sten had run for help instead of letting his twin boss him into the smoky room? What if Moshe had saved Oskar—if Sten were the one lying in the graveyard behind the garden? How different would Moshe's life be? How different would all their lives be?

He wonders how much guilt Sten feels, as the twin who survived. Is this why he's taken on the role of errand boy? Does he feel he is suited for nothing else? Moshe looks him up and down and sees himself: a skinny, talentless boy crippled by guilt and passivity, wracked with indecision and stupor. Moshe's impulse to slap him morphs into an urge to take him into his arms. But he knows the boy will resist. Instead, he puts a hand on Sten's shoulder and they close up the store before walking into the house for dinner.

They eat silently.

"This is good, Rika," Moshe says.

Rika glares at him. Fritz glares, too, at Moshe's attempt to ingratiate himself with Fritz's wife.

Sten says, "I don't want potatoes."

"That's all there is," Rika says. "Either you eat those or you go to bed hungry."

Annika says, "Pahtehtoo." Moshe nods at her.

"So what did you order, Rika?" Moshe asks.

Rika gets up from the table. She returns with the list she sent out with the train. Moshe and Fritz lean over the sheet of paper. Moshe notices that Fritz smells musty, his breath spicy with tobacco and liquor. His ears host a thin layer of dirt.

Rika has vastly overordered. She has confused, as usual, bushels with bags and has ordered four times the number of potatoes needed for the next month. She's made similar mistakes with apples, nuts, flour, sugar, sorghum, and lemons. The excess canned goods will keep, as will the tobacco and clothing, the kitchen implements, and the household appliances, but the food items will perish. Moshe sighs heavily. The store is not so profitable that they can afford to waste money. They can survive this error, but not without sacrifice. Moshe feels simultaneously angry and guilty.

Fritz, on the other hand, is incensed. He stands up and flings his chair across the room. He begins to yell at Rika in Swedish. Moshe hears her name, the word for "idiot," and a word he recognizes as something Fritz says when the hammer slips and hits his thumb. Sten covers his ears; Marira begins to cry. Annika watches with wide eyes. When Rika responds she is belligerent, Moshe can see, jutting out her chin and pointing her finger. At the end of her speech, she tacks on a final sentence, low and snide.

Fritz does not hesitate. He flies at her, over the dinner table. Dishes scatter as they fall to the ground. Dora pulls Marira close. Fritz begins to hit Rika, who is lying on her stomach, covering her head with her hands. He pounds her with his fists—her neck, her back.

Moshe feels the familiar paralysis. He knows he should do something, but he feels as though he has been nailed to the floor. His limbs are heavy, fettered.

Sten pulls Moshe's sleeve, crying now, begging him to do something, anything. And so Moshe takes a step forward. He trips on a pitcher and catapults forward, landing on Fritz. Immediately the man abandons his wife to hit Moshe. He sits on Moshe's chest, pounding his face.

Rika stands up, dazed. Freed from the abuse, she grabs the Dutch oven and throws it down on Fritz's head. Blood spouts red like Indian paintbrush.

At once, the room grows quiet. Rika can hear Marira's hiccups as though they were inside her own head. She has struck her husband. Her fear wells up, and she knows she must move, must get away, but she is tired, and dizzy. She slumps backward against the cabinet.

Fritz staggers to the door. "You fucking bastards, all of you," he slurs, pointing all five fingers into the kitchen. "You all go to hell." He spins out of the door and stumbles against the well before correcting his path toward the mill, leaving a trail of blood drops in his wake.

Moshe bolts the door behind him. No one speaks. He begins to clean the room, righting the table and picking up the silverware and salvageable plates. Sten and Dora help him, while Annika crawls into Rika's lap, where she sobs into her neck. Rika whispers, "Shh, it's all right now, it's all right." She tries to meet Moshe's gaze, but he keeps his head down, avoiding what he suspects will be recrimination. Rika's words sound empty, even to him: It's not all right, it will never be all right.

13

arfield has been pinched once, and once was enough. Many hobos contrive to get arrested at least once during the winter for a chance to warm up and be fed for a while, but Garfield felt stifled in jail, as though an engine were sitting on his chest. He would rather starve. And the police took his extra pair of socks. He could use extra socks right now.

All the trouble he's had to fight off—hunger, cold, men who invite little boys into their sleep rolls to do whatever it is that Casher alluded to—is not so bad as to nudge him off the rails, back home, say, or into a city, working a job. He loves riding the trains. It's everything he thought it would be. At nearly sixteen years old, Garfield has seen the skyscrapers of the East, the canyons of the plains, the California beaches. He has fanned himself at a brass band performance in Louisiana Territory. He watched in Chicago as the cattle that rode up North with him were led to the slaughterhouse, and then as the huge slabs of meat were loaded back onto the train. He got hold of some whiskey and spent several days in the western desert, emerging thirsty and somehow changed.

He runs into Casher occasionally. Once, in Omaha, the older hobo leads him to a pub where women dance on the table in their bloomers. They have oddly red lips and cheeks, as though they've just eaten a bushel of strawberries. Of course he's seen his mother put on rouge, but these women look almost like paintings. One takes him by the hand to a room upstairs, and Garfield is not sure what exactly he is supposed to do. He is drunk, and the woman has the same redness on her fingernails as Alice had. He watches her nails all through it. He must have done all right because the woman falls asleep after a heavy sigh, snoring loudly.

Garfield enjoyed what he assumes was sex, though he found the woman slightly overwhelming. There was a fleeting panic, in the middle, that the heavy body astride him was the sky bearing down, but just as quickly the fear passed. The best part of the evening, Garfield thinks, was the comfortable bed, with sheets and blankets, out of the wind. And the hour in which the woman snaked her hand with his, joining them.

Once, in Denver, he debates taking the train to Orerich. Perhaps Tallulah is still there; maybe Alice has come back. But then he sees a boy he knows jump a train to Cheyenne, motioning for Garfield to join him. Garfield chases the train down, leaving all thoughts of Orerich in the rail yard.

In March, Garfield is hungry. He spends several days on a slow-moving freight in Missouri, each town a small hovel with no hobo jungle and no Christian Women's Aid Society in which to take refuge. The farmhouses he begs at look worse than he does, tattered and skinned. The children inside share his hollow eyes and sunken ribs. As the winter food supplies dwindle almost to extinction, it is hard to beg for bread at a family's expense.

From Vicksburg, Garfield decides to go to Houston. He waits three days for the next train. By then, his stomach has ceased to rumble. He steals a pie cooling in a window. It is a potato pie, the dessert of the poorest of the poor. Still, Garfield licks the tin, which he is kind enough to return to the window. That staves off hunger for a few more hours.

Houston is a mean town. The jungle outside the city is deserted, the fire long cold. Garfield feels like he's started a race behind everyone else, and when he gets to each checkpoint he's too late. He tries to light the fire, but his flints are wet. Carved into a post are the signs of the road. There is a circle with two arrows through it, meaning "hit the road," and a box with a dot in the center, meaning "danger." Garfield decides to move on.

All the jungles up to Dallas are similarly deserted and bear similar dire warnings. Garfield feels dizzy. He hasn't slept more than a few hours in a week. He loses his footing leaping onto a car and almost falls. His ankles are sore and bruised. If he had let go, he would have been run over.

He is dozing in the empty freight car when panic seizes him. What train is he on? The station names rattle past him, and he realizes that the train is going through Oklahoma Territory, heading straight for Owenasa. At the next station Garfield jumps off the train without looking, and lands practically in the arms of the railroad police.

Here is Dora's reasoning: She cannot go on. Something must change, back to the way it was. And what was different before? Dora does not point to the obvious differences: her brother has died, she has had a child out of wedlock, her father has begun to drink and is slipping into the morass of his failed cotton mill, her mother has been treating Moshe as her husband. Instead she ties everything to Garfield and his disappearance. Garfield was her friend, her confidant, her ally. When he left, everything began to deteriorate. The way to take back her old self, then—to regain her laugh, her buoyancy, her childhood—is to find Garfield.

Because she doesn't know where else to turn, she enlists Sten's help. He sees her eyes, glistening and wide, and does not want to disappoint her. So he tells Dora a place, a name he heard the stationmaster say once, a locale that sounds about as far away as one can get. Dora pays him for this information, then pays him to keep quiet until she's gone. He plans on squeezing his parents for money too, but after the first smack of the paddle against his bare skin he tells his father everything, and Fritz, in a rage so blind he sees only endless rows of mills, colossal and empty, beats Sten until Rika begs him to stop.

Garfield spends ninety days in jail in Nebraska, during which he eats and sleeps so much they begin to call him "Bear." Despite repeated assertions that he is not Christian, he is visited frequently by the Sisters of the Holy Cross. They dote on him; there is still something about Garfield's teary eyes that provokes sympathy, an aura of motherlessness about the boy that makes people want to take care of him. The sisters' goal is rehabilitation, and Garfield, resigned, decides to accept their help. They beg favors from the railroad brass and arrange a post for him on the Rock Island, as a general gopher for the rail hands. The job doesn't seem that bad. It is fairly close to being a hobo, only he will get paid for his travels. He will miss the camaraderie of the jungle, the freedom to turn around midtrip and decide to go the other way. But by the time he leaves jail he is almost excited.

Garfield puts all the energy he spent running from bulls into his new position. He is the preferred rail assistant. The rail hands have a grudging admiration for the scrappy boy. He makes himself useful, sitting with the engineer, watching as he cranks the speed up or slows to bank a turn. Sometimes, the engineer will let Garfield blow the whistle when they go through a town.

Now sixteen, Garfield is old enough to become a coupler, the least enviable and most dangerous position on the rungs of the rail hierarchy. The rail yards are full of one-armed men who used to be couplers, and they are the lucky ones. When the train changes freight cars, each must be hitched to the engine. This is accomplished by lining the cars up and backing the engine into range. As the engine slows, the coupler must insert the iron hoop into the drawbar of the next car and hammer the pin down before scampering out of the way as the engine keeps rolling backward. A slack rolling engine is an excellent way to be decapitated.

But Garfield is still small and lithe, and he is good at his job. He learns caution, and prudence, and by his eighteenth birthday he has been promoted to second engineer. He is popular on the train; his gruffness and arrogance are viewed merely as eccentricities. The men know they can count on him. No one needs to recheck his assembly or telegraph again for instructions. He is standoffish, yet there is no task he considers himself above. He'll carry freight, he'll shovel coal, whatever needs to be done to get the train rolling.

For the first time in his life, Garfield is a success; he is respected. And as obscure as written letters and words still seem to him, the inner workings of a train have laid themselves utterly open to his scrutiny. He simply understands how a steam engine runs, implicitly knows what coaxing these machines need. Like a wrangler, he believes he can hear his charges speaking to him. He answers back. His peers begin to call him "the Machine."

If Garfield doesn't show emotion, it is because he feels none. It is as though he left any feelings in Owenasa. Hunger and fear came with him, but now he has discarded those as well. He feels a certain satisfaction in his job, which he has convinced himself is all he needs to feel. And the movement of the train, from state to state to territory to state, quells any momentary pangs of melancholy, grabs them in the swirl of exhaust to bounce along after the departing train, forgotten.

Dora is faced with two choices: test her luck riding the rails, braving rape or worse, or find a job. She chooses the latter. When she arrives in San Bernardino, worn out from three days of travel in coach class, sleeping with her bag on her lap in case someone should try to steal it, she asks for Garfield. A little boy, she describes him, skinny and wild-haired. Of course, no one knows who she is talking about. An Asian storekeeper—whose slanted eyes fascinate Dora, so much are they like her own droopy lid—points to a map of the United States of America on display behind him. "Is too big, one small boy," he says. "Too big."

She realizes she will never be able to find Garfield, and the realization is not as dispiriting as she would have imagined. Leaving was never really about finding Garfield. Leaving was about leaving, and Garfield was the excuse. Creating a life without Garfield should not derail her plans.

Dora becomes a Harvey Girl. She wears the uniforms provided: white skirts with frilly pink aprons and a pillbox nurse's hat. She serves the men and women who stop in San Bernardino, get off the train to stretch and walk over to the Harvey store to take a meal or browse the selection of books, candy, and clothing items for sale.

There's a preset menu, so there's little Dora has to remember. One of three appetizers and main courses, a drink and a dessert, then coffee or tea. No substitutions; the guests are on a tight schedule. Dora becomes adept at carrying trays piled high with food, weaving her way around the other girls, and setting the plates down without spilling. A major accident can be grounds for dismissal, and Dora wants to avoid that at all costs.

She is happy. The work is hard but fair. She lives in a dormitory where all the girls bunk, and shares a room with five others. They laugh and sing and braid each other's hair. Sometimes they sneak sips of liquor. On her days off, Dora wanders through town buying small items, just because she can.

The other pastime the girls indulge in is flirting with the boys. In the dormitory next door, Dora can hear the boys hollering and laughing. She watches them roughhouse in the courtyard between the two buildings, showing off for the girls. There are strict rules about fraternization; monitors live in the dormitory to enforce the "no visitors" rule. But still, the boys and girls can synchronize their days off, and they disappear into San Bernardino to spend their time however they choose.

Dora also flirts shyly with the men who come into the diner. At first she tried to hide her face, but now she realizes it is what makes her so intriguing. The other girls marvel at her ability to earn enormous tips, once a whole five dollars for a cup of coffee and a roll. Her deformed face lends her a shy innocence, like a wounded bird. Men want to take care of her.

What Dora does not realize is that many of these extravagant tippers want her for less noble reasons. Harvey Girl uniforms are made in limited sizes, and the largest is much too small on top for Dora. The buttons strain against her undergarments. Men see her melting face and pity her, feel they have a chance with her that they don't have with Dora's symmetrical friends. She must be desperate, with a face like that, they think. This one will be easy.

So Dora endures groping hands and retrieves silverware that she knows has been dropped on purpose. There is one boy who takes her for walks on her day off. He likes to talk to her, and Dora is a good listener, he thinks. Actually, Dora is shy; she doesn't like to talk.

Because Dora has a secret. Harvey Girls are good girls. They don't kiss boys, let alone do what Dora did with the boy in Owenasa. A letter arrives, with a child's lock of hair, and Dora cries upon seeing it. Some of the girls guess it must belong to a secret daughter. It has the potential to be a scandal, the rumor passing like a feather in the wind between the dormitories. But Dora is rescued by being inconspicuous, inconsequential. There are juicier rumors, and this one dies down quickly. Dora throws the lock of hair into the ravine. She tries to forget about the past, except that the secret gives her power, consoles her, and revives her like smelling salts. She speaks of it to no one.

Monthly letters arrive from Rika, full of news about the garden and the town. If Dora feels any guilt or sorrow at leaving her child or her siblings or her parents, she is able to push it down to a place where it pains her no more than her back at the end of a long shift. She is owed this, she feels, this freedom, this happiness. It is her due.

Garfield steps off the train and coughs into his hand. He has been inhaling coal dust since Albuquerque; there must be a slit in the bin. He reminds himself to tell his relief. Garfield has three days off. He considered taking them in Los Angeles, but decided instead to come here, to San Bernardino, where he can get some rest. He imagines he will sleep for all seventy-two hours; that's how tired he is. And he has heard there is a hotel here, the Crystal Palace, where he can order whatever he wants to his room: food, drink, women. He has wired ahead for reservations.

He waits for his relief, and soon the second engineer appears, his uniform crisp with washing, unlike Garfield's soot-covered overalls. Garfield slaps him on the back with his cap and decides not to mention the coal bin leak, since the man's cleanliness annoys him.

It is a short walk from the station to the Crystal Palace, and Garfield marvels at the city's growth. It seems like the last time he was here it was just a late-fading gold rush town, rickety thrown-together shacks and dirt wagon-trails for roads. Now it is a bona fide city with cobblestones and sidewalks. There is a line of shops, and off the side streets horses linger,

tethered to hitching posts outside white mansions. On the outskirts, orange groves line the railroad tracks.

He turns left and there it is. He shades his eyes; the hotel's exterior is
trimmed in what look like millions of diamonds. Though Garfield knows
they are false gems, hematite or quartz, it still looks like a giant diadem. He
approaches the front desk, careful not to get dirt on the oriental carpets.

"Garfield Harris," he says. As the country entered into a new century, so
did Garfield. He was tired of the raised eyebrows, the barely polite refus-
als, tired of fighting just to get the same food or service everyone else did.
Just because he had a Jewish surname. Easier not to be a Jew, simpler. Lots
of people change their names. This is America, the land where you can be
made anew. This name, Garfield thinks, suits him much better.

Still, he thinks often about the past. Once, marooned in Denver overnight, he decided to go to Orerich. In the second-class compartment he
silently critiqued the engineer's inferior handling. But his feeling of superiority vanished when he stepped onto the platform at the abandoned
stationhouse; there were no signs of life. He set out toward Gilges Street,
the route he'd traveled every day now deserted. Then he saw that one
blast too many in search of buried treasure had triggered an avalanche,
covering the street in boulders. If anything had been there when the hill-
side slid, it was crushed now. Garfield, used to the din of the train, found
the ghost-town silence eerie. He trudged back to the station. He was not
sure what he expected to find, but he was positive that this was not it.

He places ads in all the major papers—the *Times,* the *Herald,* and the
Bee: "Anyone with knowledge as to the whereabouts of Mrs. Alice Haurowitz née O'Malley, please contact Garfield Harris," with a P.O. box number
in St. Louis. But he has never received any mail. He's not sure what else
there is to do. He hasn't broken the old habit, however, of searching for
a familiar face in every crowd, ever hopeful that one will belong to his
mother, just as he used to search for his father.

The man behind the hotel desk curls one side of his lip. Garfield fights
the urge to rip off his handlebar mustache. "I'm an engineer," he says instead. "Here for my three days of leave."

"Of course, sir, right this way." The man's change is almost comical, his
demeanor suddenly obsequious. He snaps his fingers, and a bellboy appears, taking Garfield's old duffel from him. "Our bellboy will show you to
your room."

"I can carry that," Garfield says.

"Of course, sir," the boy says, and makes no motion to give it back.

They step into an elevator. It is Garfield's first, though he has heard tell of the cages that go up by themselves. The operator closes the two heavy doors and throws the lever to the left. It is a strange sensation to Garfield, like a series of bumps in a carriage. His ears and stomach seem to condense, collapsing down toward his feet.

"Third floor, sir." The elevator operator pulls the lever back to the right and opens the doors. Garfield's room is spacious. It overlooks the main street, which bustles with afternoon traffic, wagons and horses, women out shopping, farmers in from the fields, children coming home from school, playing ball in the street. There is a large bed with a canopy, beckoning Garfield with its velvet bedspread. It looks three feet deep in down. It is the nicest room Garfield has ever stayed in.

"Where's the washroom?" Garfield asks.

"Here, sir." The bellboy opens a door, and Garfield can see his own private washroom with marble floors, toilet, bidet, and tub. He sighs with happiness.

But the bellboy is still in the room, and it occurs to Garfield that he is waiting for a tip. Garfield puts his hand in his pocket and pulls out the entirety of its contents: a smudged handkerchief, a candy wrapper, a note from the coal loader that Garfield has not had time to decipher, and, finally, a couple pennies and a dime. He gives the change to the boy, who spins and walks out without a thank you.

Garfield is unsure what he should do first. He decides to run water for a bath. He is amazed at how hot the water leaves the tap. He should shave, but he'll do that later. Right now he wants to slide into bed and sleep forever. The sheets feel cool and soft. This room, this bath, this towel, this bed might be the nicest thing that has ever happened to him. He lets a smile creep across his face as he closes his eyes.

He wakes up ravenous. He has no idea what time it is, but there is sunlight struggling around the curtains. He gets up and draws them. Then he realizes he is unclothed and lets the curtain drop again. He dresses in his best workpants and shirt and goes downstairs to the dining room. At the entrance Garfield sees the white tablecloths, the men in suits, the women in gloves and hats. He ventures out onto the street to find a more humble place to eat.

There is bound to be a Harvey store near the station; in a town this big it's almost a certainty. There will be a reasonable lunch, including coffee. He's eaten at Harvey restaurants all over the United States, and he knows this one will be similar, if not identical, to the others he's visited. The thought is comforting.

Sure enough, he finds the restaurant easily and takes a seat at a booth. He looks at his pocket watch: two thirty. An odd time for lunch; they won't mind if he sits a while. He takes out his pouch of tobacco and begins to roll himself a cigarette.

He peruses the menu, makes his choice. He waits for the waitress to come over. He turns his coffee cup right side up to signal his readiness.

She says, "What can I get you?"

"Cup of coffee, Salisbury steak, creamed spinach."

"And for dessert?"

"Do I have to choose now?" Garfield looks up. There is Dora. It can't be her, except that it is. Who else has the same lopsided face, the fine, thin hair?

Garfield stands up. Dora's eyes widen with recognition, and her mouth falls open. They embrace.

"Hey," Garfield says. "Don't cry."

"You're so changed," she says. "When you left—"

"I'm twenty years old now."

She studies at him. He is taller than she by more than a couple of inches and broader than she would have expected. Dark hairs line his arms. His eyes are creased around the edges and, as always, rimmed with tears. "It's incredible," Dora says.

"You look just the same," Garfield says. "Just the way I remember you." He brushes her hair back with his fingers. Dora shivers.

Mr. Harvey—not *the* Mr. Harvey, but rather the boss of this particular restaurant (who demands all the same to be called Mr. Harvey, though in reality he is a German immigrant named Schmidt)—strides over. "No fraternizing, Miss Dora."

"Mr. Harvey, this is my . . ." Dora pauses. How to introduce him? "My brother."

"Pleasure, I'm sure," says Mr. Harvey. "We don't allow guests."

"I didn't know she was here, sir," says Garfield. He wishes he had his uniform on; then the man would not speak with such rudeness. "I just came in for a meal."

Mr. Harvey frowns. "Oh, sir," Dora says, "couldn't I just sit with him for a minute? There's no one in the restaurant."

Mr. Harvey looks around. "Fine," he says. "But don't say I never did nothing for you."

Dora and Garfield sit. "Do I still get to eat?" he asks.

"Oh!" Dora springs up. She returns with a tray of coffee and a large steak, creamed spinach melting like spring runoff on top.

There is so much to catch up on. Garfield shovels steak into his mouth as he tells her of his time riding the rails—how he landed in jail and how jail turned into a job that turned into a life. Then Dora relates how she left to look for Garfield and ended up as a Harvey Girl. "No one knows," she whispers, referring to the secret they both keep. She is excited to have someone to talk to about it, at last. She has not forgotten Garfield's kindness. And here he is in front of her, a fantasy incarnate.

"Have you heard from them?" Garfield asks. "Do they know where you are?"

"I hear from my mother, sometimes. Don't they know about you?"

Garfield shakes his head no. "Don't tell them you saw me."

Dora opens her mouth, but doesn't say anything. There is a silence.

"Pa was drinking," Dora says. "And Ma . . ."

"He hit her," Garfield provides.

Dora nods. "Ma didn't say so, but it was there in the letter all the same. Then he left."

"Where?"

Dora shrugs. "Who knows?"

Garfield finishes his coffee. Dora gets him more and returns with his dessert. "And Annika?" he asks, having held back from saying her name all this time. He has not forgotten the oath he swore to protect her, which he has so far neglected.

"They've sent her to the deaf school in St. Louis. Ma says she can read and write and everything."

Garfield breathes a sigh that is simultaneously relief and an attempt to expel the guilt he feels.

Dora's shift finishes at five. She has been apprenticing in the kitchen on alternate evenings. Perhaps one day she will be allowed to cook, but so far all the chefs are male, the waitresses female.

They walk along the Zanja Canal. The sun feels warm, though it is only March. Garfield takes Dora's hand to help her over a fallen tree, and they remain touching, like young lovers. They visit the Carnegie Public Library, where Garfield is more impressed with the ornate moldings and carved doorways than with the literary masterpieces housed within.

Garfield takes her out that night to the Majestic Theater, where Dora has never been. She clasps her hands tightly as the melodrama reaches its climax. By the end the heroine lies dead on the stage, and Dora is crying.

"Did you like it?" Garfield asks.

"So much."

The following morning Dora trades with her bunkmate to have the day off. She prepares a picnic, and she and Garfield take a coach to Wildwood Park to see the famous arrowhead carved into the mountains. Dora is thrilled; she cannot stop smiling as she feeds Garfield grapes and takes sips of cool lemonade. A photographer takes their portrait. Garfield is tickled to see her so happy.

He walks her to her dorm, and she tears up. "I'll never see you again."

"Of course you will. I'll come and visit each time I'm in San Bernardino."

"Promise?"

"Sure."

Dora closes her eyes and lifts her chin. It is clear to Garfield she wants to be kissed. He leans over and places his lips on her forehead. "Good night, Sister."

"Good night," she breathes.

When he returns to his hotel that night he puts his bag on the bed and packs. He is worried about the look in Dora's eyes as he said good-bye. Garfield realizes what that look meant. He's seen it before on the faces of eager young porters, on women traveling to meet their fiancés for the first time, on men looking out the window for their wives and children as the train speeds through their hometowns, too busy to stop. He wore that look, too, once. It is hope. Garfield's throat constricts. He wants no part of someone's dream. It feels too much like obligation, like being tied down.

He knows that he will not be back, not anytime soon. Dora's upturned face haunts him like having stared at the sun, bright spots behind his closed lids. He pictures her odd face, one side smooth, the other sliding, pulling Garfield down. Anger rises in him, and he curses.

He throws his bag on the floor and rings for the bellboy. He will order a woman. That was what he came here for, was it not? Later, as he's on top, inside, he will cover the woman's face with his hands so that he won't have to look at her mouth, her cheeks, her eyes.

PART 5

The Machine, Spectacular and Solid
1903–1907

14

Fritz has been gone for five years when Moshe surprises Rika by proposing. It is a hot day in April, an early precursor to summer, and they are in the store, heads together over a seed catalogue, breath mingling.

Moshe takes her hand. "Rika, would you like to be my wife?"

Rika thinks he's joking. She's already married. So is he, for that matter. She laughs, pulls her hand away.

"I mean it, Rika," he says. "We're as good as married as it is, only I sleep in the room next door. We own a house together; we raise our children together." Here Moshe conveniently forgets that his only child ran away from home almost eight years ago. He considers Annika and Marira his daughters, Sten his son.

Rika's face loses its laugh. "You're serious," she says.

Moshe nods.

"I'll think on it," Rika says. She stands up, and though there are three more catalogues to go through, she goes back into the house to make supper.

The following day, Rika acts as though nothing is different. She stacks the new inexpensive porcelain dishes carefully into the glass case. Moshe wonders if she has forgotten, or if the idea was so ludicrous that Rika is pretending she didn't hear him. But then Rika walks over to him and smooths her hands down her apron.

"Aren't we both already married?" Rika asks.

Moshe, surprised, can only stammer that he'll look into it.

"I won't divorce," Rika says. "But if you can find another way, I'd be willing."

Moshe wants to leap out of his chair and hug her. But that's as far as his fantasy goes. Unlike his desire for Alice or Dora, his love for Rika is calm, without ardor. He loves her as though they have been husband and wife for twenty years, as though they know each other's bodies too well and are past the urge to touch them. Instead, Moshe stays in his chair and nods. "I appreciate it."

He writes a letter to the Department of Social Services in Guthrie explaining their situation. He receives the following letter in reply:

May 1, 1903
Moshe Haurowitz
12 Fiddler's Creek Lane
Owenasa, O.T.

To Mr. Moshe Haurowitz:

In response to your missive of April 26, 1903, we herewith offer the following clarification of the rules and laws of matrimony of the Oklahoma Territory. As to the solicitation of emancipation from a marriage, the reason hereby being given as abandonment, the Territorial government requires the following affidavits: A legal demonstration of the preexisting marriage, if so entered into out of state; an affidavit of desertion of a spouse, and a supporting affidavit if applicable and possible; and form RFI8132 swearing the same to a proper legal representative in possession of a state seal, that proper and thorough means have been employed in an attempt to locate the spouse in question.

Once the applicants have satisfactorily proved to this office the indictment of abandonment, the government cannot lawfully impede your union. Please present your person in Guthrie on the Fifteenth day of June, Nineteen Hundred and Three, in the Year of Our Lord, to swear to the preceding statements. You will be provided with papers dissolving your respective marriages as well as the appropriate documents recognizing the new union, at which point a true copy of the receipt for the registry letter so sent will be issued directly.

Yours sincerely,
Michel J. Hamlin

"I don't understand what that means," says Rika. Annika, home from school for the summer, takes the sewing from her hand and with one deft motion rips out Rika's nervous stitches. Within seconds, the sock is darned so expertly that the hole is all but invisible.

"It means it's dissolved, broke up."

"Like a divorce."

"But different." Moshe tries to explain. "Like we're widowed."

"But Fritz isn't dead, as far as we know."

"Well, it's like the marriage *was*," Moshe says, "and now it's not."

Rika sighs. "Just tell me if it's all right. I trust you."

"It's all right."

They hug, aware that Annika is watching them. Moshe looks over at her. She is smiling, then averts her gaze to her sewing.

Moshe goes to Guthrie to retrieve his wedding papers, where he pays his last visit to Lily. He does not expect her to cry when she hears the news. Moshe hands her his handkerchief, which she places on her lap, dabbing at her eyes with her own lace, which she has pulled out from somewhere. Moshe has always admired that about Lily, her secret hiding places. How she manages to make something appear that wasn't there before, how she is eternally fresh to him, new. He will miss her.

"I know we're not supposed to cry, but *merci!*" She blows her nose. "It's been a lot of years, M." Lily calls him by the initial under which he registers. She's been calling him that for ten years.

"What will you do?" Moshe asks.

"I do have other clients, you know." Lily smiles.

"I meant, in the future, you know, when you're . . ."

"When I'm old?" Lily laughs again. This time Moshe hears something new to her voice, a twinge of bitterness she has never allowed to show through. "This is the only thing I've ever done. I'll do this till I can't do this no more. And then I'll find some other *déjà vu*."

Moshe doesn't know what this word means. He wonders if it some derogatory term for a patron, a sad old man who has to pay for whores. More likely, it's a word that Lily has made up.

"Will you take me out?" she asks, her eyes suddenly bright. "Like you did that once? That was the best night of my life."

"I can't," Moshe says, with sincere regret. "I'm sorry."

Lily looks down at her lap. She fingers the lace. "That's all right."

There is a quiet moment while Lily folds his handkerchief into a small square. Moshe looks around the room he's spent so much time in. It's as though he's never seen it before. The lurid pictures are familiar, but the fleur-de-lis wallpaper is shinier than he remembers, the lighting is softer, or the window coverings new.

Lily begins to unbutton her dress. Moshe shrugs away. Though the ceremony is not for another month, in some ways he feels already wedded to Rika. Sleeping with Lily is a betrayal. But then Lily exposes the small mole above her right breast, and it seems to Moshe that he is visiting her for the first time, sex-starved and awkward, and he feels his desire swell.

Inside her, he feels wild, feral. She guides him expertly, gymnastically, until they are both covered with sweat and are spent. He turns to kiss her good-bye, but she is already out of bed and in the small adjoining bathroom. Moshe can hear the sound of the bidet. It stops, and he knows she is getting out clean bed linens. She is making so much noise, rattling and singing. She wants him to leave. He hurries into his clothes and slips out the door.

Fritz's old cotton mill makes an oddly inspiring place of worship; its cathedral ceilings, which were vaulted in anticipation of mounds of cotton the mill never held; its round, widow's walk gallery and the makeshift chairs they've fashioned draw gazes up toward the heavens. Moshe feels closer to God here than he does anywhere else. It is an appropriate space for Moshe and Rika to be married in by a traveling priest Moshe has hired. First he baptizes Moshe, who obediently dunks his head into the large bowl provided for the occasion. He tells himself it means nothing. It is a bath, like the male version of a *mikvah*, a cleansing before his marriage. He had wanted a rabbi, but none would come to perform the ceremony between a Jew and a gentile.

The following morning, the newlyweds get up at their usual time, and Rika, modest, goes behind the screen to dress. She kisses Moshe chastely before she goes downstairs to start breakfast. Moshe lies in bed a little longer, thinking about the day ahead. He will spend it in the store, the same as every morning. Little has changed. There are still the same numbing tasks to do every day, every week, every month. But something is calmer within him. The ceiling sits higher above his head. There is a cushion, now, and his steps will be forever padded.

Annika's wedding takes place on November 9, 1906, soon after she returns from the St. Joseph's School for the Deaf, in St. Louis, and the town sorely needs the diversion. The railroad's economic crash of 1903 severely reduced the amount of rail traffic passing through the Territory, and Owenasa has felt the recession's ache. The store hasn't sold anything other than food in months, and even that has trickled off as people scrimp. Canned goods are considered a luxury. There was a death last month, a small boy, from beans preserved incorrectly at home.

Once he gets over the feeling that she is too young, Moshe decides that Annika's wedding will be the event of the year. He has to admit that she has returned from school mature, even wise. He envies her confidence, the grace with which she holds herself that he has always lacked. So he calls in all the favors he is owed and forgives several debts in exchange for labor and goods. Annika's house will be built for her. This is something her husband should do, Sten reminds him, but Moshe replies that young people need all the help they can get.

Annika sings to herself. It's something that always surprises Moshe when he comes upon her without her noticing. It is not what the rest of the world would call singing, but she makes noises she has learned not to make when other people are around— belching whines, the ugliness of which she cannot hear. She likes the way it feels, she has explained to Moshe in her language of gestures and expressions, when her throat vibrates and her lips move and her throat contracts as she blows out air. And she giggles at her own private jokes. She glows; Annika is happy.

The town is unsure what to make of Annika. Her skill as a seamstress is legendary, but she is regarded as somewhat of an idiot savant. The farmers treat her as a child, speaking slowly and loudly, as though her problem were comprehension and not deafness. The Indians seem more comfortable with her defect. They come into town more often now; they need to purchase food like everyone else.

She has sewn a series of dresses out of fabrics ordered from New York: muslin, gingham, cotton, a mix of the flowing Indian style and the stricter American fashion. Thus the dresses are colorful solids with series of pleats and decorative ribbons. She has sold every one she has made. Annika has also started taking special orders for fancy dresses and for weddings. First she sketches what she thinks the woman is trying to describe, and they make adjustments to the sketches together. If there is a problem, Rika acts as a translator, interpreting Annika's gesture language.

Annika's betrothed is named Irwin Reece, whose family lives on the other side of Plumbly's ranch. He is older, wealthy. When he was four years old, he fell off a horse, which then kicked him in the head. For two weeks he did not wake. When he finally rose from his bed, his speech was slurred and his laugh too eager. He does not read and cannot live by himself; yet there is something sweet and childlike about him. The town thinks they make a good pair, the two damaged children.

Moshe and Irwin's father know each other well enough to nod when they pass in town. They are both "old" families in Owenasa. The town is big enough, and Irwin goes out so seldom, that Moshe has not seen him in two years when he is presented as Annika's suitor. The man is dark, with curly eyebrows and short legs. His grin awakens in Moshe something violent, something Moshe suspects is fatherly protection. He can't understand what Annika sees in him, and then it occurs to Moshe that perhaps she is lonely. Perhaps in Annika's world, Irwin Reece is good company.

Moshe sees them kissing, once, behind the store. A colored man who works as the Reeces' house servant has driven Irwin into town on the small wagon, and the man waits out front, throwing rocks into the ditch beside the road to kill the time. Annika and Irwin are holding hands, pressed close to each other. Annika is kissing his neck, and Irwin is trilling his tongue for her to feel the vibrations. She laughs and kisses him wide on the lips. Moshe turns his head; the lovers remind him of Alice, who in turn reminds him of Garfield.

"Moshe?" Rika calls from the store. "Are you in back?"

"Here," he calls. Inside, he takes Rika into his arms, puts his lips to hers. She opens her mouth, obedient, but keeps her teeth together. It is like kissing her hand. They have made love a few times, but neither feels much passion for the other. Moshe pulls away, pretends he is not disappointed.

If Rika has an opinion about Irwin, she has not expressed it. Annika has always been independent; Rika merely facilitates her communication with the outside world. Marira, on the other hand, feels to Rika almost like a child of her own body. Marira is her baby; she will not have another child, and she smothers the girl with affection, excusing her from chores at the slightest whimper or whine.

Now that Marira is thirteen years old, it has generally been forgotten around town that Rika is not her natural mother. Marira calls her "Mama," unless she is making fun of Annika, and then she calls Rika "Mehh"; or if she is angry she calls her "Mother." Marira is dark, striking, which is not the same as beautiful but commands the same attention from men nonetheless. She is shockingly mature for her age. Catalogues that are as commonplace as hay bales serve as inspiration: Marira has become a fashion plate. She shows the photographs to Annika, who is able to virtually duplicate the dress on the page. Marira complains that she cannot get the magazines fast enough. By the time she is wearing a gored skirt, they've gone out of style in Paris. When she adds a sailor collar to her shirt, it's long passé. Rika sighs to remember a simpler time, when there weren't photographs and magazines to distract young people.

Rika suspects it is the school on the edge of town that feeds Marira's insatiable urge for fashion. There are more than fifty young people, all competing for attention and recognition. It was never like that for Rika, whose small town had picked out her husband for her before she even knew what boys were.

Rika attends all the school's plays and recitals, to help support the educational effort. Usually she makes Marira, who has no theatrical inclinations, accompany her. This is where they meet Irwin. His mother has brought him to a piano recital in the hopes that it will be therapeutic. He stares at Marira all the way through the program. It makes Rika nervous, the way he fixates on her—as though he is looking at something fascinating on the other side of the girl. If Marira notices, she says nothing, but eagerly nods her head at her mother's suggestion that they leave at intermission. As they are gathering their coats, he walks up to them, trailed by his mother, hurrying to catch up.

He speaks, what sounds like "Elloo cumta der."

"I'm sorry?" Rika says politely.

The man smiles, repeats himself.

By now his mother has arrived to translate. "Excuse us," she says. "Winnie, you mustn't bother strangers."

"Buh I wawnim cumta der," Irwin whines. He shakes his hands as though he's burned them.

"What is he saying?" Marira asks, looking at his mother and not at him.

"Oh, nothing. He wants you to come to dinner. I'm sorry, please excuse us."

Rika stands in the foyer amidst the cigar smoke. Mother and son walk away.

Next to her, Marira says, "Wait! I'll go."

She is doing this to vex her mother, Rika knows. They fought earlier about the full-length stockings Marira wants that Rika thinks are too sophisticated for her. Now she is accepting an entirely inappropriate invitation just to see what her mother will do.

"You wiw?" He swings around.

"I don't think that's such a good idea," Rika says.

"I do," Marira says.

The man's mother lays her hand on his arm like an old dance partner. "C'mon, Winnie, there's a good boy. Forget this whole business."

But before they turn, Rika sees his face fall; the glint of hope that tenses his entire figure leaves him, and he looks absolutely crushed. She feels pity. "Perhaps you'd like to come to our house," she says.

Marira narrows her eyebrows. This is not the reaction she has hoped to provoke.

"Say, next Thursday evening?"

"You don't have to . . . ," his mother protests.

"No, really, it will be our pleasure," Rika says. "We'll expect you around six."

As they nod to each other, Irwin bounces with glee. "Why did you do that, Mother?" Marira asks. "Why are we having that idiot in our house?"

"Don't call him that, Marira," Rika says. "That's what people call Annika. He's just another of God's creatures, is all."

At dinner, Irwin is uncharacteristically shy; Annika is strangely outgoing. It becomes apparent that Irwin's fascination with Marira is just a momentary mesmerism, like a baby to a bright object. Mrs. Reece gives apologies for her husband; Mr. Reece is in Guthrie on business. She hopes it is all right that she has come without him. The Haurowitzes are a well-known and respected family in town; otherwise she never would have ventured out so far alone.

They bring with them a dense, pocked bread that Moshe remembers his mother making. When asked if she would like a beverage, Mrs. Reece says she wouldn't mind some wine.

"Go out to the store and get some." Rika motions to Marira.

"Oh, no, not if it's a bother," Mrs. Reece says. "Only if you're having some, too."

"We're not so fond of the taste of it," Moshe explains. He puts his arm around Rika's waist, worried, as though their dinner guests are somehow inspectors, coming to investigate their marriage for fraud.

Irwin and Annika share something, a sort of propinquity. Annika taps her head when he leaves: smart. Moshe shakes his head. Annika stops him by wiggling her finger. "No," she says with her hands. "He can't talk, but he's smart. Like me."

There is nothing objectionable about Irwin, per se, except that he has never lived alone and is practically twice Annika's age. Irwin's father made his fortune in farming, taking advantage of those too poor or weak to bust sod, squeezing them out. The amount of land and fortune he was able to amass hints at other, less legitimate business dealings. He grows cotton and makes money off the high-stakes cash crop. He imports workers from Indian Territory to do the manual labor, paying them a pittance. It is all legal, but, Moshe thinks, not highly ethical. The government is trying to stop this influx of dubious businessmen, but there is a clandestine admiration of those whose tactics are so dirty, so low-down; thus the loopholes are never tightened. So Irwin Reece is rich, and his father is happy to get rid of him.

Moshe gradually starts to understand his speech. The first thing he is able to decipher is "Please don't call me Winnie." So now he teases him, calling him Mr. Reece. Irwin thinks this hilarious. Moshe sighs whenever he thinks of the pair of them, Irwin and Annika, making their odd-sounding lives. The idea fills him with a sense of nostalgia. Change is like this, he thinks. It makes him feel as though he's losing something, as though Garfield is running away all over again. When Rika senses this mood she takes his hand, and the soft pressure is grounding, comforting.

15

Sten spots him first. He is at the station to pick up the fabric and wine for Annika's wedding. The boxes are marked as soap, so no one steals them. He is tired of Annika's nuptials. He loves his sister; he wants her to be happy, but there are things on his mind more important than ribbons and cakes: People are talking about statehood. And all anyone at his house can think about are gloves and shoes.

The train sighs impatiently. Sten yells to the hands, "Mind you count four boxes, all marked 'Reece'!" he shouts. The Negro laborers don't reply. A figure steps down from the train—a man with one leg, who lands heavily on a crutch. The empty leg of his trousers is pinned neatly to his seat. He walks as though every step is a surprise; every time he swings his weight forward he is astonished to find that there is no limb there to support him. The man scowls with the realization.

It takes Sten a minute to suspect that this lopsided man is the boy who tormented him. As Garfield struggles with his bag, Sten squints at him. Garfield is older, of course, his face deeply lined by wind and sun, but the glower is unmistakable, as are the intense, watery brown eyes. A quick stab of fear runs through Sten, the old feeling of being bullied and teased. He has to fight the urge to run away and hide behind the machine shed. Sten approaches him. "You're Garfield," he says.

"Yes," Garfield says sharply. He is trying to lengthen the strap on his satchel so he can carry it over one shoulder.

"I'm Sten."

Garfield looks up from his bag, shades his eyes with his hand. "You grew up," he says accusingly, as though growing up were something Sten did expressly to confuse him. Instead of extending his hand, Garfield points: "Can you carry this?"

Sten hesitates, then decides to be polite. "Sure."

They walk in silence to the end of the platform. Sten has trouble match-ing his gait to Garfield's swinging step. The crutch is long; he walks faster than Sten.

Both Rika and Moshe start to cry when they see Garfield; they run into the yard and envelope him in unwanted hugs. Garfield resists, though something in him softens. Never has anyone been so glad to see him. Never has he felt this wanted, loved.

"A coupling accident," Garfield answers their unasked question. "Four years ago. Two train cars wanted to get together. My leg was between them."

If Garfield is surprised to find Rika married to his father, he doesn't show it. He is focused on the real reason for his visit. When they go in-side, he notices the mezuzah, still attached to the doorway. He waits until they are all at the table watching him eat as though he were an exotic ani-mal, until he thinks that his question might be perceived as idle curiosity: "Where is Annika?"

Annika is the reason he took a leave of absence from Rock Island. An-nika is the reason he has come where he swore he never would again. It was chance's fault: At the depot in Topeka he found a copy of the *Owenasa Gazette* that curiosity made him pocket. While waiting for the rails to be repaired outside Cheyenne, he took it out to read. On page eight an an-nouncement section listed Annika's engagement. When he saw that her fiancé was Irwin Reece, he did not pause even to resign his post but im-mediately caught the next train toward Owenasa.

"She's at the Reeces' today," Moshe says. "Mrs. Reece is pinning her veil."

"Oh." Garfield can't contain his disappointment, or his impatience.

"She'll be back tomorrow morning."

Tucked into bed that night in Sten's room, with Sten shifting uncom-fortably on the floor, Garfield wonders if he makes too much noise clomp-ing with his crutches to slip away before morning. It feels suffocating, this affection and attention. He expected to be angry; anger has sustained him for so long. But he finds that his rage has played itself out and given way to a new feeling, which he struggles to identify as regret.

Dora arrives the day before the wedding. She was not going to come, but when Garfield sent her a letter, finally, and it bore an Owenasa postmark, she gave her notice. Mr. Harvey is sorry to see her go. She is the second head chef (to make her head would be insulting to the men in the kitchen), and he has grown to depend on her, indeed to like her. Perhaps more than he should. Certainly more than his wife would like.

But, at twenty-six, she is ready to leave. San Bernardino feels too small, though it's growing all the time. She is tired of living in the girls' dormitory. She has seen so many come and go, meet their husbands on the trains or among the bus and shop boys who come to work for a summer or two before going back to wherever they came from. She has made new best friends a hundred times over, and it makes her sad to get letters with enclosed photographs of girls in wedding dresses.

When she steps off the train, she sees a mass of people she doesn't know. Owenasa has gotten so big she doesn't recognize anyone. Didn't they send someone to fetch her?

And then there are familiar features, but they are attached to a strange body. Why is this one-legged man wearing Garfield's face? Dora wonders. And then he waves at her, and she realizes it's him. She stands still in shock, then forces her legs to move toward him. When she stands a horse's length away, she drops her bag and runs to him, burying her head in his shoulder. She is crying.

"What?" she asks. "When?"

"Four years ago. It's all right, Dora. It's fine." Garfield smooths her hair. He sighs. He is sick of sympathy. The Machine made a mistake, and when you work with trains, mistakes are irreversible. The accident was his fault. He doesn't need pity.

Dora feels her heart soar with familiar longing. If anything, now that there is less of him, she loves him more. Now they are both imperfect. Now he will belong to her.

"Nice trip?" he asks, bending to pick up her case.

"I'll take that." Dora grabs it from his hand.

Marira views her mother with suspicion. This is not what Marira has expected. In her mind, the absent mother is a fairy tale, multiplied by the years so that Dora is now mythic—exquisite, beloved, statuesque. The reality is so disappointing as to be shocking. This incarnation of the absent mother is squat, a little on the portly side, with a melted face and a tired part down the center of her hair. Her smile is eerie, lopsided. Only after a threatening look from Rika does Marira force herself to return Dora's embrace.

Dora does not consider Marira her daughter; rather, the girl is a younger sibling. Dora offers to braid her hair for the celebration dinner that night at the Reece homestead. Dora pulls, Marira pulls back, and they bicker, like sisters.

The women pile into the buckboard. Moshe tries to make Garfield go with them, because of his leg. Garfield turns a bright shade of purple as he barely conceals his fury. He'll gallop alongside like the rest of the men. But it has been some years since he's been on a horse, and he hasn't counted on how much legs serve for balance and support. He bounces toward the Reeces' farm gripping the mane like a scared child. Still, he manages to stay on—a small victory.

In the wagon, Rika cannot believe her good fortune: She has all her girls together. She puts her arms around Marira and Dora. To have Dora back lessens the blow of giving away a daughter. And Garfield has returned home, too, completing the family. Only Oskar is missing. But Rika reminds herself that she is lucky. She has buried only one child, which in O.T. makes her one of the fortunate; nearly everyone has lost at least one child, some several, to disease, starvation, or accident.

The Reece family is gathered in the entryway: Mr. and Mrs. Reece and their three sons and four daughters, five of whom are married with children of their own. There is a moment of confusion amidst long skirts and pies and puddings and gifts, and finally they are in line to receive each other and everyone is happy and laughing and chatting so that no one notices Dora's small gasp when she meets the groom. She has prepared herself, but it is still a shock to see him.

"Dora." He pumps her hand enthusiastically. "Ahh gittin mahweed!"

"I know," she says. "To my sister."

He smiles and continues to hold her hands in his. Dora remembers the last time they held hands, at the dance that seems a million years ago, and she let him have his way with her because he had said in his slurred way that she was beautiful. He wanted her, and Dora had felt so special, being wanted in the way no man had ever wanted her before.

It is clear now, though, that he doesn't remember the specifics. He has forgotten Dora, forgotten kissing her in back of the store. Or perhaps he does remember, Dora thinks, looking into the light brown of his eyes, where the candles are reflected back at her. Maybe he understands all too well, and this is his way of hiding it. Dora swallows tears.

Garfield catches her eye, then turns to Mr. Reece as though they hadn't met each other's glance. At dinner, Dora can barely taste the food, though everyone murmurs over the quality of her pies and the excellence of the carrot pudding.

16

Everyone in Oklahoma is talking about the same thing, like a crotchety old man: statehood. It is said so much that it elides to form a new word: stayood. There are meetings and formal discussions. There are fistfights at the saloons, arguments at the market. Once someone threw a lantern in frustration in Moshe's store.

Even the women, traditionally too busy to fool with men's politics, have an opinion. All except Rika, who thinks that no matter whether Oklahoma is a state or remains a territory or becomes a Portuguese colony, or is captured by pirates, she'll still have dishes to wash and socks to darn.

Now that it is clear that the Oklahoma and Indian Territories will enter as one state, it is time to squabble over the details: the inevitability of Republican domination, how and when to impose Jim Crow laws, and whether I.T.'s prohibition should be continued. Each topic leads to the next like days in a week, and spurs normally placid men to their feet to put their fists where their opinions are.

In general, statehood makes Garfield clench his jaw. There have been many changes for the worse, in his opinion, since he was last in Owenasa. There are sidewalks for him to trip on, big curbs so ladies won't muddy their skirts. Colored men come and go along the street as they please, then go home at sundown to their own town with their own set of shops and foods and styles. The Indians he sees dress like white men; in fact, with hats on and without their horses, they could be mistaken for white men. He realizes he himself is passing as a white man, that his blood is not as pure as he would like to think. It makes him hate them even more.

Plumbly surprises himself, though not his wife, by deciding to vote the way Eloween wants. He justifies this action by claiming he has always voted

Republican. The president of the United States is a Republican, and if it's good enough for Mr. Roosevelt, it's good enough for Arnel Plumbly. To the cries of "nigger lover," Plumbly pleads selective deafness. What does he care if a thousand Negroes move to Oklahoma Territory? A million? They're good workers; they own their land. He himself has employed many of them, including Emily Anne's husband. His wife organizes women's suffrage groups in his living room, and Arnel's only complaint is, "Why are you serving them the good liquor, woman?"

When the mob ignites a pile of brush on his front lawn, Plumbly calmly gathers his servants and makes it clear that they should turn in the culprits. Gladly, they do so. It's the deacon of the small church in town, a couple of parishioners from Denton Station, and a particularly humorless pro-Prohibition farmer. Plumbly cuts them off—they are no longer allowed in Moshe's store, or Chicky's blacksmithery, or the dairy, or the saloon. The iceman won't deliver to their farms; the peddlers stop plying their wares. It's as though Plumbly is laying siege to them. Plumbly's the richest man around, the father of Owenasa: he who owns the railroad owns the town. Many others in the county are thus persuaded to vote Plumbly's ticket.

Statehood seems inevitable to Plumbly, or at least that's what they say at the saloon. Plumbly would rather not be joined in unholy matrimony with Indian Territory, but the men say that's not negotiable either. With Indians as American citizens, the Territory has to be considered as part of Oklahoma. Plumbly shrugs. Politics is not his game. As long as he gets to keep his land, the socialists or unionists or even the anarchists could have their way for all he cares.

In the eight months since Garfield returned, Moshe's and Rika's lives have changed utterly. First, Garfield announces he will stay. He has considered his options, he says. What he does not admit to his family is that his pain is getting worse, and it is increasingly hard to maneuver on even level ground. What he does not admit to himself is that he is worried about Annika and her "simple" husband. He feels the need to be near her as she starts her new life. His promise to protect her is reinvigorated each time he enters the house and sees the mezuzah, pointing like an accusing finger.

Garfield then insinuates himself into the store so that a mere three months later they have expanded their wares to include contraband spirits, luxury goods like perfumed soap, and a parade of ready-made items that

Moshe predicts will never sell to hardworking Oklahomans. They fly off the shelves.

Garfield thinks he is doing Moshe a favor. If he takes over, Moshe won't have to work as hard. If the store makes more money, Moshe and Rika can relax. Garfield will shoulder the burden. It gives him pleasure to play the martyr; it gives his life purpose. But all Garfield succeeds in doing is bossing his father around, making him feel superfluous, old. Moshe and Garfield discuss constructing a series of higher floors, and a lift to take customers from one to the other, or from the bottom to the top. Again, Moshe can't see the purpose of all the space, but Garfield tells him he's blind.

One day Garfield is minding the store while Moshe nurses a cold in the back room. An Indian who reminds Garfield of his first boss on the rails, a sharp, uncompassionate man, complains when Garfield measures light on his tobacco: "Don't Jew me, now."

Garfield clenches his jaw. "This is how the white man counts a pound, and if you want your tobacco, this is how you'll learn to count it, too."

The Indian spits at his foot, and Garfield grabs his crutch to swing around, but the Indian grabs it faster.

"Get out of here, you squawfucker!" Garfield yells.

The Indian throws Garfield's crutch across the room and storms out. Garfield immediately regrets having lashed out, but the violence felt almost involuntary, the rage as immediate as the need to vomit.

Moshe has heard the yelling. He comes running in. "What did you call him?"

"Filthy Injun," Garfield mutters.

"Your grandmother was an 'Injun.'" Moshe speaks low. "When you insult them, you insult yourself." Moshe leaves Garfield to hop, tumble, and finally crawl across the floor for his crutch.

There are almost 750,000 people in Oklahoma Territory alone, and after it joins with Indian Territory to become a state there will be twice as many people jostling for land and space. Garfield still sees a huge potential for profit, especially if the store is an attraction itself. He plans an indoor waterfall, an ice palace, a series of human deformities contained in glass jars, all to draw people inside. Moshe stands by, helpless in the face of so much preposterous industry. He wonders, Is Garfield building a store or a sideshow?

Garfield puts Sten in charge of supervising the improvements to the house. They are putting in a water closet on the second floor, in the room Moshe used to occupy when Rika was married to Fritz. Then there is a set of stairs that connect to a new back porch. The first floor sees the addition of two rooms, each with its own entrance, for Garfield and Sten. It is as though Garfield has never left, as though they are boys again, twelve and nine. Whenever Garfield commands, Sten scurries to take action.

Suddenly the savings are liquid. Suddenly there is a housemaid, an accountant for the store. Suddenly the Haurowitzes are rich, though their bank accounts are empty. There is capital to improve the land, to purchase more. Garfield has ways of coercing landowners to sell at reduced prices, or at least to rent at cut rates in exchange for protection from the spontaneous bad luck—in the form of fires and blights, broken fences and lame horses—that seems to plague people who hold out on Garfield Harris.

Garfield's tactics are underhanded, he knows, but he tells himself he is doing this for his family's well-being. This is how the world works, as unpleasant as it may seem, and everyone is shocked only because they have been living in a hamlet, protected from the nature of business. If the family wants to get ahead, it has to play the game. It's not Garfield's fault he's good at it. He'd like to explain this to his family, but for some reason when he opens his mouth, the words come out all wrong. He means to be truthful, but ends up insulting. He means to be complimentary, responsible, but his sentences are hurtful and alienating. It is as though there is a switch between his head and his mouth that flips what he is saying into its unintended opposite.

Garfield hires a series of security guards, Negroes, whom he then accuses of stealing and dismisses without back pay. He calls them all "Joe." He then rides his horse through the nearby Negro town, seeking another employee. Though he does not know it, he is listening for the songs Tallulah used to sing; he is hungry for the smells of her kitchen. He is angry at Tallulah. He feels as though she abandoned him, though he knows it was he who left. He has tried to find her, even went so far as to hire an investigator to look for a large black woman without a family name (a different investigator from the idiot who could find no trace of Alice). But Tallulah has been carried away by America's tides.

When Moshe walks through the town where he has been elected mayor twice, only recently stepping down to give someone else a chance, a hush precedes him. People part to make room. It makes him uncomfortable, being singled out. He knows it is not out of respect but out of fear for his son's power. Again, as always, Moshe feels unable to stop Garfield. Garfield is a human avalanche, felling mountains as he travels on his imperative trajectory.

Though statehood comes as no surprise, it is still a reason to celebrate. Garfield orders a tent and erects it behind the store. He invites the whole town —the white section of town—to watch the fireworks and to eat barbecue and drink whiskey. Oklahoma is part of the Union now. Oklahoma, USA.

The Portuguese men arrive with the fireworks. They are a motley crew, missing fingers and teeth. For each dollar they're paid they demand a pint of whiskey. Dora takes a break from the hot kitchen and watches them set up. She says a quick prayer that nothing will catch fire.

There are too many women in the kitchen, Dora thinks. She is tired of being surrounded by women, their high-pitched laughter and their easy emotions. She misses the Harvey House, where all the chefs were male. She prefers, when she is able, to sit with the men on the porch, watching the stock animals or the movement of the moon across the sky. She prefers to sit with Garfield. She feels a rush when he passes near. She likes to watch him ride his horse with his special one-stirrup saddle. She suspects she might be in love, if this is what love feels like—suffocating tingling like a dry hand touching metal.

The sky darkens, and the town gathers on the slight rise behind the Haurowitz place. There is a small country orchestra, made up of musically inclined citizens of the town—the blacksmith on fiddle, the cobbler on horn, a trio of singing farmers. The music swells, and people begin to dance, demurely at first and then wildly, until it seems the whole town is out of breath. There are whiskey and beer (disguised as lemonade and iced tea in deference to the Bone Dry Law), and many of Plumbly's cowhands are nearing drunkenness. Soon enough there is a fight, and teasing shots are fired at someone's feet. Garfield confiscates the arms and sends both parties home to bed.

Dora puts out all the food she has made: pork chops and beef ribs, biscuits and pies and carrot salad and pashofa and deviled eggs. Everyone eats greedily. When it seems the town has had its fill, Dora takes the leftovers around the house to where the Negroes are standing apart from the festivities. The sundown laws are lifted for the night; still they gather in familial clumps, close enough to hear the music but not close enough to be the bull's-eye of a drunken cowboy's target practice. Then she sees a face that looks familiar. It is Emily Anne, the midwife who helped her give birth to Marira. She is older than Dora would have thought, her hair ashen and her face lined. This is the woman who has shared with Dora the most intimate moment of her life, who has seen inside her. But if Emily Anne recognizes Dora she is able to disguise it. Her face is as expressionless as a cleared field. Dora sets the food down without speaking. When she turns her back, she can hear the swish of dust as they move toward the offering.

The dancing has resumed, and Dora sits by Garfield as he watches, scowling. She places her hand on his knee, but his glare warns her off. She feels stung.

"Tell them it's time for fireworks," Garfield says.

Few in town have seen pyrotechnics before, and as the Portuguese light them there is a flutter of excitement. When the first one goes off, a burst of white fire in the sky, children begin to cry. Women hide their faces in their husbands' shoulders, and boys cover their ears with their hands. Garfield worries that the fireworks, like all of his plans, have turned on him. He has meant to delight, to treat the people in town, and has succeeded only in scaring them.

But then the works turn colors, red and green, shooting up like geysers. It is a beautiful November night, cool and clear, and the explosions look to Dora like bursts of perfection, like proof of God.

In a pause while the Portuguese reset the line, Dora turns to Garfield. His face is skyward, lit by the torches they've set around the perimeter. It is the same face she's known since childhood, marked now by deep squint lines and a couple small scars.

"Do you . . . ?" Dora begins.

"What?" he says impatiently.

"Do you—could we . . . get married?"

Garfield doesn't turn. The fireworks begin again, and Dora isn't sure he's going to answer.

"Well?"

"No," he says. There is another long pause. "It's impossible."

"But not—," Dora starts.

"No."

"You offered once . . ." She is surprised at how hurt she is by his refusal. Hadn't she suspected that he would say no?

"That was a long time ago. I was a child. We were both children."

"But—"

"Don't make me say more." Garfield's voice is rough, angry. He doesn't know how to explain to Dora that it is his fault he can't marry her. He tells himself that she deserves more than what he is able to offer. But, truly, it is that he does not want her. Her fidelity makes him feel unworthy, inadequate. It is as tiresome as his limp.

Dora is so hurt that tears are beyond her. Her sorrow is farther down inside, in her gut, her lungs. She feels winded, like she can't move, and she looks at the ground, not at the fireworks until Annika comes to get her: Did Dora remember to put out the ice cream?

The light from the fireworks illuminates and then shadows the town's faces. There are audible gasps. But Garfield's delight comes not from the fireworks' beauty. Rather, what thrills him is the cataclysmic bang, the gunpowder smell, and, above all, the fire's cathartic violence as it plunges through the night sky.

PART 6

A Track Upward to the Clouds
1908–1930

17

It isn't pretty, this black sludge buried deep within the earth. It reminds Garfield of blood from a cavernous wound, coagulating in a long drip down ripped flesh. The essential difference: blood is cheap, oil expensive.

After the strike at Glenn Pool, everyone is a specialist in oil discovery. Some use divining rods—hickory wood is especially recommended. Others have trained hounds to identify the peculiar smell of gas and kerosene that seeps through the soil. Still others consult tea leaves, auspicious swells of land, magic cards, and special dice.

Garfield prefers a more direct approach, which he calls "spike and strike." His theory is that among his vast tracts of land there must be oil somewhere. So every morning, Garfield throws his custom saddle on his favorite horse and rides with a team of geologists and specialists, systematically drilling every hundred yards to find the hidden well.

They have struck several times, but never astoundingly. Never has gas forced the oil to the surface in a spectacular spume of cash. He has purchased equipment to drag it from the earth, huge scaffolds of twisted metal like mutant sewing machines. The wells pay, but not enough. Garfield wants to be rich—for Annika, for Dora, for Marira, for his father, and for himself. Somehow, though, the altruistic original purpose has been forgotten, replaced by the goal of money itself. This aim, then, is always elusive; there will always be more dollars to amass. It will never be fulfilled, and therefore Garfield will always feel like a failure.

Garfield drops the crew off and rides to the limit of his expanded property. He lets his horse graze; then they wander down to Fiddler's Creek. He looks out across to Plumbly's bare range. He must have recently burned the prairie grass to allow new growth. Ranching and farming have never really made sense to Garfield. The first seems unpleasant: Cows are messy, smelly, stubborn, and stupid. They need to be wrangled and herded, gelded and doped. They are susceptible to wood ticks and screwworms. They require branding and palpating of the innards. And farming simply seems too uncertain. Depending on the weather is an idiot's folly in Oklahoma. A clear sky can turn to rain in the flick of a horse's tail. There is rain in winter and hail in summer, and drought just as often. There are snowstorms in March and frosts in September. The Canadian River might rage and flood while the fields dry up from lack of rain. In Oklahoma, Plumbly frequently says, the weather's only there when you don't want it, like leftover hotcakes.

His horse whinnies now, and Garfield's leg is beginning to throb, a sure sign of oncoming rain. Garfield pulls the reins. It's not that he will melt in a little water, but the last time he rode wet he caught a cold and stayed in bed for a week, his temper growing fouler with every day. Dora waited on him—brought him tea and massaged his foot, fed him soup and emptied his bedpan. Her devotion embarrasses him, makes him short with her.

Annika is the only one who can make him laugh, swatting him playfully when his face reveals surliness. Their affection is obvious to those around them. Rika envies their attachment, though she doesn't understand what draws Garfield and Annika to each other. Garfield has grown up from a difficult boy to a hard and sour man. Yet all that melts away when he is in Annika's presence. Moshe wonders if Garfield has designs on Annika, but Rika can see that his attraction to the girl is not physical.

Despite Garfield's fears, Annika and Irwin seem happy. Irwin helps his father on the ranch, and Annika runs her shop. She is the most sought-after seamstress in the state, perhaps even in southern Missouri and western Arkansas too. Women mail her sketches, measurements, and descriptions, and Annika sews their dresses, adding additional flourishes. She waits for the money to arrive at the post office, then mails the dress. She offers a guarantee; she has never had a return.

Garfield gallops back to where he left the men, intending to gather them in before the storm breaks, but they are not there. In their place, however, is a veritable gusher. Columns of crude shoot into the sky like a Roman candle. Garfield feels a surge of happiness, of vindication.

Moshe stands at the edge of the platform, unsure what he is supposed to look at. It's loud, he'll say that about it, and very tall. Garfield points his crutch at the various parts of the oil rig while he narrates. "And that is the derrick that houses the traveling block . . ."

Moshe nods, trying to focus his attention, straining to hear.

"From there the pipe takes the oil to the barrels in the wagon, which brings it to the train, which takes it to the refinery," Garfield concludes. "Sten, what's the price today?"

Sten consults his clipboard. "Closed at three dollars a barrel."

"Three dollars," Garfield repeats. "She's gushing a hundred barrels an hour right now."

Moshe nods.

"We're rich," Garfield says, banging softly on a metal strut.

When Moshe doesn't respond, Garfield tries a different tactic. "Betcha didn't imagine this, Pa, when we built that little house and cleared that sorry garden. Could you have imagined all this?"

Moshe wants to say that he doesn't recall Garfield helping out at all with the "little" house or the "sorry" garden. Instead he says, "The house wasn't that little; we all fit."

"Pa," Garfield scoffs, "it was hardly a mansion. And the chimney was defective. We're lucky we didn't *all* burn to death."

Moshe's face reddens. He swallows and turns away. If his son weren't a cripple, he'd consider grabbing the crutch and hitting him with it.

Garfield can see he's gone too far. He's only brought his father out here to show him that what he has done was worth it, and now it has backfired. He wanted to prove to him that the loans they took out against the equipment, hocking everything that wasn't nailed down and a few things that were, would be worth it, would pay off. Once the money comes in, the town will see improvements in the form of schools, industry, and culture. Then, Garfield thinks, they'll be thanking them. Then his father will see that Garfield was right.

But Moshe isn't appreciative or grateful or impressed or any of the things Garfield has been expecting, and in retaliation Garfield's gone too far, referring to Oskar's death.

"I'm going home now," Moshe says, turning to climb down the deck to where the horse is waiting.

"What?" Garfield asks, but there are fifteen Kellys pounding into the earth, churning beneath sediment to find black gold; the echoes reverberate across the plain. His father's words drown in the sound.

* * *

A half dozen townspeople enter the store one day in a group, bringing with them the scent of outdoors—dung and horses. "Can we talk for a minute?" Cud Reece, one of Irwin's brothers, speaks for them.

"Surely," Moshe answers. He stands up from his desk and walks to the counter. Dust mites float in the strip of sunlight coming in through the open door.

"It's about that son of yours," J. R. says.

"And the drilling," Cud adds. Everyone nods.

"It's loud, I know," says Moshe. "We all think it's loud. I was telling him just the other day, 'Son, that drilling's too loud.'"

"It's not the noise, Mr. Haurowitz," says one of the younger men. "It's those leases he made us sign."

"What do you mean, 'made you'?" Moshe asks. He has purposely stayed out of Garfield's business, though he knows Garfield has struck some sort of deal with the men.

J. R. says, "He paid us fifty dollars to put a well on our property. Then he says we get one-eighth of the proceeds. 'Better than what the Indians get,' is what he said."

"And then," Cud takes up the explanation, "he drills, but the wells are no good, he says. So he caps them."

"If they're no good . . ." Moshe shrugs.

"That's just it. How's he making so much money if our wells are no good?"

There is a silence. Moshe worries that his son is cheating these men. He feels a hot blush of shame cross his face. These are his neighbors, fellow settlers who worked as hard as he did to make Owenasa a real town.

"I can't prove it," Cud says, "but there's gas seeping out infecting my farm. My soil's worn out, soaked with kerosene. Nothing wants to grow in that sludge. It's like he's stealing food from the mouths of my children."

Moshe considers. He is sympathetic, but he can't side with the men against his only child. "He's a grown man. Why don't you try talking to him yourselves?"

Cud lets out a guffaw. The others sigh in exasperation. "You ever try talking to that boy?" Cud asks. "I'd rather reason with a steer. At least the steer don't shoot flames out his nose."

"He's not reasonable," J. R. says. "It's like pissing into the wind."

"What do you want me to do?" Moshe asks.

"Talk to him. Reason with him. I don't know what your Hebrew customs are, but around here . . . ," Cud says. Moshe bristles. He was born right here in Oklahoma, which is more than these greenbugs can say for themselves. Cud continues, "I'm just telling you because you and me are relations."

Cud's statement sounds like a threat. Garfield may well be guilty of everything the posse accuses him of, and perhaps more. But Moshe has no more control over Garfield than he does over the weather, or the price of coffee in Vermont. He never has. He is full of anger, Moshe's child, and like an oil deposit, he's just waiting for a strike to start spewing black venom. There's nothing Moshe can do.

J. R. leans over the counter. "You tell him that if he don't give us what's our due, we'll just have to come and take it."

The warning hangs in the air like a puff of smoke. Moshe's sympathy for these men evaporates. Maybe Plumbly's right—Oklahoma is a state of savages: if you don't take it and defend it, then someone else will take it from you. He says, "If there's property being violated, maybe you should build yourselves fences."

Cud takes a step toward the counter, finger pointing. "Now see here—"

"C'mon, let's go," says the younger man. "We've said our piece."

In the doorway, Cud spits on the floor.

Moshe goes into the back for the mop and the bucket. He swabs the spot over and over, long after it is clean.

Moshe and Rika sit up in bed, the lantern casting a full-moon glow over the room. Moshe is reading the latest installment of a serialized novel; Rika is copying recipes for her card folder.

When they turn out the light, Moshe says, "Rika?" The plaintive tone to his voice lets Rika know he wants a serious discussion. She does not look forward to these. Moshe invariably likes to have them in the dark, which makes Rika feel as though she's being spoken to by a ghost. She'd rather converse in the light, during the day, when she feels less enervated, not so old. She missed her cycle last month, and though she suspects it is because of overwork, it is not out of the question that she is beginning her change.

Moshe leans away and puts out the light. She feels the bed shift as he turns to face her in the darkness. There is just enough moonlight to see the outline of his face, his bulbous nose and rounded chin.

"Rika, some folks came to see me in the store last week."

Rika nods, then realizes he can't see her face. She adds, "I know."

There is a silence.

"Dora heard from them in town." When she is tired, the Scandinavian creeps back into Rika's voice.

"What do you think I should do?"

"Nothing. What should have been done should have been done years ago."

"He's so angry. All the time." Moshe ignores the reproach in her voice.

"The leg," Rika sighs. There's nothing she can say to right the situation. "He's like a hailstorm . . . Find some cover and wait it out."

So Moshe talks to Boggy when he thinks no one is listening. He speaks out loud, picturing his father, small and gray and sturdy. He tells Boggy about Garfield, Rika; how, impossibly, he still misses Alice. He chats to Boggy as he dusts the shelves or stacks inventory or waits for customers at the counter. Boggy is the best conversation partner; absent, he listens intently but does not answer.

Garfield decides he's not going to care a continental about what the town thinks about him. The oil is his; it's his birthright. If it's not quite on the land he owns title to, then wouldn't the larger crime be to let it slush there underground, bathing the prairie dogs where it can't do anyone any good? Those men signed those leases because they were too shortsighted to see what the ground was offering. He is providing the country with power, with might. He is doing a public service.

Why should it upset him that people turn their backs on him in town? They can't understand what it is to make a life without the most integral part of humanness. Humans are the only animal he's ever seen with just two legs; the fact that he has only one makes him less human, somehow. This must be what the townspeople object to, he reasons. He is inferior, substandard, a job left half done.

Annika is the only one he lets see the stump. It is pointed like an el-bow, and still red and irritated where the doctor cauterized it. He hadn't thought it would taper like that and is still shocked when he takes down his trousers and sees what's left of his limb hanging there like a sausage.

It surprises him how much something that is not there can pain him. It throbs like a headache, radiating sharp pain as though he is constantly stubbing it. Also, his knee hurts. His foot is perpetually swollen, his ankle sprained, his shin bruised. This is impossible, he knows. There is no foot, ankle, shin, or knee to feel this pain, yet it's there, palpable as rain, an amalgamation of injuries, keeping him awake nights, tied in knots.

Some nights, when it gets too bad, he downs a fifth of whiskey and rides the mule to Annika's house in town. She can feel the vibration of the door as he lets himself in, and she always wakes up, receives him in her robe, and stokes the fire to put the kettle on. She doesn't talk to him, and for this he loves her more than he loves anyone or anything on the planet. More than he loves trains, more than he loves coal engines, more than he loves oil or money. Only with silence can he say what he means.

She bends down and takes his stump in her hands, massaging it expertly. The first few times she does this, Garfield feels a thrill not unlike the ladder of tickles that is sex, but gradually the feeling subsides as the pain disappears in her fingers. Then she moves down the leg that is not there, rubbing the air, relieving the knee, the shin, the ankle, and the foot of the agony that must be all in his head but feels so real. Finally he can relax, on these occasional evenings. Finally he can let go and remember what it feels like to sleep a night without throbbing, stinging punishment. Only then does he find peace.

Once he entered the house and heard the unmistakable groans of love-making. When he slammed the door behind him, the sounds stopped, and by the time he settled into the chair in front of the fireplace Annika was there, robe tied tightly at her waist, tucking her hair behind her ears. He was thrilled. He was more important to her than her husband, than a family, than desire. He is the most important.

He likes to stand alone and watch the oil rig pump up crude. He loves to follow it with his eyes, the power of the thruster as it reaches deep into the earth and forces out the nectar. The machine is fine-tuned, the way Garfield used to be. Watching the rig is like watching a vertical train, running a track upward toward the clouds, then crashing down again in a choreographed blow. It gives him the same pleasure that a train used to, after he'd tweaked the bolts so they reamed at the proper angle, bedding squarely on their seats inside the smoke box so that it was airtight, a wall against the outside world.

He admires the machine's strength, impenetrability, and the fact that it can pierce the hard soil, against which the farmers have been struggling all their lives, and with one yank extract that which no one else can. It is a power he no longer possesses in his own life, and so he spends the day watching what he has created, trying to make it his own, feeling the ground pulse with the sound of his fortune being ushered from below.

18

Now that war seems inevitable, the hope of a peaceful resolution sinking like the *Lusitania,* there is a rush to get married, like a run on flour before a big winter storm. Marira, ever conscious of fashion, betroths herself to a young army lieutenant. When Garfield meets him the boy blushes, his hairless cheeks given over to a sharp redness. He has the same pink skin as the other Scandinavians and wrists so thin that Garfield thinks they might snap when he shakes the boy's hand and hands him an envelope of cash.

The wedding has been hastily planned, since he reports for duty on Monday, two days after the ceremony. It is performed by an army chaplain at the Palmer House in downtown Chicago. Annika's children, Oskar and Mary, serve as ring bearer and flower girl, solemnly making their way down the makeshift aisle. The food after the service is almost inedible. Garfield would give two dollars for a bowl of Texas chili.

And then there is a woman, and Garfield stops chewing, his mouth half-full of cured fish. She is telling a story in a breathless manner that he will come to associate with her, and love about her, and then detest in her. The words come in gasps, the squeaky rust of an accent peeking through. Then she laughs, throwing back her head to reveal an endless expanse of white, white neck. China white, not the unnatural translucency of the Swedes. He has never seen skin so white next to such light blond hair—the color of wheat in need of harvesting.

Usually, he pays women no attention at all. He's not interested in marrying, and he can have whichever whore he wants, whenever he wants. But this woman stirs him. He wants to do more than just place himself inside her; he wants to own her. With all the money he possesses, he still wants something else, more property, another place to plant his flag.

Her name, he learns, after hobbling up to her indecorously, insinuating himself in front of her conversation partner and introducing himself, is Sophie. She is accompanying her father, a professor of economics at the University of Chicago and an acquaintance of the groom's family. Garfield puts his hand on her arm, and she rebuffs him by lifting one finger, the way she would a dirty rag or a dead vole.

Their courtship is brief and passionate. She hates his gruffness and vulgar speech. He hates her superciliousness, her fancy words, and her prissiness. She argues, which delights him. No one has dared say no to him in years. He finds her accent exotic, delivered in that breathy tone that promises a treat on his wedding night.

Garfield orders a custom crutch with gold inlaid staff and an ivory handle. He wears a tiepin studded with diamonds. He oils his hair and buys a pocket watch that he never once winds. He sends for a valet at the hotel, a swishy man with hands soft as flower petals, who clucks his tongue and scrubs the insides of Garfield's ears, trims his nails and nose hairs, and smooths the arms of his suit jacket. All these preparations are calculated. It has not escaped Garfield's notice that Sophie's dress is worn at the hem, and her father's suit has been patched many times. And as much as the fuss over his appearance disgusts Garfield, he has to admit that the mirror now reflects a much more citified and sophisticated version of the person he was when he woke that morning.

He hands the valet ten dollars. "You keep your mouth shut," Garfield says, in a tone more command than request. The man bows and leaves, closing the door silently behind him.

Garfield later clumsily copies this obsequious bow, nearly toppling over when he asks Sophie's father for her hand. He has forgotten that Friday nights celebrate the Sabbath, and so he is asked to stay for dinner, a simple roast chicken served by Sophie's grandmother. He eats nearly nothing so as not to reveal his lack of table manners. Sophie's family performs maneuvers with their utensils that seem more complicated to Garfield than tatting. After dinner, he retires with the professor to his study for a cognac, which they drink out of vaselike goblets. He notices that the furniture is threadbare to the stuffing in places. The professor stares out the window, though Garfield is sure he can't see anything with the light shining behind him and the moon not yet out. "Sophie says you come to ask for her marriage," the professor says in his thick accent. "She is not so agreeing with this."

"And you, sir?"

"Of Oklahoma, I know nothing. Of oil, I know nothing. Of love . . ." The professor trails off.

"I love her, of course," Garfield says quickly. He is not sure if this is true, but what he feels is strong and new; it might be love.

The professor continues as though Garfield has not spoken. "Here it is expensive to live," he says. "In Germany we were accustomed of much more. Here is too much family, too much people with hands out."

"I've got money," Garfield says. "Barrels of it. And my wife's family is my family."

"You are not Jewish."

"I was raised Jewish," Garfield says. It is the first time in a long while that he has admitted to his past. "My father is Jewish."

"A half apple is more apple than an empty cupboard," the professor admits. His eyes are droopy, as though he has not slept in years. "But you are not a man is whole."

Garfield assumes the professor is speaking of his missing leg. He feels his ears go hot, forces himself to control his temper. "There is nothing any man can do that I can't do, and I'll probably do it better than most."

The professor sighs. "I am doing business on Shabbat. This is what this country bring me to." There is a long pause. Finally the professor says, "I will talk with her."

"Thank you, sir," says Garfield. He attempts to bow and has to catch himself on the worn arm of the chair.

"You come on Sunday afternoon."

Garfield makes sure to kiss Sophie on the cheek on the way out. He can feel her breath in his ear and a concurrent surge of lust. His chest just brushes her breasts, and at that moment he feels he will do anything to make her his.

"I can still smell the horse on you," she says.

"Soon it will be your smell, too," he whispers back. He turns to Sophie's grandmother and thanks her for the meal. Then he steps into the dark street. Out of respect for the Sabbath there are no lights until he reaches the end of the block. His desire is strong, awakened like a horse's thirst after a long ride. The feeling of victory is also intense, of capture and power.

He goes to the brothel on Maxwell Street and buys the woman there with the longest hair. He makes her bend over and takes her from behind, slapping her bottom as though riding a bronco, as though each time he plunges he is an oil well railing at the earth to give up its precious wealth.

* * *

A relationship built on precarious planks, the union of Garfield and Sophie promises to be volatile, and does not disappoint. Sophie seems to view her marriage as a sort of indentured servitude imposed upon her by her father. She will serve out an unspecified number of years, and then, released, she will walk away into the bright light of an undetermined promised land. In the meantime, she must admit, there are advantages to being suddenly wealthy, even in the godforsaken forty-sixth state. Since the birth of her first son, Tomas, a month ago, she has only had to change diapers a handful of times. Dora is a live-in nursemaid; the servants clean up the mess.

Sophie has insisted on Tomas's circumcision, and Garfield was forced to pay for a *mohel* from Missouri to come by train. He cringes as the knife meets his son's flesh. The five other Jewish families in Owenasa also attend: a Ukrainian man and his wife and three youngsters, a haughty German immigrant and his stiff family, a bachelor tailor and two cousins who own a lumberyard.

Sophie then arranges for a traveling rabbi to lead them in Shabbat services once a month. She drags a reluctant Garfield to sit through the interminable rituals. "I wasn't aware I was marrying a heathen," Sophie says to Garfield's complaints.

"What's this note?" Garfield demands one afternoon, thrusting a bill into her face.

"A bonnet," Sophie says, shoving the bill away absently with the hand that isn't holding her book of sonnets.

"Ten dollars?" Garfield asks.

"And some licorice."

"What, gold licorice?"

"German licorice. The anise in this country is inferior." Sophie manages to point her nose in the air while simultaneously hiding it in her book.

"Here's what's inferior—your housekeeping," Garfield says. He tosses the bill into her lap. She lets it slide down her legs to the floor. "You pay it," he says.

"With what?" Sophie says dully. "Besides, it's got your name on it. The head that will roll will be your own."

"And you'd like that, huh? To have a headless husband? Who'll make your money for you then?"

"Frankly, your head is not your best feature anyway."

Garfield grabs his right hand with his left so he won't hit her. The few times he has done so she shuts him out for days, making the usual rumble of their household seem like paradise in comparison. Much better are the times Garfield comes to her contrite, or falsely penitent. Then she is superiorly loving.

Garfield groans in frustration and pivots. He stumbles slightly and grabs the mantel for support. He has recently been fitted for a prosthetic leg, a wooden contraption with a permanent shoe that straps to his thigh like a garter with painful canvas belts. He is still shaky on it; he misses his crutch. Without it, he feels as though a limb has been taken from him again.

He thinks he hears Sophie let out a small puff of air—a derisive laugh. He can feel his face redden, but he does not turn. As he leaves the living room, she says, "I also ordered Father new spectacles, a Dutch oven for Eva, and a blood-fortifying serum for Mother."

Upstairs in the house Moshe built, but that is no longer his own, Moshe complains to Rika, "I can't stand it. The fighting. Constantly."

"Bickering," Rika says. "There's a difference. Ignore it and go to sleep."

"It's barely dark."

"Think about all the things you have to do tomorrow. Count flour sacks."

"Maybe we could go live with Plumbly."

"At the ranch?" Rika says. "Are you out of your mind?"

"Or Marira, in Chicago."

"You're talking crazy. Go to sleep, old man," Rika says. There is an uncharacteristic asperity to her tone.

"I don't like it when you talk to me like that," Moshe says. "Reminds me of Fritz."

"Don't you dare bring him into this bed." Rika sits up, suddenly heated.

"This *is* his bed," Moshe says, literal to a fault.

"Of all the stupid—," Rika begins, but her insult is drowned out by baby Tomas crying next door.

Dora bangs on the wall. "Hush!" she yells. "Now you woke the baby."

Moshe sighs and heads to the water closet. He closes the door and sits in his nightshirt on the lid. He puts his face in his hands. He can hear the rhythmic noise of the bedboard hitting the other side of the wall—Garfield and Sophie's room. His grunts and her moans sound to Moshe like a continuation of their bickering. He hears a cry—male, female, it's impossible to tell—and the pounding stops. Soon he hears Garfield's loud snores. How is it that they've gone to sleep while Moshe sits awake and alone?

He wonders if he will ever reach an age when he no longer hopes for justice in the world. Or maybe, someday, the world will balance itself into fairness. Not likely, he muses. A better question: Will there ever be a time when he accepts that he will always be the one who stays awake while others take their rest, grabbing it as though it is a debt the world owes them?

19

Garfield is nearly certain that his wife hates him. He is trying to decide how much this matters. They've been together nearly thirteen years, enough to let faults become annoyances, annoyances become intolerable tics, which lead to gibes, which harden into rancor. They agree only on the fact that they agree on nothing.

They are on the train, having left Dora behind like a maid, en route to Oklahoma City "to get some culture," Sophie says. She eyes him now from across the compartment, narrowing her lids disapprovingly. Garfield wonders what he's done wrong: Shifted his weight? Sighed too heavily? Sniffled? There is no pleasing her.

She gathers her skirt in under her legs. Though it is hot, Sophie has decided there will be no open windows to let in dirt and mess up hair. Two of the children, Mina and Alice, complain and are silenced by their mother. The oldest, Tomas, stares sullenly through the glass. The baby is sleeping finally. Excitement prevented them from resting the previous night, and as a result all are cranky. It is not a long ride, but the compartment is small and stifling, and everyone is eager to arrive, most of all Garfield.

"Tomas," Garfield calls. "Go to the dining car and get your father a whiskey."

Tomas doesn't turn his head. He is studying to be a bar mitzvah next year, an affair Garfield so disdains that he is threatening not to attend.

"Tomas, I'm talking to you."

The boy continues to sulk.

"Tomas!" Garfield raises his hand. The girls flatten back against their seats.

Tomas turns his head.

"I said, go get me a whiskey."

"Papa, I'll go," Dalia, the oldest daughter, says.

Garfield doesn't respond. There is a pause during which Garfield can see the boy considering. He hopes Tomas will agree to fetch him a drink, first of all because he needs one and the lurching train makes it almost impossible to navigate the cars with his prosthesis, and second because Tomas has challenged his authority, and he neither wants nor has the energy to punish him.

Tomas stands and puts his hand out for the money. Garfield hands him a dollar and watches as the boy slumps away. "And get your sisters a lemonade," he calls after him.

Garfield has a new empathy for his father. Tomas treats Garfield exactly as Garfield treated Moshe thirty years ago. The difference is, Garfield takes action. When the boy mouths off he receives the beating that Garfield deserved as a child.

Tomas looks like Sophie, light-haired and fair-skinned. The boy sunburns like an infant every time they ride their horses to even slightly distant prospects. Plus, Tomas is incapable of making his hat stay on his head. He is a poor horseman, clumsy and careless; he lets his horse bloat on grain and water. He is skinny, like Garfield as a boy, and, they recently discovered, very nearsighted. Garfield is sure his incessant reading has done this to him.

Sophie picks up the book on her lap and begins to read to the children in German. Garfield can't understand it, though he hears it in his house every day. His father understands most of it, says it is similar to Yiddish, and Moshe and Sophie talk in it when they think Garfield won't hear them and forbid it. She is reading the children Goethe, pronounced "Gerta." They giggle at the same time when Sophie turns the pages.

The baby fusses, and Sophie doesn't break her reading, jiggling him on her lap. Garfield watches the fields go by. The furrows are even, straight as two-by-fours, and the only way to tell one from another is a change of crops or a difference in height. The wheat at this time of year is low and still more green than gold. When the sun glints off the stalks it seems as though there is dirt in the sky, as though the land were giving off steam like bathwater. This train isn't running as smoothly as he would have demanded if he were the engineer. If he had his leg and was still running the rails instead of developing oil fields, manacled to this growing family.

Tomas returns with the whiskey and three lemonades. "*Danke*," the girls chorus. Dalia and Mina are dark like their father, with his curly hair.

Alice, on the other hand, is blonde, with thick hair to her waist and questioning brown eyes. Jacob is still bald at almost two years of age, but has the same sharp features as his mother, her aquiline nose and thin, pursed lips. Sophie's reading grows more animated; her voice rises, and words take on the familiar gasping.

There is a minor crisis as they step off the train. Alice forgets her rag doll and wails until Sophie promises that her father will buy her a new one. Garfield has forgotten how a big city sounds, its constant sneezing, whirling wheels, and worried horns. They hire a cab, which takes them down the paved streets to the elegant Skirvin Hotel. Its size and prominence remind Garfield of the San Bernardino Crystal Palace, the time he met up with Dora, what seems like a thousand years ago, a different life.

In the dark dining room at dinner the Harris family looks as though it stepped out of the last decade. The other women are all wearing what look like their mothers' undergarments, silky shapeless shifts held up by mere suggestions of straps. They look like little boys, breastless and unwaisted, while Sophie's lace V-neck only serves to augment her impressive bust, and the bodice of her dress hugs her small waist. She would never go out in a dress as short as these women are wearing, as though they were in bathing costumes at the beach instead of at dinner in a fine hotel.

The next morning they order a picnic from the dining room and go to the fairgrounds to take in a baseball game. The weather is fine, with an inoffensive blue sky stretching on for miles. As soon as they sit, Sophie takes out the sandwiches and passes them down the row until all the children are armed with bread. Garfield shakes his head when Tomas offers him one, and Tomas shrugs and puts it in his pocket for later.

The game is slow, with interminable pitching and few hits. Alice and Mina grow fussy as the heat mounts. They bounce their dolls on the bench until Garfield yells at them to stop. Dalia and Tomas take turns keeping score on the program with a nub of a pencil that cost three whole pennies.

Garfield would have liked to take them to a rodeo, so they could see an all-American sport, but Lucille Mulhall has long since stopped riding in Buffalo Bill's Wild West Show. All that's left of rodeo culture is the 101 Ranch, a sorry, run-down tourist attraction. Gone are the days when baseball was just one pastime among others. Now baseball is the national sport, a countrywide obsession.

Garfield rubs his thigh, sore from sitting so long. He hauls himself to his feet. Saying nothing, he hobbles to the end of the row. The stadium stairs skyscrape above him, and he starts up them, lifting his good leg onto each step and then swinging his prosthesis around to meet it. He is almost at the top when he pauses for breath. The inning ends, and all at once people bustle around him, moving fast with their two good legs. The stadium tilts. The sweat under Garfield's armpits turns clammy.

He feels himself fall, and then there is a sharp pain on the side of his head. He brings his hand to it and feels something sticky: blood.

"Papa?" a voice asks. "Papa? Are you OK?"

Tomas helps him sit up. Blood snakes lazily down the side of Garfield's face. Tomas presses his handkerchief to the wound.

"When I saw you fall I—"

"Someone pushed me," Garfield says. His head hurts more than anything he can remember. He'd like to punish whoever did this to him. Whoever made him seem weak, fallible. But there is no one save himself. "I'm fine."

He tries to stand and realizes his prosthetic leg is not where it should be. It has twisted around on his thigh. As Garfield manipulates it, he sees that it is broken in two, the tube freakishly hollow inside. Tomas hands him the lower half.

"Fuck," Garfield swears. There is no way he can move now. Legless, crutchless, he is like a baby, completely dependent on others. Tomas extends a hand, and Garfield groans as he takes it. He has bruised his back as well as his head, and his limbs feel tender as though he's spent the day cutting bulls. Garfield's humiliation and ire grow with each step.

That night, he insists that Sophie take the children to the cinema. He will stay in, attend to some business. That business, Sophie knows, will be Garfield canning up his rage, sealing it up in some private place and letting it fester. He will never admit his pain or frustration, just shove it down deeper until it joins the tumor of rancor that is growing inside him. She closes the door to their hotel room and rests her forehead against it for a minute. The children call her from the elevator. This event might conclude it, she suspects, might be the proverbial final straw. It will take away whatever good remains in her husband. She can see it on his face, white with pain. She debates going back inside, then taps the doorframe with her hand as though smoothing a child's blanket and walks down the gilded hall.

This morning, it's his hip. Every day it is something, arthritis in his knees or pains in his back or soreness in his shoulders. But this morning there are dull aches radiating from the place where his leg meets his torso, as though the ball has popped out of its socket. Moshe takes an aspirin.

He shuffles around the store, straightening clothes, marveling again, as he does daily, over the new electronics section. Radios as small as bread-boxes, hand-cranked phonographs and records to play on them, waltzes and ballads and something new: this Charleston dance that makes the kids look like chickens bobbing for grain.

It seems abruptly as though the world has started to spin faster. It is nearly a new decade: 1930. Nothing remains of the wilderness he grew up in. The open prairies are dotted with houses and ranches, the Indi-ans safely "subdued" on their allotments. There are horseless buggies. He knows he is supposed to call them "automobiles," but the word sticks on his lips. They rule the paved streets; there are now more gas stations than blacksmiths.

The house he lives in is completely taken over. It feels like an orphan-age or a reformatory with all the children running around underfoot, the crying and screaming and strewn toys and maids and nannies and family members running after them. Sophie and Garfield fight over the smallest thing: birds dueling over a worm. The house is in constant uproar.

He doesn't understand how Dora puts up with it. Sophie treats her like a servant. Why doesn't Dora get fed up? Why doesn't she leave? What ties her to the house, to Garfield? There is nothing as complicated as the hu-man mind, Moshe thinks.

The world is getting cloudy at the edges—things that should not be small are getting smaller; things that should be visible are now hidden. Moshe feels too old for this new world.

His son, he knows, would not disagree with him, though he, too, has aged significantly. Garfield's hair is going gray at the temples and thinning on top. He smokes heavily and has a cough to match, a rasping dry hack that drives his wife crazy. Garfield keeps the store open so that Moshe will have something to do. Moshe knows this and is grateful. It does keep his mind off things, keeps him occupied. And the store still serves a purpose in town. They could sell it off, he knows. They could all live forever on the money Garfield has amassed. But Moshe doesn't want to live forever.

If Rika were alive, she would help him keep busy. She, after all her years of hard work, would know how to enjoy the "twilight" of her life. She'd play with the grandchildren and weed the garden and draw salt baths for Moshe's aching feet. It was she who knew how to make do, she who held the family—and the town—together during the war years.

It was harder, almost, for the men who stayed behind. They were somehow less than men because of it. Moshe was too old; Garfield was exempted for his leg, Irwin for his injury, and Sten because of his lungs. The family survived it, intact, whereas so many lost their sons. And then those who survived the war fell victim to the influenza that followed. Outside his bedroom hangs Moshe's gallery of loss: photos of Rika, Sten, and Annika's baby boy, Melvin.

First Moshe got the flu, so sick that they broke the quarantine to say good-bye to him. Moshe thought he had already died when he saw the faces of his loved ones gathered around the bed, wearing expressions of worry and grief. And then one morning he woke; the fever had lifted, but by then Rika had already passed, and Sten followed her the next week. Melvin lasted a little longer, and they buried him next to Sten—so many freshly dug holes that it looked more like the site of a prospect than a graveyard.

But Moshe doesn't want to dwell on tragedy. Marira is coming to visit soon, bringing her children for the summer. Then the house will be filled with tiny voices—Garfield's five children, Annika's two, and Marira's three. Moshe will have to write their names down so he can remember who they all are. "You there," is the name he calls most of them. Melvin, his namesake, was the only one he could remember.

The other sad part about growing old is seeing your contemporaries die, thinks Moshe. Though he and J. R. from across the stream were never good friends, Moshe still felt sorry for his wife when they brought his body back to her, pocked with bullets like measles spots. And then Irwin's father, who, like his son, was injured by a horse; it dragged him miles after his foot caught in the stirrup. And the others, the original citizens of the town who succumbed to consumption, malaria, heart failure, liquor, fighting, or just bad luck. There are too many to count.

The door opens now, and the buzzer that Moshe hates, installed at Garfield's insistence, signals an entrance. Annika says her warped hello. She rushes to him and kisses his cheek, tickling him. She swats him on the back and takes a basket, going around the shelves and straightening as much as shopping.

She smiles and laughs readily, but something darker lurks behind her veneer of playfulness. Moshe saw it at Melvin's funeral, when he was barely able to stand for weakness. Her face was expressionless, but the sadness beneath it was almost unbearable. Sometimes, when she thinks no one is looking, Moshe sees that face emerge, and it breaks his heart all over again. She never lets on. She goes on with her life, making clothing and keeping house, raising two children with a damaged husband without complaint.

Moshe writes down her purchases slowly; he doesn't want her to leave. As he enters the last line—hair tonic, 75¢—she puts her hand on his and squeezes. It hurts, a little; the knuckles are swollen and sensitive, but he appreciates the touch, and he leans over to kiss her hand. She smiles and walks quickly out of the store.

Moshe wishes Owenasa had not gotten so large. In other towns in the Territory—no, the *State*, he reminds himself—children come home for lunch so they can get a proper midday meal with their parents. Now Moshe's grandchildren travel by streetcar to the other side of town to a school that looks like a prison, in Moshe's opinion. He slumps into his chair behind the counter. It's true what they say, that old age is return to infancy—the world works in ways Moshe cannot understand. The difference between the two states is the knowledge that eventually a child will catch up, whereas Moshe knows he has already missed the proverbial train.

It's late, and the figures are swimming before Moshe's eyes. They squirm like worms in a bait can, wriggling out of reach before he can catch them with his pen. He rubs his eyes; lately he has been seeing double or not at all. Now the figures retreat, hiding in pools of meaningless ink.

There is not much work to do tonight. The shelves are straight and dusted, the inventory taken, the ordering complete. Invoices have been drawn and distributed; there is no need to make sure the ledgers are current— they have a bookkeeper for that now. No, he is not needed, Moshe thinks, except as a memory nobody wants.

So he simply sits in the store, his refuge. He has lit only one candle. The store has electricity, of course, but Moshe prefers the flickering light.

Then he is on the floor on his back. There is a great weight on his chest, and he searches his mind to see what it could be. He realizes that the weight is coming from inside, and then the pain hits harder than anything he's ever felt.

The world around him is black; his body is spinning, falling. He reaches out to grab hold of something solid and finds the table leg. When he grasps it, it begins to shake. The candle falls off the edge.

Inside the flame Moshe sees Alice. He is surprised; he thinks of her less and less often these days. Yet here she is, in her flowing white nightgown, her hair curled and loose. She has not aged. What he wants most, even more than he wants the incredible pain to leave his body, even as his lungs beg for air, is to reach out to her. But his arms will no longer obey him. She stands there, motionless, undisturbed even by wind, and finally Moshe breaks free of his paralysis and feels his body lurch toward her. And then there is nothing.

The candle hits the ground hard, dislodging the wax from its holder. The flame licks the wood floor, searches blindly for something to light, and, finding nothing, is extinguished.

Garfield's eldest daughter, Dalia, finds him the following morning. Her breath catches in her throat; she sits down and weeps quietly. Then she rearranges his limbs into a dignified repose. She rights the candle and removes the pen from Moshe's inert hand. If Moshe could see her, he would be proud of the way she knows what to do, how comfortable she is in her surroundings. He would be glad of her confidence that this store, this town, this land—an assurance never shared by her father or grandfather— is her home.

PART 7

Staring into the Past
1935–1937

20

arfield picks up the fallen ledger and, light-headed, rights himself. He sets it on the desk and hobbles back to the counter. He has the latest prosthesis, but he has readopted the crutch as well for better balance. Dalia is sweeping the back of the store, singing "Jump, Jump Jim Crow."

"Stop it," Garfield says, cross.

"Why, Daddy?"

Garfield doesn't answer her.

"I heard it on the radio." She continues to sing softly, switching to "Poor Paddy Works the Railroad."

"Don't sing that anymore, please."

"Then what should I sing?"

"How about you don't sing at all?" Garfield turns on the radio. He sits on the high stool and puts his elbows on the counter, resting his chin in his hands.

"Move your foot, Daddy." Dalia sweeps around his stool.

An announcer's deep voice intones: "Will we hear the great rumble of our collective stomach?"

Garfield spins on his stool, but she has gone around the counter to the front of the store. From his perch, Garfield can see out the back door all the way to the molasses drip of the creek in its bed.

The announcer continues: "Will we let them call us Okies? Will we let them grind us down, drive us out?"

A gaunt figure appears in the back door. His boots are held together with twine, and his overalls hang loosely from his shoulders.

Garfield stands. The man is heads taller so that Garfield has to shade his eyes from the sun as he looks up. "We don't give," he says. "This ain't the government. We buy or sell."

"I don't got much worth selling, 'cept my back. Maybe you'll need a little help, the leg and all."

Garfield's face turns into a scowl.

"I'm a vet, too," the man says. "Northern France. Twenty-third Regiment."

"I don't need your help," Garfield says. Being reminded of his exemption from the Great War makes him even more cross. "You can go elsewhere."

"I been elsewhere," the man insists. He sits down in the soil. "This here is elsewhere."

From behind him Garfield can feel movement; Dalia hands the man a can of beans. He clasps it as though it were a gold bar and puts it in his large pocket. The can looks bigger than his thigh.

"Could you move the shelves so I can sweep behind 'em?" she asks.

"Gladly." The man speaks to Dalia, ignoring her father. They both push past Garfield into the store. The wind is picking up again. Sometimes Garfield thinks that the wind will drive them all mad with its persistence. At night, he removes what seem like buckets of sand from his ears.

The man emerges, carrying an overflowing dust pail that he dumps into the ditch. Futile, Garfield thinks; she'll be sweeping it out again tomorrow. The three of them meet just inside the door, the dark hallway a shock after the insistent sun. Dalia pulls Garfield's sleeve, then stands on tiptoes to speak a stage whisper into his ear.

"Can't he stay in here tonight?"

Before Garfield can answer no, the man says, "Oh, I don't like to sleep indoors none. It gives me the all-overs. You've been plenty kind, thank you."

"Well, c'mon in for supper then," Dalia says. Garfield purses his lips. His home is not a Ladies' Aid Society, and his daughter does not run the household.

"Thank you, miss, sir. Y'all're real kind."

Garfield locks the store and follows them to the house. Dalia's excited hops look like his own lumbering. The man walks straight, back rigid. He must have once been something, Garfield thinks. Oklahoma is full of people who were once something and are now indistinguishable from the dust and the wind.

Even Garfield's circumstances are diminished. Though the family is far better off than most of the state—most of the country, even—the desiccation of the oil wells and the collapse of the banks hit him hard. They've had to cut back drastically.

The man showers in the old ranch bunk, and Garfield asks the maid to bring him some clothes and a razor. She returns, blushing. When the bell rings to bring everyone to the table, the man is clean-shaven. He looks fuller without the grime emphasizing the hollowness of his cheeks. And he is handsome, even dressed in Garfield's clothes, the hems and sleeves of which end halfway down the man's limbs. He introduces himself as William Driscoll, but people call him Buddy. Garfield shakes his hand.

The man eats as though his stomach were an empty vault, packing it away in his cheeks like a chipmunk. He grins between swallows, sips milk as though it were brandy.

When the meal is through, Buddy sits back and reins in a belch. Sophie finally turns to address him. "What brings you to Owenasa, Mr. Driscoll?"

"I'm a little down on my luck." Buddy leans toward her. "I'm a trained silversmith, but nobody has a need for silver now. Nobody has a need for nothing that can't be ate. I was making my way out West, you know, maybe Californians got some silver there, or Colorado, I don't know. But it beats starving to death doing nothing."

Sophie nods.

"I thank you for this meal," Buddy says. "And the shower and the loan of the clothes and the kindness. I'll just change and be off then."

"Before you go, Mr. Driscoll," Sophie says, ignoring her husband's narrowing eyes, "do you think you could pound out a few dents in the service? It's from Europe. I don't trust anyone around here with it. No one here appreciates the delicacy."

"Surely!" Buddy stands up, eager to be of service. "Yes, ma'am. If there's anything I can do, I can do that. If you've got a hammer and maybe a polishing cloth, I'll have the service looking better than when it came to you."

"Thank you," Sophie says. She looks him right in the eyes. "That'd be a big help. Clara will show you where everything is."

In bed that night, with Buddy Driscoll bedded down in the yard near the ranch bunk, Sophie can't stop talking about him. "Did you know he knows all about German decorative arts?"

Garfield grunts.

"He knew where my grandmother's silver came from, the house that designed it, the patterns and swirls. All of it."

"Did he say how much it was worth?"

"It's not about that," Sophie sighs. "He's smart. We'd do well to employ him."

"We don't need employees. It's all we can do to keep the store running. Unless we find a new gusher."

"It's dryer than the Mojave out there. You heard the geologist."

"They don't know everything." Garfield isn't sure what the Mojave is.

"And you do." She pauses. "All I'm saying is a man like that might be useful. Just put that in your pipe and smoke it."

In the morning, the telephone rings at the store. Garfield knows it must be Plumbly; though the lines have been installed for several years, few in town have a private phone. If anyone wants to make a call, he comes to the store and makes an appointment with the long-distance operator.

"Hello, Plumbly," Garfield answers.

"Y'all got any Mason jars in the store?" Garfield can hear Eloween in the background: "Ain't you gonna say good morning?"

"Good morning," Plumbly adds.

"Good morning. We got Mason jars."

"Do you think you could have your boy run them up? We're a little busy here with the preserving."

"We?" Garfield asks.

"Well, yeah, you see, I'm in a little trouble with the missus, and I promised to help . . . Shit, can't you just bring up the jars without making fun of a man?" Eloween demands an apology for the foul language. "All right, I'm sorry. Good Lord . . . I'm sorry for that, too."

Garfield hangs up. He hobbles over to the house and yells from the entryway, "Tomas!"

Sophie rushes out of the drawing room. "Don't you dare walk in here with your dirty shoes and cane," she warns. "And Tomas is at school today."

Garfield says, "I have an errand for him. Plumbly wants some jars delivered."

"I heard he's got kitchen duty," Sophie says. "In town Eloween was saying she was so angry she was fit to leave him, and he begged her what could he do and she said, 'Well, it's fall, you could do the preserving,' and he said yes." Sophie waits for a response. When there is none, she says, "Why don't you ask Buddy to go?"

"Buddy?" Garfield asks. The name rings no bells. "Oh, Mr. Driscoll. I don't want to trust him with the team. Plus he doesn't know where he's going."

"We'll send Dalia with him. She has a half day today."

Garfield has run out of arguments. He returns to the store. The morning is cloudy with dust. There is a small line outside the front door—disheveled farmers, a couple of Indians—they all line up at the counter as though at the bank. No one has anything to purchase.

"Yes?" Garfield asks.

"I got no money, Mr. Harris. We got nothing. I was just wanting some potatoes so the family don't go hungry."

There is a general murmur from the half dozen people assembled. "Just want some beans . . . a little tobacco . . . some flour for bread."

"I don't give credit," Garfield says. "Times being what they are."

"Can I trade you for something?" An older farmer holds out a pocket watch. It is gold, or gilded; Garfield can hear the mechanism ticking loudly. Certainly it'd be worth a few potatoes.

"All right," he says. And with this transaction, Haurowitz Sundry returns to a primitive barter system. By evening, when Plumbly calls to thank Garfield and remark on the professionalism of his delivery services, Garfield has accrued the watch, a brooch, a small oil painting, and a waffle iron in exchange for some meager supplies. This, then, is how he'll make money during these lean times. He'll exchange groceries for heirlooms, and when the Depression ends he'll be rich again.

After dinner, Sophie is struck with a new attack of homesickness for Germany, and they fight about Garfield's intractability. In his opinion, the idea that they would move to Germany is ludicrous. Germany is the enemy. She lost the war; she's still paying reparations for chrissakes. It's not worth discussing. In tears, Sophie runs out of the room and beds with Dora for the night. Garfield stretches out across the cool sheets; he can hear Buddy Driscoll whistling in the yard.

How did Garfield become someone who waits for others, he wonders? In the store, the shades pulled down low, he sits on the stool and rubs his stump. Buddy should be here by now. Though there are a million things that might have detained him, they had arranged to meet at 4:00 p.m., and here it is almost 5:00 p.m. and the store is quieter than a church on Monday. This is Buddy's third round in the county surrounding Owenasa. Plumbly's request gave Garfield the idea: What if Buddy ran a traveling store? A sort of peddler, except that Buddy would return to Garfield's shop to restock. Garfield gave him instructions to trade for whatever might be of value. So far he has returned with stoves and jewelry, typewriters and radios. After both circuits, Garfield chided him for giving away too much for too little, and he tossed a number of worthless items into the dry bed of what used to be Fiddler's Creek.

All he hears is how wonderful Buddy is, how kind, how fair, how charming. Sophie goes on and on about it like a human katydid. Even Dora seems susceptible to his charms. Her eyes water for Buddy's tales of his experiences overseas. It's as though Buddy is rubbing Garfield's nose in it, the fact that Garfield didn't go to war, couldn't go to war.

But now here is the telltale rumbling of the approaching wagon. He hears Buddy call, "Whoa," and the thud of his boots hitting the ground. "Ho, there, Mr. Harris." He opens the door.

"How," Garfield says, sarcastically affecting an Indian hello.

"Had a good trip this time, Mr. H," Buddy says. When there is no response, he repeats, "Good trip."

Garfield walks past him, out into the dregs of dusk. He looks at the wagon, piled high with junk. Junk and more junk. Garfield has become a garbage man, picking through refuse for things of value that others have discarded. He feels the bile rise as a wave of self-loathing. The wagon seems threatening, as though the trash will dislodge and fall on him, covering him with the scent of others' desperation.

He takes his cane and begins to beat the teetering load with it, ignoring the whinnying of the horses still hitched. Things begin to fall off—pots, pans, irons, brooms—and Buddy comes running to his side.

"Hey!" He tries to pull Garfield off, but Garfield is surprisingly strong. "Now stop that, stop it."

Garfield turns and begins to hit Buddy now. He is too close to the man, so most of his blows fall on Buddy's back and arms, and not on his face and head. He would like to see the man bleeding in the dirt. Any man would do, but Buddy is here, and Garfield is trying to split his skull.

Finally Buddy wrenches the cane away. He hits Garfield once, and Garfield drops to the ground unconscious. "Goddammit," Buddy swears, swinging his arm to shake the pain from his hand. "What you made me do."

He hoists Garfield onto his shoulder, takes him inside, and sits him down, leaning against the counter. Then he goes back outside and calms the horses, takes them around to the watering trough in back. He begins to unload, bringing the lighter items in. He'll get Tomas to help with the rest later tonight.

When he goes inside he sees that Garfield's awake. "You all right?" he asks.

"Go away," Garfield says. "Go away to a place so far I never have to see you again." Buddy merely nods and goes into the house, where he washes his hands for dinner.

* * *

Garfield stays in bed. His symptoms are nebulous. Things hurt, old injuries are inflamed, he has grippe, a low-grade fever. Dora comes into his room at regular intervals to empty the bedpan and try to force a little more soup down his throat. She ignores his insults and snide remarks.

"Get out," he says. "I want to be alone."

Dora's love is different than it used to be. It has grown less ardent with the years, but deeper, as though it has burrowed to someplace more essential in her body. It is a love that requires no response, almost like a love for God. Therefore she is not jealous when she thinks of Sophie and Garfield together. Nor does she think about marriage herself. She is married to Garfield the way a nun is married to Christ. He and his family are everything. He has kept her secret like he promised, and for this she is devoted to him.

She has ceased to have any perspective where Garfield is concerned. She looks at his unshaven face and sees no wrinkles of time. She can no longer smell him. His sweat doesn't affect her. Neither does his waste. It is merely a part of him. She lives for the moments when he opens his eyes and smiles at her for an instant before remembering to replace it with his scowl.

Sometimes she comes in and he is sleeping, mumbling. She wonders what he dreams about. Moshe told her once that Jews don't believe in heaven. If that's true, then where is Moshe now? Where does Garfield dream he is? Do Jews believe in dreams?

He is not dying; this she knows. He does not have enough sickness to die. But he is not living, either. He is hiding. Dora is not sure what he is hiding from, and she doesn't have the courage to ask. He lies under the covers shivering, eyes closed, arms folded. One day, she suspects, he will come downstairs and demand his breakfast. This day will be soon, she hopes.

And then it arrives. Garfield gets up on a cold day a month before Christmas and dresses himself. He clomps downstairs and reads the newspaper in front of the fire. His children, returning from school, stop laughing and roughhousing when they see him. They tiptoe around him and go up to their rooms. When the bell rings for dinner he stands up, folds the paper, and makes his way to the table. It is set for nine, but when the five children, Dora, and Garfield sit down, there are two place settings left.

"Where's your mama?" Garfield asks.

"She's gone for the afternoon," says Dalia.

"With Mr. Driscoll," Mina says.

All movement at the table stops. "Shhh," whispers Dalia.

"What did you say?" Garfield asks Mina.

She doesn't respond, and Garfield doesn't expect her to. He's heard what she said. "Where?" He breathes through clenched teeth. When no one answers, he bangs his hand on the table. The silverware jumps. "Where is my wife?" he demands.

Tomas looks up at him. "Traveling," he says, nonchalantly. "Please pass the meat."

Garfield grabs Tomas's outstretched hand and squeezes. "How long has this been going on?"

"Ow, Pa," Tomas says. His eyes well. "Let go."

Dora says, "It's been a month or so they've been doing the rounds together."

Garfield clearly doesn't believe this euphemism. "And you knew?" Garfield lets go of Tomas and turns to Dora. "You knew and you didn't say anything? Goddammit! All of you. Goddamn y'all to hell." Garfield imagines his wife entwined with Buddy Driscoll, enveloped in his long arms and his two good legs. He is inflamed, his limbs flail; he no longer has control over himself. Years of anger, rage, and hurt flood out of him.

Garfield yanks the tablecloth. Dishes tumble to the floor and break. The soup tureen tips and spills split pea down the center of the table in rivulets, like the intestines of a cow left to rot in the sun. All the children stand up in shock.

"Fuck!" He grabs the underside of the table and tosses it with all his might. Everything ends up in a ruined pile on the floor. The children begin to cry.

Dora takes a step forward, and Garfield slaps her. "It's your fault. You taught Sophie this." In his voice he can hear the echoes of Fritz's frustrated tirades, his poisonous vituperations.

Dora sobs. She makes sounds that don't qualify as words.

Garfield leans close, grabbing Dora's hair at the nape to pull her head back. "All these years I've kept your secret, you whore. All these years I told no one that your sister is married to the father of your baby. I've lived with the image of you and that disgusting retard smearing each other with spit in the woods. You're no better than a two-bit hussy."

Dora's sobs stop. "No," she whispers. "No."

"I kept your secret, and for what?" Garfield says. He releases her hair and with one swift motion backhands her across the cheek. It glows red.

"What goddamn good did it do me?" He slaps her a third time and throws her against the edge of the table so that she doubles over.

Dimly, he hears the children gasp behind him, Alice's small whimper. He could vomit from what he has done. Dora stays folded over the table. Garfield bends for his crutch and notices the spilled bowl of soup, its contents lumpy, and then he does vomit, which makes him feel slightly better. His blood quiets.

As he stands up, he pauses, but what can he say? An immense sorrow overcomes him, stronger even than the anger he felt a moment before. He knows he has irreparably altered all their lives. He has broken his promise to Dora. He has destroyed her love for him as surely as his wife has destroyed his trust. More important, he has betrayed his vow to protect Annika from the news. In a town this small, it will all come out, as surely as if he'd painted a sign on the side of the courthouse. It has all ended, as everything has for Garfield, in rancor, unhappiness, and violence. Garfield lets one tear squeeze out, the first he's cried in thirty years, before regaining control, shutting off his emotions completely.

Dora stands up and grips her skirt in her hands, using it to dry her face. Her cheek is hot from Garfield's slap. It throbs as though she has been burned, and she can feel the tender bruises starting where his knuckles made contact.

The event feels too large to comprehend. She walks into the kitchen, where she begins to wash the pots absently. The maid must have heard the ruckus and fled. Maybe she has gone to hide in the pantry. Dora herself has sought shelter there on occasions when Sophie and Garfield argue. It is small and close and smells of old potatoes, a soothing earthy smell.

The water rushes over her hands, and she feels a heavy sense of loss. Her secret is no longer hers. It is out, like a dried dandelion on a windy day, dispersed. She knows the children will tell Sophie and Annika. She could run to them, if she wanted to, swear them to secrecy, ply them with sweets. Perhaps that would work. But it's not important. The hidden knowledge, the one thing she cherished as hers to keep, is gone. She has built her life around guarding it; it has kept her company at night when the hot-water bottle she has brought to bed fades to cold. And now she has nothing. Nothing to tie her to Garfield. It's amazing how something she has held onto so ardently for so long can disappear in one violent instant.

She begins to scrub the soup pot, elbows deep in the suds. Her knees are wobbly; they start to buckle, and she wills them straight. It is then that the unnatural quiet dawns on her. There are no children's footsteps overhead, no one yelling for favors or help, no demands. It is blissfully quiet, and she would do anything to prolong this space, her arms in warm water, before she is confronted with all that has happened to her, the ruin of her life.

When Sophie returns that afternoon, it is immediately obvious that something is wrong. The house smells of overcooked vegetables. The silence is profound: There is no noise from the phonograph or the radio, the children or her husband. The store was closed, she noticed when Buddy dropped her off on his way to unhitch the team. Sophie looks into the dining room and draws a sharp breath in as she sees the disarray. "Children?" she calls up the stairs. "Garfield? Tomas?"

The children come down like boulders cut loose from a cliff. "Mama, Mama." They are all talking at once, except for Tomas, who is stubbornly silent. The younger ones are in tears.

Sophie pieces together the story; Garfield has found out she was with Buddy. He said awful things about Dora. He hit her and destroyed the dining room. The children are afraid. Her ribcage feels too small for her heart. She soothes the children, tells them it will be all right. If only she herself were so sure of the outcome. She sends them to their rooms and stands in the dining room gathering courage to face her husband. Smashed dishes lie in a heap, bits of food clinging like bugs. Sophie sees her future in the broken shards and chips, her life as shapeless as the puddle of soup on the floor. She hears his uneven footsteps descending the stairs.

Sophie has expected violence—planned on it, in fact—but the vehemence and suddenness surprises her. He hits her once; his ring thuds against her cheek. It hurts so much it doesn't really hurt. She feels merely an echo of the pain. Her mouth, when she opens it to breathe, since her nose doesn't seem to be drawing in air, drips blood, and she spits out a tooth.

He falls away slightly, and Sophie grabs at his peg leg, dislodging it from his stump. And now it is a weapon; she swings it back and forth, a bludgeon.

He seems to glide toward her, as though the prosthesis has been making him limp these many years, and now that it is off he can walk smoothly again. He is there before she can react. He is holding something—the old candelabrum that has sat on the mantel all these years. He smashes her across the face with it. The pain is sharp, bright.

And then he is pulled off her as though by a tornado, hurtled back against the far wall. Buddy is there, pummeling him with closed fists in the chest and stomach. Garfield seems held up only by those punches. His breath exhales as a humid whine. "This is between my wife and me," Garfield spits. "Get the fuck out of here."

"I ain't gonna stand by and watch you beat a woman, even if she is your wife."

Sophie tries to stand, but the room is turning circles around her and she sits back down. She is aware of someone crying in the kitchen. "Buddy," she says softly. When he doesn't seem to hear, she says his name again, louder.

He pauses mid-punch.

"Just go," she says. "It's all right, just go . . . away."

He stares at her, slack-jawed. Garfield takes advantage of his lapse of concentration and uppercuts his jaw, slamming his mouth shut. Buddy returns the blow, dropping his adversary to the floor, where he stays, crumpled.

"Goddamn," Buddy swears. "Goddamn." He pivots and leaves, slamming the door behind him.

Sophie is aware, in the silence that settles now, that the fighting has stopped, that someone is standing over her. Instinctively she covers her head, but the figure moves behind her, and the hands that slide under her armpits to pick her up are soft and strong. Dora's hands.

In the kitchen, Dora wipes Sophie's face. The cloth comes away bloody.

"Maybe we'll have to sew it."

Sophie groans. She opens her eyes, and only then does she register that Dora's face is red and swollen like a cow's udder. "You, too?" she asks. She doesn't even wait for Dora's nod before she says, "That son of a bitch."

Dora wrings the cloth again. "I just wanted him to notice," Sophie says. "It was nothing with Buddy. I would have stayed with him." Sophie's eyes begin to fill with tears. "He was my husband," she says. "I would have stayed . . ."

"I know."

Sophie pats her hand. "I'm going back to Chicago," she says. "You should come."

"Oh, I—," Dora protests.

"If you don't want any more of this," she strokes Dora's face lightly, "then you'd better come with us."

Dora considers. For as long as she can remember, her life has been about Garfield. About looking for him, about finding him, and then about being near him, making a life with him in whatever way he would let her. What would her life be now, without him?

What would it be like to move to Chicago? It will be cold there, she knows from attending Marira's wedding. But she can be close to Marira and her children (Dora's grandchildren!). She could dote and knit and sing Swedish songs to them. When she thinks about it, does she have a choice? She might as well go pack. She nods at Sophie, who is weeping silently. And then her gaze drifts to the door, where Garfield is watching them. He is still holding the candelabrum, its base shiny with blood. Dora reaches down and draws Sophie to her chest, cradling the woman's sobbing form. She continues to stare into Garfield's brown eyes until, unable to look any longer, he is the one who turns away.

21

arfield listens to the radio. He listens all day, to whatever stations he can find—news, baseball, music. One day he finds a station at the end of the dial playing that new jazz, and he listens to the Negroes as they scat up and down the scale. Then there is a woman vocalist who seems to be singing about Garfield himself. About the weighty cloud he is lost in all the time, about the nostalgia that hits him unawares like a blow from an assailant, the anxious flutter of the long day ahead. The singer calls it loneliness, and finally Garfield can give it a name, though he is too embarrassed ever to say it out loud. Garfield has lost his wife and children, even Dora's love, which he thought was as constant as the sun, and he is lonely.

Each morning he drags himself down the stairs, where he lights the stove and puts the kettle on for coffee. He takes out the remains of yesterday's dinner—a few cold rolls—and eats them quickly with bacon fat. Then he trudges across the yard to the store, pulling up the shades and turning the sign to "Open." He rarely bothers with the prosthesis; he moves just as well with the crutch. He lets his pants leg hang empty.

Opening the store is futile, though. No one has any money to shop. The safe in the back is filled with the townspeople's jewelry and possessions, and still most of them are going hungry. It is a bad time to be an Okie, Garfield thinks. Most would be better off declaring themselves Indians; then they'd have the government subsidy, meager though it is. Pride prevents most of them from claiming Native heritage, for almost everybody, if he is native to Oklahoma, is a mix of Indian, white, and Negro blood.

When the door opens it is invariably a farmer who has driven his emaciated team to Garfield's store to beg provisions. Garfield has hardened his heart to these pleas. He refuses to listen to the farmers beg.

"Goddamn kike," a drunk yells from outside the tavern.

"Usurer!" a woman screams from her kitchen window.

"May God help you," says another, gathering her children close.

Garfield no longer goes out on the street.

Another daily visitor is Annika, bringing Garfield his dinner. She has grown older, a little stout, her hair tinged with gray. She is uncomplaining, or at least smiling. Her contentment is infectious, and he feels the tightness in his chest lift. She doesn't stay long—she is planning her daughter Mary's wedding—but she leaves more than Garfield can eat, and he tries to keep her in the store as long as he can.

He isn't sure if the rumor that she is married to her niece's father ever got back to her. She seems all-knowing, yet he realizes how cut off she is. If she does know, it would be like her to never say anything, to accept it as one more fact about the world, like drought or influenza. Though he delights in her presence, every time he sees her he feels a twinge of shame, humiliated that he has failed her so drastically.

Today the door opens and the buzzer sounds, signaling someone come to beg, or to buy a half cup of flour with a few coins. A man steps in, takes off his hat, holding it in both hands. He seems old, but it's hard to tell. In the dust, all men look old. Corrupted by hunger, all look wrinkled.

This man tilts his head up at the ceiling as though inside a cathedral. He scrapes his toe along the wood floor. He runs his hands along the glass cabinets as he walks. When he reaches the counter he stops, puts his hat down. A small cloud of dirt rises in a circle. "Well, lookit you," he says.

"You're looking at me," Garfield says.

"Wouldn't hardly recognize you . . ."

"Do I know you?" Garfield asks.

"Sure," the man says. "I'm Fritz."

Garfield looks up from his ledger. "Fritz?" And then in the shadows of the store he can recognize Annika's nose, Dora's chin, and Sten's tall, gaunt frame. Before he knows what he's doing, he sticks his hand out and grabs Fritz's, patting him on the arm.

"It's all so different here," Fritz says. "How's your pa?"

"Passed on," Garfield says.

"Oh." Fritz looks at the ground. "I was going to . . . And Rika?"

"Dead, too. With Sten and one of Annika's, of the flu."

"Oh," Fritz says again into his shirt. He lifts up one wrinkled hand and runs it through his hair.

Garfield feels bad to have delivered this news. "You want some lunch?" he asks, surprising himself.

"Sure." Fritz's face brightens.

"Come along to the house then. Won't be much."

As Fritz steps around he sees Garfield's leg. He does nothing more than nod to acknowledge it, and for this Garfield feels an overwhelming gratitude. It is as though Annika were here, the same parting of the clouds.

They walk to the house, but before they go in, Fritz asks to stop and see the mill. In the intervening years his Swedish accent has all but disappeared, evident only in the long vowels, and even this drawl could be mistaken for a midwesterner's flat speech. Garfield undoes the lock and swings open the door. Fritz steps inside, his head so far back Garfield is afraid it will fall off his thin neck. They've done little to maintain it. The catwalk that used to wind around its crown is rotted away, and the roof has parted in places to reveal thin slats of sky.

"Praises be," Fritz says.

They step outside, and Garfield relocks the door. "I've gotten religion," Fritz says. "The Salvies finally got to me. I was sitting in the meeting one night—you know, they make you go to the meeting if you're getting food or spending the night there, and there He was."

"Who?" Garfield asks.

"Jesus Christ. And right there I repented. I come back to make amends before I die."

"Are you dying?" Garfield asks.

"My liver. Now I have to take my booze regular as tonic or I get the shakes. You happen to have some?"

"Half a bottle of scotch."

Fritz sits at the kitchen table like a gossipy old woman while Garfield makes lunch. Garfield tells Fritz about his family as he fries bacon. As he sets syrup on the table, Fritz prattles on and on about the wonderful works of Jesus. "You see the light yet, Garfield? Cause if you ain't saved you can't get to heaven. It's a simple equation, like what goes up must come down."

"I don't know about heaven." Garfield takes a bite of bacon, chases it with a biscuit. The can of beans sizzles on the stove.

Garfield notices that Fritz has barely touched his food. For someone so thin, he seems little concerned with eating. Garfield watches his hands, gesticulating wildly, trembling with the effort.

"You got that scotch?" Fritz asks.

Garfield sets it on the table with two glasses. Fritz pours unsteadily, spilling on the table. Then he lifts the bottle to his lips and swallows it in three gulps.

"Hey," Garfield says.

Fritz puts his head in his arms. There is a lull during which Garfield wonders if Fritz has died, or fallen asleep. Then Fritz looks up and says, "See? All better." He holds out a steadier hand. Then he stands up and counts five paces. He kneels, knocks on the floor once, then again on a different board. "Aha," he says, and crooks his fingernail into the groove between planks, pulling the floor up. Inside, there is a small hollow with three dusty bottles of clear liquid.

Garfield lets a smile run over his lips. Fritz catches it and opens his mouth to laugh, and then the two men are in hysterics, doubled over. When it finally subsides, Garfield has to wipe his eyes. "I forgot about that. I wish I'd known that was there."

There is a pause. Garfield asks, "Where are you staying?"

Fritz looks around him, as though his bed might be there somewhere behind him, hidden as a prank when his back was turned. "I don't think I got too long," Fritz says. "Salvie doc told me three months, tops."

"You can stay here, I suppose," Garfield says. "Have yourself a bath and lie down. Annika will come with dinner soon. I'll come get you when she gets here."

With the mention of Annika's name, Fritz's face grows a shade more ashen. "You think she'll see me?" he asks.

"She can't hear you," Garfield says, attempting a joke.

Fritz nods as though this is a nugget of wisdom.

On his way back to the store, Garfield thinks about what he has just done. A part of him feels proud of having invited Fritz to stay. He feels a strange sense of obligation to this man, who has given him Annika and Dora, as well as the house he lives in. The least he can do is give the man a place to die. Plus, the company might be nice, now that Garfield has listened to the radio programs so much he knows them by heart.

The store seems darker than usual, emptier. There will have to be rules, Garfield thinks. The man can't prattle so much. Garfield isn't used to talking. And Fritz will have to do some of the cooking. Garfield is no one's nursemaid. He closes his eyes and has almost nodded off when the door opens. Annika runs in, signing furiously with one hand. Garfield can't see her clearly; the sun is behind her, backlighting her. When she gets to the counter and puts down the basket, he tells her to breathe.

She signs that she's sorry she's late, and tells him a story he can't follow, other than the word for dress and Mary's name, and something about white and shoes.

"Annika." He tries to interrupt her with his voice. When she doesn't respond, he waves his hands as though signaling for rescue. "I have a surprise," he signs. "In the house."

She follows him out. In his haste, he missteps on the rutted road. She reaches out to take his arm, but he bats it away. As they near the house, Garfield can hear Fritz singing: ". . . where the grapes of wrath are stored. Dum dum dum dum terrible swift sword . . ." No singing will have to be another rule. Fritz is standing in front of the fireplace, fingering the candelabrum. Beside him, Annika grows rigid. Her smile, which Garfield has thought permanent, slips slightly.

"Your father," Garfield begins to sign, but without looking at him, Annika reaches out and grabs Garfield's hands, squeezing them tight with her own to silence him. She takes a step forward, touches Fritz's shoulder. She seems so tall, or else Fritz is stooped now. He lets his head hang down while Annika examines him.

She turns to Garfield. "He's sick," she signs.

Garfield nods. "Beer," he signs back. It's not quite what he wants to say, but Annika will understand.

Fritz lifts his head. "Tell her . . ." He pauses. "Tell her . . ."

Annika lifts her hand and re-parts her father's hair, which has zigzagged over his skull. Garfield can see the patch of baldness on the pate. Then Annika pats her father's face twice, and as she turns to leave her smile is back, though Garfield can see her eyes are wet.

"No whistling," Garfield is saying. "And don't try to cook any vegetables."

"OK," Fritz says. "Should I be writing this down?"

Garfield glares at him. "And don't just take; ask first." Garfield thinks hard for a moment. Is there anything else he wanted to mention? "Is something burning?" he asks.

"Oh." Fritz turns and takes the biscuits out of the oven, fanning them with a towel. "No harm done." He takes a sip from the small bottle he keeps in his hip pocket.

"No, no, you sit." Fritz pushes on Garfield's shoulder when he tries to stand to help. "Today we are here to serve you, *monsieur.*" Fritz affects a horrible French accent.

On the table he sets crispy ham, a solid, gelatinous mass of some sort of grain, runny eggs, the burned biscuits, and a mystery dish, identifiable only by its color: green. Garfield grabs the large spoon, but Fritz stops him by taking his hand. He bows his head. "Dear Lord, thank you for this bounty we are about to receive. And thank you for redemption and bless us evermore. Amen."

Garfield clears his throat, uncomfortable. Fritz serves him some from each of the platters, except for the grain, which seems to be permanently attached to its pot. Garfield takes a small bite of ham. It does taste something like the meat he knows, but there is an odd floury flavor to it.

Fritz has served himself but doesn't pick up his fork. Instead he sips from a mug that Garfield knows contains brandy. "How's the grub?" Fritz asks. Garfield searches for the proper word, something that won't offend. "It's . . . It's . . ."

"Tastes like mud, don't it?"

"Yeah." Garfield smiles apologetically. He pushes his plate away.

"Dumbest thing I ever did in a life full of dumb things was leave my family." Fritz waits for Garfield's reaction. Garfield pretends not to have heard, gets up, and takes the dishes to the sink. "When I found Christ it was like I could see my life clearly, like I was a bird, flying over it. And I saw how empty it was. But it's too late now, body wearing out and everyone but Annika gone."

There is a silence. "You've changed," Garfield says. "You're different."

"You're not." The words are directed at the floor.

"What do you mean?"

"You're still the same stubborn spoiled summa bitch as when you were twelve."

"What do you know about it?" Garfield turns, angry.

"Plenty." Fritz turns his face up, his white-blue eyes yellowed but still arresting.

"How dare you come into my house—"

"*My* house," Fritz interjects.

"—and insult me."

"Just telling you the truth." Fritz moves past Garfield to put the kettle on. He is not afraid of Garfield. "Make you some coffee?"

"No," Garfield says sharply, turning to walk out. He wants to formulate some response, but Fritz's calmness diffuses the offense. Fritz is like all those missionary fools, he thinks, all holier-than-thou and do-as-I-say-not-as-I-do. What does Fritz know about it? What does he know about losing a leg, about having tried so hard and failed at everything, alienating everyone? About being born wrong and getting wronger with every passing year like bad preserves?

"I'll see you for supper," Fritz calls.

Garfield gnashes his teeth as the door closes, and through it he can hear Fritz sing a Swedish tune. By the time he reaches the store his aggrievement has left him. It is replaced with a deep, nagging feeling of disappointment, a knot in the bottom of his lungs. He pounds his fist on the counter and succeeds only in bruising his hand.

Today's mail includes a letter from Dalia in Chicago and a dated newspaper. The letter is routine: everyone is well; they've heard from Tomas, training to be a master mariner in Russia. Dalia is full of teenage gossip about people Garfield doesn't know.

Garfield opens the paper and reads the headlines: "Derby Corrections Dash News of Luck"; "Wheat up Seven Cents on Bad Crop Talk"; "Enid Man Found Guilty of Wife's Murder." The store is silent. On page two, something catches his eye. The Federal Food, Drug, and Insecticide Administration is cracking down on so-called tonics; snake oil salesmen are being rounded up and prosecuted. And there among the names is Napoleon Pickney. Garfield remembers the ugly, skinny schoolmaster who took his mother away. The paper says it's likely he'll do time in jail. He must be old, Garfield thinks, if it's even the same person. The knowledge that Pickney is being punished is not as satisfying as Garfield would have imagined. He hasn't even thought about the man in years.

Garfield looks up. There is a new sound—silence. The wind seems to have stopped, finally. Could it be true? He steps outside and shades his eyes. Yes, the flag on top of the post office is still, and the weather vane on the saloon roof has ceased its squeak too, an eerie change. Garfield stands for a minute, letting the stillness settle.

Fritz takes to his bed. He says his stomach is knotted and his liver has broken up into small pieces. Annika comes by once a day to change the sheets and wipe Fritz's brow, but the majority of the nursing is Garfield's responsibility. It disgusts him to have to empty chamber pots and feed soup to the weak man. It is repulsive that Fritz could show so much need.

One night, Fritz cries out. Garfield descends the stairs to see Fritz on the kitchen floor, curled up in a ball, rolling in vomit. The sickness has large chunks of a smooth, brown, spongelike substance. Garfield helps the man sit up.

"Christ, it hurts." Fritz writhes for two minutes, three, and then the pain is over and he leans back on Garfield. "I'm sorry."

"It's all right," Garfield says. He wipes his sweaty brow with a kitchen towel. He is reminded of Tallulah, how she cared for Garfield when he was sick. He remembers how her hands smoothed the covers, tucking him in. How he slept next to his mother and felt a security and peace he has never managed to re-create since. The memories sting like salt. Garfield craves a return to a life that doesn't include Fritz.

"I think I'm eliminating my liver," Fritz says, looking at the chunks on the floor.

Garfield doesn't see how that's possible. "I'll clean it up," he says.

"Not just yet. Let's just set a minute."

The men listen to the dogs calling across the prairie and the settling of the house. Fritz's heavy breath smells of sulfur. "Devil's belch" Tallulah used to call it.

Fritz says, "I retract what I said before about you being a son of a bitch."

Garfield doesn't answer. Fritz's breathing slows.

"You sure you ain't found Jesus?"

"Positive," Garfield says.

"Right." Fritz's eyes flutter. "Hebrews don't have Jesus." He gets heavier in Garfield's arms. "Maybe . . . make you an exception."

Fritz slumps back, asleep. Garfield is not strong enough to carry him to bed, but he drags him nearer the fire, puts a pillow under his head, and covers him in a blanket. Then he takes out the mop and cleans the floor. He puts a kettle on for coffee, sure that he won't be sleeping any more this night.

When Garfield wakes the next morning and finds Fritz dead, he sends a telegram to Dora, wires money so she can come down and see her father buried. He convinces himself that he is doing this as a favor to her. But he never hears back. She does not return the money, he notices.

He feels the loss in his belly, like a belt pulled too tight. He narrows his eyes and thinks about crying, but no tears come. Searching through Fritz's things, he finds only old clothes and a pipe and a well-thumbed Bible. Fritz has underlined various sections, dog-eared the pages. Garfield looks for the "dust to dust" passage but can't find it. He knows that Fritz would want him to pray, but he doesn't know what to do other than to kneel, which is impossible with one leg.

So on a windless, scorching summer day, Garfield, Annika, Irwin, and their children, Mary and Oskar, bury Fritz in the same makeshift cemetery that marks Rika's and Moshe's, Sten's and Oskar's, Melvin's and the two little girls' final resting places. Annika and Garfield sit on the front porch after the short funeral and drink mulberry wine. All land that does not belong to Garfield has sprouted houses and businesses, automobiles and sidewalks, electricity poles and telephone cables. But now that the oil wells are dry, Garfield's land has returned to its wild state. Over the long grass, wrens glide and alight. The two sit on the back porch. They are not looking at the view; they're staring into the past.

22

When the letter arrives from Annika, Dora opens it slowly. Good news, bad news, it is all the same to her. If it's good, the birth of a baby or a lucrative new commission for a dress, then Dora feels jealous. If it's bad, well, Dora's had enough bad news to last her a lifetime. The neat handwriting is recognizable even in the address; Annika's control over a pencil is remarkable.

Annika gets right to the point: Garfield is sick. He even went to Tulsa to get a second opinion because Doc Smalley is getting so old. But the results came back clear: stomach cancer. There is not much hope, Annika writes, and he's already pretty far along in his sickness. He was doubled over in pain before Annika could get him to see a doctor, and now he lies in bed counting the minutes until he can take his next dose of morphine.

Annika needs help. Irwin is a handful, and her daughter, Mary, is living next door with her new baby. And Annika has housework, not to mention her storefront. Her hands are so full they're overflowing. Garfield needs constant care. Could Dora come down to Owenasa?

Dora thinks about what ties her to Chicago. Sophie's and Marira's children are nearly grown, and Marira is too busy for her—she is running a salon. It has been made patently clear that Dora is not invited, but she has passed the ladies on her way out, and they are uniformly slim and lovely, with feathered hats and leather gloves, minks splayed across their shoulders as though the animal has simply fallen asleep there. Dora sleeps in what was built as the maid's room in the attic—ostensibly to give her more privacy but really because she is not exactly part of the family and not exactly hired help.

This in-between state is made plain when Isidore Rosen comes to call on Dalia. Dora is introduced as an aunt, but when he pushes for details,

Dalia is forced to explain that actually Dora is no blood relation. It sounds to everyone in the room as if Dora is a charity case, though Sophie is quick to say how helpful it was to have Dora around when the children were younger.

When Isi proposes, down on one knee in the living room, hair already beginning to thin on top so that glimpses of scalp reflect the lamplight, pleading brown eyes when he looks up squinting with emotion, Dalia panics.

The positives are obvious: It is a suitable match. Dalia's grandfather (Sophie's father) and Isidore Rosen's grandfather have known each other since they worked together coordinating freight on the docks of the Chicago River when they first arrived in the United States. Herr Rosen has made good for himself with his zipper factory. But the Rosens do not live ostentatiously. Like the rest of the Depression children, Isi puts money away for the next time there is not enough. He walks most places to save on gasoline; he lives at the factory to save the time and expense of commuting.

He is obviously grateful for Dalia's company. Isi holds his breath while she speaks; he buys her presents, little trinkets so as not to embarrass her: a locket, flowers, a coin purse in the shape of a dog. The family gets used to having him around.

Dora had thought she would never recover from the exposure of her secret, that the revelation would destroy her. But gradually the pain has faded, and she has reconstructed some sort of a life up North. And ultimately, does it matter if the laundry and the cooking take place in Chicago rather than Owenasa or San Bernardino? Is her life substantively any different?

Dora considers, then, going back to the only place that ever felt like home. Her first memories begin in the long boat passage from Sweden, and then there was a year of hardship and traveling, and then Oklahoma. Maybe that's where she should live out her days.

Dora feels herself softening toward Garfield as the intervening years form a buffer. Memory is tricky, maybe kind; their last, violent encounter is less vivid and less immediate to her than the time they spent together in San Bernardino, where she was sure he loved her the way she loved him. The pleasure of that thought brings a smile to her face even now, as she looks out onto the snow-covered street through the narrow garret window.

Isidore Rosen has been a perfect gentleman. Until just before he proposes to Dalia, he hasn't even tried to kiss her. In the past couple of weeks, they've done a bit more than kiss, but still, clothes stay on. Once, when Dalia tried to unbutton his trousers, he sprang back as though she had stung him and looked at her with wide, disbelieving eyes. He loves her, this much is clear.

On the other hand, Dalia has hoped for so much more. Though she is working in the typing pool at the Rosen factory, she dreams of going to college. She dreams of being an actress, a socialite. She wants to attend cotillions and belong to country clubs and dine out twice a week, and Isidore Rosen is not the man who will fulfill those dreams.

But she could do worse, she knows. She is a Jew. She is not an American. She was born here, yes, but she is not a member of the country. Protestants are members, Negroes even, but those whose parents still have accents are not fully accepted. They exist in an alternate reality, their lives parallel to, but not coinciding with, American lives. So she will marry someone from her world and not try to subvert the natural order.

At dinner, Isidore and Dalia announce their engagement. Sophie accepts the bottle of champagne that Isi has been hiding in his rolled-up jacket and struggles to open it. Dora takes it and with one deft twist pops the cork. Dalia's grandfather's face turns red with joy.

As preparations commence, Dora is superfluous. She is amazed to find herself crying, something she hasn't done for years. And once she starts she is convulsed with sobs. Her life has dwindled to this: she is unwanted, lonely, alone. Maybe she should go away. She's not sure she could stand to see Dalia, whom she has cared for since she was a baby, be married without Dora's having any part in the ceremony. Who knows if she'll even be allowed to attend the temple, a non-blood-relation, a non-Jew?

Then a telegram from Annika arrives, begging Dora. It says the magic words: He asked for you, personally. Whether it is true or not, Dora doesn't know, but it is enough to make her decision. She goes upstairs and begins to pack.

Annika's boy drops Dora at the house. It is dark inside, and Dora wonders if perhaps she is too late. She opens the door to the kitchen and sees everything neat as though it were going to be photographed in a magazine. Annika's handiwork is in this organization, as well as in the immaculately stitched curtains that let only a small piece of sunshine filter in.

Dora takes the stairs slowly. Her knee is swollen and stiff from the long train ride. She stops and rests halfway up. Her breath is loud in her ears.

Still there is no sound from upstairs. The air feels dry and old, as though she were inside a barn.

Dora turns left down the familiar hallway. Along the walls hang pictures: of Annika and her family, of Sophie and the children, of Rika and Moshe, and, most surprisingly, the picture of Dora and Garfield on their picnic in San Bernardino. Dora had had it framed, but never expected to see it displayed so prominently. Something softens in her then, and she hopes to find Garfield alive, says a quick prayer that will bring him back from the death she has imagined.

His room smells of decay, of rotting bowels and watery vomit, and Dora sucks in air through her mouth until the gag reflex stops. The room is dim. She thinks it empty until her eyes adjust, and she sees a small form under the bedcovers. He is as tiny as a child, his face gaunt and pale, his shoulders bony as though all the tissue has been sucked out of him, leaving only the skin.

"Who's there?" Garfield asks. It is more a rasp than a question.

"Dora."

"Can you get me some water?"

This is how he welcomes her back into his life, back to her home. Somehow it makes it easier for Dora that he doesn't try to bridge the distance between them. It's simpler for her to fall back into the old role. She pours a glass from the bedside pitcher and leans over him to put it to his lips.

"Will you stay awhile?" Garfield asks.

"As long as is necessary."

"Good," Garfield says, and he drifts off to sleep.

Dora goes downstairs and opens her bag. She brings the most essential items up by lifting the hem of her skirt to form a bowl. The rest she leaves downstairs for a time when her knees don't hurt so much. She goes to her old room, the one overlooking the front of the house and the store. Owenasa is unrecognizable. There are paved streets, dozens of stores and houses, a cinema, a pool hall, and another side of town, over the train tracks, where the Negroes live. She remembers, fleetingly, without being able to recollect her name, the colored woman who helped her give birth. The roads are almost obscured by billboards advertising everything from veterinarians to portraiture. There are stop signs, and even two stoplights, which means there is actual traffic.

She roots around in the kitchen and then goes over to the store, taking the key from its hook. The store is as dark as the house, the glass cases draped in white sheets, a thin layer of dust atop them like gray powdered sugar. On a shelf near the window she finds what she is looking for: a can of chicken broth. Later, as she feeds Garfield, the tenderness comes back to her. He is so diminished, so shrunken and small and so helpless that his sickness unleashes in her a flood of forgiveness.

With Annika's help, Dora cleans out the store. Behind a cabinet in the back they find a safe. Dora tries several numbers: the address of the house, Garfield's anniversary; it is Annika's birthday that finally opens it. Inside is a jumble of objects: watches, bronzed baby shoes, spoons, dishes, the old candelabrum from the mantel. These must be the things Garfield collected on barter during the Depression. What's left has little value now. Still, Dora and Annika put everything in the glass cases. When they have free time (which is code, both of them know, for when Garfield dies, which will be any day now), they will have a small sale where people can buy back their goods at a low "storage" price.

Dora and Annika discuss what will happen to the store. Annika's daughter, Mary, is married to a butcher who already has a family shop. Her son, Oskar, is enlisting in the army. Dora says she will ask if Dalia would like to come down to Owenasa, but it isn't likely, she admits. Dalia's new husband works at his father's zipper factory.

Dora and Annika clear out the accumulated merchandise and junk: canned goods past their expiration dates, archaic sewing tools and stove parts, clothes with moth holes in them. They heap these outside the store. Annika assures Dora that the poor of the town will come and take everything before sunrise, and sure enough, when Dora returns the next day the pile is down to one pair of holey socks.

Dora carries Garfield to a chair and removes the soiled sheets from the bed. As she brings them to the basket by the door, she catches sight of her reflection in the mirror. Dora sees a deformed woman grown lumpy with age. Her gray hairs wisp back against her head, and her spine is slightly curved.

"My mother . . ." Dora is surprised to hear a small voice behind her: Garfield, wheezing with exertion. "Used to stand looking at herself, too."

Dora turns. She has never heard Garfield mention his mother. She knows only that her name was Alice, and that little Alice is named after her. And now, so close to the end, another fact: Alice was vain.

"She is so beautiful," Garfield says, and Dora does not correct his use of tenses. She remakes the bed and puts Garfield back in. He is so thin now that he weighs less than a child.

Two weeks pass. Dora goes into Garfield's room to see if he needs anything. To her surprise, he is crying.

"I don't want to die, Dora."

Dora nods, unsure what to say. She sits on the edge of the bed. Garfield winces.

"Can you stay here?"

"Sure I can," she says. She pats his hand softly and turns out the light. Garfield's breathing is labored.

"I didn't . . . ," he begins. "I shouldn't have . . ."

"Shhhh," Dora says. It doesn't matter what he is trying to say. There's nothing it could change.

The next thing Dora knows it is morning. She has spent the night next to Garfield for the first time. It has been her dream for so long, yet she feels only sadness and regret. Garfield wakes feverish, delirious. He calls her "Mama," then, mysteriously, "Tallulah." He hits the air when she comes near him.

By night he has calmed down, and Dora again falls asleep next to him. In some ways, it is as she hoped it would be. The two of them are growing old together. This thought sustains her through the next week.

Eight days later the half-moon is casting dim light over Owenasa. Garfield has not spoken for three days; Dora knows it can't be much longer. Still, when she sits upright in the bed she shares with Garfield, knowing something is terribly wrong, she is devastated to find no breath, no heartbeat.

She lies awake next to him until first light. Then, still in her nightclothes, she strips him naked. There is so little of him left. The stump where his leg should be seems to have withered. She starts there, running a soapy washcloth over the body. Then she straps on his prosthesis, dresses him in his suit. She folds his hands over his chest and smooths what hair he has left across his forehead. She does not cry; she feels empty, dry. She has passed over some threshold to a place where all tears have already been shed.

She stands at the door and looks at him. She never imagined he could be so still. From the squirrelly little boy to the grimacing young man to the frustrated, wrathful adult he became, he was always active. It is odd to see him motionless. Though she is not a religious woman, she says a prayer that finally, at last, Garfield will find peace.

She makes the bed around him and then goes into her room to dress in the long black skirt and shawl she brought for this occasion. Then she walks the silent, sleepy streets to Annika's house.

Annika opens the door and puts her hand to her mouth when she sees the black clothes. She reaches for Dora's hand and takes her inside, sits her at the kitchen table. She offers Dora coffee, and Dora cups her hands around the mug as though it were for warmth and not for drinking.

Annika's husband comes down the stairs. He says hello to Dora and, sensing the mood, asks Annika what happened. Annika makes the sign for dead, closing her eyes with her fingers. Irwin immediately bursts into tears—long, racking, tired child sobs. Annika takes him into her arms, rubs his head into her chest, runs her fingers along the back of his neck.

Strangely, it is this display of intimacy, this husband and wife clinging to each other, seeking comfort in each other's arms, that brings Dora to tears. She averts her gaze as they roll down her cheeks.

23

Annika's son, Oskar, picks up Dalia and Isi at the station. He is reluctant to shake hands. "Sorry I'm such a mess. I was digging . . ."

Isi puts his hand on his wife's back to steady her, although she isn't trembling. "He should have been buried as soon as he died, according to Jewish law."

Oskar shrugs.

They climb into the car. The city is bustling; its squat storefronts and houses fight for sidewalk space. In the road are all manner of vehicles: wagons, tractors, automobiles, horses, buggies, wheelbarrows. Oskar swerves to avoid a pig and her brood, then again to miss a little boy whose ball has wandered into the street.

"Is that an Indian?" Isidore whispers. "Or a Negro?"

"Bit of both, most likely." Dalia doesn't even look where he is pointing.

The house's wood frame is just as Dalia has remembered it, no more or less wounded by winds and winters. Isi whispers to her: "This is the desert."

"This is my home."

She gives Dora a tight hug and kisses Annika on both cheeks. "Didn't Sophie come?" Dora asks. Dalia shakes her head.

Dora surveys Dalia, smart in her suit, a brooch on her lapel. She seems too elegant for her surroundings. Or perhaps the rest of them aren't elegant enough for her.

Garfield's funeral's most noticeable trait is its lack. There is no music, as no one in the family is musically inclined. Plus, what would they play? Garfield had no favorite songs, no preferred instruments. Also missing is a crowd. Letters will come, in the next week, from vendors and townspeople, expressing, if not exactly condolences, then at least an appreciation for who Garfield was, who his father was.

Plumbly, confined now to a wheelchair, arrives with his daughter. At the house, before the funeral even starts, Plumbly begins to cry. "Well shit," he says, then turns back to look at his daughter, Maura. "Don't tell me to watch my language, young lady. I think I was the only one who liked the son of a bitch. I knowed him a long time, and his father. And every one of my friends who dies means it's that much closer to my time, too. God rest your mother's soul." He pats Maura's hand.

"You there." He points at Isidore. "You'll get an old man a drink, won't you? My daughter respects this Prohabitation."

"Prohibition, Daddy."

"Whatever it's called, I need a drink."

Isidore goes to the cabinet and pours Plumbly a whiskey.

"Thank you, son," he says. "Are you one of the deaf girl's boys?"

"No, sir," says Isi, bending to Plumbly's level. "I'm Dalia's husband, Isidore."

"Hebe name, ain't it?"

"Uhh, yes, sir."

"Well, you look strong enough. You'll make it. You need to be strong to live in Oklahoma."

"I don't know if we're going to live—"

"Sure you are." Plumbly waves him closer. "Can't you see your wife wants to? Always do what the wife says. Because she's the one that makes your food and cleans your drawers. If the wife's happy, the husband's happy."

"I don't know that we'd fit in here."

"Nonsense." Plumbly pokes Isi's chest. He has more strength than Isi expects, and Isi almost topples backward from his crouch. "That's the thing about Oklahoma. You think I fit in here? You think they do?" His hand sweeps the small group assembled in the living room. "This is the land of misfits and can't-get-alongs. We got Injuns and Catholics and Hebrews and cripples and criminals and Negroes and Chinamen, and everyone hates everyone else. Don't no one fit in. Don't think you're special." Plumbly's words are starting to slur.

"That's enough now, Daddy," Maura says.

"Are you married?" Plumbly asks Isi. "My daughter, here, is—"

At that moment the rabbi clears his throat. Sophie insisted on a Jewish burial, though she didn't make the trip herself. "We go to the grave, yes?" he asks Dora in heavily accented English.

Outside, it is a beautiful day. Storm clouds are gathering in the west, but for the moment the sun is shining. The wind blows lightly, bringing the familiar mixed scent: crops and brush and horses and hay. The whir of the wind through the scraggly brush is vintage Oklahoma, too; the occasional bird call pierces the droning undertone of the breeze in the fields.

There is a hole next to Moshe's and Rika's graves, near Fritz, Sten, and the others whose names are no longer remembered. A pile of dirt sits next to it. The cottonwood tree provides shade. Distant sounds of horns and hawkers, engines and children can be faintly heard. The funeralgoers can see Fiddler's Creek, swollen with the recent rains, and its neighboring tangle of green bushes, blocking the sight of the ranch land beyond. An overgrown garden, ripe vegetables pulling the plants toward the ground, rims the house. And beyond it, just on the edge of eyesight, train tracks slide over the slight rise.

The rabbi begins the kaddish. Isi joins in, as do the handful of Jews who have come to pay respects. They sway, looking at the grave as they recite. Mary is supposed to translate for Annika, but none of the prayers is in English. Then Oskar and a hired hand lower the coffin. Her face betraying no emotion, Dora takes a handful of dirt and lets it fall through her fingers onto the wooden lid. They each take a turn dropping dirt into the hole. Then Oskar and the man shovel all the dirt back in and tamp it down as best they can. Everyone finds a small rock and places it on top of the grave. Dora crosses herself as she performs this task.

Dora realizes that she is being treated as Garfield's widow. She has made the funeral plans, has thrown the first fistful of soil on the coffin. The rabbi addresses her when he speaks. The few attendees are keeping a respectful distance. Annika takes Dora's arm as though she is delicate, fragile. Finally, in his death, Dora is married to the man she loved, a cruel irony that does not escape her.

The ceremony is brief; it finishes just before sunset. No one wants to speak. The flies are biting; the funeralgoers shift and slap. Then everyone walks back toward the house, where Dora, Annika, and Dalia have set out a small repast: meats, breads, and wine, hard-boiled eggs and salt. The rabbi touches the mezuzah on the way in, kisses his fingers. The family will wait seven days for the callers who don't come. The town itself is a eulogy, cataloguing Garfield's and Moshe's indelible handprints on Owenasa. So even though there are no speeches, the town's noises—its rumbling streets, strident shouts, slurping gutters, and the screech of the train as it passes through—sound an elegant chorus, louder and more lasting than human speech.

EPILOGUE

I sidore and Dalia will indeed stay in Oklahoma. They will add four floors to the store and change the name to Harris-Rosen's. An elevator, operated by a colored man with white gloves, will ferry passengers up and down. Inside, the walls will be carpeted in velvet, with ornate railings. There will be pictures, portraits of Isidore and Dalia and their children. Also a woman with a twisted face and a man who looks angry. A family of blond children.

Each floor will have a theme. The first will be China, decorated with yellow Asian characters and tiered pagodas that house furniture and beds. Ethereal flute music will play. The second will be Egypt, with its columns and sphinxes, where homewares nestle on gilded trays. The third will be New York, where skyscrapers display shoes, and streetlights direct imaginary traffic toward the men's department. There will even be piped-in street noises on this floor: honking horns and revving engines, cranes and elevated tracks. The fourth story will be Spain, with flamenco music and brightly colored clothes for children.

The fifth floor will be the Old West. It will hold the makeup section, women's clothing, lingerie, and perfume. It will look like Oklahoma itself, back when it was still a territory. Guns will decorate the walls between dresses; fake cacti will act as displays for hats. Skins will serve as carpets, and the fitting rooms will open like saloon doors. The air should smell smoky, like men and sweat, but instead it will smell sweet, flowery. Here, clothes will sparkle and shoes will shine brilliantly. Hats will scream color, and nightgowns will rustle in an artificial wind.

Gradually, people will begin to shop at the larger chain stores. The train will become a freight line, then lie dormant. The Indians will continue their retreat until their land is mostly memory, a puddle shrinking in the sun. The Rosens will donate money to the Owenasa synagogue; the sanctuary where more than five hundred families worship will bear their name on a brass plaque polished weekly by the janitor.

When Harris-Rosen's eventually closes, Isi will sell off his land. It will be eaten up by housing and shopping malls. Just before they raze the house, Isi will remove the mezuzah from the door. He will tell the contractor to put it up on the new house. The contractor will do so, but will nail it to the wrong side of the door. No one will notice. The store itself will remain vacant for many years while the city's economy grinds almost to a halt, and then a developer will buy it for almost nothing, turning it into luxury apartments. He will keep the photos hanging in the elevator; he will like the idea of the ugly buxom woman and the rough, uncomfortable man presiding over the elevator as it travels up and down.

ACKNOWLEDGMENTS

The author wishes to thank the following people and organizations for their contributions to the creation and publication of this novel:

Michael Griffith and John W. Easterly of the Yellow Shoe Fiction series, Louisiana State University Press
Lee C. Sioles, managing editor, Louisiana State University Press
Allison Parker and Susan Murray, copyeditrixes extraordinaires
Gina Frangello, Stacy Bierlein, Dan Wickett, and Steve Gillis of OV Books
The Delta Schmelta Sorority: Sheri Joseph, Dika Lam, Margo Rabb, Lara JK Wilson, and Andrew Beierle
Leigh Feldman and Elisabeth Dyssegaard
Hannah Tinti, Maribeth Batcha, and *One-Story Magazine*
Jay Baron Nicorvo, Thisbe Nissen, and Peter Orner
Mark Baillie, Margot Grover, Lynn McPhee, Lindsey Marcus, Stephanie Pommez-Djerejian, Samantha Schnee, Duncan Smith, and Sarah Tombaugh.
Cousin David Adelman and Cousin Joan Griffin and their children: Cousin Sam, Cousin Vivian, and Cousin William
Kirk Bjornsgaard and "Mr. Grouchy-Pants" of Oklahoma University Press
Beatriz Badikian-Gartler, author of "Mapmaker," from her collection *Mapmaker Revisited*

The following conferences, organizations, and residencies were instrumental in my conception and development of the novel:

The Corporation of Yaddo

Edward Albee's The Barn (William Flanagan Memorial Creative
    Persons Center)

Fundación Valparaíso

Gibraltar Point Centre for the Arts

Maria and Peter Matthiessen Long Island Idyll

Saltonstall Foundation

Sewanee Writers' Conference

Tin House Writers' Conference

The Jack Wettling and Mitch Karsch Home for Hungry Writers

The prologue and chapter 1 were published in a slightly different form as "Stations West" in *One Story Magazine* 13 (2002).

Despite my best efforts to be as true to the historical record as possible, I am a novelist and not a historian. If this novel contains any factual errors, they are mine alone. Bogy (or Boggy) Johnson really was the first Jewish settler in Oklahoma. Beyond that, the characters are my invention. I want to thank my family: Sheila, Jim, and Anthony Amend, for their continued support and encouragement. And my grandparents Ethel and Edward Cohen, whose experience as Jewish Oklahomans and collection of Oklahoma Judaica inspired this story.